# NO MERCY

**Also by Joanna Schaffhausen**

*The Vanishing Season*

# NO
# MERCY

## Joanna Schaffhausen

**TITAN** BOOKS

No Mercy
Print edition ISBN: 9781789090567
E-book edition ISBN: 9781789090574

Published by Titan Books
A division of Titan Publishing Group Ltd
144 Southwark Street, London SE1 0UP

First Titan edition: January 2019
10 9 8 7 6 5 4 3 2 1

A CIP catalogue record for this title is available from the British Library.

Printed and bound in Great Britain by CPI Group Ltd.

*Did you enjoy this book?*
We love to hear from our readers. Please email us at
readerfeedback@titanemail.com or write to us at Reader Feedback
at the above address. To receive advance information, news, competitions,
and exclusive offers online, please sign up for the
Titan newsletter on our website:
**TITAN** BOOKS.COM

For all the Wendys

# NO MERCY

# 1

*You kill one guy, one time, and suddenly everyone thinks you need therapy,* Ellery Hathaway thought as she stood in the biting wind of the subway T platform overlooking the icy Charles River. *Doesn't matter if everyone is glad he's dead.* She debated again whether to follow through on her shrink's orders to show up at the group meeting for survivors of violent crime. "You want to get your job back, yes?" Her court-appointed psychiatrist, Dr. Sunny Soon, had kept her tone pleasant with the question, but the underlying threat was plain. Ellery shoved her hands in her pockets and turned her collar up against the cold and the curious gaze of the passing commuters as she headed for the long escalator down to the street. Her face had been on TV for weeks over the summer as the public tried to render a verdict on whether she was more of a victim or a killer. The man she'd shot would be devastated to know he'd been nearly written out of the conversation—the viewers only ever wanted more of Francis Coben and Ellery, the girl who got away.

On crisp fall days, the T station for Massachusetts General Hospital boasted one of the loveliest views in Boston, with the city skyscrapers on one side and the MIT buildings on the other. Trees and boat docks lined the banks, wending back and forth along with the river's curve. Today, however, everything was the same washed-out gray, from the polluted melting snow to the naked tree branches scratching overhead at the gloomy sky.

Ellery noted with some irony that this supposed survivors' group met inside a hospital, like the victims had all been infected somehow. Like violence was a virus. Then she remembered how she'd landed there herself, and considered maybe it was true.

"You should come to the group sessions because there's someone I want you to meet," Dr. Sunny had said. "I think you'll have a lot in common."

Ellery had tried not to roll her eyes at this idea. "No offense," she'd told Dr. Sunny. "But I really don't think that's possible."

"It can be helpful to talk to other people who are walking your same path," Dr. Sunny had countered, but Ellery knew all crimes were not created equal. There was getting mugged on the street, and then there was surviving an abduction by one of the world's most infamous serial killers. Ellery wondered if any of these other people had had their perp show up as an answer on Final Jeopardy!

She edged carefully around a murky puddle and jaywalked with the crowd across the street toward the hospital. Officially winter wasn't supposed to arrive for a few more weeks, but it had crashed the party early, blowing the doors off the city with howling winds and a foot of heavy snow. Ellery embraced the icy landscape, because a frozen world suited her just fine. Frozen was the crunch of snow under your boot and the glint of icicles on crystal-coated trees. It was clean and unspoiled and beautiful. *The problem,* Ellery thought as she trudged through the slushy streets of Boston, *is the thaw.*

She reached the glass doors and the forced-air heat hit her like a wall as she stepped inside the hospital. She unwound her scarf and went down the hall in search of the appointed therapy room. The police brass holding her job hostage could make her go to these stupid sessions, but they couldn't make her cooperate. *Talking is pointless,* she'd told Dr. Sunny at their first meeting. *It doesn't change the facts.* Ellery could ramble on until she was blue in the face and it wouldn't bring back any of the girls Coben had killed; nothing she could say now would keep her off the Chicago streets the night she'd turned fourteen years old. Nothing would change what had happened in Woodbury last summer.

She found the meeting room without any trouble. It was in

the basement of one of the older buildings, and the scuffed-up linoleum floor and lone, crankshaft window reminded her of an elementary school classroom. The circle of chairs and blank whiteboard added to the effect, although the table at the back of the room appeared to have a hot plate with coffee on it. Dr. Sunny looked up from her notes with a pleased expression. "Ellery, welcome. I'm glad you could make it."

The others turned to look, too. Ellery glanced around at all of them in turn, curious about which person Dr. Sunny wanted her to meet. There was a tall, slim, African-American man wearing a conservative pullover sweater and Malcolm X–style glasses; a heavyset older white guy with shaggy graying hair and worn-out work boots; a couple of women, one Hispanic perhaps about Ellery's age who sported a shaved head and—Ellery squinted—a neck tattoo? The other woman looked like an average Boston suburban housewife: white, plump but not overweight, with soft hands, a tired perm, and a Target sweatshirt that did not match the designer handbag at her feet. They were all strangers to Ellery, but she found they were regarding her with recognition or expectation, as if her arrival had been scripted. She felt her face go hot and wondered if Dr. Sunny had told them her story, irritation flashing through her because she was at a disadvantage now, knowing nothing about them. Then she remembered they would have to have lived under a rock the past few months not to know who she was—which was why it was so stupid to have her come in the first place. *Try being raped and then watching Hollywood make a movie about it,* she told them silently. *Where's the group for that?*

Ellery crossed the room with her head down, making a beeline for the coffee table. She didn't actually like coffee but at least it would give her something to do with her hands. Her fingers had become clumsy from the force of her embarrassment, and she had difficulty getting a single paper cup free from the stack.

"Let me get that for you." Ellery glanced up to find the black guy standing next to her, holding his own cup of steaming coffee, which he set aside to assist her. He had the coffee poured before she could object.

"Thanks," she said, careful not to touch him as they made the exchange.

"Happy to help. My name is Miles, by the way."

"Ellery," she replied with a short nod. She wondered if she was supposed to ask what brought him to the group, or if it was off-limits, like asking a con in prison, *So, what are you in for?* She said nothing and instead set about adding cream to her coffee, filling it to the very brim, after which she added four straight packets of sugar.

Miles gave a low whistle. "I take it you don't really like coffee," he said with a smile. "You could set that outside in the snow right now and it'd turn straight into ice cream."

"Then maybe I would eat it," Ellery admitted. She took a sip and made a face.

Miles chuckled and sipped his own coffee. "It's not good enough to force it," he advised her. "This here is your very basic cup of joe."

"It all tastes like dirt to me."

"Hmm." He scratched at his chin thoughtfully and she looked him over for scars. She saw no obvious marks on him and became more intrigued for his story. "I suppose the java beans come from dirt," he said. "Like we all came from dirt— and one day we'll go back into the ground all together." He lifted his paper cup in mock salute. "To the cycle of life."

She raised her cup in solidarity, enjoying the morbid slant on the discussion. So far this was easier than she had expected, and she hoped that Miles was the one she was supposed to talk to so that she wouldn't have to make direct conversation with any of the others. "Have you, uh, have you been coming here long?" she asked, thinking he might volunteer something that hinted at a Dr. Sunny–arranged meeting. After all, he had been the one to approach her.

"About a year," he said soberly. "That's actually what I want to talk about today."

Miles didn't get a chance to say anything further because the door opened across the room and two people entered:

an old woman in a wheelchair and an old man pushing behind her. They both wore hats—his, a tweed newsboy-style cap, and hers, a colorful knit that looked like it might be homemade. "That's Myra," Miles explained in a low voice as the old man helped the woman off with her coat. "She's been coming here the longest of any of us."

Even from a distance, Ellery could see that this woman had not emerged unscathed from whatever her ordeal was. Her facial features did not line up correctly, and the skin color on the right side did not match the color of the left. *Burned,* Ellery realized with a start. *She's been burned.*

"I think we're all here now, so let's get started," Dr. Sunny said, and Ellery chose a seat next to Miles. "We have a new face with us today, as I'm sure you've noticed. Ellery, would you like to say anything to the group?"

Ellery shook her head and slouched farther in her seat.

"That's quite all right," Dr. Sunny replied easily. "You are welcome to just listen, but of course feel free to join in the conversation if you would like. Everyone else, let's please go around the room and introduce ourselves to Ellery."

It was like circle time in kindergarten, Ellery thought as they all complied with Dr. Sunny's request. Miles went first. The shaggy-haired guy was Alex. Wendy was the one with the shaved head, and the housewife was called Tabitha. Myra volunteered her name with a smile, and Ellery noticed that the old guy who had pushed her in, presumably her husband, had not stuck around. "So you may remember that Miles asked us to talk about anniversaries this week," Dr. Sunny said. "Miles, would you like to start the conversation?"

Beside Ellery, Miles took a deep breath and leaned forward slightly in his seat. "Yeah, okay. I've got the one-year anniversary coming up. The crash was December eighteenth. I think on some level I've been trying to prepare for it all year long. How would I feel? How was I going to handle it when the calendar flipped over to December? I'm supposed to be in school teaching that day. Which is better—stay home and take the day for myself or go in and let the kids distract me? Like, maybe if I make a good enough plan I can get through the day without feeling destroyed."

The housewife, Tabitha, snorted. "Good luck," she said, and crossed her legs.

"Feeling destroyed," Dr. Sunny said. "What would that be for you? What do you think would happen?"

Miles was silent for a moment and then shook his head slowly. "Like before. Like right after Letitia died. I lay in bed in the dark, acting like I was dead, too. Maybe I was hoping I could be. Like if I faked it good enough, the Lord would take me with her."

Ellery looked hard at the floor and held very still. She remembered that feeling, lying on the closet floor in her own blood, praying God would kill her so Coben wouldn't do it himself. She wished suddenly that Miles would stop talking, but he continued.

"We can all tell since I'm sittin' here that it didn't work out that way," he said wryly. "Those kids at school needed me, so I got up one day and I just kept on getting up every day after that. Now it turns out it's almost a year later and I can't quite believe it's happened. This big chunk of rock has traveled all the way around the sun again with me here on it and Letitia gone. Makes me want to be Superman—pushing it back and back and back until we get to the place where we turned down Harvard Street and Ed Kleinfeldt came roaring through the intersection, high as a kite in July."

"That bastard," Tabitha muttered. "The drunks, they always walk away without even a scratch."

"He got taken to the hospital," Miles replied absently. "Probably for detox."

"He gets out pretty soon, doesn't he?" the man called Alex wanted to know.

"Next spring if he makes parole. That's what the lawyers told me. Five years, out in less than one-and-a-half. But don't worry: he's real sorry he killed her."

"Bastard," Tabitha said again. "How long before he's loaded up and behind the wheel of another car?"

"I think we're getting off course a bit," Dr. Sunny

interrupted. "Miles wanted to talk about how to handle the anniversary of his wife's death—isn't that right?"

Miles nodded and sat back in his seat. "The thing is, I was prepared to be freaked by the date on the calendar. I didn't expect the rest of it."

"What do you mean?" Dr. Sunny asked.

"It's all the same," he answered, gesturing vaguely around him. "The tinsel decorations on the streetlights. The smell of frost in the air. It was so cold that night. But clear, you know? You could see the stars. Letitia put Christmas music on the radio, like she always did starting in about mid-November. It was playing 'Jingle Bell Rock' when those headlights came right out of nowhere. Now ... now when I try to cross a street in the dark, I see headlights and I flinch. I hear Christmas songs and they make me want to cry. Ed Kleinfeldt didn't just take Tetia from me: he took the snow and the music and the pine trees and every little reminder, because it's all tied up together."

Ellery forced down a swallow of coffee to clear the lump in her throat. For her, it was the summer, especially when it got so hot the concrete remained warm even after dark. The smell of her own sweat. The sight of a girl riding a bicycle always made her cold inside.

"I know what you mean," Alex said. "Nate and I weren't even supposed to be in the store when it got hit. We were just walking by and he said, 'Let's go in a sec. I want a Snickers.'

We were only going to be there like maybe two minutes. Only two minutes later, he's lying on the ground, shot to the gut. It's been three years and I still can't friggin' stand the sight of Snickers."

"What did you do on the anniversary of the first year?" Dr. Sunny asked him. "What got you through the day?"

Alex grinned and Ellery saw he was missing a couple of teeth. "Jim Beam and ESPN." Then he faltered, his grin slipping away. "Nate hated ESPN."

"Let's talk about other strategies people have used to deal with tough anniversaries," Dr. Sunny suggested smoothly.

Ellery tuned out the resulting chatter because she became aware that the young woman with the shaved head, Wendy, was staring at her. When Ellery turned to look, Wendy glanced away in chagrin, as if she'd been caught with too many items in the express lane at the supermarket. Ellery wondered again whom she was supposed to meet at this gathering, and if Wendy could be the one. The others had all spoken during the session but Wendy hadn't said a word after introducing herself. She sat with one leg drawn up defensively on the chair in front of her. From this angle, Ellery could see that the neck tattoo read NO MERCY.

Privately, Ellery agreed with the sentiment. Take down the monster when you have a clean shot because you might not get a second one. This philosophy had landed her in hot water now, but she felt confident it would blow over eventually. Her crimes were small compared to those of the man she'd killed.

When the meeting broke up, Ellery cast a dubious look around at the other group members, men and women with their own small crimes. She edged closer to where Dr. Sunny was putting some papers away in her briefcase. "So who is it?" Ellery asked her. "Who's the one I'm supposed to meet?"

To Ellery's surprise, Dr. Sunny waved over the old woman in the wheelchair. "Ellery, meet Myra. Myra, this is Ellery. The two of you have something in common."

*I can't imagine what,* Ellery thought as she appraised the other woman up close.

Myra extended a gnarled hand that was covered on one side with bald, shiny skin—too tight to match the rest of her softly aging physique—and that's when Ellery realized the woman had been burned across more than just her face. "Pleased to make your acquaintance," Myra said in a hoarse voice. She tried to smile but the scorched half of her face wouldn't cooperate, so the result was akin to a grimace.

Ellery gave the woman's hand a perfunctory shake and then stepped backward again, shoving her hands in the pockets of her coat, lest she show off her own scars. "What is it we have in common?"

Ellery asked the question of Dr. Sunny, but it was Myra

who answered. "I read about you in the paper," Myra said, looking up at her. "I read what happened with Francis Coben."

"Yeah?" Ellery glanced at the door, wondering if it was too soon to make her good-byes and escape back to the solitude of her apartment.

"You were the one who lived," Myra continued. "So was I."

Ellery swiveled her head around and regarded the woman with new eyes. "What did you say?"

"Myra received a lot of unwanted media attention as a result of what happened to her," Dr. Sunny explained as she took up her briefcase to leave. "I know the scrutiny is new for you, but she lived with it for years. Perhaps she has some advice."

Myra gave a harrumphing sort of sigh, as if denying her own supposed wisdom, and for the first time, Ellery felt something like grudging respect. "You're probably too young to remember," Myra said. "Heck, look at you—maybe you weren't even born back then. It was the mid-1980s, and Boston was on fire. Seemed like every day, the papers would carry a new story about a building that went up in flames overnight. No rhyme nor reason that anyone could see—warehouses, a couple of churches, abandoned or empty houses. There was a major investigation but they couldn't seem to find the guy. Then one night I went back to our furniture store after closing. My husband was sick, hanging his head over the toilet half the day, but taxes were due and we needed some papers. I took Bobby, our son, and went to fetch them. I—I only put him down for a minute. You know how wriggly toddlers are, especially the boys. I turned my back to get the papers from the cabinet, and the next thing I knew, the place was on fire and Bobby was gone." She drew a shuddering breath and placed one hand to her chest. "I tried to look for him. I called his name, over and over, but there was so much smoke and the place got so hot, real quick. I couldn't find the way out. I only survived because a passing firefighter saw the smoke and busted through the nearest window. He tried to get to Bobby, too, but it was no use."

Ellery tried to imagine it, the dense smoke and searing flames. How terrified the woman must have been when she couldn't find her son. "I'm sorry."

"Thank you, dear. So am I." They lapsed into silence for a moment. Ellery had no idea how to navigate a conversation that included the death of a toddler. Thankfully, Myra seemed to have had practice. "It was a huge story because of Bobby's death, my dramatic rescue, and because they caught the guy that night."

"They got him?"

"He was standing there watching the place burn. Apparently they do that," she said, her voice quavering. "The firebugs. They want to watch their handiwork. The police said he still reeked of gasoline when they arrested him. The reporters hounded us for comments—camped right outside our house, like cats waiting for the mice to come out of the hole. I bet you know what that's like." She glanced up at Ellery for confirmation, and Ellery noticed for the first time how bright the blue was in her eyes, like they were the eyes of a much younger woman, full of light. *It was,* Ellery mused later, *like the fire was still inside her.*

"I do know what they're like," Ellery said of the reporters. "'The story will go on with or without you,' they say. 'Make sure you tell your side.'"

"Exactly." Myra pointed a finger at her. "I didn't want to tell my story. My story was about my dead little boy. Who would want to talk about that?"

Ellery shook her head. "I'm sorry you went through that. I hope they eventually left you alone."

Myra gave a sad smile. "Oh, sure. They move on to the next big thing. There was a TV movie in the 1990s, and every ten years they do some sort of retrospective. But mostly, folks stopped talking about it once Luis Carnevale was locked up. That's why I still come here to the group." At Ellery's inquiring look, she explained. "Now, this is the only place I can talk about it. Otherwise, I'm a sad old lady dwelling on the past, and no one likes a sad old lady. Here, I can talk about my Bobby, and it's like . . . it's like he comes alive again, if only for a little while."

Ellery, who had a young brother gone too soon, one who

lived now only in her memory, understood this all too well. The dead could only speak if you spoke for them.

"They say time heals all wounds," Myra said after a beat. Then she leaned closer to Ellery and dropped her voice low. "But we both know that's a lie, don't we?"

Ellery didn't quite know what to say to that. She straightened back up and cleared her throat. "Is he still alive—the man who did it?" Francis Coben was sitting on death row in Terre Haute, Indiana, writing her letters he could never send.

"Oh, yes. He's coming up for parole again soon—and they tell me he might make it this time. It's been so long that no one remembers anymore how it was, the year the city burned. They aren't afraid of him anymore."

Her voice drifted off at the end, and Ellery could tell Myra didn't share this reformed opinion of the arsonist. "You never know," Ellery said, hoping to be reassuring. "There would be press again if they released him—that alone might keep him behind bars."

"I've no doubt there'd be stories," Myra said grimly. "Bad ones. They'd start up again when he set his first fire." The old man returned, presumably Myra's husband come to take her home, but he didn't actually enter the room, just stood there frowning from the doorway. Again, Ellery felt as if she and the rest of the group were lepers, contagious somehow. She couldn't wait to get out of there. "I hope you'll come to the next meeting," Myra said, as if reading her thoughts, and Ellery tore her gaze from the door. Myra gave her a twisted smile. "It's nice to get fresh blood into the group."

"Maybe." Ellery felt sorry for the woman, but she didn't want to be like her, showing up at these support group meetings a quarter century after the fact. How utterly depressing. Dr. Sunny might want to rethink the wisdom of pawning Myra off as some sort of life lesson for other people, given that she didn't appear to be a success story. Still, Ellery had one question she wanted to ask, just in case she never saw the woman again. "What will you do if he gets out? Carnevale?" This was Ellery's big fear: as long as Coben was still breathing air, there was a chance he might get free somehow. If that happened, he would know exactly where to look for her, because now, thanks to last summer, everyone did.

Myra halted with her hands on the wheels. Her chin quivered. "I guess I'd have to find a way to bear it, the same as everybody else."

Ellery left the hospital preoccupied from her talk with Myra. The slush had refrozen as the sun went down, making the path hard and slippery. As she walked toward the T station, she caught a flash of movement on her right—the impression of a person more than anything else—and she whirled on the figure, prepared for battle. She stopped short when she saw it was the girl from the group, Wendy. Her shaved head was covered in a black hoodie and she held up her hands in a gesture of peace. "Whoa," she said, skidding to stop about five feet from Ellery. "It's just me."

"You scared me."

"Sorry. I was waiting for you."

Ellery didn't know this girl from a hole in the wall. "Waiting for me?"

"Yeah. I saw on TV what happened to you last summer— what you did."

*Oh,* Ellery thought. *That.*

Wendy licked her chapped lips and took a tentative step closer. "I just needed to ask you . . . can you sleep at night, you know, now that you shot him? Is that what it takes?"

*Oh hell.* Ellery scrubbed her face with both hands. *I ought to move to Mexico or Denmark or something.* "I'm currently unemployed and being forced to do court-mandated therapy," she told the woman darkly. "Make of that what you will."

Wendy's eyes became wider, her gaze unfocused. "I lost my job, too," she whispered. "I can't even sleep. I thought—I thought maybe you could tell me what to do next. How to go on."

Ellery thought longingly of her apartment across town, but she dropped her hands with a sigh and nodded down the street. "Come on," she said. "I'll buy you a slice of pizza."

Soon she and Wendy were seated in a tiny pizza joint at a table for two right up against the store window, the kind of place that ran so cold in the winter that you didn't bother to take off your coat while you ate. Ellery welcomed the extra layers of winter clothes because it kept away the prying eyes, and she expected from the enormous hoodie Wendy wore that her new companion felt the same way. She and Wendy had each ordered a slice of cheese and an ice-packed cup of Coke, but Wendy didn't touch her food. "He came in through my bedroom window," she said without preamble, and suddenly Ellery wasn't hungry anymore, either. "I was stupid. I left it cracked. It was early spring but we had a weird heat wave going on. My apartment got roasted. It was so stuffy that I opened the window to get some air. I lived on the second floor of a house, in a nice neighborhood. There was a balcony outside the windows but it was high up and I never thought . . . I didn't think anyone would get up there. But I was sleeping, and all of a sudden, I just woke up. Like there was no transition. I was asleep and then wide awake. Maybe somehow I knew he was there?"

She seemed uncertain, searching herself for the details, and Ellery didn't have the heart to tell her the particulars didn't matter. The story was always the same.

"It happened so fast," Wendy continued. "I didn't have

time to look around or turn on a light because then he was on me. He had a knife and he put it against my throat, right here. He said, 'If you scream, I will kill you. No mercy.'"

*No mercy.* The same phrase as the woman's tattoo. A strange choice on Wendy's part, Ellery thought, to wear his words on her body.

"He didn't kill me," Wendy continued bitterly. "But he may as well have. Before, I had a job and a boyfriend and my own apartment. Now I'm alone, on disability, and living with my sister and her kids. I'm too afraid to be alone. They didn't catch him so he's still out there someplace. Not enough evidence, the detective says to me. All I could tell them was that he was big and strong, like a linebacker. He wore a ski mask and I didn't see his face. I went through hell at that hospital to get the rape kit, only turns out, it has nothing in it. He didn't leave semen, no hair, no DNA. It's like he was a fucking ghost."

"I'm sorry." Ellery couldn't fathom how she would get through a day if Coben were out on the streets.

"I thought," Wendy said, hesitating. "I thought since it happened to you, too, kind of, and since you were a cop, that maybe you could help."

"Oh," Ellery replied, realization dawning as she leaned back in her seat. "I'm not—I'm not working right now. I'm on leave."

"So maybe you have free time?" Wendy asked hopefully. "The detective on the case has given up. He can't do anything until he gets another lead. That means another woman gets raped, right? That's what he's waiting for."

Ellery couldn't deny it. "It's not my case," she said gently. "I don't have access."

"Please. I'll tell you everything I know. I'll call up my doctor and Detective Manganelli and tell them I want you to have access to my records if that will help. I just . . ." She put her hands to her head. "I just want him caught so that I can get my life back. I thought maybe you would understand that."

Ellery barely heard her. Her mind was already whirring. "Did you say Detective Manganelli? Joseph Manganelli? Works in Somerville?"

Wendy's expression gave the barest hint of brightening. "You know him?"

"A little bit. He taught part of one of my training courses five years ago." Ellery had pestered him with extra questions outside of class, and Manganelli was always obliging with his time. "Listen," she told Wendy, "I'm sympathetic to your position, believe me, but if you've followed my story, you know that most cops are doing their best to get away from me right now."

"You had the guts to shoot that guy. They're just jealous because you're in the papers and stuff."

*No*, Ellery thought, *that's definitely not it.* She could just imagine what would happen to her if the brass caught her mucking around in someone else's case. If Dr. Sunny got wind of what she was doing, she'd tattle to the brass, and Ellery's career would be over for good. Forget about any second chances. "I'd like to help you. I really would. But . . ."

Wendy's lower lip trembled and she bit it back. "The stories on the news, they made it seem like you were different. They made it seem like you knew what it was like. If you're not going to help me, who will?"

The plaintive question reminded Ellery of her plea last summer, when she'd called up Reed Markham at the FBI and tried to cash in on a fourteen-year-old favor. Reed could've told her to get lost, that he had his own problems to deal with, but instead he'd risked his career to come up to Massachusetts to help her. "I suppose I could call Detective Manganelli, just to see where the case is," Ellery found herself saying. "But I can't promise anything."

Wendy straightened in her seat. "That would be amazing, thank you. Anything at all you can do to help."

Ellery drank a long swallow of Coke and crunched the remaining ice cubes between her back teeth. If Wendy had seen the stories on the news, then she must have known the truth: the last time Ellery had tried to help, two more people ended up dead.

\* \* \*

Back at her apartment, Ellery crouched down to greet her basset hound, Speed Bump. He wriggled up against her and stamped his paws in enthusiasm, like she'd been gone to outer Siberia for six months. "Yes, yes, I missed you, too. Let's get your dinner, okay?" She fed the dog and turned on the stereo for added company, opting for something mellow from The Cure. She ate her own dinner—microwaved mac and cheese—standing at the kitchen counter, since she'd left the pizza slice she'd had with Wendy virtually untouched. She glanced around at her empty, shadowed loft, with its sparse furnishings and huge windows. Normally she loved the tall ceilings and hardwood floors, the sense of isolation that came from living far above the city, but tonight she kept glimpsing her reflection in the black windows and thinking someone else was looking in on her. Impulsively, she picked up the phone and dialed a familiar number, a series of digits that still felt like "home," even though she hadn't set foot there in more than a decade.

"Mom," she said when the other voice came on the other line. "It's me."

"Ellie! It's been ages since you called." She could picture her mother in the same threadbare green chair, the TV news on mute, an open beer in her hand.

"I know," she said, suddenly shamed. "I've been so busy . . ."

There was a short silence as her mother processed this lie.

They both knew Ellery had no job at the moment. "How are you doing? Are you eating?"

Ellery looked at the cardboard container sitting in her trash, the one coated in a particularly nuclear shade of orange cheese. "Yes, I'm eating."

"Good, good. I worry about that. When you were little we had to work so hard to get food into you, and then you'd just pop outside and run it off again."

Ellery stroked her flat stomach and leaned against the wall, still watching the windows. "I promise I'm eating fine."

"Good. A man likes a woman with a little meat on her bones, you know?"

"Yes, Mom. I know."

"Yes, you know? You have someone special?" The hopeful tone in her mother's voice made Ellery wince, and she remembered anew why she didn't phone her mother more often. They always spent the entire call disappointing each other.

"No, there's no one special."

"Oh, that's such a shame. Soon, I'm sure. You just have to put yourself out there. Smile and you'll make friends. You know who is getting married? Timothy Adler. Remember him? He was Daniel's best friend in grade school—that little red-haired boy? I met him in the grocery the other day with his fiancée, and I wouldn't have even recognized him, he's got so tall. But he said I look exactly the same."

"I remember Timothy."

"I can't believe he's old enough to be getting married. Seems like yesterday he and Danny were swinging from the trees in the park."

"That was twenty years ago, Mama. Timmy's all grown up now."

"Yes." Her mother sounded wistful. "Of course he is."

Timmy would be thirty-two now, Ellery knew, although it seemed impossible because Daniel had died before his seventeenth birthday. She felt alien sometimes as her own birthdays mounted, as she turned ages that her big brother never knew.

"Christmas is coming soon," her mother announced. "You know what I'd like more than anything."

Yes, Ellery knew, because it was the same wish her mother had for every birthday, every Christmas, since Ellery had left home a dozen years ago. "I'm not going back there, Mom. Not ever. You're more than welcome to come out here for Christmas. It's—it's real pretty. They have a tree on the common and we've had snow already and everything. I can pay for your ticket."

"Fly? I don't think so. You won't catch me hurtling through the sky in some bucket of bolts that's probably driven by a liquored-up pilot."

Ellery repressed a sigh as she sagged against the counter. "The train then."

"Did you see the news last week? A derailment outside of Philadelphia killed three people."

Caroline Hathaway saw danger everywhere but the city streets outside her apartment. Meanwhile, Ellery spent the remainder of her growing-up years looking out on the park where she'd been abducted. "Mom?" She wiped her eyes with the heel of her hand. "I've got to go. I've got to take the dog out."

"So soon? We've hardly talked."

"I'll call again."

"You always say that."

"I know. I always mean it."

When she hung up with her mother, Ellery did take the dog out into the night for a brisk walk. Down close to the ocean, the winter air set on her like a sea monster from the blackest depths, wet and icy cold. It froze the inside of her nose and burned the tips of her ears. She heard a siren in the distance, the belligerent honk of a fire truck, and it made her turn for home. She quickened her steps but she couldn't outrun Myra's painful grimace and melted face as she'd said those words, *we both know that's a lie.* The woman had been in therapy for more than twenty years and she obviously wasn't healed yet. It didn't give Ellery a lot of confidence in Dr. Sunny or her methods.

Back inside, pink cheeked and breathless, Ellery put on water for tea and resolved to focus her attention on someone she could help: Wendy Mendoza. She looked up Wendy's case on the internet while she waited for the kettle to whistle. Wendy had provided enough identifying details that Ellery was able to find the news stories with no trouble, and what she read largely matched Wendy's narrative. The rapist broke in through an open second-floor window. The police had no clues, at least that they were sharing publicly, and no physical description beyond the fact that he was big and wore a ski mask. Detective Manganelli said they were looking to match the M.O. to other open cases, and he urged anyone with information that might be helpful to the case to come forward. That was eight months ago, with nothing since. Maybe Manganelli would be able to offer some additional tidbits in person.

The kettle warmed from a noisy vibration to a full howl, and Ellery hurried to pull it from the stove. She singed her thumb in the process, leaving a red mark that again made her think of Myra. Unable to resist this time, she took her mug of tea to the couch and started a new search on Myra and the fires. Myra was right that there had been a lot of press, so Ellery had many links to peruse. She got the basics easily: there had been more than two dozen four- or five-alarm fires across South Boston over the course of two years in the mid-1980s, with eight firefighters injured during the fires, including one hurt badly enough that he had to take early retirement. The target buildings were all empty at the time of the blaze until the final one, at Gallagher Furniture, a small business that specialized in hand-carved wood pieces. Deceased in that fire was Robert Gallagher, aged two. He was survived by his mother, Myra, who was badly burned in the fire; his father, Patrick; and an older teenage brother, Jacob.

Ellery noted that Myra had survived only because fireman Kevin Powell was passing by and happened to see the smoke and flames soon after they started. Powell was also the one to spot Luis Carnevale, a two-bit criminal who had been on no one's radar as the arsonist, among the onlookers at the scene of the fire. He'd been arrested on the spot, stinking of gasoline. When she looked him up, she found Kevin Powell had been richly rewarded for his bravery and was now fire commissioner for the City of Boston.

Ellery looked at Bump, who wagged his tail happily whenever her gaze set on him. "Lucky he happened to be passing by at the right time," she told the dog. She hoped for Myra's sake that Carnevale remained locked up, because Wendy's desperation showed how crazy-making it felt when your tormenter was free. Ellery had one predator in the grave and another one on his way, assuming they ever did give Coben the needle. Still she lived in an apartment with no closets and a gun on her nightstand, and yet half the nights she could not sleep at all. *No,* she would have told Wendy if she'd been entirely truthful. *It does not stop when they are dead.*

The next night, Detective Joe Manganelli was more than happy to meet her for a drink, as she'd suspected he would be. Yes, he'd been generous with his knowledge all those years ago, but now she was infamous and not telling her story to anyone. Cops, like reporters, loved a good story, and she knew that Joe would show up for hers. "Ellery," he said warmly when she slid into the booth across from him. "Long time, no see. You look great."

She wished she could say the same, but Joe was balding, ruddy cheeked, and always looked about eight months pregnant. "Thanks for meeting with me," she replied. "Drinks are on my tab—what'll you have?"

"Another one of these," he said, nodding at his empty beer glass.

Ellery bought them both a round and settled in for shop talk. "You might have seen something about me in the news," she began, and Joe threw back his head with a laugh.

"Something? Darlin', you were leading the six o'clock hour for two weeks straight. Most cops don't sniff a serial case their entire career, and you bring down two of 'em."

His tone was somewhere between admiration and envy.

"And two's my limit," she replied lightly. The last thing she wanted to do was get sidetracked into the gruesome details of the Coben case or its reprise from the summer. But Joe was curious and she had to pay the piper if she wanted to dance to the tune, so she had to accept at least a few of his questions.

"I read a book on Coben a few years back," he said. "That was some twisted shit, the way he cut off all those girls' hands. Did he try that with you?"

Reluctantly, she showed him the scars at her wrists.

"Wow, incredible. Guess he messed with the wrong girl, huh? Have you seen him since it happened?"

"No, and I don't care to."

The finality of her tone made him blush. "No, no, of course not. Why would you?"

She took advantage of his discomfort to press her agenda, leaning conspiratorially over the booth. "Anyway, the thing is—they've got me doing mandated therapy now, on account of what happened over the summer."

Joe made a face. "Yeah, I read about that, too. The bastard got what was coming to him. Why're they yanking your chain about it?"

"Because they're just as glad he's dead but they're afraid to give me back my gun for fear I might shoot someone else."

There, she'd said it. It was kind of liberating to have the truth out loud.

"I hear ya. It's always cover-your-ass mode with the brass, ain't it? We do the dirty work and they'll look the other way so long as the collars keep rolling in and nobody ends up on the wrong side of the news."

"Yeah, well. That's where I went wrong, I guess."

They clinked glasses. "So tell me what I can do you for," Joe said as he licked the foam from his upper lip.

"This therapy group I'm in," she said, figuring she would play it straight. "Wendy Mendoza is in it, too."

Joe knew the case right away. Just the sound of Wendy's name seemed to deflate him in his seat. "Aw, hell. That poor kid. I wish I had some good news for her, I really do. You don't know how hard we worked that case—night and day for a solid month. It was priority one. Sick freak like that, you figure he's going to do it again if we don't stop him, right? And the city was panicked there for a while. Women calling all day long, wanting to know why we haven't caught the guy yet. We tried. We're still trying. There's just nothing to go on."

"I heard you were trying to tie it to other open cases," Ellery said, fishing delicately now that they were in open waters.

"Yeah, there are a couple that seem possibly related, but it's hard to say. One of 'em, the victim is an old lady of eighty-two. I mean, we're talking gray hair, walker—the works. In that case, no weapon was used. In another case, it wasn't nighttime but the middle of the day. A woman came back from a jog and found the perp waiting for her in her bedroom with a gun. He had rope, too. In the Mendoza case, it was nighttime, a young, attractive victim, and he had a knife. We have no hair or fluid from any of these cases, which is one reason we think they might be related—but at the same time, we have nothing solid to connect them. Goddamn frustrating, I tell ya."

"Maybe I could look at the cases," Ellery suggested.

Joe's eyebrows shot up. "You pass the detective's exam in Somerville and I didn't notice?"

"Just trying to help out a friend. I have the time."

He looked her over skeptically and then took another drink. "I appreciate the offer, Ellery, but we've had a dozen eyeballs on these files already, so I don't think it's worth either of us risking our heinies just to get one more, *capisce*?"

Ellery turned her glass around in her hands as she considered her next move. She could just give up here and tell Wendy, *Hey, I tried,* but the desperation in the woman's eyes and the way she'd said *I thought maybe you'd understand* kept eating away at Ellery. "What if," she said slowly, "what if I could get you access to an FBI profiler? Someone who might take a look at the case and move the investigation forward."

"FBI? They don't get involved in this low-level shit."

"He would if I asked him to," Ellery said, sounding more confident than she felt. It's not like Reed Markham owed her any favors. This time, it was definitely the other way around.

"He," Joe repeated, putting the pieces together. "You mean Markham. The guy who caught Coben."

"If I can convince him," Ellery pressed. "Will you let us see the cases?"

"Let you? I'll throw a goddamned ticker-tape parade."

Ellery smiled in triumph and drank down her beer. Tomorrow she would figure out how to call up the decorated Agent Reed Markham and tell him she had pimped him out to the Somerville PD.

# 2

"You're doing it all wrong!" Reed's six-year-old daughter, Tula, clutched her cheeks and used her fingers to pull down the lower lids of her eyes to express her full displeasure at his dubious hairstyling technique.

"What? It's a ponytail," Reed protested as he met her eyes in the mirror.

"It's all lumpy on this side," she complained as she patted the supposedly offending bump, whose presence Reed could not detect at all, and he was an FBI-trained investigator. The doorbell rang downstairs, and Tula took off with the hairbrush. "That's Mom! She can fix it!" Tula fled the room at the same breakneck speed at which she'd done everything else in her short life, including being born four weeks early. Reed smiled faintly, wondering how long he'd be able to keep up with her, and followed Tula downstairs to greet his ex-wife, Sarit. By the time he arrived in the living room,

Sarit had redone the ponytail and Tula was smiling again.

"Are your things gathered for school?" Sarit asked her, and Tula looked at the floor.

"Not yet."

"Off with you then, and hurry—we don't want to be late!" Sarit patted Tula on the backside as if to spur her into action, while Reed lingered from his place at the edges of their old life, still unsure how he fit into this new version. The divorce had become final two months ago, the ink barely dried on the pages, but Sarit seemed to be completely at peace. Her warm brown skin had a pink undertone of happiness, her shoulder-length hair had a new, stylish cut, and the new man in her life seemed to be sticking around. Reed still hadn't found anything to put on the bare walls of his condo.

"Reed," Sarit said, and then bit her lip in the way he'd used to find so adorable. "I wanted to talk to you about something. Randy is surprising Amanda with a trip to Disney World over Christmas, and I know it's technically your time with Tula, but I think she would be over the moon with happiness if she could go, too, and—"

"You want to take her for Christmas?"

"I know. We agreed it was your year. It's just this trip popped up at the last minute, and Randy, Amanda, and I will be going no matter what, so I thought I would see if you might be flexible this one time. We'd be back on the twenty-seventh and you could have her the rest of the school break, if you wished. That's eight days."

His usual ration was six days per month: a three-day weekend twice per month, plus dinner on Tuesday nights if he wasn't away or Tula didn't have some school function to attend. Although they shared legal custody fifty-fifty, the physical custody was heavily slanted in favor of Sarit due to Reed's erratic schedule. Plus, Sarit remained in the family home where Tula had been raised thus far, and it seemed best for her to let her stay in familiar surroundings most of the time. Still, Reed had been looking forward to taking Tula to his parents' home for the holiday, where she could run around with all her cousins. It had been his inner mantra for weeks now as he'd sent his daughter away on Sunday nights. *At least you'll have Christmas,* he told himself.

"You've put me in an impossible position," he said to Sarit. "If I say no, I'm the monster who kept his kid from spending Christmas at Disney World with her mother, her best friend, and her mom's cool new boyfriend. Have you told her about it already?"

Sarit looked offended. "Of course not. I wanted to speak to you first."

Reed put his hands on his hips and turned his gaze to the bare, beige wall, which he stared at until his vision started to blur. They both knew he could kick up a fuss about this if he wanted to—for once, he had the power here. "Maybe I wanted to be the one to take her to Disney World," he said finally, turning back to look at her.

Sarit appeared perplexed at this idea. "Did you?"

He stuck out his chin. "Maybe."

Sarit seemed to consider this a moment, but then she shook her head brusquely. "Let's be realistic for a moment, shall we? We took exactly one family vacation in six years—a trip to the Grand Canyon that got cut short when you had to fly to Seattle because a teenage boy had been murdered there."

*The third one,* Reed remembered. Gary Warner, age fifteen, a runaway and street hustler who picked up the wrong trick. It had taken them another three months to find his killer, during which time Reed flew back and forth across the country a dozen times.

"As for Christmas," Sarit continued, "half the time, you weren't even home."

He looked at her sharply. "One time. I missed Christmas one time." It was a kidnapping on that occasion; eighteen-year-old Kacie Daniels left to buy a last-minute gift for her boyfriend and never came home. Her body turned up in a nearby swamp just after New Year's.

Sarit looked sad but sympathetic. "It felt like more," she said gently, and what could Reed reply to that?

"Fine," he said with a sigh. "Take her. Have a great time."

"Thank you. Thank you for me, and for Tula. I owe you one," she said as their daughter came bounding back into the room with her school backpack in hand.

"I'm ready!"

"Is that so?" Sarit chucked her lightly on the chin. "Take a look at your feet, my sweet."

"Oh . . . shoes. Right." She went skipping out of the room again, and Reed gave in to the baser temptation to lob a surprise back at Sarit.

"McGreevy's retiring this year," he informed her. "They're going to need someone else to run the unit."

She blinked at him. "You mean . . . someone like you?"

"Why not? McGreevy indicated to me recently that the job might well be mine, and they'll take his recommendations into account. I've certainly got the experience."

"Yes, of course. It's just that I didn't think you wanted a management-type role. Someone has to go out and catch these monsters. Isn't that what you always told me?"

"Someone would still be doing that. It just wouldn't be me getting on the plane for every case. I'd be sticking closer to home, which means I could spend more time with Tula." He said the last part casually, but the implication was clear— he might be soon able to cash in on any debts Sarit owed him.

Sarit's expression appeared clouded for a moment, but all she said was, "I think she would love that."

Tula entered the room again, this time with shoes on her feet. "I'm ready now."

"Say good-bye to your father," Sarit commanded, and Tula launched herself at Reed.

"Bye, Daddy. I love you."

"Bye, sweetheart." He barely had time to kiss her warm head before she was off again, disappearing out the door in a whirl of chatter and a sudden gust of winter air. "I love you, too," Reed whispered to the room. But there was no longer anyone around to hear it.

At his desk, Reed focused on the background workup on a suspect in a car bombing case in Birmingham, Alabama, that one of his colleagues had finished that morning. Reed had mastered the ability to tune out the world around him, disappearing the other agents and their tap-tapping on keyboards or ringing phones, so it took him a minute to realize his pants were buzzing. He fished out his phone, and a little jolt went through him at the sight of Ellery Hathaway's name on his caller ID. He had not spoken to her since the summer and all that ugliness up in Woodbury.

Gingerly, he pressed the button to accept the call. "Reed Markham," he said, and then looked around to see if anyone was watching him. For some reason, Ellery still felt like his secret, even though the rest of the world knew who she was now.

"Reed? It's Ellery. I, uh, I hope I didn't catch you at a bad time."

"No, no, not at all. It's fine. I'm glad to hear from you. I've been meaning to give you a call, but . . ." He trailed off because he didn't really have a good excuse. Mostly, after the Coben story blew up again in the wake of the new murders, this time with Ellery's identity revealed, Reed felt like the best thing he could do for her was to get the hell out of there. Hanging around in her orbit would have only helped keep the story alive. He groped around in his head for some amount of truth, something real that wouldn't scare her off entirely. "I've wondered," he said at last. "How you were doing."

"Oh." She gave a short, dark laugh. "Well, I haven't shot anyone since you left. So there's that."

"I read that you were suspended," he replied.

"Yeah, they have me shrinked up at the moment. First, they tried offering me an early retirement—no pension or anything, just a couple of years' pay to hush up and go away, and I think they were praying I'd take it. They don't want me back but they don't want to fire me, either. I mean, how would that look on the news, right?"

"Not pretty." If it hadn't been for Ellery, the town of Woodbury might have lost a good many more citizens.

"Exactly. So I'm in limbo at the moment." She paused.

"That's kind of why I'm calling."

"Oh?" The last time she'd phoned, Reed had ended up face-to-face with a serial murderer. "No one is mailing you menacing Christmas cards, I hope."

"No, it's nothing like that," she assured him quickly. "But I could use your advice. Your professional advice. Well, not me, a friend. No wait. She's not really a friend, but I think if you heard her story, you'd want to help, too."

Reed closed his eyes and leaned back in his seat. Of course he always wanted to help. This was his problem, at least as Sarit had framed it to him. "What is it?" he asked with his eyes still shut.

"Her name is Wendy Mendoza," Ellery told him, and then she sketched out the basics of a case that was both horrible and entirely hopeless: there were no witnesses, fibers, DNA, or fingerprints. Just a victim whose life had been destroyed. Of course her story seemed powerful. It was literally all that was left. "She can't eat or sleep," Ellery was saying. "She lost her job and she's afraid to leave the house because he's still out there. The detective on the case says there's nothing more they can do right now, but he would love to have you take a look at the file and offer your opinion."

Reed's opinion was that Somerville had an anger-type rapist on the loose, that the man had assaulted women before and likely would do so again before he was caught. He felt confident that the detective on the case already knew all of this, however. "You talked to the detective? About me?"

"Your name came up. Listen, I know it's a lot to ask, and you don't owe me anything—"

"How do you know her?" Reed cut her off. "The victim—the one who is not your friend."

Ellery was quiet on the other end of the line for a long moment. "We're in group therapy together," she muttered eventually. "A group for people who experienced violent crime."

Something in her words made his throat seize up. He had a flash of his own hands shaking as they'd pried open Coben's closet. He saw Ellery lying half-dead on the floor. He'd been sure he was too late, that she would not be saved. "I can be there tomorrow evening," he announced with sudden decisiveness, already calling up the flight schedules. "But just don't expect any miracles."

"No, I don't. Not anymore."

When he hung up with Ellery, Reed booked a flight to Boston, found a hotel, and only then went to ask permission for the side trip he'd already arranged. Russ McGreevy, colloquially known as "Puss" since he'd come out of an armed standoff with the victim's pet cat under his arm, barely looked up when Reed knocked on the door and stuck his head in the room. Maybe he would be too distracted to parse the details. "Hey, boss? I just wanted to let you know I'm going up to Massachusetts tomorrow for a quick consultation on a serial rape case." Ellery had mentioned just the one known victim, but Reed knew there had to be others.

McGreevy looked up from the paperwork he was reading and took off his glasses so he could regard Reed fully. "I don't recall seeing anything on the docket about a rapist in Massachusetts." McGreevy might have been retiring later in the year, but he was only in his mid-sixties and was exiting at the top of his game. The man missed nothing. "You're working the bombing in Birmingham with Alan Turk."

"We have that report ready to go," Reed said as he eased into the room. "Alan can handle any follow-up."

McGreevy scratched the back of his head and squinted at the ceiling. Reed had seen the routine enough times over the years to recognize that McGreevy's next question would be rhetorical. "Did I assign you a case about a rapist in Massachusetts? No," he said, indeed answering his own question. "No, I am sure I would remember if I had done so. We don't have any active investigations at all up there at the moment, so what is this about?"

Reed took a seat and gave Puss the basics of the rape investigation. McGreevy waved an impatient hand at him, cutting it short. "Terrible story, yes. But if the local PD needs assistance, they can requisition help through the usual channels. This is a matter for the state bureau, Reed. You know that."

"I'll be up and back in a day or two. I can do it on my own time if you prefer."

McGreevy frowned, deepening the lines at the corners of his mouth, and the scowl made him look his age. "No, I very much don't want you investigating official cases in your free time," he said. "Let's take a moment and remember how that worked out last summer."

Reed heard the shot ring out in his memory, saw the body at his feet. He shifted uncomfortably in his chair. "We stopped a murderer. Last time I checked, that was part of the job description around here."

"Don't get cute with me, Markham. There's brave and then there's stupid, and we both know your stunt last summer was an equal mix of both. I'm surprised you're in such a hurry to get back up there." As he said the words, a realization dawned over his face. "This is about that girl, isn't it? Abigail."

"Ellery," Reed corrected, now even more uncomfortable.

"Ellery. Right. She lost her job, if I remember correctly."

"She's on paid leave, and it's just temporary." Reed sat up straighter, happy to defend her since he'd been suspended so recently himself. "And anyway, this isn't her case. The investigation is being run by a Detective Manganelli from the Somerville PD."

McGreevy raised his bushy eyebrows. "Yeah? Is he the one who called you?"

"In a manner of speaking." Ellery had said it was Manganelli who wanted him to look into the case; she had just been the one to make the call.

"Hmm," said McGreevy, clearly not buying it. He tapped his fingers on the desk a moment and then sat forward with a sigh. "Two days," he told Reed. "That's all you get."

Reed grinned and leaped to his feet. "Thanks, Puss."

"Don't thank me. Just go do your job and get back here with your nose still clean. And Reed . . ." He waited until Reed turned around again. "Whatever itch you have for that Hathaway girl, make sure you scratch it this time, okay? She's not someone you want to be mixed up with on a continuing basis."

"She's not—"

"We both know that bullshit story the two of you cooked up this summer is exactly that—bullshit. I don't give a damn what the record says because I've seen the evidence firsthand. She shot an unarmed man. She put a bullet through his head while he was in physical custody."

Reed gripped the door handle more tightly. "She saved my life."

"For which we are all sincerely grateful." McGreevy put his glasses back on and returned his eyes to his work. "You go on up there to Massachusetts and thank her for us any way you see fit. But then you get your ass back down here for good."

* * *

The clock hadn't touched six when Reed landed in Boston, but the sky was already dark as night. The descent into Logan always made him vaguely queasy, as it looked for all the world like the plane was going to set down in the ocean, black water rising ever closer, until the very last second when the landing strip appeared out of nowhere beneath them. Reed breathed a sigh of relief at the bump of the wheels on the tarmac and then began collecting his carry-on items with the rest of the crowd on the East Coast airbus. He had been planning to take a taxi to his hotel and phone Ellery from the room, but that idea evaporated when he caught sight of her waiting for him near the bottom of the escalator.

She appeared exactly how he remembered her, with long brown hair tied in a knot at the back of her head and clothed in unisex, no-nonsense jeans and work boots, which were now paired with a leather jacket that looked one size too large for her. She was leaning against the airport wall but fidgeting with her hands as though she were either impatient for his arrival or nervous about the herd of people streaming past her in the corridor. She looked up sharply and froze when she saw him. Her gray-blue eyes had gone dark, like the color of a bruise, and she did not smile at his approach. "Thanks for coming," she said, falling into step beside him.

He allowed himself a wry smile. "When I texted you the flight information, that wasn't a summons for you to pick me up."

She didn't slow down. "Yeah, well, I've got some extra time on my hands these days."

"All the same, it's good to see you." He glanced sideways at her, drinking in the sight. Sixteen other girls had died, but this one lived. She would always be a wonder to him. "You're looking well."

"Am I? Thanks, I guess. Maybe later I can have you send a note to my mom as an affidavit."

"How is your mother?"

Ellery gave a dismissive shrug of her shoulder. "The same. Always the same."

Reed followed her through the airport to the parking garage, to her familiar old truck. He peered through the passenger window to make sure it was vacant inside. "No sign of the fur beast," he remarked as he opened the door.

"Bump's at home. We have to go straight to Somerville to hook up with Detective Manganelli. But don't worry— Bump told me to tell you hello."

"Is that so?" Reed said, brushing some stray dog hair off his coat.

"Yeah, remind me to lean over and lick you later."

She said it so matter-of-fact, not even glancing his way,

that it made Reed do a double-take. Her eyes were on the road but there was a ghost of a smile playing at her lips. *Maybe this was going to be some fun after all,* he reasoned. McGreevy seemed to think it was some sex thing that kept Reed coming back to Ellery, that if he just took her to bed he could "scratch that itch" and get her out of his system. In reality, Reed had barely touched her. The most physical contact they'd ever shared was the night he'd scooped her up from the closet floor and run like hell with her into the woods, half-convinced she was dead in his arms. When she'd lived, Reed became a hero, and for years, that was the end of the story. Now he'd seen up close how the scars still lingered and knew the truth was far more complicated: he'd gotten her out of that closet, but no one could really bring her back home.

"Tell me more about Wendy Mendoza," he said to her, because as terrible as Wendy's story was, it was still an easier topic than the personal history he shared with Ellery.

"I've told you pretty much everything I know," she replied. She inched her truck forward so they could join the stop-and-go traffic on the busy Boston freeway. "I've only met her one time."

"I thought she was in a therapy group with you."

Ellery squirmed. "She is. But I've only been to one meeting."

"I see."

"I've been following all the rules," she protested, meeting

his eyes to prove she meant it. "I've been doing the one-on-one stuff just like the agreement said. It was only this week my shrink said I should come to the group because she wanted me to meet someone."

"Wendy?"

"No, this other woman named Myra Gallagher. Her son was killed in a fire back in the eighties, and I guess the case made a lot of headlines—kind of like mine. The fire was part of a string of arsons that had occurred over a couple of years, so the city was in an uproar over it even before the boy died. Myra said they caught the guy at the scene."

"Luis Carnevale," Reed supplied as the memory came back to him.

Ellery looked surprised. "You know him?"

"No, I've heard of the case. My boss—you remember McGreevy—he used to lecture on it. You're right that the case was famous."

"He worked the case? I didn't see his name in the news stories."

"It would have been a long time ago, back when he was a junior agent—probably fresh to the team. It's not like he would have been giving a lot of interviews. Anyway, what did you think of Myra?"

"She's all right, I guess." Ellery paused, as if considering. "Kinda weird, though—it's been more than twenty-five years and she's still going to weekly therapy. I know her son died and everything, but at some point, you have to move on. Sitting around singing Kumbaya with a bunch of crime victims isn't going to bring him back."

"Maybe it makes her feel better."

Ellery rolled her eyes at him. "You sound like my shrink. Everything's always about feelings. I'll tell you what will make Myra feel better: keeping Carnevale behind bars."

"They're letting him out?"

"He's up for parole, and Myra seems to think they'll roll the dice this time. He's old and the fires were a long time ago. May as well free up his cell for someone younger and more dangerous. At least you and I don't have to worry about that, right? Coben will stay locked up until he rots."

Reed noted the way she said "we," as though Coben posed an equal threat to both of them. Reed might have been the one to call in the cavalry, but Ellery was the girl who got away. When Coben wrote letters from inside his cell, they were only ever addressed to one person.

Ellery had mentioned they were meeting the detective straight-away, so Reed was surprised when she turned down a quiet residential street and pulled the truck to the side of the road. "This is the spot," she told him, craning her neck to see out the windshield. "This is where it happened."

"You looked up the crime scene?" *Of course she had.* He

remembered her meticulous records on the disappearances last summer.

Ellery was already getting out of the truck, so Reed followed her out to examine a long stretch of traditional New England homes that had been divided up into multiple apartments. They were crammed side-to-side, with barely enough space for narrow driveways between them. Each was a slightly different shape or style but boasted the same aging shingles and wide front porch. "Tufts is just a few blocks over that way," she said, indicating the local university with a wave of her hand, "so these houses have a high percentage of students. Some are condos that are rented or owned by young professionals commuting into Boston or Cambridge. That one right there was Wendy's."

Parked cars lined either side of the street. Tall trees with barren branches spoke to the history of the dense neighborhood. There were warm yellow lights on in people's homes, including the brown three-story home that Ellery had singled out as Wendy Mendoza's. "Which window was it?" Reed asked, and Ellery pointed to the one on the left at the front of the second floor. It was easy access from the large balcony, but first the rapist had to get up there. The lack of a railing on the lower porch would have made it somewhat challenging. "How did he get to the second floor?"

"Don't know," Ellery replied, shoving her hands into her

pockets. The winter wind came blustering down the dark street. "Maybe he just climbed."

"A taller person could do it," Reed agreed. "It wouldn't be easy, but it's possible." He looked up and down the street, paced first one way and then the other.

"What are you looking for?"

"All these houses look essentially the same. He picked Wendy's apartment out of three dozen or more other potential targets. The question is why."

"Most of these places have multiple people living in each apartment," Ellery said, catching on, "but Wendy was alone."

"Precisely. He'd no doubt been here before. He knew what he'd find inside her room." Reed turned around in place and surveyed the houses. Most of them didn't even have a front yard as such, just maybe a patch of dead grass and half-melted snow. This was city living at its finest, where you could reach out your side window and shake hands with your neighbor. "It was an unusually warm night, you said," Reed remarked to Ellery as he squinted up at Wendy's window. "She probably wasn't the only one with her windows opened. Given the short distance between homes, there was a good chance that, if she'd screamed, someone would have heard it."

Ellery's face darkened. "You're saying it's her fault for not screaming."

"No. I'm saying he knew that she would never scream."

Detective Manganelli turned out to be right out of central casting for a Boston cop, with a rotund middle, close-cropped dark hair, and darting, watchful eyes. They met up at an Irish pub that featured high-backed dark wood booths and Boston Celtics prints on the wall. Manganelli's red cheeks suggested he'd had a head start on the alcohol. He greeted them both enthusiastically, pumping Reed's hand and thanking him profusely for his help. "I haven't done anything yet," Reed said mildly as he took a seat across from the detective. Ellery demurred until Reed was seated so that she could have the outside spot. She was not going to be trapped, not even by him, not even for the length of one dinner.

Reed ordered a beer and the shepherd's pie, while Manganelli selected a burger. For her part, Ellery had a Coke and an order of deep-fried pickles. Reed looked at her askance. "I see your eating habits haven't improved a bit," he said.

"Pickles are a vegetable," she retorted as she pulled the basket toward her. "They're good for you."

"I've never met a real-life profiler before," Manganelli said, leaning over the table eagerly. "God, the war stories you must have to tell, yeah?"

"No more than you, sir, I assure you." Reed knew there was plenty of strange behavior to be found in your average police blotter.

"Yeah, sure, we got our kooks. The boys picked up an

old lady last week who was walking buck-naked down the middle of the road in the snowstorm. She thought she was Lady Godiva looking for her horse. Then once, I had a husband who shot his wife in their backyard because—you won't believe this shit—she was arguing with him about how to read a sundial. But that's your run-of-the-mill crazy. You chase serial offenders and child abductors—they're a level of sicko we don't see every day. I mean, what's the craziest thing you've seen on the job?"

Reed resisted the urge to glance at Ellery, but he felt her go momentarily still in the booth next to him. She'd been a small-town cop, too. All her experience with serial killers and child abduction was of the personal kind, so she probably didn't know: it was an amazing testament to her strength that she could sit here across from this guy, having reinvented herself so completely that Manganelli forgot he was prattling on about Coben-type crimes right in front of one of the victims.

"I don't rank the crazy," Reed said at length. He'd been at this job long enough to know he had to play the game, had to give to get what he wanted from the local law enforcement personnel. "There was one case I consulted on many years ago now. A wealthy couple in Texas had their home broken into during the daytime. The perpetrator slashed up some expensive paintings, threw some sort of acid on the grand piano and other furniture, and spray-painted badly spelled vulgarities and satanic-type symbols on the walls."

"Wow, a real nutbag," Manganelli said around a mouthful of burger. "Did you catch the guy?"

"We got called in to consult because of the possible satanist angle," Reed said. "Some of the locals were afraid they had a cult on their hands. But it was quickly apparent that was not the case. The crime scene made no consistent sense. The perpetrator was both organized and disorganized in his or her behavior. They hot-wired the alarm at the front gate but then used a rock to break the back patio door. Once inside, they clearly identified the most valuable items—but some they stole, like the jewelry, and others they destroyed, like the paintings. The rest of the damage—the torn couch cushions, the overturned chairs, and the crude sayings on the wall—seemed mostly to be for show. It was like we had an educated, organized offender pretending to be a disorganized, uneducated offender."

"So what happened?" Manganelli wanted to know.

"We arrested the homeowners. As it turned out, a quick check of their financial situation showed they were deeply in debt and at risk of losing their business. They hid the jewelry and damaged the rest of the goods to try to cash in on the insurance. The tip-off was the one painting that had not been slashed—a portrait done of the couple's daughter when she was a child. It had no value to anyone other than the family, and that's precisely why it was spared."

"Holy crap." Manganelli sat back in the booth, shaking his head. "People will do just about anything for the almighty dollar—am I right? But at least with those guys, it's easy to suss out their motive and work backward from there to nail 'em. This rapist we've got on our hands, he's like a ghost. We've got nothing to go on." He heaved a great sigh that made his large belly bump the table and slosh his beer. "I know Wendy Mendoza thinks we haven't been trying, but the problem is, we've run out of stuff to try. So, you know, thanks for taking a look. We'd love nothing better than to nail the sonofabitch." He reached down and pulled out a sheaf of folders, which he handed across to Reed. "I made copies of what we have, both on this case and the few that might be related. The thumb drive in there has the digital files. I'd tell you that you have to come down to the station to view the physical evidence, but the truth is, we don't have any."

Reed opened the file and started leafing through it. Ellery sidled a bit closer so that she could see, too. "Ellery said the man told Wendy he would kill her if she screamed, that he would show her 'no mercy.'"

"That's right."

"Did he say anything else?"

Manganelli made a disgusted face. "Only that she'd better not tell anyone, or he might come back. He took her driver's license to show her he meant business. We hoped like hell he would come back. We parked an undercover unit on that street every day for a month and got zippo."

Reed pulled out a photo, a candid shot of a pretty young woman with dark hair sitting on a picnic blanket at a park somewhere. She had a warm, open smile and friendly eyes. "That's her," Ellery murmured to him. "That's Wendy."

"That picture is from before," Manganelli clarified. "She don't look that way anymore. You'd hardly recognize her now. After that bastard attacked her, she shaved off all her hair and got herself tattooed—one on her neck with his words, 'no mercy.' He made her hate herself that much."

"She didn't do it because she hates herself," Ellery said flatly. Reed turned to look at her. "It's protection," she murmured to him. "The rapist picked her because she looked like that," she said, nodding at the smiling picture of Wendy. "She made herself as ugly as she could so he wouldn't want her anymore."

Manganelli blinked. "She told you that?"

Reed cleared his throat and looked at his lap. He knew Wendy didn't have to tell her; Ellery had lived it herself. "So he took things from the scene," Reed noted, changing the subject. "Her driver's license, some underwear."

"Trophies," Manganelli agreed. "Probably beats off to them every night."

*Yes,* Reed thought grimly, *every night until the memory*

*isn't enough, and that's when he has to go find someone new.* "I can give you the basics on the classic anger rapist," he said aloud, "but it's probably nothing you haven't heard before or guessed already. He's pissed off at the world, and at women in particular, because he blames them for his lack of achievements. He's prone to angry outbursts, which means his employment history is probably erratic. His fury is merged with his sexuality, so the aggression is part of his fantasy. He has violent erotic fantasies that build up over time until the fantasy is not enough; he has to start acting it out. Some inciting incident—an argument with a coworker or girlfriend—may be the trigger. Once he has his victim, he will use as much force as necessary to subdue her. He doesn't imagine he's enjoying a romantic encounter with her; her humiliation and fear are part of what gets him off. Now that he has started acting on his fantasies, he is unlikely to stop until someone makes him stop, although his trophies may see him through a long period between attacks."

Manganelli was nodding along. "Yeah, that's what we figured. This asshole hates women and gets off on hurting them. He obviously knows the area well enough to realize Wendy would be home alone. We've shaken all the usual trees on this one, looked at anyone in the area with a similar sex offense on their record, but there's just nothing we can prove. My guys knocked on every door in a six-block radius after the attack; no one saw or heard anything."

"I can take a look at these," Reed said as he held up the reports, "and give you my opinion on which of them might have been committed by Wendy's rapist. I would also suggest you expand your search for similar cases back five years and include anyone arrested for peeping or stealing women's undergarments. This offender probably started slowly and worked his way up to the full-out assault on a grown woman."

"Good, good, I can do that."

"Detective Manganelli said we may have to wait until he rapes someone else," Ellery said, her tone faintly accusatory.

Reed hesitated. "He might be right. This offender has been extremely clever, not to mention lucky, thus far. He will be difficult to catch unless he makes a mistake that allows us to pinpoint his identity."

But Ellery had stopped listening to him. Her eyes had become fixed on the television behind Reed's head. Manganelli's gaze slid up to join hers, and so Reed turned around, too. The TV was tuned to the news, showing what looked like old B-roll of a fire from an era when cameras shot with real tape. The picture shifted to a mug shot of a bleary-eyed Hispanic man with a pockmarked face and a thin mustache. The chyron identified him as Luis Carnevale.

"I saw this story in the *Herald* today," Manganelli said, pointing at the TV. "They're talking about letting him out.

His niece or cousin or something is a lawyer and she's putting pressure on the parole board. If they don't let him go, she's going to try to get the whole case retried. Says the Innocence Project might be interested in his story." His disgusted tone suggested how little credence Manganelli gave this idea.

"Poor Myra," Ellery said softly. "This must be killing her."

As if on cue, the news story switched to show a picture of the murdered little boy, Bobby Gallagher. Reed turned back around and reached for his beer. "It's been a long time," he said. "People's opinions change."

Manganelli's face hardened. "Not mine. That asshole burned half the city, and he can stay locked up for the rest of his days as far as I'm concerned."

"His lawyer said it was a setup," Ellery told Reed. "I looked it up online last night. The defense was that Carnevale was a handy fall guy for the cops, who were desperate to catch an arsonist—so desperate, his lawyer said, that they made one up. Carnevale's attorney claimed they had a witness who had seen the fire and would testify that it was not Carnevale who set it. The trouble was this supposed witness was a homeless drifter by the name of—you can't make this stuff up—The Blaze. No one had ever found him or verified his story, so Carnevale went down for the Gallagher fire. I guess everyone figured he'd made up the whole story about The Blaze."

"The Blaze?" Manganelli threw back his head to drain

the rest of his beer. "The Blaze was as real as you or me. Had a patch on his face right here that looked like a campfire." He indicated his left cheek. "But he was a drunk and a hustler, no kind of witness. He'd tell you whatever story you wanted for a quick buck."

"He existed? For real?" Ellery's eyes widened as she regarded the television again.

"Threw him in the drunk tank myself once or twice, back when I was walking a beat in Southie. He was a figment of his own imagination, but he was real enough to stink up the joint."

"Why didn't the cops track him down to get his story?" Ellery asked.

"What story? Some crap about witnessing a fire? We already had the bastard who burned that little boy. Besides, the way I heard it, the cops did look for him, but The Blaze had hit the road again. That or someone rolled him for his last two dollars, and he ended up as a John Doe in the morgue somewhere. Either way, it didn't matter. Luis Carnevale was guilty as sin—it was true then and it's true now. He'd better shut his hole and enjoy the comfort of prison while he can because where he's going, there's gonna be fire for all eternity."

Ellery did not reply, but she looked troubled. Reed followed her gaze to the television again, where the large screen played the old video in cinematic glory as the city burned.

# 3

In the morning, Ellery waited with Bump outside her apartment building for Reed's taxi to arrive. The unusually mild temperatures reacted with the leftover snow to create a low-lying fog that resembled the skin of hot milk. Ellery leaned against the rough brick exterior while Bump sniffed around, trying to catch the trail of one of the eighty-seven local squirrels. Reed showed up after only a few minutes, his briefcase in hand. "I thought we could get something to eat first," she said as her dog wagged an enthusiastic greeting around Reed's shins. "I'm starving, and he could use the exercise."

"Yes, hello to you, too," Reed muttered, trying to sidestep Bump. "You seem entirely recovered from your ordeal."

Speed Bump had taken a bullet for her last summer but, amazingly, survived. "He's doing great," she said, leaning down to give Bump's ears an affectionate scratch. "The vet can hardly believe it. He's like some sort of super dog."

"Super slobbery," Reed replied, making a pained face as Bump licked his shoes, but there was no animosity in his tone. Reed knew better than anyone what Bump had endured. As they fell into step together, Reed glanced up at the large five-story brick building that was her new home. "You have some impressive new digs."

"I sold my house in Woodbury to the first person who made an offer," she told him. "There was no way I could stay there." She didn't have to say more because Reed would understand this part, too. "This is the Foundry Building," she explained. The stalwart warehouse had been a fixture in this South Boston neighborhood for almost a century. "It was built in 1920, and the Hershey Manufacturing Company used it for more than sixty years to make everything from steam engines to soap. It was converted to lofts sometime in the 1980s."

Reed glanced at her, amused. "You've become quite the local historian."

"There's a Facebook page," she replied grimly. "All the neighbors are encouraged to join and introduce themselves."

"I'm dying to know what you said."

"Nothing. Why would I?" She tugged on Bump's leash to urge him from his dawdling. "Everyone already knows who I am."

At Dunkin' Donuts, she bought a Boston cream donut and cinnamon cruller for herself, and a large black coffee with a honey-oat bagel and cream cheese for Reed. They took the provisions back to her loft, where she put on water for tea while Reed used her coffee table to spread out the files that Joe Manganelli had given them the night before. He picked up each report in turn, read it silently, and then put it aside. Occasionally, he paused to write some notes on his laptop.

Ellery, feeling useless, curled her legs under her and set her mug of tea on the other end of the couch. "Are you finding anything?" she asked after he had viewed several of the additional reports.

"This one is interesting," he replied, not really looking at her. When he didn't elaborate, Ellery left him to his reading and got out her own laptop. She started poking around the internet again for more information about the other members of Dr. Sunny's group. She found a story about the death of Miles's wife, Letitia. Letitia Campbell was a petite woman with a pixie face and long, dangling earrings. She had been a much-loved music teacher in the Medford Public Schools, and her picture suggested why: she had a twinkle in her dark eyes and an impish, friendly smile. The story of her death was just what Miles had said, that a drunk ran a red light and T-boned the Campbells' car last December.

Ellery also found a news report about what she presumed was Alex's story: he and his best friend Nate Norman had stopped into a convenience store one night just before it was held up by a single gunman. The clerk pulled his own weapon, and the robber opened fire on everyone—wounding the clerk, killing Nate, and missing Alex entirely. The cops had arrested the guy two days later.

Strangely enough, Ellery couldn't find a single story about whatever had brought Tabitha to the crime survivors' group. Without the woman's last name or some element of the crime, it was impossible to narrow down. So Ellery switched back to Myra Gallagher and the fires. She found an interview with firefighter Kevin Powell that recounted his heroism. Apparently, Powell had been out drinking at Lucky Sevens with his work buddies and they'd all been fantasizing about being the one to catch the arsonist. Then later, Powell was heading home to his place in Dorchester around midnight when he saw the blaze. "God saved that woman, not me," Powell said in the interview. "He just put me in the right place at the right time to make it happen."

Ellery closed out the story with an angry click. *And what about the dead toddler?* she wondered. *Did God just not care enough to save him?*

On the other end of the couch, Reed sat back and rubbed his face with both hands. "There are five of these that merit further investigation," he said. "The two rapes that Manganelli flagged initially—the one with the elderly woman and the other daytime attack involving the gun and the rope—and then also this report of a prowler three blocks from Wendy Mendoza's apartment, and two other incidents Manganelli emailed me last night involving a possible peeping Tom. If you're up for it, I'd like to go take a look at the exact addresses. I have the beginnings of a theory, but it needs fleshing out."

"I'm in," she said, springing off the couch. Bump sat up with renewed excitement as well. "What's the theory?"

Reed shook his head. "I need to see the houses first. Then we'll know."

"Know what?"

"How he may be picking them."

They went to the old woman's apartment first. The victim, Edith Bellamy, lived not in Somerville but in nearby Arlington. Her street could have been a carbon copy of Wendy Mendoza's, with the multifamily houses packed all in a row on both sides of the narrow road. "This is the one," Ellery said, indicating a blue-gray four-square house with white trim and a loose, hanging gutter.

"So number forty-two is on the second floor," Reed said as he walked right up onto the porch. Ellery glanced around once to see that no one was watching before she followed suit. Reed peered in the glass in the front door and then inspected the wooden porch railings. He tugged them each in turn to see that they were sound.

"Manganelli said there was no weapon used in this case," Ellery said.

"Not on the victim, no. But whoever attacked her used a knife to slit the screen on the window before climbing inside." He glanced around the property once more and then set off down the steps. "Let's go see the next one."

They crisscrossed back and forth between Somerville and its neighboring communities until they had viewed all the crime scenes. Four were houses identical to Wendy Mendoza's, but the last was a traditional apartment building, brick and six stories high. It abutted a small parking lot that was half-filled with snowbanks and surrounded by a sagging chain-link fence. "Carla Watkins, age twenty-five, reported a guy in a ski mask peeping in her bedroom window on the fourth floor," Ellery read off of the report. Reed was already walking around toward the back, where the fire escape was. "This place doesn't look like the others," she called out as she followed him. The surrounding area was more commercial than residential. The deli across the street advertised a five-dollar sandwich special that included chips and a large soda.

"No, it doesn't look the same, but the other details match," Reed said. He stood at the bottom of the fire escape and jumped to try to reach the lowest edge, which was one story off the ground. After three tries, his fingers tipped the edge of the metal bar but he had not managed to grab hold. He halted, a little winded. "That's not as easy as it looks."

"It's not meant to be easy," Ellery replied with a frown. "Otherwise anyone could just climb up there."

"Ah," Reed said, holding up one finger. "Precisely. Physically, this offender is not just anyone, at least that's how he sees it. He's quite acrobatic. He picks his targets partly out of opportunity and partly as a personal challenge. It probably helps to keep the victims off guard as well, because ground-floor dwellers are liable to be more cautious with their doors and windows."

"Hey!" Someone shouted at them, and Ellery and Reed turned in the direction of the voice. A young African-American man had materialized at the back of the parking lot, and he was walking toward them in a confrontational manner. Ellery judged him to be about twenty-two years old. He was wearing baggy jeans and a sweatshirt that bore the fading image of Tupac Shakur. "Somethin' I can help you with?" he demanded in a tone that was the opposite of helpful.

"Just looking around," Reed replied.

"Yeah? This is private property." He looked from Reed to Ellery, and his eyes narrowed a bit. "Hey, wait a second. I know you. You're that killer cop."

"Ellery Hathaway," she supplied evenly. "And you are?"

"A concerned citizen who doesn't want no trigger-happy cops on my property."

"You're the owner?" Reed asked, and the young man scowled.

"I live here. I got rights."

Reed withdrew his FBI identification and showed it to their new friend. "Let's try the introductions again," he said. "I'm Reed Markham. Your name is . . . ?"

"Markus," the man said reluctantly. "Markus Evans."

"Mr. Evans, do you know anything about the reports of a prowler on the fire escape last year?"

"Prowler? You mean that dude who was peeping in our windows? Yeah, I seen him. He seen me, too, when I chased his ass clear down the street."

"You saw him? Did you get a good look?" Reed asked.

Markus shrugged one skinny shoulder. "It was dark, right? I ain't got night-vision goggles. All I know is that Carla started screaming, and I was standing around the corner, having a smoke. I came running to see what she was hollering for, and I seen him coming down the fire escape. Big dude. Dressed in all black, with a ski mask on in late September. He was clearly bad news. So yeah, I chased him. He was a fast mofo, let me tell you." He looked Reed up and down skeptically. "I don't get it. What's the FBI want with some lame-ass peeper?"

"Maybe he was out to do more than peeping," Reed replied.

Markus glanced toward the fire escape and beat his left palm with his right fist. "Yeah? He'd better not try it, or we could fix him up real good."

"Was there anything else you noticed about him?" Ellery asked him. "Seeing as how you're a concerned citizen."

"He was about my height," Markus said, indicating the top of his head, which would put the peeper about six feet tall. "Bigger, though, kinda meaty-like."

"Skin color?"

Markus scoffed at her. "I told you he was wearing a ski mask."

"What about his hands? Did you see his hands?"

Markus appeared to think about this. "Man, all I got was a quick look. He was bookin', you know what I'm saying? I think he had gloves on." His eyes widened at a new thought. "He had a watch or a bracelet or something that caught the light. It showed when he had his hands raised up like this when he was climbing down, and his sleeves came up. The thing was gold or silver or some shit, shining all the way around his wrist. I remember thinking he might've lifted it from some other apartment, creeping through their windows."

"A watch," Ellery repeated, less than thrilled with this additional non-identifying information.

"Or a bracelet," Markus said defensively. "It was thick-like. Expensive looking."

"Right hand or left hand?" Ellery asked him.

Markus thought for a moment. "Right. It was the right hand. Look, I'd love to stand out here with you all day talking sicko creepers, but I ain't seen nothing else and my balls are freezing off."

Reed pulled out a business card. "You see him or anyone else suspicious hanging around the place again, call 911. Then call me."

"I see him again up there, and you can bring the body bags with you."

"Just call the police," Reed said mildly. "Let them handle it."

Markus hunched his shoulders. "Yeah? You call and give them this address, and just wait to see how long 'til they show up. He'd have raped and killed the whole damn building, and then thrown himself a parade, if I'd waited on those fat donut dunkers. I see that guy climbing up there again, I'm taking him out. He won't be your problem no more."


Back in the truck, Ellery idled with the heat on. It was mild for December but the damp air held the remnants of snow and her fingers had turned to ice. She held them over the vents and looked at Reed. "You think that was our guy he chased off from here?" she asked.

"Ski mask, and a tall building that required some athletic

ability to master," Reed replied. "It's certainly a possibility. Either way, I'd say Carla Watkins was lucky to escape unharmed that night."

"If it wasn't him, that means there are two of them."

"If only it were just two," Reed said, shuffling through his notes. He pushed his wire-rimmed glasses up the bridge of his nose. "I think as a next step, I'd like to talk to Wendy Mendoza, if you believe she'd be willing to meet with me."

"I'm sure she would. She said she'd do anything to get this guy." Ellery considered. "There's a group meeting today at five, and we don't have to meet Manganelli until eight. You could swing by after the meeting to talk to Wendy."

"Sounds good. What do you want to do in the meantime?"

Ellery put the truck into gear. "There's a sandwich place we can go for lunch," she said, "and after that, there's one other crime scene I want to see."

They ate lunch on opposite sides of an expansive booth, downing thick deli sandwiches that required two hands to hold them. Ellery watched Reed raising the roast beef roll to his mouth and remembered the last time she'd seen him, when his hands had been swathed in bandages. Reed caught her staring and moved to brush any traces of lunch from his fingers. "Did I get something on me?" he asked as he groped for a napkin.

"No, sorry. I was just thinking—your hands, they're

completely healed. You can't even tell what happened."

Reed put down the napkin and held out his hands between them, palms up. "It turned out to be just a bunch of small cuts. Nothing that leaves any scars."

As usual, the word "scars" made Ellery drop her own hands into her lap, although Reed had seen the marks on her wrists plenty by now. "I'm glad," she said finally. "I'm glad you got away clean."

They both knew this was another lie; she had shot a man, and Reed had covered it up. He rested his hands on the table a moment, his fingers inching forward as though he might reach for her. She held her breath and he stopped.

"I was happy when you called," he confessed in a low voice. "I've been wondering how you were doing."

"I'm fine," she said, raising her chin, daring him to deny it. He'd rescued her twice now, and she certainly didn't want him to think she was fishing for a third round. "How—how are you? How's your daughter?"

"Tula's wonderful." He smiled such a delighted, unselfconscious grin that it hit Ellery right between the ribs. Her own father had left when Ellery was ten, and that was the start of all the trouble to follow. She had a few nice memories, times when he'd hoisted her high on his shoulders while they'd walked through the city or when he took her and Danny down to the lake to swim, but these images were hazy and far away and she no longer trusted them. Reed was still smiling as he talked about his daughter. "Her current ambition is to be a race car driver–princess when she grows up, but I think she's much more likely to follow her mother into journalism. After she visits, my house is covered in bits of scrap paper documenting everything that happened from a six-year-old's point of view. The quality of the snacks figures heavily into the narrative."

Ellery forced herself to return his smile. "She sounds like a great kid."

Reed hesitated, seeming unsure about whether he should say more. "McGreevy's retiring this year," he said finally. "I may take his position so that I can travel less and see more of Tula."

"You'd be the boss?"

"In a sense. Why? Do you not think I'm cut out for the role?"

"Who would do your job?"

He shifted in his seat, looking uncomfortable. "The FBI has many talented behavioral analysts. I'm hardly the only one qualified for the job."

Ellery was quiet, thinking of the hundreds of law enforcement personnel who had turned out to look for her fourteen years ago. "Yes," she agreed at length. "But you're the one who found me."

They had eaten a late lunch, and traffic poked along

slowly back through the city, so the gray sky was already deepening toward night when they arrived at Ellery's destination. "You forget how blasted early the sun sets up here in the wintertime," Reed said as he eyed the rolling clouds overhead. "It's the middle of the afternoon."

"You get used to it," Ellery said distractedly. She was scanning the row of buildings in front of her. "I guess that's the one."

"One what?" Reed asked as they stood in a pile of dirty slush.

"That sporting goods store and that Mexican takeout joint used to be Gallagher Furniture. This is where the fire was." Watching Reed in action all morning had shown her the importance of walking the scene of the crime, but the original building had been razed after the fire. Most of the surrounding shops had turned over in the intervening twenty-six years. She wasn't actually sure what she was supposed to be looking for after all this time. She closed her eyes briefly and tried to imagine it—the acrid smell of the wood smoke as the furniture went up in flames, the loud wailing of the fire engines bearing down on the scene. Ellery turned her head to look down the street as if in search of them.

"What happened to the place after the fire?" Reed asked her.

"Insurance paid out—a few million if I recall the story correctly. The Gallaghers didn't need to reopen a new store."

"Hmm," Reed observed. "Interesting."

"But it's not like it could have been arson for profit," Ellery continued. "Not with the little boy there."

"You're right, it wouldn't make sense. Business owners looking to cash in usually hire a torch man, not send their wife and kid downtown with a can of gasoline." The air had grown drier and colder as the day wore on, and he rubbed his hands together to warm them. "So what are you hoping to find here? You think that drifter is still hanging out on the street somewhere?"

"No." She looked around again. "It's just something's been bothering me . . ."

They both heard it then, a siren in the distance. It was a police car, not a fire engine, and Ellery turned to watch as it wove through the traffic and then disappeared out of sight.

"This is a one-way street," she said suddenly.

"Like over half the streets of this godforsaken city," Reed concurred.

"Lucky Sevens is over that way," she continued, pointing as though Reed had not said anything. "Dorchester is to the south. Kevin Powell said he was on his way home from the bar, heading back to Dorchester, when he saw the flames. This street doesn't go toward Dorchester—in fact, it points away from it, toward the harbor. He'd have no reason to be on it."

Reed froze and the implication of what she was saying

hung in the air between them. "Maybe," he said carefully, "maybe he got lost."

"A Boston firefighter? It's his job to know the streets. Besides, the papers said he grew up here. He had to know his way home."

"He'd been drinking . . ."

Ellery opened her mouth to protest further and then shut it again. She was suddenly cold. "Let's get out of here."

They climbed back into her truck, and she pointed it in the direction of MGH, where the group meeting would be starting soon. In the close confines of the cab, a heavy silence descended over them. Ellery felt her heart beating inside her throat, a sick feeling roiling in her stomach. Myra would be at the meeting, and Ellery wasn't sure how to face her with this new guilty knowledge.

"It doesn't prove anything," Reed offered at last. "Witness stories don't always make sense. People leave out important details, get the times wrong, all sorts of narrative missteps. That doesn't mean the sequence of events that night didn't occur roughly the way Powell claims they did."

"Right. Of course." She waited a moment. "But that's a thing, right? People who set fires on purpose so that they can be the hero?"

"Yes, it does happen," Reed allowed after a beat. "You'd need a lot more evidence than what you've got even to raise the suspicion, though. Right now, you have a tipsy fireman who maybe took a wrong turn down a dark street and ended up a city hero."

"He's the fire commissioner." She glanced at him. "I guess he must have been really into his work."

"Or really successful at it."

More silence. "I wish I could talk to him," Ellery said.

"Ellery . . ."

"Like you said, maybe it all makes sense. Maybe there's something in the story he left out that explains everything."

"It's not your case. It's not anyone's case! This was all investigated by dozens of seasoned professionals years ago."

"Like McGreevy. That's what you said, right? He was on the case."

"In some capacity, yes."

"Then maybe he could get us in to see Powell."

"Us? I have a plane to catch tomorrow at noon."

She spotted a parking space that was just opening up and swooped in to grab it. Reed clutched the side of the truck as she threw him off balance. "You're not curious? Those seasoned professionals you mentioned wanted this case closed real badly—maybe badly enough that they didn't look too hard at Powell's story."

Reed pressed himself against the car door, as far away from her as possible. "You're suggesting I telephone my boss and float the theory that the FBI may have botched a high-profile arson investigation, and then, because that's going to go over so well, I should follow it up with a request to check up on his work? That's what you're asking for?"

Ellery blinked. "Is that a no?"

"That's career suicide, is what it is."

Ellery slumped in her seat, her hands loose on the wheel. She had torched her own career so thoroughly, she might never get it back. It wasn't fair to ask Reed to do the same thing, not when they barely had anything to go on. "Sorry," she said. "You're right."

Reed let out a lengthy sigh. "I'll make the call," he said. "Just . . . give me a little time to try to get the wording down."

Ellery grinned. Reed's father, she knew, was a politician. Surely Reed could craft a winning speech. "No hurry," she replied as she opened her door. "It's only been twenty-six years."


The survivors group met in the same room as last time, and most people had already assembled by the time Ellery hurried in at five past. There was no time to grab the terrible coffee, but she need not have worried, because Miles waved her over with a smile. "I brought you a hot chocolate," he said, handing it to her. "Figured you might like the taste of this a little better."

"Oh, thanks," she said, feeling touched and awkward. She was treating these people like research subjects and here he was extending a bit of human kindness. She felt her face grow warm as she accepted the paper cup. "This was really nice of you."

"You need something to make these meetings go down a little easier." He took a sip of his own coffee.

"Yeah. I, uh . . . last time, I meant to say—I'm really sorry about what happened to your wife."

"Thanks. She was a special lady. She didn't deserve this, not that anyone does." He paused and pushed up his glasses with one finger. "After it happened, I couldn't think about what happened without being so angry, so furious I felt like I could kill that guy with my bare hands for what he did."

"I don't blame you."

"But it's hard, carrying that anger around. It's so heavy you can't get out of bed some days." He sighed. "I realized when I started coming here that I didn't want to be angry every time I thought about Tetia. I wanted to think of her and be happy, because we were happy."

"Is it working?" Ellery asked doubtfully.

"A lil' bit," he said with a smile. "A lil' bit every day. What about you? You think you'll talk today?"

She shrugged one shoulder. "What's to say? Everyone here already knows my story. The newspapers printed every detail. There's been at least two movies by now.

What the hell can I really add at this point?"

Miles looked thoughtful. "I'd say . . . forget about the papers. The papers don't own your story. Hollywood doesn't own it, either. It belongs to you, and you're the only one who can tell it."

Ellery didn't get a chance to answer this because Dr. Sunny asked them all to take their seats. Ellery looked around the group but did not see Wendy. This was going to be a problem since Reed wanted to talk to her. Dr. Sunny started out with some follow-up from the last meeting, asking Miles if he had worked out a plan for the one-year anniversary of his wife's death. Miles said he was taking the day off from teaching and that his brother was coming up from New York to spend the day. He detailed a few plans they had to honor Letitia's memory, but Ellery tuned him out. She watched the door, hoping that Wendy would walk through it.

Then Myra started talking, and Ellery jerked her attention back to the group. ". . . seeing the fire on television again after all these years, it's so difficult. Patrick got up and left the room when the news came on. He can't even stomach looking at it. And that woman, going on and on about how she's going to fight for Carnevale to be released—she's even threatening a new trial!"

"What if she might be right?" Ellery blurted out before she could stop herself. All eyes shifted toward her, and

Ellery swallowed twice in quick succession. "What if Luis Carnevale might be innocent?"

Myra's mottled face twisted into a deep frown. "What are you saying? The police caught him right at the scene."

"What if he was there, but he didn't start the fire?"

Dr. Sunny was frowning, too. "Ellery, where are you going with this?"

"Nothing . . . I was just reading up on the fires, since they've been in the news, and it seems like Carnevale's niece might be right that there were questions about the case. Carnevale has always maintained he is innocent."

"So did Ted Bundy," Tabitha replied with a snort.

Myra's blue eyes watered and her chin trembled. "Of course he did it. He was there, he had a history of setting fires, everyone said so, and he reeked like gasoline . . ."

"Okay, Myra, okay." Dr. Sunny's tone was soothing. She shot a warning look at Ellery. "Myra wasn't raising the question of guilt or innocence," she said. "She was talking about how it feels to have the case back in the public eye."

Ellery'd had about enough of feelings. "It doesn't matter, don't you see? The question is out there whether she likes it or not."

The group stiffened in stunned silence, and Myra raised a trembling hand to her face. "Ellery, I think that's enough on this subject," Dr. Sunny said steadily. "I am asking you to move on. Who else would like to share today?"

At that moment, the door opened, and Wendy slunk into the room, her hoodie drawn up over her bald head. She took a seat and fixed her gaze to the floor. Ellery felt relieved at the sight of her, and not just because she had promised Reed to bring him the witness. She was worried about the girl.

No one else seemed to be leaping at the chance to share, so Dr. Sunny turned to Ellery with an assessing look. "Ellery, since you are in a chatty mood today, perhaps you would like to tell the group a little bit about why you're here."

"I'm here because you asked me to be."

"I mean, what circumstances in your life caused you to be suited for a group like this?" Dr. Sunny corrected smoothly.

Everyone turned to look at Ellery, even Wendy. Ellery tugged the sleeves of her sweater down over her hands and fidgeted in her chair. "I was abducted the night of my fourteenth birthday by a man named Francis Coben," she recited at last. "You've probably heard of him, on account of there were sixteen girls before me. They didn't make it."

"What happened that night?" Dr. Sunny wanted to know, and Ellery felt a flash of irritation because the woman damn sure knew the details by now.

"I was riding my bike. He stopped me to ask for directions."

"What were you thinking, right then, when he stopped you?"

Ellery faltered. No one had ever asked her this question before. "I, uh . . ." She let herself remember it, the sweltering night and her T-shirt stuck to her chest, how the only way to get a breeze was to pedal fast through the dark neighborhood. She'd wished she had seventy-five cents to get a soda at the corner store. "He had a nice car," she said wistfully, remembering how naïve she'd been. "That's what I thought when he pulled over. It was new and shiny and expensive-looking, much nicer than the usual cars in my neighborhood. So when he rolled down the window, I thought he'd be nice. I thought everyone with money had to be nice—if you had money, you'd be happy, right? Maybe if I was nice back, he'd give me a dollar or something for helping him, and I could get a drink."

She stopped there, lost in the memory. She saw herself getting off the bike and approaching Coben's car. Saw his smile and his dark, floppy hair.

"What happened next?" Dr. Sunny asked softly, and Ellery snapped out of her reverie.

She sat up straight and went back to the facts. "He grabbed me by the throat and choked me until I went unconscious. I woke up in the closet. And everyone already knows what happened after that."

The bare walls reverberated with her furious words. Ellery looked around the circle of faces, defiant, daring them to judge her or pity her over the details of Coben's torture. One by one, they all slid their gaze away. Coben's story made for great TV, but no one ever wanted to sit in a room with his living victim and admit they had consumed her pain for entertainment. Everyone in the group had survived a nightmare; only one of them had to do it daily on the public stage.

When the meeting broke up, Wendy hurried over to Ellery. "Did you talk to him? Did you find anything out?"

Ellery nodded and started walking the other woman toward the door. "I talked to Detective Manganelli, and he hasn't forgotten about your case, not at all. But more importantly, Agent Reed Markham from the FBI has agreed to take a look at your case and possibly related incidents to see if he can offer some insights. He's waiting outside to talk to you, if you're willing to speak with him."

Wendy looked uncertain, but she said, "Yeah, sure, whatever will help get this guy."

Outside under the cover of a gunmetal sky, Reed stood by the lamppost, looking like some sort of caped avenger in his black overcoat. Ellery led Wendy over to him and made the necessary introductions. Reed extended his hand in greeting but Wendy would not touch him. Reed retracted his hand and cleared his throat. "I'm very sorry that you've had to endure all this, Ms. Mendoza," he said with genuine warmth. "I have just a few quick questions for you."

Wendy nodded and hugged herself. "Go ahead."

"It seems likely that the offender had some knowledge of the layout of your apartment. Did you have any workmen through the place in the few months before the attack? Repairs, a cable installation—anything of that nature?"

Wendy shook her head. "No, nothing. The cops already asked me that. There was a plumber who did some work in the downstairs apartment, but he was an old white guy with a bunch of missing teeth. The guy who came in my window was young and built like a tank."

"Did you have the sense of anyone following you or watching you prior to the attack?"

Wendy looked at Ellery, who gave her an encouraging nod. Wendy took a long, ragged breath. "I don't know. If you're a woman living on your own, you kinda always feel like you're being watched. Guys whistle at you on the street. You feel their eyes on your body." She shuddered. "You almost never feel 100 percent safe."

Ellery looked away from the conversation and saw Myra's husband, Patrick, wheeling Myra down the ramp from the hospital. "I'll be right back," she murmured before darting off in their direction. "Myra, wait up just a second?"

Patrick stopped in his tracks, his gaze bleak as it settled

on Ellery. "We've got to get home. Myra can't take bein' out in the cold."

"Please," Ellery said. "I just wanted to apologize. I shouldn't have badgered you like that during the group, and I'm sorry."

Myra drew her mitten-covered hands together as if gathering up her dignity. "I accept your apology," she said stiffly. "I know you come from law enforcement, so you have different views."

Ellery hesitated, not sure whether to press the old woman any further. "If Carnevale isn't guilty," she said, "it means someone else was—someone who has gotten away with it for years."

"Enough of this nonsense," Patrick said, pushing Myra past Ellery. "We need to get going now."

"They said he was the one," Myra said helplessly as Ellery scrambled along next to the wheelchair.

"They may have lied," Ellery told her. "Wouldn't you want to know?"

Myra covered her face with her hands. "I just want it to be over," she said. "Twenty-six years now, and Bobby still can't rest in peace."

"Leave her alone!" Patrick snapped, pushing the wheelchair so fast he nearly ran over Ellery's foot in the process. "She's been through enough."

Ellery backed away then and let Patrick help his wife into the car. Myra was crying softly now, and Patrick's eyes shot daggers in Ellery's direction. Ellery turned back, intent on rejoining Wendy and Reed, but Miles materialized at her side. He had apparently been waiting to talk to her.

"That took guts today," he told her. "Speaking up in group like that."

Ellery glimpsed the disappearing taillights of the Gallaghers' car and was not so sure that Myra would agree. "I shouldn't have pushed her," she said.

"What? No, I mean what you said about your past, about what happened to you." He looked up at the sky for a moment. "Listen, I just wanted to say . . . I teach fourteen-year-old kids, you know? They're funny and crack wise and they're tryin' to be so tough all the time, but really, they're just babies. Barely figuring things out. For someone to grab a kid like that and do those things . . ." He shook his head as if to clear it. "You should own the shit out of your story, Ellery, because to have survived and thrived the way you have, you must be one amazing lady."

Ellery felt her face go pink again. "Oh. Well, thanks. I think."

He smiled and touched her lightly on the arm. "Same time, next week?"

"Uh, yeah. We'll see."

"I'll bring the hot cocoa."

Miles wandered off in the direction of the T, and Ellery jogged back to where Reed was standing. Wendy had given him a wide berth, about three people's worth of personal space, but she hadn't run off. "How's it going?" Ellery asked them.

He nodded at Wendy. "Wendy remembered something she left out of her original narrative. The offender tasted sweet."

Ellery looked to Wendy. "Tasted sweet? Like how? Like he had sugar on him, or are we talking about some sort of metabolic disease here?"

Wendy shrank backward. "I don't know. He—he had gloves on, but when I turned my head away his wrist kind of ended up in my mouth for a second. He tasted sugary, I guess, like breakfast cereal."

"Wendy," Reed said, "do you recall if he was wearing a watch or a bracelet of some kind?"

Wendy searched herself and came up looking surprised. "Actually, yeah, on his right hand. It got stuck in my hair when he held me down and he cursed me out for it, like it was my fault. Why? Is that important?"

"Maybe," Ellery said, trying to match Reed's neutral tone. "We don't know yet."

Wendy clenched her hands and sucked in her bottom lip. "When will you know? When?"

Reed and Ellery exchanged a look, and Ellery reached for Wendy's shoulder. The other woman drew away. "We're doing everything we can," Ellery said softly. "I promise you."

"Promises are great," Wendy replied, her voice bitter. "But I need something quicker than that."

"We'll get him," Ellery said. Reed turned his head away at her words, like he wouldn't be party to this lie. He didn't understand that sometimes the lie was necessary to make it through one more day.

"Sure, you'll get him," Wendy said, like she no longer believed it, either. "That's what Manganelli told me, too." She shoved her hands in her pockets and jogged off toward the street, disappearing into the dark.

Reed and Ellery met up with Manganelli that night at a different pub, one closer to home for Ellery, but the change in venue came at the behest of Manganelli. "I may've mentioned to the guys that you were here to look at the case, and now they all want to meet you," the detective explained to Reed. "I figured they might all try to show up at the regular bar to get a look-see."

"I appreciate your discretion," Reed replied solemnly. "I have the files for you, if you'd like them back."

"Nah, keep 'em. I have copies. Did you get anything?"

Reed explained his theory about their daring, athletic rapist, and Manganelli frowned.

"That's it? He's a guy who likes to break into second-story buildings or higher? What am I supposed to do—put out a BOLO for a guy carrying around *Architectural Digest*?"

"I warned you not to expect miracles," Reed replied. "I can offer you this profile of your offender, based on what we know so far." He slid a piece of paper across to the detective. "He's young, probably early- to mid-twenties, physically strong, and flexible. He probably works out regularly at a gym and is known to show off feats of strength for friends and family. He lives in the area and is familiar with the general outlay of multifamily homes. He may have grown up in one or resides in one now. I've indicated on the list there those incidents that have a high probability of being committed by this same offender, but it's almost certainly not comprehensive. I would urge you and officials from the surrounding towns to compare notes again to turn up any similar cases, especially ones where physical agility seemed to be a strength of the offender."

"Great, yeah. I'll get right on that." Manganelli sounded deflated. "I want this guy bad. I do. But I have six other cases on my desk right now. I was hoping for something a little more concrete to go on."

"Well, according to Wendy Mendoza, he tastes sweet."

Manganelli made a face. "What the hell does that mean? He's candy-flavored or what?"

"I couldn't get any more detail from her," Reed said with a sweep of his hand. "Maybe it will become clearer with additional context."

"Right now, it makes no goddamned sense," grumbled Manganelli.

"Reed has given up his time to come all the way up here and look at the cases," Ellery reminded him. "He's offered you some new angles."

"What I really need is new suspects," Manganelli said, sounding defeated. "But yeah, thanks. Thanks a lot."

Later, as they left the bar and climbed back into the truck, Reed threw his scarf across his lap with a sigh. "I have a feeling that once Manganelli relays our conversation, the local law enforcement would not be so keen to turn out to visit me if I were to make a return visit to the great city of Somerville."

"He's frustrated," Ellery said. "He wants results and he wants them yesterday. Once he stops and thinks about what you've told him, he'll realize it's more helpful than it seemed initially."

Reed chuckled. "I can't tell if you're supporting me or damning me with faint praise, Hathaway."

She gave a half-shrug. "You know how it goes. Profilers always look best in hindsight."

"Oh-ho! Now I know I've been burned. You're doubting my abilities now, are you?"

"Not at all."

"Let me see if I can redeem myself then. That gentleman you were talking to tonight after the meeting . . ."

"Miles?"

"Miles. Yes. He's going to ask you out."

Ellery coughed in surprise and clutched the wheel a bit tighter. "He wasn't asking me out."

"I said he will ask you out. I can't tell you when. I'm not actually a fortune-teller, you know."

"Obviously not," Ellery replied, striving to keep her tone light. "Or you would know—I'm never going on a date with Miles."

There was a beat of silence and she could feel Reed stewing on the other side of the cab. Finally, his leg jerked and he sat up straighter. "Okay, I'll bite: why are you never going on a date with Miles? Is he unattractive? Uncouth? Allergic to hounds?"

"He seems very nice," Ellery allowed. "I just don't date."

"What do you mean, you don't date?"

"I've never been on a date. Don't have any plans to start, either." They arrived at her building and she parked the truck. Reed was looking at her strangely as she came around and joined him on the sidewalk.

"What about Sam Parker?" he asked, referencing her old boss.

"That was sex," she replied. "Not dating. He was married."

"I noticed that part," Reed replied with a scowl as she let them into the building. "But surely there are suitable men in the greater Boston area who are not married."

She eyed him as they waited by the elevators. "Why do you care?"

"I—I don't. Not really. I just hadn't heard this 'no dating' philosophy of yours before and I'm curious to know more about it."

"It's not possible for me to go on a date like a normal person," she said. "You of all people should know that." She unlocked her front door and pushed inside, leaving him standing in the hall. He came sputtering in a few moments later.

"What? Me? I don't see what my opinion has to do with anything, but since we're on the subject, I don't think—"

She didn't get to find out what he thought because Speed Bump came skittering over to them with something stuck to his left front paw. "Hey, boy, what's this?" she asked as she bent to free him. It was a folded piece of paper, now wrinkled and covered in dog slobber.

"What is it?" Reed asked as he moved to stand near her shoulder.

"I don't know." She opened it up and then sucked in a sharp breath. The printed note had just one line: GET BACK IN THE CLOSET WHERE YOU BELONG.

# 4

Reed watched as Ellery crumpled the hateful note in one hand and sent it sailing into the trash can across the room. "And there you have the answer as to why I can't date," she said, not looking in his direction. "Come on, boy, let's go out." She bent to clip on Bump's leash as the dog wagged his tail happily, unperturbed by what had just taken place.

"What are you doing?" Reed blocked her path to the door. "You can't just go back out there."

The look she gave him was both tired and resigned. "I have to go out there every damn day," she said. "Tonight is no different."

She stepped around him and Reed followed her back out into the dimly lit gray corridor. His gaze swept up and down, probing for anyone lurking in the shadows, as Ellery marched toward the elevator without a backward glance. He hurried to catch up with her before the elevator doors closed. She leaned against the metal wall, studying her fingernails, while Reed just stared.

"That's not the first one," he said finally. "Is it?"

She said nothing as the elevator dinged its arrival on the ground floor; she merely pushed off the wall and brushed past him toward the outside. Reed realized he wasn't going to be able to force her to talk, so he just fell into step beside her as they walked the cold, dark streets. The jingle of Bump's collar sounded overly loud in the frosty night air. When he paused to sniff at a snowbank, Ellery turned to look at Reed. "There hasn't been a note before," she said. "Not like that. Reporters sometimes slip their cards under my door, asking me to please call them. Everyone wants to write the next true crime bestseller, it seems." Her voice took on a touch of irony, and Reed was forced to glance away. His own book about Ellery had sold more than a million copies; of course, back then, she'd had a pseudonym and no one knew her address.

"This wasn't some reporter who wrote that note," Reed pointed out. "That was a threat."

Ellery again said nothing. She stalked off down the street with Bump scrambling behind her to keep up. Reed loped after them, his breath fogging in the cold air. "On Halloween, someone thought it would be funny to leave a pair of rubber hands outside my door," she said when he'd rejoined her. This was the Ellery he knew: the one who recited terrible facts without a trace of emotion. "Sometimes people try to take my picture when they think I'm not looking. After the summer, when I first moved here, I was in line at the grocery store, and the checkout girl stopped the conveyor belt and just started staring. I turned around to see what she was looking at and found out I'd been standing next to a tabloid magazine with my picture on it. Then a few weeks ago . . ." She stopped suddenly, and looked up at the sky.

"What?" Reed asked softly when she did not continue.

She shook her head and kicked at the icy slush on the edge of the sidewalk. "I was waiting for the T when this guy came over to me. He was dressed in a suit and carrying a briefcase, kind of like you. He asked if I could tell him the time. I didn't realize until I had my arm out to check my watch that he wasn't interested in the time—he wanted to see the scars. I guess I should be glad he wasn't taking pictures, too." An edge crept into her voice at these last words, and she made a pivot back toward the apartment building, leaving him momentarily alone on the street.

"I'm sorry," Reed said as he caught up with her again. "I'm truly sorry for all of it. But Ellery, this note tonight wasn't sick curiosity—this was a power play by someone hell-bent on rattling you, at the very least."

"They'll have to try harder, then." She yanked open the door to her building and Reed followed her back inside. She glanced behind her when she realized that he was still there. "I thought you had a plane to catch."

"I'm worried about you." They rode the elevator up to her floor. He looked around the hallway for any sign of security cameras. "Is there any way to see who left the note?"

"No," she said as she unlocked her door. "People here value their privacy."

Reed was glad to see at least that she double-locked the door behind her, but his heart was heavy as he watched her set about making tea. Her shoulders were square, her mouth a determined line, but her eyes were downcast and hidden from him. He was beginning to understand that all the locked doors in the world weren't going to fix the problem, that it wasn't possible to shut out Francis Coben on the other side. Even from his prison cell, he trailed her like a ghost because the world looked at her and saw only him. "The ogling and paparazzi will die down as people get tired of the story," he said with sympathy. "But the note tonight still concerns me."

She looked up and met his gaze. "You're thinking of the summer, of the birthday cards."

"Truthfully, yes." The last time someone started harassing Ellery about her macabre past, it had turned out to be the prelude to a series of brutal murders.

Ellery put two mugs on the counter, so at least she wasn't kicking him out. "You really think I'm unlucky enough to attract the attention of a third serial killer?" she asked dubiously as she dropped in the tea bags.

Reed had to admit it would be a stretch. "It's unlikely this note is from a serial offender," he agreed, "but you have to keep in mind that these men are admirers of one another's work."

"I think I know that," she replied evenly, and Reed's face went hot. Of course she wasn't some rube patrolman that he had to explain this to; she'd been there, unwittingly, the night one serial murderer had birthed another.

"He doesn't have to be a serial killer," he said quietly, "to be someone very dangerous." He wondered if she had searched for herself on the internet, the way he had from time to time, and seen the explosion of results since the summer. She had a full Wiki page now, one that was of course linked back to Coben's, but that was just a drop in the bucket compared to the more gruesome commentary. There were message boards and social media groups devoted to her—some admiring, some just hungry for more of her story. They speculated on precisely which farm tools Coben had used to rape her. They knew she had nailed her closet doors shut. They discussed openly whether she, out of all the victims, deserved to be the one to live. There were Photoshopped pictures and derogatory sexual slurs, and even a few disgusting anonymous monsters who claimed they'd like to take up where Coben had left off. "Maybe I should stay here tonight," he said, "just to be sure whoever it is doesn't come back."

"Absolutely not." She took up her mug of tea and walked past him toward the living room.

"Ellery . . ."

"I have a gun, and you know I can use it."

He shut his mouth, recalling the last time he'd seen her with it. Ellery curled into one end of the sofa, nothing more dangerous than tea in her hands, and after a moment, Reed gingerly lowered himself to sit on the other end of the couch. There was a long, uncomfortable silence.

"You're not responsible for what happens to me," she told him. "Not anymore."

"Yes, pardon me for giving a damn," he shot back, irritated now. He was about to say more when his phone rang from inside his pants pocket. The caller ID read Kimmy, and Reed would have loved to ignore it, but he knew at this point she would only keep ringing him until he picked up. He'd been dodging her calls for more than a week, and his sister had surely had enough. "Kimmy," he said, forcing some cheer into his voice. "How nice to hear from you."

"Sure, so nice you haven't replied to any of my messages," she answered, but she sounded only mildly annoyed by this inconvenience. Reed's loved ones were used to his erratic schedule.

"Sorry, I've been really busy."

"Uh-huh. I've got two kids with the flu, a cat that needs four teeth removed, Jack's out of town until Tuesday, and oh yeah, I've taken on three new divorces this week. Merry effing Christmas to all of us, every one." Kimmy ran a family law practice in Roanoke, Virginia. She had volunteered to handle Reed's side in his own divorce, but he had declined her kind offer to *show Sarit that she can't just walk off with Tula—she's a Markham whether Sarit likes it or not.* "You're not so busy that you're skipping Christmas, are you?" Kimmy asked him now.

Reed glanced at Ellery, who was sipping her tea and scrolling through messages on her phone. "No, no. I'll be there."

"Good. What do you think this big announcement from Daddy is all about?"

Reed had received the holiday summons along with his three sisters, but he'd honestly not given the matter much thought. His father, Virginia State Senator Angus Markham, would have been a preacher if he hadn't gone into politics. A born orator, he could whip up a speech-cum-sermon in the blink of an eye, and he didn't care whether his audience was on a street corner or in the state capitol building. "You know Dad—he loves a stage."

"I keep waiting for him to have a lectern installed in the family room," Kimmy replied.

"Mama would never stand for that."

"Speaking of Mama, I talked to her the other day, and she

said she thinks Daddy will love the genealogy tree, especially since it confirms what he's been saying all these years, that he's related to George Washington." Reed sat forward and cradled his head in his free hand as if to ward off the conversation to come. He knew full well the reason Kimmy had been trying to reach him. "On her side, Mama's ancestors go back to Mary, Queen of Scots. Can you believe that? Our mother is like royalty."

"I've never doubted it," Reed said, his eyes closed as he waited for The Question. Kimmy didn't keep him in suspense.

"Have you gotten your results yet?"

Reed clenched his jaw and then willed himself to relax. "No, not yet," he lied. The email from DNA Discoveries, Inc. had been sitting in his in-box for a couple of weeks now, but Reed had not been able to make himself retrieve the results.

"Reed," his sister said reproachfully. "We're running out of time to get this done before Christmas, and we need you."

"You don't," he replied, more harshly than he'd intended. "You don't need me for this."

"Of course we do," Kimmy said, sounding wounded. "You're a part of this family, no matter what—Mama and Daddy would spit hellfire if we left you out. And think of the surprises you might find! Maybe we have a blood relative in common after all somewhere back through the ages. Wouldn't that just be amazing?"

"Right, amazing."

"So you'll get the results and send them to me?" Kimmy prodded. "Soon?"

"Soon," Reed answered, regretting again his initial agreement to participate in this project. When he hung up with Kimberly, he found Ellery had put her phone aside and was watching him with naked curiosity. "My sister," he said by way of explanation. "The youngest one, Kimmy. She's got a bee in her bonnet about our family history, so she had us all take a DNA test so she could make an ancestry history book for our father for Christmas. You know, where you spit in a tube and send it off and then you get a report back telling you that you're one-quarter Dutch, one-eighth Native American, and so forth."

"Oh," Ellery said, and then she looked into her tea. "That's nice, I guess, that she wants to document your family DNA. But, um, aren't you—?"

"Adopted," Reed finished for her with a sigh as he sank back into the couch. "Yes."

"Wow," Ellery said after a beat. "That's some Christmas gift to you, then. Your sister has got a set on her the size of Saturn, huh?"

He couldn't help his grin, because, yes, Ellery had nailed Kimmy in a nutshell. "She means well," he said. "She's not trying to make me feel excluded so much as she's catering to our father's love affair with his own history. Now that everyone can trace their heritage back practically to the Neanderthals, Kimmy's taken on the 'big picture' view, which is that we're all related, more or less. I'm just on a different branch of the family tree."

"And what do you think about that?" Ellery's tone suggested she wasn't impressed.

Reed hesitated. His adoption had never been a secret, to him or anyone else, since Angus Markham lived his life in the public eye, but few people had ever asked Reed how he felt about it. The assumption seemed to be that he was lucky, having been plucked from the apartment of his murdered Latina mother into the warm and loving care of the well-to-do Markhams. Most days, Reed felt that way, too. Sitting across from Ellery, who had her own rocky family history, Reed could admit it wasn't always so easy. "Kim thinks we might find we have a common ancestor," he told Ellery. "That's part of the process, you see—you can put your DNA into the system and it will tell you if there are others who have taken the test who might be related to you, and if these people can trace their ancestry back to the Pilgrims, why then, so can you."

"So that would legitimize you," Ellery guessed. "Is that it?"

"No, no, I don't think that's it. It's just . . . I don't think Kimmy understands. I'm not worried about stumbling across some long-dead relative. I'm concerned about the ones still walking the earth." It was touching, in a way, that his family seemed to forget Reed had ever belonged to anyone else. Kimmy and his other sisters, Lynette and Suzanne, didn't have to look beyond the walls of the Markham home to see their DNA in action. They had the same narrow nose, bright blue eyes, and dimpled chins. It wasn't until Tula was born that Reed saw his features clearly echoed in another human being. He'd wondered from time to time if his other family was out there—siblings or cousins, aunts and uncles. Somewhere, he had a biological father.

"If you found them," Ellery asked, "would you want to meet?"

"I don't know. Maybe they would be able to tell me something that explains what happened to my mother." The one relative Reed knew about, his mother, had been murdered at age nineteen in Nevada. The case remained open and unsolved. "Or maybe I could find out medical information that could be useful to Tula. As it is, I'm a blank slate."

Ellery drew her leg up and rested her chin on her knee. Watching her bend and shift like a teenager reminded Reed how far apart in age they were. "I'll tell you what I think," she said, "if you want to hear it."

He made a sweeping gesture with his hand. "By all means."

"If you get your results, it has to be because you want

113

to know. Not to help your birth mother. Not for Tula. You. You're the one who has to live with the knowledge, whatever it is. Not anyone else."

She got up off the couch and left him there to think about it. When he went to find her again, she was washing out the mugs in the sink. "So are you going to call McGreevy and ask about the investigation into the Gallagher Furniture fire?" she asked without turning around.

"I'll call on one condition," he said, and this statement did make her turn and face him.

"What?" She dried her hands methodically on the checkered towel.

"You let me spend the night here on your couch."

They looked at each other for a long moment, but Ellery finally relented. "Okay," she said. "One night."

She brought him out a blanket and pillow to make up the sofa, and he began working on his makeshift bed. Ellery watched him with her arms folded across her middle. "You're not one of those people who believes that nonsense about how, if you save someone's life, they belong to you forever, are you?"

Reed paused with the end of a blanket in his hands. He'd rescued a few people from probable or certain death over the span of his career. But he felt drawn only to Ellery. Not because he'd saved her, but because of all the ways he couldn't. "Well, if that's true," he said slowly as he turned around to face her, "it means we're both stuck with one another."

She frowned. "One night," she repeated. "That's all."

In the morning, Reed awoke to a tongue bath over his face. "Gah! Back off, you stinking hound," he cried, pushing blindly at Speed Bump's sturdy, waggling body.

Across the room, he heard Ellery's voice, full of amusement. "You're the one who wanted the couch," she said. "It comes with some perks."

Reed arose creakily from the couch, his stiff back aching. "May I avail myself of your bathroom—and perhaps some disinfectant?"

"He's had all his shots," Ellery retorted. "Can we say the same for you?"

He scowled at her as he walked past her to the bathroom, where he washed his face and redressed in his clothes from the day before. He would have to stop by the hotel before leaving to collect the remainder of his things. Later, he scrounged together the makings for blueberry pancakes while Ellery visited the gym inside her apartment building. He deliberately waited until she was in the shower to make his call to McGreevy. It was Friday and a slow week, so his boss was in an expansive mood when Reed reached him at the office. "Markham," he said heartily, "did you catch yourself a rapist?"

Reed frowned, because McGreevy knew as well as he did that there was essentially zero chance a perpetrator this skilled would be caught within twenty-four hours of Reed's analysis. "The local PD are hard at work on the case," he replied.

"Good, good. So you're back here this afternoon, then." It wasn't a question.

"The plane leaves in a few hours," Reed said, without committing one way or another to being on it. "But something else cropped up here and I wanted to ask you about it—the arson investigation from the 1980s, the one with the furniture store fire. You worked that case, didn't you?"

"I played a part." McGreevy's tone had become guarded. "I was working out of the Boston office when the fires started happening—late 1987, it was. By the end, nearly every LEO in the state was involved in that case in one regard or another. What's it to you?"

"Luis Carnevale is up for parole."

There was a strange note of silence. "Yes," McGreevy said at length. "I'd heard that."

"His niece is a lawyer who is putting pressure on the parole board. She says Carnevale was railroaded, and if they don't let him go, she's going to petition the courts for a new trial. It's all over the news up here."

"And what would you like me to do about it?"

Reed chose his words carefully. "The victim, Myra

Gallagher, is concerned that Carnevale might be released, that his niece might have an argument on her side."

"Bullshit. Carnevale was guilty as sin. It took the jury just an hour to convict him, that's how strong the case was."

"His niece says it was engineered that way."

This time, McGreevy's end went quiet for a long time. "His niece is saying it, or you are?" he asked finally. "If you have something you want to say to me, Markham, I'd appreciate it if you just stated it directly."

"The local authorities were desperate to solve this case," Reed replied. "We both know how sometimes that pressure can cause people to make mistakes."

"You're not talking about a mistake. You're implying a frame-up."

"I'm implying nothing. I'm just asking questions."

"Yeah? Go on, then. Ask."

"Why was Kevin Powell on Emerson Street the night of the fire? He said he was on his way home, but his house was in the opposite direction from Gallagher Furniture."

"Jesus Christ, Reed. Maybe he took a wrong turn. You ever try to navigate the streets of Boston in the dark after you've had a few under your belt? Those roads were laid down by cows three hundred years ago."

"You're saying no one investigated him."

"Investigated him?" McGreevy scoffed on the other

end. "He was a goddamned hero. He not only rescued the woman from the fire, he caught the guy who started it. The man probably hasn't had to buy a drink in Boston his whole life. If you want to try to rewrite that canonized piece of city lore, you'd better come up with something more than maybe he took a wrong turn on a dark street."

"There was a witness who disappeared," Reed said. "A drifter."

"The Blaze? Half the task force was convinced that guy never existed."

"I've got a city cop who will swear he did."

"Now listen here," McGreevy said, his voice low and urgent, "I don't know what you're up to with this crap, but I don't like it. I granted you a couple of days to go up there and consult in a possible serial rape investigation, and instead, here you are muckraking in a case that is ancient history. Calling me up with a bunch of innuendo and nonsense, running down a good man's name in the process. So you listen up, and you listen good because I am not going to repeat this: the niece is going nowhere with her case. Luis Carnevale is a sociopath who gets his jollies burning up little kids and watching firemen risk their lives to put out the fires he started. He was guilty as hell twenty-six years ago, and there is one way you can be a hundred percent sure of it: the fires stopped when we locked the sonofabitch up."

Reed cleared his throat. "Noted," he said.

"Your ass better be on the plane in two hours," McGreevy said. "And then I'll expect you back here Monday morning, with your attention focused where it belongs."

"Yes, sir," Reed replied, looking up as he spied Ellery walking toward him. She was redressed in street clothes and running a towel over her wet hair. She raised her eyebrows at him when he hung up with McGreevy. "McGreevy is convinced they got the right guy in Luis Carnevale," he told her.

"Figures," she said. "I look forward to hearing the other side."

"What do you mean?"

"Bertina Jenkins, Carnevale's niece. I gave her office a call this morning, and I'm meeting with her in forty-five minutes to talk about the case." She walked back toward the kitchen, the towel over her shoulder, and paused at the counter to pick up a cold blueberry pancake. He watched as she broke off a piece and ate it.

"Bertina Jenkins agreed to see you? Just like that?" he asked, somewhat incredulous.

"Turns out there is an upside to being infamous," she replied, a hint of mischief in her gray eyes. "Everyone wants to meet you." She dusted off her hands and regarded him. "I can drop you at the airport first, if you want."

Reed checked his watch, debating whether he could still

make it back to the hotel to fetch his belongings. "How about you drop me off at the airport after?" he countered, and Ellery's mouth widened into a grin.

Bertina Jenkins, of the upscale Jenkins & Associates Law Firm, worked out of a sleek office in a building right in the heart of downtown. The waiting area featured comfortable chairs, tasteful art, and actual living plants, as well as a partial view of the snow-covered Boston Common. Reed was most impressed by the TV screen playing what was essentially an extended advertisement for the firm, with Bertina Jenkins and her fellow lawyers nodding sympathetically at would-be defendants, striding purposefully up the courthouse steps, and glad-handing grateful clientele who had apparently beaten all charges. The production values were high, the staging savvy, and Reed could see why this woman had managed to raise attention about her uncle's case in the media. She clearly knew how to craft a message.

Reed rose along with Ellery when Bertina emerged from her office. She was shorter than she'd appeared in the video, barely over five feet, but angling to seem taller with three-inch heels and a smooth, elaborate top-knot hairdo. She had a warm, firm handshake and a quick smile. "Ellery Hathaway," she said. "I've read a lot about you."

"I could say the same for you," Ellery answered as Bertina led them back to her office.

Reed wondered, if Ellery hadn't shot the man who'd tried to kill her, who'd tried to kill them both, if this woman would have been happy to take over the murderer's defense. The walls of her office were covered in plaques, diplomas, and various smiling pictures of Jenkins and local celebrities. Reed recognized the late Mayor Menino and Red Sox slugger David Ortiz among the photographs.

"So you're interested in my uncle's case," she said as they took their seats. "Why is that?" Reed gave her points for sitting with them on one side of the desk rather than placing herself in opposition on the other side.

"Ms. Jenkins," Ellery began, but the woman cut her off.

"Call me Bertie, please. Everyone does."

"Bertie," Ellery tried again, sounding a bit more uncomfortable with the informal moniker. "I recently made the acquaintance of Myra Gallagher, the woman who was injured in the fire."

"Terrible, awful thing. That poor woman."

"Yes," Ellery said. "As you might imagine, she's been upset by all the recent news coverage."

"I'm sorry for that," Bertie said, laying a hand over her heart. "Truly, I am. But I have to get justice for Luis somehow."

"I've seen you on the news," Ellery said, "and you seem very convinced he's innocent. I was just wondering why that is."

Bertie gave Ellery an appraising look, and then glanced at Reed. "You're law enforcement," she said at length. "I know how you guys think, how the system operates. It only matters what you can sell to a jury, not what really happened. If the prosecutors convinced twelve citizens that Luis was guilty, he must've done it, right?"

"If we thought it was that easy, we wouldn't be sitting here," Reed replied, spreading his hands.

Bertie considered this a moment and then shifted forward in her seat, until she was practically out of the chair entirely. "Here's the truth: the task force has no idea who set that fire because they never investigated it. They fixated on Luis right at the scene and then built up their case around him. They never even considered any other suspects."

"What other suspects?" Ellery asked.

"The Gallaghers, for one. The two brothers, Patrick and David Gallagher, inherited that store from their father but then mismanaged it to the point where it was going under. The rumor was that David wanted out, but Patrick couldn't afford to buy him off. Both brothers were going to lose their shirts, except then the place burned down and they collected a cool two million dollars in insurance money."

"Patrick Gallagher lost his son," Ellery protested. "His wife was nearly killed."

"Yeah, and maybe he wanted it that way."

Reed tilted his head, considering. "You have any proof of that?"

"Just a neighbor who'd be willing to say that Myra and Patrick fought a lot. But maybe he didn't intend to have them killed. They weren't supposed to be there that night, right? She went back to get some tax papers. Maybe Patrick or David hired someone to torch the place, and the hired help just picked a really bad time to do the deed."

"Interesting theory," Reed said, although his tone indicated he didn't find it wholly plausible.

Bertie narrowed her eyes at him. "Maybe you'll like this one better: Myra and Patrick's older son, Jacob. He was a punk-ass kid who had been suspended from school twice—once for fighting, a second time for setting a fire in the cafeteria trash can."

"He was a teenager at the time, right?" Ellery asked. "That's a big leap from high school vandalism to burning down the family business."

Bertie shrugged. "I'm not saying he did it. I'm saying no one ever checked to see whether he might have done it. He wasn't at home the night of the fire. Where was he? I don't know. The cops never bothered to follow up. They already had Luis in custody—a nice brown-faced fall guy from a poor neighborhood that guaranteed he'd have no resources to fight back. I was four years old at the time, so I don't remember any of it, but it practically destroyed my mother. She lost her job at the restaurant because no one wanted to be waited on by the sister of Luis Carnevale, convicted arsonist and murderer."

"That may well be true," Reed said. "But you won't be able to get Luis a new trial without new evidence."

"Between you and me, I'm hoping the parole board just releases him," she said, her posture softening a little. "But I am serious about reinvestigating this case. I have a private eye working on finding Earl Stanfield."

Reed exchanged a look with Ellery, who gave a slight shrug. "Who's Earl Stanfield?"

"Better known as The Blaze," Bertie said dryly. "Earl supposedly told Luis's defense attorney that he had seen the arsonist start the fire that night at the furniture store, and that it wasn't Luis. Funny thing is, after he said that, Earl disappeared."

"You know where he went?" Reed asked.

Bertie leaned back in her seat and sized him up. "No. Do you?"

"Me? Why would I know?"

"Someone does. Someone with a badge. Earl Stanfield didn't have two nickels to rub together—it's not like he was boarding the Concorde and jetting off to the Riviera to start living the lifestyle of the rich and famous. No." She shook her head. "Earl Stanfield didn't just suddenly disappear after that fire. The way I see it, someone disappeared him."

By the time they had left Bertina Jenkins's office, the sky had thickened with clouds. "Storm's coming in," Ellery murmured as she glanced overhead. "You're lucky to be getting out before it hits." She started up her truck so she could take him back to the hotel and then to the airport.

Reed gave a noncommittal reply, lost in his own thoughts as they bumped and jostled over city streets torn up by salt and winter plows. He did not feel glad to be leaving; rather, he felt intense disquiet, as though he were departing with nothing in order. The rapist was out there somewhere, perhaps with a new target in his sights. Luis Carnevale—maybe a reckless killer, maybe an innocent man—was on his third decade of prison. And someone was sending Ellery threatening messages again. Reed's unease grew as he collected his suitcase from the hotel and let her drive him toward the airport. He had no concrete reason to stay and many good reasons to go. McGreevy would definitely remove his name from consideration for the promotion if Reed failed to show up on Monday.

He glanced sideways at Ellery. She didn't belong to him, not at all, but he didn't want to let her go just yet. Once he got on the plane, there was no way of telling when he might see her again. "If anyone slips a threatening note under your door again, please let me know," he said as they swooped down into the tunnels and his anxiety level ticked up a notch. The airport was mere minutes away.

"They won't come back," she replied dismissively. "Whoever it is, they're a big coward. They got their cheap thrill and that's that. I know how it goes."

"I hope you're right. But for my peace of mind, please promise me that you'll be careful."

"I'm always careful." She took the exit for Logan Airport and entered the lane for departures.

He looked at her again, took in the delicate curve of her face and the shorter tendrils of dark hair that had escaped the knot at the base of her neck. She had a leather jacket on and gloves so no one would see the scars. *I'm always careful,* she'd said, but what he really wished was that she didn't have to be.

She navigated around all the taxis and other cars to the side of the road, where she let the truck idle. "So," she said with a deep breath. "Here you are."

"Here I am," he agreed, glancing at the sliding doors to the terminal. He made no move to get out of the truck. "Keep me informed about the cases, will you? If you hear of any new developments."

"Of course. Thank you again for coming up here."

So formal they were all of a sudden. Reed groped around for what he really wanted to say. "When that man from your group asks you out—and he will ..." He paused while Ellery rolled her eyes in dramatic fashion. "I think you should say yes."

"And I think that it would be a disaster."

"You don't know that."

"I do," she said crossly. "You don't know what it's like."

"Dating is scary for everyone," he told her. "Trust me. I'm back on the market for the first time in ten years, and I practically need to take a Valium before asking a woman out."

"Oh, yeah," she said skeptically, "I'm sure it must be real tough for you out there—the poor little handsome FBI agent with his own trust fund. I feel your pain."

"You think I'm handsome?" He hadn't thought she'd noticed him physically at all, really. He fought the urge to check his look in the side mirror.

"I think you're full of crap," she said good-naturedly, and gave him a playful shove. "You're also going to miss your plane."

"Say yes," he told her suddenly. "See what happens. If it doesn't go well, you can call me up and tell me how very wrong I was."

She arched an eyebrow at him. "Really. You'd want all the gory details?"

"I want—I want you to be happy."

She blinked in surprise, her expression softening into a

sad smile, as though this was the one thing she knew she could never give him. "Go," she said, her voice hoarse. "Get out of here."

He opened the door and stepped out into the biting wind. The storm was getting closer. He was going to lean down to the window and say his last good-bye when his phone rang inside his coat pocket. As he dug it out, Ellery started to pull away, and his words got stuck in his throat. Reed glanced down and saw the caller ID: Powell, Kevin.

In his haste and shock, Reed completely forgot to take the call. He chased after her taillights, waving his phone in the air as he yelled after her. "Ellery, wait!"

# 5

Ellery kept one eye on the tunnel traffic and one eye on Reed as he finished his side of the conversation with Kevin Powell. A cab cut her off, crossing the double yellow line, and Ellery laid on the horn in retaliation. Reed made a *do-you-mind* gesture at her as he clutched the phone tighter to his ear. "Yes, we could meet," he was saying. "Uh, Southampton Street?" He gave a helpless shrug in her direction, and Ellery nodded.

"It's a half hour away," she told him.

"We could be there in a half hour," Reed said with more authority. "Okay, then. One o'clock it is. I look forward to the conversation."

Ellery regarded him with open curiosity as he hung up the call. "Well? What did he want?"

"He didn't say much over the phone," Reed replied, sounding distracted. "Just that McGreevy had called him and said he didn't need to answer any questions we might put

129

to him. On the contrary, Powell seems eager for a meeting."

The Sumner Tunnel dumped them out into the North End, where the first few snowflakes were beginning to swirl in the air. "If we don't have to be there until one," she said, eyeing the crowded rows of cars parked on the sides of the street, "maybe we could grab lunch." Already they had passed four Italian restaurants, cozy-looking places with brick storefronts and names like Vito's or Villa Francesca, and Ellery could almost smell the roasted tomato sauce in the air. She finally nabbed a parking space big enough for her truck, and then she led Reed a block away toward a tiny hole-in-the-wall place called Trattoria Il Panino that she remembered from her earlier days in the city. The place held just six tables and wooden straight-backed chairs, but the heady mix of garlic, basil, and fresh-baked bread made it clear that no one came here for the ambience. She ordered the spaghetti carbonara while Reed opted for the octopus salad. Her dish arrived in the pan it had been cooked in, retaining every luscious drop of the creamy sauce, and Ellery's eyes rolled back in pleasure as she took the first bite. "I don't get over here enough," she said of the North End. "I forget how amazing the food is."

"It's very good," Reed agreed as he speared a green olive with his fork.

Ellery took another few quick bites to quiet her rumbling stomach. "So Powell wants to talk even though McGreevy said he didn't have to," she said. "Doesn't sound like a man who thinks he has something to hide."

"Or he wants to find out what we know."

"Which isn't much." They both chewed on that for a few moments. "We could go in there and hit him with the one-way street problem," Ellery mused. "But he'll probably just blow it off, say he made a wrong turn."

"Which could still be the truth," Reed pointed out. He crunched on a narrow slice of garlic bread. "No," he said when he had swallowed. "He's going to want to tell us the story of the Gallagher fire. It's his story, and it's the best story he's ever told. That's why he wants to talk to us—so he can tell it one more time."

The surety of his words made Ellery pause with her fork in hand as she regarded him. She knew very well what Reed's best story was. It had sold a million copies and gotten him interviews on dozens of talk shows. It occurred to her suddenly that there had been no second round after the summer, despite the feeding frenzy in the media. Reed had replied to reporters with a terse "No comment," and returned back to Quantico almost immediately. "Are you going to write another book?" she asked him now, and he looked up in surprise from his plate. "About what happened this summer," she clarified. "It would be another bestseller, practically a sequel." She put down her fork, her appetite gone.

Reed cleared his throat. "Ah, no. I don't think so."

"Don't hold back on my account."

"No, it's that . . ."

"What?" she demanded, almost belligerently. His memoir about the hunt for Coben and her ultimate rescue had served as the template for at least two movies over the past fifteen years. The public would eagerly devour this juicy new chapter.

"I think maybe these monsters don't need any more ink devoted to them," Reed said after another moment. "At least certainly not by me."

Their eyes met and held. There was no denying that Francis Coben had enjoyed his fame, strutting for the cameras during his trial, smiling and waving like he was a celebrity charming the paparazzi. His crimes were his alone, but his legend had required help.

"So I say we give Kevin Powell the floor and let him tell his tale," Reed said, taking a deep breath as he broke the spell. He reached for his water. "If he has some secrets he's harboring about that night—if indeed he has any regrets at all—time may well have brought them to the surface."


Southampton Street, Ellery noted with some irony, was another one of the city's ubiquitous one-way roads. "This must be the place," she said dubiously as she parked the truck outside the address Powell had given them. The run-down brick building looked like a relic from the Truman administration, with its stained concrete base and the narrow rectangular windows in cheap metal frames. Silver lettering stretched across the front of the building, proclaiming it to be the City of Boston Fire Department Headquarters. It sat surrounded by contemporary structures—squat brick buildings that had some of their windows boarded up, as well as a gas station, a McDonald's that was doing a brisk afternoon business, and a car wash, which was not.

Inside, the young man at the front desk did not make eye contact but told them Powell was expecting them at his office on the top floor, room 508. There, they were met with another gatekeeper, this one a female secretary who was approximately as old as the building itself, and she announced their arrival. "Come in, come in!" Powell stood to welcome them, greeting each in turn with a firm handshake. Ellery knew from the stories that he had to be nearly sixty by now, but he was still a powerfully built man, taller and bulkier than Reed. Powell had rolled up the ends of his white shirt to the elbows, as though the cuffs were too narrow to contain his muscular forearms. His dark hair was slicked back and thinning, and his face lined around the edges, puffy and less defined, like a cartoonist's sketch, but Ellery could still see the imprint of the young, handsome firefighter who had dominated the news cycle a quarter century ago. "Please, have a seat," he said, indicating two basic office chairs in front of his desk. "Sorry about the mess. I spend my days buried in paperwork." As if to make his point, he shoved a stack of folders to the side of his desk.

"Thank you for taking the time to see us," Reed said.

Powell waved them off with one beefy hand. "Please. It's my honor. Russ called and said I didn't have to take your calls, but I told him—like I'm going to turn down the chance to meet the guy who nailed Coben?" He gave a low whistle. "What a squirrelly little bastard he was, eh?"

"It was really the combined effort of many people that led to his capture," Reed demurred.

"Like hell it was! I read your book. No one else was even suspicious of that freak before you started following him."

Ellery saw Reed shift slightly in his chair, clearly uncomfortable, but Powell either didn't notice or didn't care. He turned to her instead.

"And you! You're the one who got away! Impressive fortitude, surviving everything that sicko threw at you. How many girls were there before you? Ten? Fifteen?"

Ellery didn't answer. Powell's tone was admiring, his smile and body language open and friendly, but there was an underlying steel in his words. He was reminding her that she had been the girl in the closet. Helpless and afraid.

"I can get you an autographed copy if you like," Reed cut in smoothly. "Of the book."

"Yeah? That would be terrific of you. My wife, Marlena, she'd get a kick out of it. A real true crime fanatic, that one. Can't get enough of that Investigation Discovery stuff, you know?"

"You must have had some stories of your own for her," Reed said, leaning back in his seat, prepared to be regaled. Ellery tried to match his posture.

Powell went silent a moment, apparently gathering his words carefully, as if sensing a trap. "Sure, sure. I've had some success here and there. There was a warehouse fire in East Boston about seven years ago—the place went off like the Fourth of July in the middle of the night—and it turned out to have all different kinds of inventory inside, from furniture to DVD players to automobile parts. We had the torch man on camera—not his face, but proof he was at the scene right before the whole thing blew—so it was obviously an arson job. But the video showed that he was carrying no chemicals on him. We come to find out, one of the companies shipped the accelerant in separately. It was already on the premises when the guy showed up. All he needed was a Bic lighter." Powell finished this story with a satisfied smirk. "The owner's doing fifteen years at Danbury."

"What about the Gallagher Furniture fire?" Ellery asked with a trace of impatience, and Reed glanced at her sharply. She flushed as she remembered the plan and forced her features into what she hoped was an obsequious smile. "I mean, that's got to count as one of your successes, right?"

Powell frowned. "In one way, yes. I was able to get Myra Gallagher out in time, and by God's own miracle, she survived. But that little boy died, and so it's hard to think of that night as a complete success."

"But you caught the guy," Reed protested as he sat forward. "Luis Carnevale. The whole state was looking for him, and you're the one who got him." He paused significantly. "I know what that's like."

Powell gave him a shrewd, assessing look. "Yes," he said. "You would know. All those girls, the ones with their hands cut off? You didn't save them."

"You're right. I didn't. I did the only thing I could, which was to keep Francis Coben from killing anyone else. And that's what you did, right? You got him off the streets. Now his niece is making a big stink and the parole board might let him free again. How do you feel about that?"

Powell reached to the side for his desk drawer and pulled out a bottle of pink antacid. "This," he said as he held it up. "This is what I think of it." He uncapped the lid and took a long swig from the bottle, and Ellery had to restrain herself from making a disgusted face. When he was done, he looked from Reed to Ellery and then back again. "Your work with the Bureau—did you do profiles on arsonists?"

"I've read a few," Reed said. "But that wasn't my particular area."

Powell nodded as though he'd expected as much. "You two ever been to a fire? Not like a beach or backyard bonfire. I'm talking about a five-alarm deal where there's ash in your mouth and the smoke can be seen for miles."

Reed and Ellery shook their heads. "No, sir," Reed said. "Nothing like that."

"It's like walking into the mouth of hell. The roar of a fire like that, it sounds like a 747 taking off. The flames are like a living, breathing thing, because that's what fire does—it feeds on oxygen to get bigger, stronger, until it can incinerate everything in its path. And you. Your job is to go right into the belly of the beast. Look it right in the eye and make it think you're not afraid. Your skin gets tight. Your body hair singes. You can barely see anything that's going on, and at any minute, a wall or the ceiling might cave in and crush you right where you stand.

"Then, if you're lucky, it's over. You're left with a black shell. A stinking husk of a building that's now covered in six inches of dark water, everywhere in ruins, and you've got to figure out how the fire got started and who's to blame. I've got to tell you—sometimes, too often, they get away with it. Knowing a fire is arson and proving it are two very different things. It's true, what they tell you on TV, that so much of the evidence goes up in the flames—or is washed away in the fight. The man who was setting fires around Boston back then, we nicknamed him the Marlboro Man. Did you know that?"

"No," Ellery said. "I didn't read anything like that in the news stories."

"We kept it to ourselves," Powell said. "A private joke. Only it wasn't so funny, see, because the Marlboro Man was using those cigarettes to set the fires. He'd douse the place in gasoline, tie a cigarette to a pack of matches, and light it up. The cigarette acted like the wick, giving him time to get out before the place caught fire."

"The Gallagher fire," Reed cut in. "Did you find a Marlboro cigarette at the scene?"

Powell hesitated. "No, not that one. But we didn't find it every time. Sometimes the flames just ate everything."

"But you were there at the scene so early," Ellery said.

"In my car, yeah. I didn't have the truck. I didn't even have my gear. I just saw the place burning and pulled over. There was a woman screaming inside, so I didn't even stop to call it in. I just grabbed my car jack and used it to break down the front window and go in after her. It wasn't until five minutes later when the first unit rolled in. It was dry, in the middle of summer, and the place was packed with wooden furniture. It went up like a tinderbox."

"When did you notice Luis Carnevale?" Reed asked.

"Not right away. I was with the medics at first, getting oxygen and having my arm wrapped up from the burn." He gestured at his left bicep. "They wanted to take me to the hospital straight off, but I couldn't leave until the fire was out. The cops had the crowd backed up down the block and I was standing on the other side of the barricade. At first, I was watching the fire just like everyone else. But then something made me turn around, and I saw him standing there with his hand down the front of his pants. His pupils were all huge and dark, his mouth hanging open. Then I noticed that the edges of his mouth were actually turned up. This asshole was smiling! So I started trying to get closer to him and see what his deal was. That's when I got a whiff of the gasoline. It was already in the air—you could smell it from the fire—but on him, it was real strong, like he'd been bathing in it. I asked him to come talk to me a second, and he bolted. Lucky for me he had kind of a bum ankle and didn't run very fast. I caught him about thirty yards down the street."

"I see why you were suspicious," Reed said. "His behavior made him look very guilty."

"Because he was guilty," Powell replied. He stared long and hard at Reed. "McGreevy told me you had some doubts. I said to him that you should come on over here, because I have something that will make true believers out of you."

Reed raised his eyebrows. "We'd love to hear it."

"You really want to be convinced?" Powell said as he got up and fiddled with the blinds on his window. "Go down to the prison and talk to Carnevale. He's a sick, twisted little bastard with no respect for human life. Most arson is done for profit. The next biggest chunk is committed by angry young men who don't feel in control of their own lives. Maybe their mommy didn't hug them enough. Maybe they didn't get a date to the prom. Maybe they've been kicked around their whole lives and so now they're going to make people pay. They get a thrill out of destroying property that other people value, at watching the firefighters scurry around because of a fire they caused."

Powell had darkened the room and he switched on his laptop, which he plugged into a projector. As he trained it on the wall, Ellery let her gaze linger on the other decorations he had hanging about the office—pictures of firefighters in uniform, several framed commendations, and what looked like an old map of Boston with the famous fire of 1872 marked across a third of the city.

"Luis Carnevale was the third kind of arsonist," Powell said as he called up a picture of the man's mug shot from 1988. "He set fires because he just couldn't help himself." Ellery had seen this same photo of Carnevale in all the old news reports, although it looked washed out when projected against the institutional blue-gray wall. Carnevale appeared scruffy and shadowed, with a couple of days' worth of stubble on his face and a healthy shiner around his right eye. He was heavy-lidded and resigned, looking beyond the camera lens to the fate that awaited him. "At the time of his arrest, Carnevale was living in the basement of his cousin's house, not working. He did handyman-type jobs around the neighborhood sometimes to bring in a few dollars, but mostly he sat around smoking and watching TV."

"Smoking?" Ellery asked, remembering the cigarettes that had been used as the incendiary device.

Powell rewarded her with a thin smile, as though pleased with her for keeping up. "Marlboros," he said as he clicked through to the next slide. "This here is the number of major fires in the Boston area from 1975 through 2012. You see how overall, the number's going down, except for that spike in '87 and '88? Yeah. That's one arsonist single-handedly reversing the trajectory. And here, in 1989, is when Carnevale was arrested and convicted. Notice the drop."

He was right. On paper, it looked like the task force had found the right man. She glanced at Reed, but his expression was difficult to interpret in the low light.

"But here," Powell continued, "here is the real pièce de résistance." He looked to Reed. "Are you familiar with geographical profiling?"

"Yes," Reed allowed. "It's based on data showing that offenders are most likely to commit crimes that are in nearby familiar neighborhoods to them, but not in their exact neighborhood itself."

"Right—don't shit where you eat. Pardon my French." He turned to the projection on the wall, which showed a map of Boston. "See that blue dot right there? That's Carnevale's place, his cousin's house. Here are the fires that the task force investigated, starting with the ones in late 1986." He clicked a button and a handful of tiny flames showed up on the wall, well away from Carnevale's place of residence. "Then here are the ones from 1987." Powell clicked again, and this time, two dozen more tiny fires, each representing a much larger one, appeared on the map. Ellery blinked as Reed shifted in his seat, and she knew he must see what she did: there was a literal ring of fire around the blue dot at Carnevale's house.

"And 1988?" Reed asked.

Silently, Powell advanced the frame, and the map shifted again. Ellery saw that the tiny fires continued the same ring pattern, but encroached closer on Carnevale's residence. "He was getting more comfortable, more complacent," Powell observed. "It had been two years and no one had caught him yet, so he figured no one ever would. This one here? It's the Gallagher Furniture fire—just four blocks from where Carnevale was shacked up at his cousin's."

"The pattern is striking," Reed agreed.

"I figured you would recognize it. I told Russ—just let me explain to them, and they'll understand. We nailed the right SOB back then. I'm one hundred percent sure of it." He then called up a series of pictures that seemed to be crowd shots from one of the fires. "A *Herald* photographer took these right before I noticed Carnevale standing there. That's him with a front-row seat. What you won't see—no matter how many times you look at these—is any sign of that so-called witness."

"The Blaze?" Ellery asked. "We're under the impression he existed."

"Sure, he existed." Powell called up another image, this one showing the mugshot of a heavyset black man of indeterminate age. He had a graying beard and bleary, unfocused eyes. He also had a patch of discolored skin on the left side of his face that, if you squinted just right, looked something like a flame. "Earl Stanfield. Indigent alcoholic. There was never any evidence that he was at the scene of the Gallagher fire, let alone that he saw the arsonist."

"Did you bother to find him and ask?" Ellery said.

Powell's jaw tightened. "Finding Earl wasn't my job. The detectives on the task force said they searched the whole damn city and came up empty. Hell, your friend McGreevy took on the search himself. I think if the FBI couldn't find him, then it's pretty damn clear he didn't want to be found."

"Or someone didn't want him to be found," Reed said mildly.

Before Powell could reply, Ellery leaped into the conversation. "It was a fortunate thing, you driving by just after the fire started," she said. "How were you on Emerson that night?"

Powell turned off the projector and flipped the overhead light back on. "The grace of God," he said, shaking his head as though he still couldn't quite believe it himself. "He put me just where I needed to be."

"But isn't Dorchester south from Lucky Sevens?" Ellery pressed him. "Emerson is one-way headed east."

Powell froze for a fraction of a second, his hands going still, but it was long enough to shift the atmosphere of the room. He had been regaling them with an oft-told tale, its fabric warm and familiar, with every conversational beat well worn and anticipated. He had his slides prepared, that's how mapped-out the visit had been. But Ellery had knocked him out of his comfortable, lofty role as the inside man with all the information. Here, for once, was a question without a pretty picture to answer it.

To his credit, Powell recovered quickly, his mouth twitching back into a smile. "Must've taken the wrong turn," he said. "I was all charged up from the conversation with my buddies, talking about how we wanted to nail the bastard.

I wasn't thinking straight. Or, I guess you could say the Lord works in mysterious ways."

Reed's face was sober. "So what you're saying is . . . Jesus literally took your wheel." He delivered the line so earnestly that Powell clearly couldn't tell whether it was a put-on, a put-down, or the quiet awe of a fellow true believer.

The momentary confusion on Powell's features dissipated as he surged ahead to safe, familiar territory. "That's right, that's right," he said, smiling broadly as he spread his hands. "All praise be to Him and those He favors. God wanted Luis Carnevale captured that night, and I was merely the instrument He used to do it."

Reed looked thoughtful. "It's a convincing line of evidence that you've laid out here," he said, "and I can see why the jury had no difficulty in convicting Luis Carnevale. But . . ."

Powell opened his mouth to protest, and Reed held out his hands to forestall him.

"Just for argument's sake—just to play the devil, as it were—who would have been the number two suspect?"

"There wasn't a number two," Powell replied with a frown. "Carnevale did it."

"But if there were. If you had to choose someone else to have set that fire, who would you pick? After all, no one knows the case quite like you do."

Powell looked like he didn't know whether to be suspicious

or flattered. His mouth worked in and out as he considered what to say. "I guess maybe that Gallagher boy. Jacob. He had a history of fire starting, if I recall the facts correctly. But it wasn't him because it was Luis Carnevale. Case closed."

"Thanks for your time," Reed said, standing, so Ellery took that as her cue to rise as well. "Do you mind sending us a copy of that presentation you gave? The illustrations of the geography of the fires are particularly well done. It's something I could imagine we might use for teaching at the Bureau."

Powell puffed up like a pigeon. "Sure, just leave your cards. I'd be happy to send it along."

Ellery had no card so she jotted her personal email on a Post-it and left it with Powell. Seeing the little sticky note next to Reed's polished FBI credentials made her face warm as she remembered anew what was really at stake here: her whole career.

They left together, and outside the snow had started to fall in earnest. Ellery hunched into her jacket as the snowflakes tickled in through the open spaces around her neck and melted across her skin. She retrieved a window scraper from her truck and started clearing the windshield. Reed, ever the gentleman, used the sleeve of his wool overcoat to brush the light snow from his side. They were both a bit breathless from the cold as they climbed inside. "He was lying," Ellery announced immediately. "He wasn't there because of a wrong turn."

Snowflakes clung to Reed's lashes as he blinked them away. "Yes, for a man who has a golden cross hanging on his office wall, Commissioner Powell seems to be rather sketchy on the details of the Commandments."

"We could track down his buddies who were drinking with him that night," Ellery said as she started up the truck and used the wipers to clear away the remaining snow. The defroster roared to life, sending a blast of chilly air at them.

"Yes, it would be interesting to hear their version of the story," Reed concurred, but he seemed to be only half-listening to her. He had pulled out his phone and was poking around on it with one finger. "I'd be keen to talk to Jacob Gallagher at this stage."

Ellery held her frozen hand over the air vents, which had warmed up to tepid. "You're buying Powell's idea that he's the number-two suspect?"

"Not Powell, no. I read a half-dozen news articles this morning before phoning up McGreevy, just to make sure I had the facts straight. One of them included a picture of young Jacob Gallagher at his brother's funeral." He held out his phone so she could take a look. Indeed, there was Jacob standing next to his father outside the church. The boy looked awkward and shell-shocked inside a suit that was one size too small for him.

"So?" Ellery asked Reed. "It's a picture of Jacob Gallagher."

"So I'm reasonably sure I just saw another picture of

him. In there, among Powell's photos." He nodded in the direction of the building. "That's why I asked him to send the whole presentation."

"Jacob was at the scene? Funny that no one ever mentioned it."

"Mmm," Reed said. "I thought maybe we might head over to the auto body shop where he's working now and ask him about it. First though, we must get some coffee—it's colder than a tin toilet in Tibet out here."

Ellery smiled as she put the truck in gear. "Your thin southern blood is showing, Agent Markham."

Reed scoffed, his breath fogging the window. "Can't be," he drawled. "It's plumb done froze."

They picked up coffee and then made their way back into East Boston, where Jacob Gallagher was supposedly employed at T&E Auto Body. Progress through the city was slow. Lumbering plows scraped along the streets even as the snow poured down from the sky. A few scattered pedestrians remained in sight, bundled up and bracing themselves against the swirling storm, while the tops of the taller buildings had vanished into the clouds. The world was erasing itself, inch by inch. Ellery drove with both hands clenched on the wheel, cautiously easing the truck around each corner as her wipers slapped against the mounting snow. She had to circle back to get to the repair shop because she missed the sign the first time due to poor visibility.

An old-fashioned bell jingled as they tramped inside the shop, snow melting at their feet, but no one immediately appeared. "Hello?" Reed called out. There was a lone desk that was covered in white and yellow papers, but no attendant. "Is anyone here?"

Eventually, a broad-faced man with swarthy skin emerged from the garage, wiping his hands on a cloth. "Can I help you?"

"We're looking for Jacob Gallagher," Ellery told him. "We were told he works here."

The man seemed unimpressed. "And you are?" he asked in slightly accented English.

Reed, as the only one of them with a badge, took the opportunity to flash it. "Agent Reed Markham," he said. "This is Ellery Hathaway. Are you the owner here?"

"Ernesto Aducci. I own this place with my brother, Tony," he said, only it came out more like, *wid my brudder, Tony.*

"Ah, that would make you Mr. E," Reed said, smiling, but Ernesto Aducci did not smile back.

"What do you want with Jake?"

"We just want to ask him a few questions," Ellery said. "He's not in any trouble."

At the word "trouble," Aducci's bushy eyebrows rose. "Oh,

yah? He's in trouble with me. He's not shown up to work here for two days. I don't know where he is. If you see him, tell him he's here at eight on Monday, or he don't come back at all."

"You have an address for him?" Reed wanted to know. "We'll be happy to deliver your message."

Aducci seemed to be weighing the benefits and risks of cooperation. Eventually, he sighed deeply and went over to the desk. He leaned down and rustled around in a filing cabinet, after which he stood up holding an employment form. "Sixteen Shelby Street, number two," he said, waving the paper. "You tell him. Come back Monday, or don't bother."

The trip to Shelby Street didn't take very long, even with the deepening snow. Ellery glided the truck to a stop not far from the address Jacob Gallagher's boss had given them. The street was straight, laid out in classic Boston style: uniform row houses lined up on either side of the road, with barely three feet between them. They were boxy and plain, like shipping containers, differentiated only by the slightly varying colors of their cheap plastic siding. Each row house contained three separate apartments, and Ellery and Reed quickly found the one marked sixteen, number two. There was no name near the bell. Ellery used one gloved finger to press it and then blew on her hands to warm them through the material as they waited. The sound of heavy footsteps on the stairs coming down made her heart rate pick up. He was home. She braced herself for what she might find on the other side of the door.

It swung open quickly, and she found herself looking into the face of Patrick Gallagher. He appeared as surprised to see her as she was to see him. "Mr. Gallagher," she said. "Hello."

His shock faded into a scowl. "What are you doing here?" He glanced at Reed. "And who're you?"

Reed glanced at Ellery, as if unsure how to play it. She cleared her throat. "This is Reed Markham. He's a friend of mine. Reed, this is Patrick Gallagher."

"Pleased to make your acquaintance," Reed said, extending his hand, but Patrick Gallagher merely frowned at it.

"You didn't say what you're doing here."

"We were hoping to speak to Jacob," Ellery said. "Is he here?"

"He's not here, so you're out of luck. What do you want with him?"

Ellery hesitated, knowing how Patrick didn't want her digging around in his family's past. In a way, she couldn't blame him. "They're worried about him down at the auto body place where he works," she fibbed. "He hasn't been to work in two days. I imagine you must be worried, too, if you're here."

"Jake's a good boy. Works hard, pays his bills. Helps me with Myra on the weekends. I don't want you coming around here, bothering him."

"Do you know where your son is, Mr. Gallagher?" Reed asked gently.

"That's not your business."

Reed pulled out his FBI shield. "Maybe it is," he said, and Patrick stiffened. He turned his head slowly and looked down at Ellery with some horror.

"What have you done?" he whispered to her.

"Nothing, I—"

"You get out of here!" His arthritic, liver-spotted hands started pushing the door closed on them. "You leave my family the hell alone."

They had no choice but to back up and let him slam the door. There was the sound of his uneven footsteps trudging back up the stairs, and then only the silence of the snow. Ellery and Reed stood on the narrow stoop and looked at each other. "He's scared," she said.

"This must be hard, bringing back all the memories for them," Reed murmured.

Ellery recalled what Patrick had said about Jake being a good boy, and how he hadn't always been that way. "The fires Jake set when he was a teenager," she said. "What happened with that?"

"Don't know," Reed said as he peered at the sky. "But let's find somewhere warmer to talk about it, shall we?"

They hurried through the snow and back to the truck,

where Ellery started the engine and steered toward home. "Don't think you're flying out of here tonight," she said.

"No, it would appear not. It's fine. I've got time."

Ellery said nothing to this, although she could practically hear the clock ticking. He had a day or two at most. "You're welcome to my couch again, if you can stand the dog hair."

Reed sighed and glanced down at his trousers. "I practically blend in as it is," he said morosely as he picked off a bit of fur and then another. "It's like he keeps a spare coat in here just for emergencies."

Ellery smiled. "Think of it as extra warmth."

As they drove, Reed played around with his phone. After a bit, he announced: "It doesn't appear that Jacob Gallagher was ever convicted of arson. Rather, he participated in the juvenile diversion process."

"That's where kids get counseling and community service and stuff instead of jail time, right?"

"Yes, if you keep a clean record, you aren't ever charged with your original crime. If you violate the terms, then the state can charge you as originally planned. Jacob Gallagher must have completed his probation without incident."

"Huh."

Reed turned to look at her. "That's a particularly thoughtful 'huh.' What are you thinking?"

"Jake would have needed a lawyer. His family would've

had to pay a fine also, and possibly restitution from the damage caused by the school fire."

"Yes, and?"

Ellery shook her head, a tad impatient. If Reed Markham had a blind spot, it was money. He'd never in his life had to think about it, and so he pretty much didn't. "The furniture store was going under," she explained. "The Gallaghers were flat broke back then—so where did they get the funds to bail out their son?"

Reed blew out a long breath. "That's a good question." He paused. "I guess two million dollars might have helped in that regard."

"You think?" She remembered what it was like to be poor, when Daniel's medical bills had taken every last bit of her mother's money and then some. Ellery had walked the streets and searched the garbage cans for aluminum cans that other people had tossed away because they didn't need that five-cent refund from returning them. She'd used the spare change money to buy food or clothes from Goodwill—one less thing for her mother to worry about. One time she'd been so hungry she'd eaten two Big Macs and a large fries all at once, practically gulping the food right there near the counter. An old man, someone worse off than her—she could tell from his tattered clothes and by the way he carried all his possessions on his back—had laughed and laughed. "Damn, girl," he'd said as he'd handed her a five from inside his army jacket. "You look like you could use this."

She recalled how she'd taken it and run out like a squirrel with a nut, how elated and ashamed she had felt, all at the same time. Back then, five dollars had felt like a million. A real million would've been simply beyond belief.

Back at her apartment, Ellery took Bump out for a short walk in the snow while Reed booted up his laptop. The dog never seemed to mind the cold, trotting amiably from one snow pile to another, his long ears making snakelike tracks in the snow. He stuffed his delighted snout deep inside a snowdrift and then withdrew with a sneeze. "Pee already," Ellery told him darkly as she hugged herself. "Or we'll both catch our death out here."

The snow had tapered off into flurries for the moment, a bit of a lull, but the street was as deserted as though it were a full-on blizzard. Ellery looked around at the warm yellow light spilling from the apartment buildings, hers and the others around her. For some reason, Joe Manganelli's irritation about Reed's profiling efforts on the rapists came back to her: *He's a guy who likes to break into second-story buildings or higher? What am I supposed to do—put out a BOLO for a guy carrying around* Architectural Digest?

Maybe there was a way to profile a building, but not in the

way Joe had intimated. Ellery hustled Bump back inside and jabbed the elevator button repeatedly. When she reached her apartment, Reed looked up in surprise as she burst through the door with an air of excitement. "That geographical profiling—could it work on Wendy Mendoza's rapist?"

"Uh, what?" He had his glasses on, his brows knit in confusion.

"The geographical profiling technique that Powell showed us today. I was thinking maybe it could be used with the cases that are linked to Wendy Mendoza's. That way we might narrow down the area her attacker lives in."

Reed's expression turned thoughtful for a moment and then he took up his laptop again. "That's not a bad idea," he said. "Five probable cases isn't a lot to work with, but I was learning last year about a new software program that can sometimes make estimates with lower levels of geographic data. I can look into it."

Ellery joined him on the couch, bouncing a little with the rush of possibility. "If we could narrow the zone, it would at least point Manganelli in the right direction," she said. Plus, it would allow her to face Wendy Mendoza again. She didn't know how to look the poor woman in the eyes and tell her they'd come up with exactly nothing on her case. She sank deeper into the sofa, relaxing for the first time that day. Beside her, Reed got up and stretched.

"If I'm impinging on your hospitality, the least I can do is cook."

"Hmm. Well, good luck with that."

He gave her a curious look and went to the kitchen. He opened a few cupboards and closed them again. Then he spent a good long minute staring into her refrigerator, really much longer than she felt was necessary, given the meager contents inside. "What the heck do you eat?" he called back to her, sounding vaguely alarmed.

"There's a Burger King up the street," she said as she pushed herself off the couch. "I can run out." No need to test the mettle of his sensitive southern skin.

"Burger King?" Reed was aghast. "I'm sorry, but no. I'll find us someplace for dinner. Someplace with actual food."

"Yeah? Good luck with that, too." She walked to the window and looked out at the storm. "The T is probably barely functioning right now. You'd freeze your *tuchus* off waiting for a train, and I'm sure not driving around in that." As if to prove her point, the wind slapped at her windows, spewing an icy blast of snow across the panes.

"So we call a cab." Reed was back at his laptop, this time consulting restaurant options.

"You think you're getting a cab to come out in this weather?"

"You pay them double, they'll come whenever you want," he replied, absorbed in his search. "Do you like Cantonese?"

"I was kind of hoping for that burger," she replied with a sigh.

"If it's red meat you want, red meat you shall have. You just go get ready."

Ellery looked down at her jeans and long-sleeved black T-shirt. "I thought I was ready."

"We're aiming for a slightly higher class of restaurant than Burger King, remember?"

"Fine," Ellery grumbled. "I'll go put on my dressy jeans."

She got to her bedroom door when a sudden, terrible thought occurred to her. She walked slowly back to the living room and stood there with her hands on her hips. Reed did not look up. Finally, she spoke up. "This isn't a date, is it?"

He still didn't look at her. "Can't be. You don't date."

"Good." She wasn't quite satisfied yet, given how he had been pushing the agenda earlier. "Because if you have some sneaky idea up your sleeve . . ."

"Ellery." He turned to face her at last. "It's not a date. It's just dinner. Okay?"

"Oh." She searched his face and saw nothing that contradicted his words, and suddenly she was embarrassed. "Okay, then. Forget I said anything."

She went to her bedroom and opened her drawers one by one, looking for something that might be nice enough for whatever four-star restaurant Reed was lining up. There would probably be a zillion pieces of silverware and the menu would be in a foreign language. "I'll end up ordering brains or something," she remarked to Bump, who lay sprawled on the floor. "Just you see."

She pawed through all of her clothes and did not find anything that seemed suitable. Date or no date, it wasn't like she had a lot of opportunities to wear fancy clothes. She flopped backward on her bed and stared at the blank white ceiling. *Screw Reed Markham for even raising the possibility to begin with,* she thought. *It's hard for all of us,* he'd said, but he had no real idea what it was like. He hunted down the monsters and then got to go home to his nice house with his wife and kid. That he even thought it was possible for her to smile and make chitchat showed how clueless he was. She could date the same way a crocodile could run a horse race.

He wanted to know what kept her from going on dates? Well, she could give him an up-close and personal lesson, one nobody would ever learn from his damned book. She got up and stalked over to the stack of cardboard moving boxes she still had piled in the corner of her room. She slid out the bottom one and dug around until she found what she was looking for: a deep purple Lycra dress and knee-high boots—paid for by the Woodbury Police Department and left over from a one-night undercover operation she'd participated in when the chief had suspected the owner of the local bar had started dealing drugs out of his pool hall. Clothes that had never belonged to her, not really.

Ellery showered and changed into the unfamiliar outfit, tugging the dress this way and that in an effort to make it sit right on her body. Most girls had this routine down by the time they were fifteen, but the ritual was completely alien to her. She hadn't been kidding with Reed when she'd told him she'd never been on a date. She hadn't missed it, either, but now here he was insisting she give it a try. The dress had long sleeves and a high enough neckline that it did not show many of her scars. She owned exactly no makeup, only ChapStick, so she put that on and combed out her hair. Having been twisted in a knot all day, it now fell across her shoulders in soft waves. Ellery hesitated as she looked in the mirror—she never spent this much time looking at herself—and tentatively assessed her handiwork. She looked ... normal? Like a woman who could be going out on a date, if she had been born into a different lifetime. A ghost of a person she would never be.

Hot tears stung her eyes. *Screw you, Reed Markham,* she thought. *It's showtime.*

# 6

"This is all I own, so it's going to have to do." Her words came at him from across the loft, bouncing off the high, hard walls. Reed looked up from his computer and saw the shape of her, with her hair down and newly rounded edges, but he couldn't make her come into focus. He slipped off his reading glasses and tried again, blinking in owlish fashion for a long moment as the vision coalesced. She was dressed to put the sizzle on a steak, with knee-high leather boots and a dark-colored dress that hugged her curves like a mountain road. "I—" He broke off in a stammer. "You— Ah, yes. It's fine."

"Good." She stalked to the window, pointed heels echoing on the hardwood, and he couldn't help tracking her with his eyes, struck dumb by this new creature with flowing hair and legs that went all the way to the floor. She'd said she'd never once been out on a date, so it begged the question: *who in the hell had she bought this outfit for?* "Cab's here," she announced as

161

she looked out the window to the street below. She turned her gaze to him, cool and assessing. "You'd better get cleaned up."

Freshly shaven and with his tie once again knotted, Reed found himself in the back of a taxi, taking care to remain on his own side even as Ellery crossed her legs and showed off an expanse of long white thigh. She smelled like shampoo and leather, and the waves of her hair obscured most of her profile so he could not read her face. A tense, challenging sort of energy radiated from her, a mood he did not recognize, and it made him distinctly nervous. Outside, the landscape was alien, snowflakes like stars whooshing past the windows as they hurtled through the dark night. It was frigid when they landed, and they stepped carefully into the snowbound street. Reed poured money at the driver until the man seemed satisfied and waved them off. As the cabbie's red taillights winked out in the distance, Reed realized he had failed to arrange for a ride home. *Leaped into this without a fully formed plan,* he lectured himself as he watched Ellery pick her way through the snowdrifts toward the restaurant. *Very smart of you.*

The steakhouse, Mooo . . . , looked like something out of a London fairy tale, with its dark wood exterior set off by decorations of cheery red branches, evergreen boughs, pine cones and white lights. The whole lot of it was half-buried in snow, which only added to the holiday aesthetic. Reed and

Ellery hurried inside with a bluster of wintry air. "I can see why you were able to get a table at the last minute," Ellery muttered in regards to the mostly empty restaurant as the male host approached with a wide smile.

The host took their coats while Reed surveyed the place. The white, modern design inside belied the pub-like exterior. It was well lit by large circular lamps that glinted off large starburst mirrors and a gleaming bar, but there were few other patrons around to take advantage. The storm had kept most sensible New Englanders indoors for the night. "Right this way," the host said, and led them to a table for two by the windows.

Ellery regarded the white bone china and shining silverware with a tiny frown before carefully placing the starched napkin in her lap. "So this is where you go?" she asked him. "When you go on dates?"

"No, Boston is a bit out of the way from Virginia. I try to start out with something that doesn't involve airfare." At her scowl, he coughed and smiled. "You talk like I have some heavily stacked social calendar, some playbook to work from. I haven't been on a proper date in ages."

"So . . . just improper ones, then? Duly noted, Agent Markham. I guess these improper women must not rate a . . ." She paused as she picked up the menu, and her jaw fell open. ". . . sixty-two-dollar steak!" She shot him a glare across the table.

The waiter gave them a concerned glance, and Reed rushed to assure her. "Dinner is on me."

She looked affronted. "I can pay for myself."

"I know that," he said, although he really didn't. She was on leave from her job and he had no way of knowing what her finances were at the moment. "I just meant that since I selected the restaurant without input from you, it seems only fair that I pick up the cost."

"I don't want to owe you any more than I already do."

"This isn't about owing."

She tilted her head, her gray eyes guileless. "Isn't it?"

The waiter returned to take their orders, and Ellery selected the steak-frites for a more modest thirty-two dollars, while Reed ordered a New York strip with asparagus and braised carrots on the side.

"My mother would be appalled if she knew you'd just agreed to pay twelve dollars for one measly order of carrots," Ellery said when they were alone again. "We used to get a two-pound bag for two bucks."

"Have you talked to your mother recently?"

Ellery shrugged one shoulder. "She wants me to come home for Christmas. I told her I'd fly her out here. So that's where we are—each of us stuck someplace the other one won't go."

Reed didn't understand Caroline Hathaway, who had lost one child forever and yet seemed determined to keep the remaining one at arm's length. Ellery's mother still resided at the scene of the crime, the windows of her Chicago walk-up just one block from the park where Ellery had been abducted. Maybe Mrs. Hathaway looked out at the swings and basketball courts and remembered her kids playing there, but Ellery would forever have a different view. "Tell me about Daniel," he said, and Ellery halted with the wineglass just in front of her lips.

"Why?"

"I never got to know him." Her older brother had died of leukemia shortly after Ellery's return, Reed knew, but he had never met the boy. He'd been low man on the totem pole back then, and interviews with the victims' families were left to more experienced agents. When Ellery didn't volunteer anything further, Reed tried again. "I'm just curious what he was like," he said, taking up his own wineglass. "Besides, if you must know, this is how it usually works on dates. You talk and get to know each other."

"This isn't a date," she reminded him, narrowing her eyes. "And you already know me. You literally wrote the book, remember?"

Reed felt an embarrassed flush go through him, as it always did whenever she brought up his bestseller about the Coben case. "It was hardly a comprehensive biography . . ."

"No," she agreed, an edge in her voice. "It wasn't."

"You've raised a fair point, though—you should ask the questions. Anything you want, I'll answer it."

"Anything?" She eyed him speculatively, and he got that wiggly feeling in his belly again. He forced himself to sit still as she pondered the possibilities. "Why did you ask out Sarit in the first place?" she asked. "Was it because of the book?"

Reed shifted in his seat. Normally, women asked him why his marriage broke up, not how it got started. "I, uh, I guess you could say she asked me out, in a way. We met at the mayor's benefit dinner and got to talking. Sarit was doing a piece on domestic violence and she wanted to pick my brain about the psychological makeup of the offenders, so she asked me out for coffee. She talked so much and so passionately about the women she was interviewing for her piece that her coffee just sat there, untouched, until it went completely cold. I didn't care because I would have listened to her forever. She had this lyrical quality to her . . ." He broke off, remembering, and shook his head. "The book came later." Reed could fill out an efficient report, a catalog of facts, but he was hopeless when it came to storytelling. Sarit's keen sense of narrative flow and sharp eye for character detail had brought the book to life.

"Does she know you're up here now?" Ellery asked.

"She knows," Reed replied, with a tone that indicated Sarit was none too pleased about it.

The food arrived in a cloud of savory aromas, the elegant white plates weighed down with more than the pair of them could ever eat. A stack of golden fries. Thick, tender cuts of meat. Asparagus drizzled with house-made hollandaise. They each enjoyed a few bites before Ellery resumed her inquisition, sparing no quarter. "Do you think you'll ever try to solve your mother's murder?"

Her question caught Reed with a mouthful of ice water, which he choked on briefly before managing to get it all down. Ellery flashed him a chagrined grimace. "Sorry if that's over the line."

"No. I said to ask me anything," he said, regretting every word of it. He picked at the edge of his napkin with his thumbnail for a moment as he considered how to answer. His birth mother, Camilla Flores, had been found stabbed to death in her apartment in Las Vegas when Reed was a baby. Reed had known she was dead all his life but hadn't learned the details until he was an adult and petitioned his parents for the truth. Eventually, he'd been able to see the murder book for himself, thin as it was. Reed, then five months old and apparently named Joey, had been found in his cot by Camilla's female roommate who'd walked in on the macabre scene. Reed still knew her initial statement by heart: *I pushed open the door because the baby was crying, and there she was on the floor with a knife sticking out of her.*

However many minutes had passed between the time Camilla lost her fight and Angela arrived home, it was just long enough for her killer to escape into history. The police had knocked on doors and rounded up a few local suspects, but never got traction with any of them. Absent any new leads, they more or less gave up.

"It happened more than forty years ago," he told Ellery. "There's nothing left to investigate."

Ellery nodded as though she had expected that answer. "Is that why . . . is that why you went into law enforcement?"

He gave a thin, rueful smile at his obvious transparency. "If you can't save the one you love, save the one you're with," he said, raising his glass in a mock toast. Then he froze as he realized the impact of his words. Her gaze traveled up to his and stopped there. It was rare enough, this lingering direct eye contact from her, that he forgot his manners and simply stared right back.

"What would you have done otherwise?" she finally asked, still watching his face. "If you hadn't joined the FBI?"

"Oh, you know," he said, looking away at last, gesturing vaguely with one hand. "I was very young, you see, so there were the usual teenage boy fantasies . . ."

She arched an eyebrow at him as she speared a bite of steak. "Aren't you kind of living the teenage boy fantasy?"

"I was going to be a rock star," he told her.

Her eyes widened and she leaned over the table toward him. "Get out. You're not serious."

"I was deadly serious. Why? You don't see it?" He ran a hand through his hair to fluff it up and turned his head so she could admire his jutting jaw and strong profile.

She squinted and tilted her head to one side, making a show of studying him. "Mick Jagger?"

He turned back to her in horror. "Just how old do you think I am?"

She grinned and gave a girlish shrug that delighted him more than it should have. "The waiter only asked one of us for ID," she pointed out.

Ellery would turn thirty next year, hardly a girl, but with her hair down and the lowered lighting, she looked younger than her years—which made him feel every one of his. "That's because you're dressed like a college student about to head out clubbing," he informed her with a lofty tone.

She looked down at her chest, so he had to look, too. "I thought you liked my outfit," she said, looking up again.

He held her gaze deliberately. "I never said I didn't like it."

"Oh. Well, then. Back to your imaginary rock band: which instrument did you play?"

"It wasn't imaginary. Cow Ascension was very real, and I'll have you know we rocked Tommy Tindler's graduation party. I played the keyboard."

"I'm sorry. Time out. Flag on the play." She made a T with her hands. "Cow Ascension?"

"Brad thought up the name. You don't like it?" He tried to look wounded.

She folded her arms over her chest. "I'm just trying to imagine the T-shirts."

"Ah, well, I don't think we ever got that far. Brad got early acceptance to Yale, and we lost our rehearsal space ... his parents' garage."

"And now the world will never be treated to the musical stylings of Cow Ascension," she said mournfully. "What a pity. Do you still play?"

The question drew him up short and his smile faltered. "A bit. Well. I, uh, I'd like to, but I had to leave the piano when I moved out. Tula's taking lessons so it really makes more sense for it to stay with her." He looked down quickly at his lap; the next part came out all in a rush. "It was the strangest feeling, you know, to close the door behind me, leaving everything I loved on the other side."

He hadn't talked about the divorce with anyone, not beyond the nuts and bolts mechanics with lawyers and mediators and all the people he'd paid to slice up his former life. He raised his head again and found Ellery watching him with clouded eyes. "Yes," she said finally. "And when that door shuts, and you hear it click, it sounds so final—

because you know." She looked away toward the outside, in the direction of her lost home. "You know you'll never come back again."

The restaurant turned out to be attached to a small boutique hotel, so Ellery wandered the intimate lobby while Reed talked with the concierge about the hope of finding a taxi. Outside, the storm had picked up again, swirling in the streets and banging on the windows like an angry guest demanding to be let in. After a couple of calls, the kind woman at the front desk found a taxi that was willing to make its way out, but it was "going to be a while." Reed went to give Ellery the news, and he found her off in a shadowed corner, contemplating a black-and-white abstract painting that might have been a ballerina bending over, or maybe a pregnant penguin. "Daniel loved to draw," she said as he came to stand next to her, looking at the art and not at him. "He had an amazing knack for capturing people. If I tried it, the noses came out wrong and the proportions would be off, but Daniel . . . he could sketch a person in five minutes flat, and it was like they came to life right on the page." She glanced at Reed. "Not just what they looked like in their faces, you know, but like who they really were inside. Does that make sense?"

"I think so."

She turned back to face the painting. "My mom didn't want anything touched in his half of the room after he was gone, but I used to get out his sketchbooks and look at them when she wasn't home. I even took one when I left for good, which I felt a little guilty about, but then why should I? It's not fair that she gets to keep everything."

He wondered briefly what it might have been like for her if Daniel hadn't died, if Caroline had had the money or time or emotional wherewithal to deal with her daughter's trauma. Ellery had survived. Once she was no longer dying, not in any way that could be measured, her mother had returned all her attention to the child she couldn't save.

"Thank you for suggesting this place for dinner," Ellery said abruptly. "You were right—it's better than Burger King."

He smiled. "You see? You could do this if you wanted. Dinner and conversation. It's not so difficult."

He expected her to remind him again that this wasn't really a date, but instead she said nothing. She drifted away, down toward a shadowed corner, a disappearing act that only begged for him to follow. He found her standing on one side of a display case, hidden from view of the front desk. She was slouched against the wall such that her hips jutted out toward him slightly, and she twirled the end of her hair around one finger. "If this were a date," she said slowly, "what would happen next?"

Reed checked either direction before taking a small step forward. "It's not a date," he said, but all of a sudden he felt less sure.

"Yes, but if it was one," she said, looking up at him from beneath a dark fringe of lashes. No matter what else changed, her stark gray eyes were always the same. His mouth went dry. She licked her lips. "What next?"

"I'd—I'd see you home." He nodded to himself, pleased with his answer.

Ellery's lips curled up with her smile. "Oh, like a proper date. I get it." She stretched out one finger and ran it over the middle of his silk tie; he felt it down the back of his spine. "But what if it was one of those improper ones?"

Blood started coursing through his ears as his brain rang out the alarm—*danger, danger, abort, abort!*—but he found himself drawing even closer, into her intimate space. She smelled like cinnamon tea and her own warm skin. "Ellery, what is this?" he whispered to her.

She shrugged again, the one he'd liked so much earlier, and ducked her gaze. "Your idea," she murmured back. "Remember? You were explaining to me how I should be going on dates."

He swallowed, trying to recall his exact words. Whatever they were, this wasn't the scenario he'd had in mind, but his neurons were fizzing like sparklers now and he had no coherent thought beyond *yes.* His hand reached out almost of its own volition and brushed tentatively against hers. Her mouth parted at the contact but she did not pull away. "I'm not meant to be doing this," he said as he threaded their fingers together slowly, back and forth.

"Mmm. Don't be you then. Be someone else."

His eyes squeezed shut at the suggestion. If only it were ever that easy. She knew very well it was not.

"You don't know me," she said softly as their fingers continued a leisurely, loose exploration. "You're just some guy on the T who saw me and asked me out."

"Yeah." He chuckled wryly. "That's definitely not me," he said, but he could not seem to stop touching her. It had been so long since he'd been here like this, this painfully sweet moment; he'd taken a few women to bed since splitting with Sarit last year, but he'd never held their hands. Ellery had beautiful hands.

"You were waiting for the train when you saw me standing there," she told him. "You saw me standing there, and you thought . . . what?"

"That you're beautiful," he filled in automatically, because it was true.

Her smile slipped, just for a second, and he wondered if she'd ever heard the words before. He didn't have time to question it because she started talking again. "So you asked me out, and I said yes, and here we are," she said, her voice low and breathless. "We're alone and you're finally able to touch me."

His fingertips dragged over her palm at the words and he felt every ridge of her skin. He was waiting for her to stop him, slap him, break the spell somehow, but her body was warm and open and so he kept going. Their breath fogged up their darkened corner, making the air hot and close. His thumb rubbed the rounded fleshy part of her palm and then ventured higher, to the impossibly soft skin of her wrist.

It was there he met the scars.

Ellery went rigid and he tried to draw back, but her hand had grabbed him fast. "What are you thinking now?" she asked tightly. She wasn't loud, but her voice had lost its playfulness. Before he could summon a reply, she answered for him. "You're probably thinking I'm a suicide survivor, right? I mean, that's the sunniest scenario—that I tried to off myself."

"Ellery, please." He tried to extricate himself but she held him still.

"I look pretty from a distance," she said. "Up close is a different story."

"I'm damned close," he whispered back, "and you look fine."

"What about if you saw these?" she demanded, as if he hadn't spoken. She used her free hand to tug down the collar of her dress. In the darkness, he truthfully couldn't even see the scars, but he knew that they were there. "Now maybe you're thinking—whoa, this lady's not your average garden-variety crazy. She must be a special breed."

"I don't think you're crazy."

"No?" Her hand tightened on his to the point that she was hurting him. "You accused me of murder once. How's that for crazy?"

He gritted his teeth. "I didn't know you then."

"You knew me well enough to write a book. You knew, and you thought it anyway. Hell, you thought it because of what you knew about me, about what happened with Coben. Some other guy without a psychology degree, what's he going to think?" Her voice was rising rapidly now.

"I'm sorry. I was wrong."

"Oh, screw your *sorry*. I don't want it. Maybe it can happen like you say, where I meet some nice guy and we have a nice dinner and then maybe even a nice kiss or two, but sooner or later, he's going to know the truth. He's going to see the scars and he's going to know about the farm tools. What if we're on a date and some nutbag throws a rubber hand at me? What if he's the kind of guy who wants to cuddle in bed at night? How do I tell him I don't sleep unless I'm alone? Hmm? What if . . . what if he wants kids? Too bad, nice guy, because I had that possibility ripped right out of me."

"Ellery, please. Please stop."

Her eyes went wider, her fingers biting into his flesh. "You still don't get it. *There is no stop.*"

"I get it," he said. "I do. I know what a monster he was."

There was a moment where he heard only her harsh breathing and the sound of his heart slamming against his ribs. Maybe, maybe he had found the right words.

"You don't know," she told him at last, her voice cracking painfully. "You hunt these guys, Reed, and you see what they do. But then you get to go home."

She released his hand in a sudden flash, pushing past him in such a burst of movement that it took his addled brain a second to parse her words and realize what had happened. His hand throbbed as blood flow returned, and he dashed after her. "Ellery! Wait!" She wasn't in the main lobby when he got there, and the lingering cold air told him she'd fled into the streets. He ran outside without bothering to put on his coat. "Ellery! Ellery, where are you?"

Snow slapped at his face, raw and wet. He put out his hands to wave it off but it just came coursing down from the sky. He could see only a few yards in either direction. He staggered first one way, then the other, calling out to her, but she was gone. There was no one but him standing in the winter wasteland. He bit back a curse and walked back to the front of the hotel, where the taxi he had summoned drifted into view. He grabbed his coat from the bench inside and ducked into the backseat of the car. Reed ordered the driver to go slowly around the block while he pressed his face to the cold window and scanned the snow for any signs of life. Every few seconds, he tried her cell. No answer.

Reed had dated enough to recognize the *fuck off* signal when he got it, so he sat back with a sigh, scrubbing his face with both hands. What the hell was he supposed to do now? His stuff was at her place for the night. Eventually, he gave the driver Ellery's address and just hoped she'd cooled off enough by the time he got there that she would let him inside.

*You get to go home,* she'd said. He gave a humorless grin to himself in the dark. *Maybe not tonight.*

He shut his eyes, partially from exhaustion, partly to block out everything on the outside. The taxi inched its way through the driving snow, an interminable silent ride into oblivion. Reed swayed with the car and let the motion carry him away.

He was jolted upright again when the taxi slammed to a sudden stop. The driver cried out something in Urdu. Reed didn't know the words but he recognized the meaning: *holy shit.* A strange light flickered ahead on the street, and Reed sat forward so that he could get a better look. *Fire.*

He grabbed his cell phone and started dialing 911 even as he leaped from the cab. Outside, he could get his bearings, and he could see it was Ellery's building—and there was Ellery, standing in front of the fire. It was a vehicle of some sort, now reduced to a metal shell inside the flames. "Ellery!"

he called out, scrambling toward her. His shoes kept slipping on the icy street.

The blaze went up behind her, ten feet in the air. The falling snow couldn't touch the burn.

"Ellery," he gasped as he reached her. "Are you all right?"

She looked up at him, dazed. "That's my truck."

# 7

Detective Ned Banyon was no one she had ever met before, but as usual, he knew Ellery, or at least the legend of her. "Car fire," he remarked when they met, only in Boston-ese it came out *cah fiyah*. "Trouble just seems to follow you around, now don't it." She recognized him only by his type: early fifties, with a rounded paunch and a buzz cut to camouflage a rapidly receding hairline. He'd arrived at the scene holding a Dunkin' Donuts cup and wearing the grim expression of someone working the overnight shift in the middle of a snowstorm. Now he was standing in her living room with his boots dripping a puddle of melting snow and salt onto her hardwood floor. He looked around at the walls as if cataloging them for evidence, taking in her framed poster of Led Zeppelin's *Mothership* album and the picture of the Chicago shoreline as seen from near outer space—as close as she dared get to her origins. She felt every sweep of his eyes on her apartment like they were up and down her body. She had invited exactly one person into her home, ever, and that was the other guy standing there with them, watching her intently. "Any idea who might've wanted to torch your truck?" Banyon asked.

"No," she said, avoiding both Reed's and the detective's eyes. She didn't plan to answer anything beyond precisely what was asked. She hadn't even removed her jacket because then she might be forced to solicit Banyon's coat, too, and she didn't want to make it seem like she was inviting him to stay.

"Did you see anyone suspicious hanging around the building lately? Anyone you didn't recognize?"

"No. I wasn't here when the fire started." She had run out on Reed at the restaurant and taken the T home, which is when she'd stumbled on the blaze. She had to have missed the arsonist by only a minute or two.

"But you showed up even before the fire engines," Banyon said. "Awful convenient timing." He had apparently done the same math that she had and reached a similar conclusion. Someone had wanted her to see the show. "Any other signs of trouble?" he asked her. "Anyone you seen following you, that sort of thing?"

She felt Reed's gaze on her acutely. "No."

Banyon turned to Reed. "What about you?"

"Me?"

"Yeah. You're stayin' here, aren't you?" Banyon nodded at the roller suitcase parked by the couch and the folded blanket and pillow sitting upon it. He obviously hadn't missed much during his visual inventory. "You see anything unusual today?"

There was a short silence while Ellery held her breath to see if Reed would bring up the note slipped under her door. "I didn't see anything," Reed said finally, and Ellery exhaled.

Banyon scrunched up his face as though he didn't quite believe them, but it was going on midnight and he plainly wasn't going to be bothered any further. He gave Ellery his card. "You'll be wanting a copy of our report for your insurance," he said. "And if you think of anything else—or you have any other issues, big or small, you call me, okay?"

Ellery took the card but made no promises as she showed Banyon out the door. When she turned back around, she practically bumped into Reed and her dog, both standing right in her path. "Jeez, the two of you," she muttered, stepping around them. "Give a girl some space, why don't you?" She shrugged out of her coat and put it on a hook as she went by.

"You didn't tell him about the note," Reed said as they followed her down the hall to the bathroom, Bump's nails click-clacking on the floor. She shut them behind the door and turned on the water to wash her face. The fire lingered everywhere on her body—ashes in her hair, the taste of burning plastic in her mouth. She had been so close to it that her eyelashes were singed.

She splashed cold water on her face for a few moments and then rose up, watching in the mirror as the droplets ran down her cheeks and dripped from her chin. She looked pale and haggard, nothing like the woman who had dressed up for dinner only a few hours before. On the other side of the door, Reed and Bump would not be ignored. Bump's blackberry nose snuffled underneath along the crack, seeking her out, as Reed continued his argument. "This person isn't playing around anymore," he told her. "It's not a prank."

She yanked open the door, and he startled backward at her sudden appearance. "We don't even know it's the same person."

"You don't know it's not," he said, following her again as she walked to her bedroom. He halted in the doorway but kept right on talking. "And let's just consider that implication for a moment, shall we? That would mean you have more than one person threatening you. How is that any better?"

"Sixteen thousand messages," she told him tartly as she pulled out her gun. The dog still needed to go out. She was going to have to face the streets once more tonight.

Reed stared at her. "I'm sorry—what?"

"More than sixteen thousand messages," she said. "That's how many emails I got after the story hit the news this summer, at least before the department shut down my account. My address at the Woodbury PD was public information, and let me tell you, the public made sure to use it. Lots of people wanted to congratulate me. Others had different ideas. 'Dear Ellery: I had a dream about you the other night. You didn't have any hands.' Or, 'Dear Ellery: I think about you all the time when I'm gardening.'" She shot him a hard look. "That one had a picture of a hoe attached to it."

Satisfied with his stunned silence, she pushed past him and went to find Bump's leash. The dog trotted after her eagerly as he picked up on her mission. "Did you save these messages?" Reed trailed them both to the door. He had never even bothered to remove his overcoat.

"No," she replied wearily. "What would be the point?"

"To find out who's doing this."

"Sure, right. We find him. Then the next him. And the one after that. Where does it stop? People will say shockingly disgusting things from the privacy of their computers, just to get their rocks off."

She went to yank open the door, but Reed put his hand on hers to stop her. The touch shocked her enough that she drew back. "This guy isn't satisfied with just sending messages through the internet," he told her in a low, urgent voice. He pointed to the nearest window. "He's right out there, and he's started setting things on fire."

"Good," she said, meeting his eyes with defiance. "I hope he is out there. If he's dying to give me a message, well, then let's have it." She pulled the door so hard it came flying open, and Bump surged into the void. She held up her hand when Reed tried to follow. "I can take care of myself."

She took the stairs instead of the elevator, burning off nervous energy as she rushed down each flight, blood roaring in her ears. Her heart was thudding by the time she hit the streets. The snow had stopped but the city was frozen under the weight of it, dark and silent. Ellery took Bump to the side of the building where her truck had been parked, but it was now gone, the smoking remnants having been towed away. She glanced up and down the deserted street but saw no signs of life anywhere. The stink of the fire hung in the cold air, noxious and acrid. *Convenient timing,* the detective had said. Someone had been on this very street, waiting for her. She shivered inside her coat as Bump ambled idly around her feet in the snow. She felt eyes on her all of a sudden. "Hurry up," she urged the dog, a flash of fear hot on her neck.

She turned around wildly but there was no one there. Only when she thought to look up did she see—it was Reed, a dark angel set against the glow of her windows, watching her from above.

\* \* \*

In the morning, her eyes cracked open against the bright white light of day. The floor-to-ceiling windows in her loft had blinds to hold back the worst of the sun, but all the snow-white surfaces outside magnified the rays and trained them as if through a crystal into Ellery's bedroom. She curled up like a mole, burying her face in Bump's soft fur. He thumped his tail on the bed and whined in appreciation as she petted him. She had corralled him in her room last night, partly to keep him away from Reed on the couch, and partly because she wanted the company. She ran her fingertips over his muzzle and he licked her hand once before flopping against her, his solid body wriggling as close as it could get. Bump was no kind of watchdog—he spent most of his day dozing in a patch of sun—but he had known no other version of her. To him, she was perfect just as she was.

She rubbed her hand over his familiar barrel shape a few times before she became aware that Reed was talking to someone, a faint one-sided conversation from the living room. Curious, she got up and padded on bare feet to the door, which she cracked open so she could listen. It took her only a moment to realize he was talking to his daughter.

"Sweetheart, yes, I agree that this boy shouldn't have taken the soccer ball if you were in the middle of using it," he was saying, "but that still doesn't give you the right to call him a—a snogglepus." He paused. "What is a snogglepus anyway?"

There was a pause, and then Reed made some sort of strangled noise that was partway between a laugh and a cough. "Okay, I see. With horns and a pig nose, you're saying? And you drew him a picture? Well, no wonder he was cross with you."

Ellery closed the door silently and leaned her shoulders up against it. The tenderness and affection in his voice made her ache in a way she couldn't name. He had a life far away from here, one she had no place in, and she should be letting him get back to it. Resolved, she waited until she heard him end the call, and then charged into the living room. Reed startled at the sight of her, fumbling his phone, and she stopped short when she realized he was clad only in his T-shirt and boxers. "Sorry!" she said, throwing up her hands in apology. She turned away. "I heard you on the phone and I didn't think . . ."

"No, my fault," he assured her quickly. She heard him rustling frantically for his clothes. "I shouldn't be hanging around someone else's living room in my underwear."

She heard him hopping around on one foot and was glad he couldn't see her smile. Reed was typically so smooth and put together that it gave her perverse satisfaction to catch him all flustered. His physicality intrigued her—he was built like a swimmer, thin and long but with powerful shoulders, but what she really envied was the way he seemed comfortable with the space he took up in the world. She was accustomed now to viewing men with wary eyes, keeping a careful distance, always on alert. For some reason, though, her inner alarm system went quiet around Reed, through no conscious choice of her own. It was as if her body remembered him.

"There," he said at length. "I'm decent now."

She turned around again and saw he had dressed in the same trousers and button-down shirt he'd worn the day before. He was going to have to go home simply because he had no more clothes with him. She also noticed that his laptop was powered up and sitting on her coffee table, along with some paper notes he'd been making. "You're off to an early start," she observed. "Rebooking your flight?"

"Not yet. I've been looking into additional sexual assaults in the Somerville area that might fit a pattern similar to the Mendoza case—anything that might give the geo-profiling program more data to work with."

"Did you find anything?" She crossed the room to look for herself.

"I'm up to eleven probable incidents, with an additional six possible cases. We can look at scenarios that include only crimes with the highest degree of match, as well as those broadened out to include more uncertainty."

"How long will that take?"

"I should be able to have something this afternoon—tomorrow at the latest."

"Good," she said, heading for the kitchen. "Then after

you're done you can catch that flight home."

Reed followed her, frowning, although whether it was because of her words or because she'd just pulled down a box of breakfast cereal with a cartoon animal on the front, she couldn't say. He watched her pour on the milk and take a few bites. "I don't like the idea of leaving you here alone," he said finally, "not after what happened last night."

She kept her gaze neutral. "The nondate wasn't that bad, was it?"

"I'm talking about the part where someone set your truck on fire," he replied with a scowl. He needn't have reminded her; she'd peeked out at the street already and seen the damage in the light of day. The intense heat of the fire had burned off all the surrounding snow, leaving a bare crater on the side of the road.

She pushed the marshmallows and Os around in her bowl. "The police are investigating," she said finally. "There really isn't anything else to be done right now. You have to get back to your job and your family."

He looked her over searchingly. "You're the one who accused me of always running home."

Her face was hot. "It—it wasn't an accusation. It was a fact, a blessed one, if we're being completely honest. I don't blame you, not at all. I would do the same, if I were you." He said nothing, just stared with those dark eyes that seemed to go right through her. "Besides, how do you think I would feel, if you stayed up here babysitting me and it cost you that promotion? If it meant you didn't get more time with Tula? I can't be responsible for that."

"And how do you think I would feel if I left and something happened to you?" His voice was quiet but determined. "I would never forgive myself."

"So—what? You just give up your whole life to move in and sleep on my lumpy couch? Follow me wherever I go? I appreciate the sentiment, I do. But let's be honest here. You have very real obligations, Reed, but I'm not one of them. Not—not anymore. The reason you go home at the end is because that's where you belong."

His shoulders slumped, and she knew he saw that she was right. "I could at least stay an extra day or two," he said, trying to rally the cause.

"It wouldn't make a difference." She kept her words gentle, but he stiffened as if struck anyway, because Reed Markham's whole life was built on the principle that he made a difference. She had a flash of the night before, of showing him her scars, and felt a guilty flush go through her. He was being so kind and she'd just wanted to rub his nose in it: *here's everything you can never fix*. "But . . . thank you." Her voice caught just a bit. "Thank you for wanting to try."

He nodded and averted his eyes, diminished by his

limitations. "I just worry about you having to deal with all this crap . . . all those creeps out there who get off on Coben's story. Probably they're harmless, sure—but you never know what might happen."

She smiled sadly. She didn't worry so much about what else might happen to her, because the worst already had. "I'll be careful," she told him. "I promise."

He gave a grudging sigh and pulled out one of her stools to sit down. "You have another one of those bowls?" he asked as he picked up the cereal box. "Or shall I skip the facade and just eat a half pound of raw sugar?"

"It has antioxidants in it," she said, pointing at the label. "See?"

"It has a grinning parrot on the front."

"He's happy about all the vitamins he's getting."

"He's happy about the fact he doesn't have any teeth to rot with this stuff," Reed retorted as he poured himself a large bowlful.

Ellery kept to her own bowl then and didn't argue any further, but she couldn't help noticing—he ate the whole damn thing.

They spent the morning holed up in her apartment, far from the frozen white world below. Reed worked on his analysis

191

from one end of the couch while Ellery paced the living room, arguing on the phone with various people from her insurance company that yes, the truck was going to be a total loss, as it now resembled a bag of charcoal. After three separate conversations, she learned that the insurance claims adjuster would still have to verify the damage for himself, thus delaying the whole process. "Maybe he could just watch the news," she said, exasperated. "I think channels four and seven both sent a truck."

She gave up for the moment and took a seat at the other end of the couch. Bump saw this as his invitation, too, and he ambled over from his spot in the sunbeam to climb onto the sofa between Reed and Ellery. Reed was so deep in his work that he barely noticed. "How's it going?" she asked him, but he just muttered an unintelligible reply and looked at something on his notes. Ellery watched him for a few minutes as he looked up information on his computer, squinted at it, and then jotted down some observation she couldn't read from her vantage point. TV shows always portrayed FBI profiling as breathlessly exciting and dangerous work, whereas Reed seemed more like he belonged in a commercial for headache medicine. Or perhaps an office supply store. She smothered a yawn just at the sight of him. "I'm going to go down the street to get sandwiches," she announced as she stood up. "Is turkey okay for you?"

"Fine." He didn't even glance her way.

Ellery suited up against the elements, scarf and all, and took the dog with her into the cold sunshine. The city had come to life again, although it moved slowly under the heavy remnants of the storm. Pedestrians had to slow their usual brisk walk as they navigated around icy patches of sidewalk and giant snow berms mounded at the intersections. Cars motored past wearing funny snow hats. Everywhere, drops of melting snow trickled from the overhangs and rooftops. Ellery followed along behind Bump as he blazed a trail, ears akimbo, always eager for whatever new scents the day might bring. When her cell phone rang, she had to pull off her glove with her teeth to answer it. "Hello?"

She was expecting Reed, perhaps with a change of order, or maybe a follow-up call from the insurance company, but it was Bertie Jenkins, Esquire, on the other end of the line. "I saw the news," she said. "Someone set your truck on fire."

"Yeah, I kind of noticed that," Ellery replied as she set forth with Bump again.

"Any idea who did it?"

"Not a clue. No suspects, no witnesses. Why?"

Bertie was quiet for a moment. "It's a hell of a coincidence, don't you think? You come over asking me about the old arson cases, and then someone torches your truck?"

Ellery halted in the middle of the sidewalk. "You think this has to do with you?"

"No, I think it has to do with you," Bertie corrected. "I've been crusading on this story for months now, and nobody's come around to set my stuff on fire. So I'm thinking maybe you rattled the right cage. Who else have you been talking to?"

"No one. Just Kevin Powell."

"Powell," Bertie repeated, musing. "I know a few people who liked him for the fire, but I wasn't one of them. He's a blowhard but he's not an imbecile. The Gallagher store always made a strange target for a firebug—relatively busy street, a whole row of businesses to choose from, and our guy picks one smack dab in the middle. It reads personal to me."

"Or like someone too brazen to think he'd get caught," Ellery couldn't help pointing out. This was the story the prosecution had put on, suggesting that Luis Carnevale was overconfident and crazed with fire lust. He'd picked the furniture store because it was filled with wood that could ignite quickly.

"Luis didn't do this," Bertie said, but it came out automatically, like her mind was already someplace else. "I don't think it's a coincidence about your truck," she told Ellery. "I think you've made someone nervous—more nervous than I have—and I'd like to know who."

"I don't know the answer to that," Ellery replied. "If I did,

I'd be having the SOB arrested for destroying my truck."

"Maybe we can get together again. Exchange information."

Ellery bit her lip. She didn't have any information to exchange. "The thing is . . ."

"Wait, I have an even better idea. Are you free this afternoon? I'm going up to see Luis, and you could come, too. Get his side of the story. If you talk to him, you'll see the truth: he didn't set this fire."

Ellery thought of the summer and how many times she'd looked a murderer in the eyes with no hint of what he was hiding. "No offense," she told Bertie, "but that's bullshit." Whether Luis Carnevale was innocent or not, it was a story he'd been telling himself for decades now, and Ellery was sure he had it perfected to an art form. "Liars lie. That's what they're good at."

"Yeah? Well, try this on for size then: Luis sure as hell didn't set your car on fire. Maybe if we pool our resources, we can figure out who did."

So this was how, by midafternoon, Ellery had picked up a rented midsize SUV and was headed out of the city to the Cedar Junction Correctional Facility in Walpole. Reed was frowning from the passenger seat. "You said you were going to be careful," he reminded her.

"It's a maximum security prison. How much more careful could I get?"

"Someone sets fire to your vehicle, and your reaction is to set up a playdate with an arsonist."

"If the fire last night is connected to this case, then it's in my best interest to figure out how." But it wasn't really her truck she was thinking of as she drove toward the prison. It was Myra Gallagher, with her gnarled hands and half-burned face. The news stories on the fire had carried pictures of Myra from before, when she had milk-white skin and auburn hair and clear blue eyes that had yet to see her life go up in flames. If Coben was the man who marked Ellery's before and after, then Carnevale was the man who marked Myra's, at least that was how Myra told it. Ellery could only imagine how she might feel if someone started sniffing around Coben for hints of innocence and inviting him to "tell his side." She'd begun digging around in the arson story with the intent of helping Myra, to reassure her that her monster would remain trapped in his cage, but now here she was going to chat up that monster with an eye toward possibly letting him out. "Have you ever been here?" she asked Reed as she made the turn to the Cedar Junction parking lot.

He shook his head. "Not personally, no. But I've heard of it." She gave him a curious look, and he filled in the grim answer. "This is where they put Albert DeSalvo—the man convicted of the Boston Strangler cases. He himself was murdered inside those walls."

Ellery got out of the car and regarded the high concrete face of the prison. There were multiple separate buildings on the property, all ostensibly painted white, but against the backdrop of the pure fresh snow, they mostly looked a grubby gray. Ellery and Reed met up with Bertie Jenkins, and together they went through security and were put in a windowless room, this one painted an odd combination of cream and turquoise green, to wait for Luis Carnevale. "I'm still not sure of our purpose here," Reed said to Bertie.

She gave a half-shrug. "I've been shouting to the rooftops for three years now that Luis is innocent. You two are the only ones who've ever really seemed to listen. Sure, if it's a slow news day, the TV stations send their cameras around to let me bang on about the case, but it's mainly an excuse to run the old fire footage—especially when the city starts talking about closing one of the smaller stations. Something like ninety-five percent of all fire department calls are for paramedic help these days, not fires. Turns out, if there's a war on fire, we've already won it. Better safety codes now. Sprinklers. You just don't see the kind of fires that happened in the 1980s anymore, not with any regularity. But the BFD budget is just as fat as it's ever been, and they sure as hell don't want that money wandering elsewhere. I think half the time, they're the ones sending those TV cameras to my door, so the news can trot out Luis like some old bogeyman and everyone remembers how scared they were. I'm the best PR team they've had in years."

There was the sound of a lock releasing and then a heavy metal door opened. Luis Carnevale entered the room, ushered by a uniformed guard. Ellery knew him only from his 1988 mug shot and from news clips that were a quarter century old, images that depicted a churlish young man built like a prizefighter. The current version of Carnevale resembled a monk, with his fringe-top hair, the deferential downward tilt of his head, the slow shuffle, and the shapeless, too-large clothes that wore like robes. Whether it was due to standard procedure or just years of earned good behavior, Ellery didn't know, but the guard released Carnevale's handcuffs and left him to sit unimpeded in the remaining plain plastic chair. She waited to see if she would feel something, anything to suggest that she was now in the presence of evil. He eyed her intensely, his mouth twitching on one side, his gaze hungry. Twenty-five years was a long time to be on the inside, with only your niece for female company. Ellery crossed her arms over her chest but Carnevale did not stop staring.

"No contact," the guard reminded them gruffly, and then he left, locking them all together inside the room.

# 8

Reed kept his gaze carefully neutral as he regarded the prisoner, but Bertie smiled warmly at her uncle. "How are you doing?"

Carnevale's answering smile did not meet his eyes. "One day in here, it's just the same as all the rest," he said with a slight shrug. "Any day I see you is better than before."

"I brought some friends with me," Bertie told him, and she introduced Ellery and Reed.

Carnevale's thin eyebrows rose when Bertie mentioned Reed's background. "FBI," he said, clearly surprised. "FBI is who helped put me in here."

"I'm just here as an observer," Reed clarified as he shifted in his seat. "Not in any official capacity."

Carnevale spread his arms as though he had nothing to hide. "Observe all you want. I ain't much to look at no more."

He hadn't been an attractive man back then, with his

acne-scarred face and one droopy eyelid that made him look either disinterested or menacing. The years in between had leeched the color from him so that now he matched his faded prison clothes, old and gray. He looked wizened and ordinary, not like someone who had terrorized a city with fire, but Reed knew by now not to trust appearances.

"You're up for parole soon," Reed said after a minute. "How do you think the hearing will go?"

Carnevale scratched the back of his head with one hand. "Those first years, they was hard. I knew I didn't burn that woman and her little kid, but it don't make no difference once the jury says you're guilty. I didn't kill no one, but the cops said I had to be locked away separate in here, for my own protection. Because of the other guys who are killers. The warden told me, 'We got guys in here that will kill you soon as look at you on account of you burned a little kid.'" He shook his head, as if resigned. "After a while, my story kinda went away. People got other things to worry about. I kept to myself and made up my mind to do my time clean. Got my GED. I ain't been in no trouble since I got here."

"It's true," Bertie told them. "You can check his record. It's exemplary."

"But it won't matter," Carnevale told her with a trace of impatience. "Everyone, they forgot right now, right? They ain't thinking about some fire that happened twenty-five years ago. But when it comes time for the hearing, they'll open my file and see those pictures, and they'll remember again. And it'll be just like last time. Someone's got to pay for those pictures, and they decided a long time ago—that someone is me."

"Pictures?" Ellery asked Bertie.

Bertie hesitated a moment before withdrawing a folder from her briefcase. "The prosecution was allowed to show pictures of Bobby Gallagher's body as it was found at the scene," she said as she slid the folder toward Reed. "You can imagine how that went."

Reed put his palm on top of the folder and moved it slightly back and forth, watching Carnevale for a reaction. Carnevale just stared right back at him. Reed made him wait a few seconds longer before he flipped open the cover. Beside him, Ellery sucked in a short breath at the horrible sight. The eight-by-ten glossy photos showed a toddler's body, badly burned and curled in on itself as though still in the womb. His face had melted away. Reed could just make out a patch of reddish hair and a little blue tennis shoe.

When he looked up again, Carnevale was staring at the wall, his jaw set. He didn't want to see the pictures, Reed realized. A dead toddler was definitely never part of the plan. "The jury saw the pictures," Carnevale said tightly, "and it was all over. Didn't matter what I said or did."

Reed closed the folder again and slid it back to Bertie. This time, Carnevale didn't even track its progress. "The cops didn't pick you at random," he said. "You were at the fire."

"So was a lot of people."

"But when Kevin Powell looked at you, you ran," Ellery cut in.

"He looked at me like he wanted to rip my head off. Hell yeah, I ran. You would've ran, too."

"He said you smelled like gasoline." Ellery was right to press him. If Kevin Powell really went after Carnevale the night of the fire, something must have set him off.

"The whole place smelled like gasoline," Carnevale said, waving his arms. "The air, the street, the trees. It was everywhere. What else you think gave that fire its juice?"

His voice held a hint of awe, and Reed could appreciate this now, having seen how fierce the fire was last night as her truck burned up, flames licking ten feet into the air. The Gallagher store fire would have been bigger, brighter, a hungry dragon devouring everything around it. "The fire started around midnight that night," Reed said. "How did you happen to be right there at the scene?"

"I couldn't sleep. I was up when I heard the sirens coming, lots of 'em. You could tell it was a big one. I just followed the trucks."

"You like fire?" Reed asked, trying to sound casual.

If there was a spark in Carnevale's eyes, he extinguished it in a hurry. "I was up already, like I said. I decided to go check it out. Biggest mistake of my life."

"Agent Markham and Officer Hathaway have been making some inquiries into the case," Bertie said, apparently trying to cheer him up. "Their questions may have made someone nervous."

"Oh, yeah? Who?" Carnevale looked interested again.

"Well, like I told your lawyer," Ellery replied, "we've only talked to Kevin Powell."

"Powell." Carnevale fairly spat out the name as he sat back in his chair. "Mr. Macho Hero Man. Yeah, he'd love to keep me locked up 'til I'm just a bag of bones. If I'm innocent, he ain't no hero no more."

"I haven't really focused on Powell," Bertie said thoughtfully. "Maybe I should take another look. I will say I found it odd he didn't testify at Luis's trial."

"He didn't?" Reed asked, clearly surprised.

"No, the state put on the firefighter who found the boy's body and the medical examiner who did the autopsy—and Myra Gallagher, of course."

"I know why he didn't testify," Carnevale said, and they all turned to look at him. He wore a smile of satisfaction. "He wasn't going home that night. He was goin' to get him some pussy—s'cuse my language." He nodded to

203

himself, adjudicating this new bit of information for the rest of them. "My lawyer, he even found the girl. Some skinny bitch Powell was banging when he was s'posed to be going home to his wife and kid. The girl, she didn't want to testify neither, just wanted to stay out of it, but just interviewing her was enough to spook 'em away from putting on Powell."

Ellery exchanged a look with Reed. Here at last was a plausible explanation for why Powell was on a one-way street going the wrong way that night. "Your lawyer back then—who did he think set the fire?" Ellery asked him.

"He liked Patrick Gallagher for it," Bertie replied for her client. "Frankly, so do I. He was in debt up to his eyeballs and that two-million-dollar insurance made a lot of his problems go away. I think he hired someone to torch the shop, and the hired help didn't realize Myra and Bobby would be on the premises. It was after midnight, after all."

"There was another brother," Reed said, remembering.

"David," Bertie agreed. "He wanted out of the family business. Took his share of the settlement and opened up a pizza shop in Providence."

"David would have had the same problem with the debt from the furniture store," said Reed. "Where was he the night the place burned up?"

"Home in bed with his fiancée, Heather Soto." Bertie

didn't even have to look it up. "She alibied him straightaway. Said he was with her the whole night."

"Fiancée," Reed repeated thoughtfully. "Did they actually get married?"

"Yep, and then divorced three years later. Just long enough that she probably got herself a sweet little piece of the pie. Why? You thinking the years might have changed her memory about where David Gallagher was that night?"

"I'm thinking that if they were getting married, she was going to be taking on that debt, too. Instead they got a financial windfall. Besides, if Patrick Gallagher could have hired someone to set fire to the store, then surely David could have done the same."

"Sure. Only problem—no way to prove that a professional arsonist ever existed. The cops arrested Luis at the scene and never looked anywhere else. His original lawyer subpoenaed the Gallagher bank records, but they were a mess. Half their trade was in cash, and who the hell knows where that money went?"

"The Blaze would've known," Carnevale cut in. "He saw the guy."

"You have his statement?" Ellery asked, eyeing Bertie's files.

"No," she replied with a heavy sigh. "He disappeared before he could tell exactly what he saw."

Ellery wasn't buying what Bertie was selling. "Wait, so

you're saying this guy, The Blaze, said he saw the arsonist the night of the fire, but he wouldn't say who it was? And no one followed up?"

"The original lawyer on the case, he tried," Bertie replied. "Initially, he couldn't get Earl Stanfield to say on the record exactly who he saw that night, and then the guy up and disappeared. No one could find him."

"Greedy SOB wanted money," Carnevale said, folding his arms. His sleeves pulled up at the wrists and Reed noticed a handmade tattoo, faded now and blurred at the edges: 111.

"If you paid him off, his story would be worthless anyway," Ellery said.

"I think Luis's lawyer knew that," Bertie answered. "That's why he didn't pay, and why he was working to find another way to convince The Blaze to give up his information. Before he got anywhere with the guy, The Blaze disappeared."

"Or someone rubbed him out," Carnevale said.

"Someone," Ellery repeated. "You mean the cops."

Carnevale fixed her with a hard stare. "They lock us up here like animals. Feed us crap that dogs wouldn't eat. I've seen stuff in here that would give you nightmares, and it ain't always the inmates dishing it out. We ain't in here by choice, but those guards sign up for this. They call us human filth and they pretend like they're better than us because they got the guns and they're lookin' in from the outside of the cage. But

I seen what they do when they know cameras ain't watching. And I can tell you: they aren't so different after all."

Later, when they were on their way back from the prison with copies of some of Bertie's files in the backseat, Ellery kept glancing Reed's way as if expecting him to talk. After several miles, she apparently couldn't wait any longer. "Well?" she asked. "What did you think of him?"

"Hard to say with such a short conversation," Reed replied. "He seems bitter but reconciled to his fate. It's clear that Bertie is the one driving this push to have him released and the case reexamined. Carnevale himself gave up hope a long time ago."

"Maybe he's not fighting harder because he knows he's guilty," Ellery suggested.

"Is that what you think?"

She hesitated a moment. "He tried to play it off, when you asked him about whether he liked fire, but he has a tattoo on his arm: 111. That's the Boston emergency code for fire."

"Is it? That's interesting. I tend to agree that Carnevale wasn't at the Gallagher fire as a mere interested bystander."

"Speaking of bystanders, you didn't say anything to Bertie about spotting Jake Gallagher in the news footage."

"I'd like to verify I'm right before we ring that particular bell. Those additional clippings Bertie gave us might help, especially if I can take them back and have our lab techs enlarge and enhance the photos."

Ellery was quiet again, clearly thinking as she worried her lower lip back and forth with her teeth. "You said it makes sense to look at the other Gallagher brother, David. You're right he would have a similar motive. Maybe he and Patrick even planned it together, if they both wanted to escape the debt from the store. They could've been covering for each other all these years."

"I have my doubts about Patrick Gallagher as the arsonist," Reed said.

Ellery looked over at him, plainly curious. "Why?"

"Myra told you she was there unexpectedly late at night because Patrick was desperate to get his hands on his tax documents—the deadline for filing was the following day." Ellery nodded, and Reed shrugged. "I can't help wondering what man bothers to prep his taxes for a business he knows is going to burn down in a matter of hours."

Reed had handled all sorts of crimes in his years with the Behavioral Sciences Unit, from noncustodial parents who kidnapped their children and disappeared with them to serial predators who left a trail of bodies in their wake. The murders were awful, of course, because there was no hope for redemption or a happy outcome, but it was the brutal rapes that Reed found most difficult to stomach. The murder victim's pain was over, silent now, while the rape survivors lived and breathed their ongoing horror. Once, he'd had to conduct an interview with a woman whose attacker had been waiting for her with ropes inside her apartment. Reed's job was to dive deep into the complexities of the M.O., but the woman started crying in response to his first question, and they'd sat there for an hour like that, with her weeping and him unable to help in any way. Another time, he had interviewed a middle-aged woman who owned a beauty parlor in Cincinnati. She had been cleaning up at the end of the day when her attacker came in through a back window. He had savaged her repeatedly, with his body and with the various tools he'd found around the shop, until just before dawn when he'd fled and left her near dead for her employees to find the next morning. She had seen the man's face but did not recognize him. *I don't understand,* she'd kept saying afterward, *he didn't even know me. Why would he want to do this?*

Reed Markham, the man from the FBI who was supposed to have all the answers, had no good reply. He'd hightailed it out of that hospital room as soon as he was able, and never looked back. Ellery was right: the first chance he got, Reed went home.

At the moment, though, he was still in her home, reading through reports detailing recent sexual assaults in and around

Somerville. The cops took down the details in clinical fashion but Reed tried not to focus on the pain behind the words. Stranger rape was thankfully uncommon, with only a few dozen cases in the greater Boston area each year. Add in the home invasion element that would link the M.O. to Wendy Mendoza's case, and Reed could even risk entering all the reports into the geographic profiling program to see what it would spit out. He started with the most probable cases and took a quick look at the basic geography. The map showed a red dot for each separate attack, and they scattered across five different cities: Arlington, Medford, Somerville, Cambridge, and Boston.

The first victim, a twenty-eight-year-old woman who'd worked as a receptionist in a dental office, had been attacked in her third-floor apartment more than six years ago. She had escaped with relatively minor injuries, whereas Wendy Mendoza's arm had been broken and her windpipe crushed. Either Wendy had fought a lot harder, the crimes weren't actually related, or, as Reed feared, the offender was becoming more violent. It wasn't enough for the rapist to violate the women sexually anymore; he had to hurt them in other ways first.

Reed rubbed the back of his neck to try to ease the knot of tension there. It was dark as pitch outside despite the early hour, which turned Ellery's giant living room windows into light-reflecting mirrors. His own image looked pallid and worn, his face pinched and his clothes rumpled from two days of wear. He decided to recharge with a bit of physical exercise and some healthy food. He'd checked out the local surroundings online and discovered there was a gourmet grocery store only a few blocks away.

He went down the hall to Ellery's room, where she sat cross-legged on her bed, reading through the files that Bertie had given them. "Finding anything interesting?" he asked from the doorway.

She sighed as she put aside the papers in front of her. "No, but I think I can tell you why nobody tried too hard to find this Blaze character. Near as I can make out from the notes, the last guy who spoke to The Blaze was a server at the Pine Street Inn, where The Blaze sometimes spent the night. The Blaze told him he was leaving town, going someplace warm."

"Did he say where?"

"Yeah. Mars."

"Uh, come again?"

"Mars. That's what it says in the notes. The guy told people he was going to Mars. So I'm guessing it wouldn't even matter what this guy did or didn't see the night of the fire. If he had mental health problems, the prosecution would've eaten him alive."

"Mars isn't especially warm," Reed replied, almost out

of habit. Before he'd set his sights on being a rock star, he'd planned to visit outer space. "Temperatures top out at around seventy degrees Fahrenheit."

She rolled her eyes at him. "Thank you, Mr. Wikipedia, for the astronomy lesson. Do you really think some street hustler who called himself 'The Blaze' was up-to-date on interplanetary climate data?"

"You could have a point." He patted the doorjamb, already restless to get outside and stretch his legs. "I'm going to jot over to the store for some dinner groceries. Do you have any objections to pasta and a salad?"

"That depends. Is it a normal salad?"

"Define 'normal' in this instance," he said.

"You know—carrots, lettuce, cucumbers, and tomatoes— that sort of thing. No weirdo vegetables like kale or artichokes or eggplant. And no octopus or anything with tentacles."

It was his turn to roll his eyes. She had the palate of a fourth grader. "Leave off the tentacles. Got it. May I borrow your keys?"

She hesitated only a moment before extracting them from her pocket and tossing them his way. "Don't forget dessert," she said.

Outside, the night air was crisp and cold. The snow squeaked under his footsteps as he set off in the direction of the grocery store. Few people were out, and those who were kept their faces bundled up away from the frosty night. Reed had come unprepared for the Boston winter, so he compensated by walking briskly to generate extra body heat. By the time he'd found his quarry at the store and returned to Ellery's place, his face was raw and ruddy. He rewarmed quickly as he worked in the kitchen, standing over the simmering puttanesca sauce he had whipped up on the stove. The most adventurous vegetable he included in the salad was a yellow pepper.

"Supper's on," he called as he tilted the pot over the sink to drain the pasta. When Ellery did not appear, he went in search of her and found her fast asleep amid the folders, news clippings, and piles of old notes. He hovered just inside the room, knowing she would hate him standing there but unable to turn around and leave. Ellery—she'd been Abby back then—she hadn't cried at all the night of her rescue. She'd been unconscious when he'd scooped her off the closet floor and run like hell with her into the woods to call for help. Coben might have been lurking anywhere on the farmhouse property. At first Reed had been afraid she might scream when she awoke, that she wouldn't understand him as her rescuer, but Ellery was silent as the grave, her eyes round and dark in the moonlight. Later, he'd seen her just one more time at the hospital, where she'd been a pale waif under the sheets. She had not thanked him for saving her. She hadn't said anything at all. *Here's my card,* he'd told her. *Call me if you ever need anything.* He'd never dreamed she would.

Cautiously, he drifted closer to the bed. On the floor, Bump whined and thumped his tail in greeting. "Shh," Reed murmured distractedly. Ellery was curled like a comma, her hands tucked protectively beneath her chin. Slowly, carefully, he pulled the folded afghan from the foot of the bed and draped it over her. He froze when she sighed and stirred, his heart thudding at the prospect of being caught as a witness to her vulnerability, but she just rubbed one eye without opening it and quieted back into sleep. He hoped her dreams were pleasant ones as he tiptoed back out into the hall. In the kitchen, he turned the sauce down to low and covered it with a lid. Dinner would keep. For now, at least, Reed wasn't going anywhere.

Ellery slept until well past eight, when she emerged squinting and flushed, her hair askew, to mutter a sheepish apology. "I guess I was more tired than I thought."

"No worries. I'm just working on the geographical analysis. It's coming along." Ellery came over to sit next to him on the couch, and he showed her the initial distribution of the crimes. "You can see the attacks span across these different cities," he said as he drew his finger between the dots.

"Well, yeah," she replied as though this were obvious. "That's the Red Line."

"What?"

"That invisible line you just drew? It's pretty much the Red Line for the subway—Boston, Cambridge, Somerville, and Arlington."

Reed frowned. He'd been so wrapped up in the small details he'd rather missed the big picture. "Oh," he said. "That's, uh, that's useful information."

"So the rapist probably lives near one of the stops, huh?"

A simple paper map could have revealed that much. Reed cleared his throat and shut his laptop. "I'll incorporate that detail into the modeling after we eat," he said.

They ate dinner at her kitchen island, and Reed smiled inwardly as he watched her wolf it down. This was part of the joy of cooking for him, the enjoyment his food gave to others. He used to love to make Sarit's favorite scones, and nothing had made him happier than when tiny Tula would dive face-first into his homemade baby food. Cooking for himself in his lonely apartment was a dismal enterprise.

After the meal, Ellery tidied the kitchen as Reed fiddled with the computer model, reworking it so that it accounted for proximity to the Red Line T stops. When he had a heat map that looked reasonable, he called Ellery over for a look.

"The blue areas are zones where the offender is less likely to reside. The yellow zones are somewhat more probable, and the red peaks you see here . . ." He pointed. "And here . . .

215

they are the neighborhoods most likely to contain the offender's address."

The program had identified two hot zones: one in East Cambridge and one in Chinatown. Ellery was looking instead at the easternmost dot, representing a forcible rape inside one of the South Boston row houses that had occurred three years ago. "That's only a half mile from here," she said.

Reed shifted because this thought had occurred to him, too. "Yes," he admitted. "It fits the pattern. The attacker went in through an open second-floor window. Your building doesn't especially match the targets. It's much larger and the windows don't open in such a way that would allow a human being to climb through them."

"Great," she said flatly. "So I'm safe. What about everyone else?"

"I've cross-referenced these addresses against the database of registered sex offenders with a history of forcible rape or sexual assault involving a previously unknown victim," Reed said. "There are eleven names."

"Eleven?" Her mouth fell open.

"The heat map narrows the area down to a few probable neighborhoods, but in a densely populated city, that still means thousands of residents. Still, it's a place to start. At least you can give Manganelli some actual names this time, not a profile of a building. That should make him happy."

Ellery looked at the list of names Reed had up on his screen. "So what are the odds one of these guys is the rapist? Fifty-fifty? Better than that?"

"I can't say." Reed looked at his lap, reluctant to confess the truth. "There is a good chance—let's call it eighty percent—that the offender lives in one of these neighborhoods. But we're working only with a list of names of men who have been apprehended before. They're already in the system." He paused. "Studies suggest that offenders with this profile have an average of six victims before they are caught."

"You have fourteen dots there. Fourteen cases."

"They may not all have been committed by the same man. We're just presuming based on some limited similarities."

"What about the dates and times?" she asked, peering at the screen. "Any pattern there?"

"The attacks mostly occurred at night, no discernible pattern as to the day of the week. The longest separation between them was eight months, and the shortest was three months. There is a slight trend toward increasing frequency."

"Wendy Mendoza was attacked seven months ago," Ellery said quietly.

"Yes." Reed had worked out the math himself. If the rapist hadn't picked a new victim already, he would do so very soon. "We can send the results of the analysis to Detective Manganelli," he said, "and hopefully he can run through this list of names quickly. With luck, he'll get a hit."

Ellery regarded the work that Reed had spread out across her coffee table. "I don't feel good pinning some poor woman's future on the possibility of luck," she muttered.

Reed was so tired that his eyes burned. He, too, felt the limits of his power in this situation, where all he could offer was an incomplete picture of someone the offender might resemble. He leaned back against the sofa and favored Ellery with a wry expression. "There's an old joke about Pablo Picasso getting held up by a robber on the street. The robber got away with Picasso's money, but Picasso told the cops he could draw them a sketch of his attacker. The cops took his drawing and ran out immediately to arrest a one-eyed man, half a violin, and a bottle."

Ellery smiled faintly. "You're saying we're the cops in this scenario? Running down false leads?"

Reed sighed. "No. I'm saying sometimes I feel about as useful as Picasso."

In the morning, Ellery tried calling Detective Manganelli to tell him about the geographic profiling that Reed had done, but he wasn't answering his phone. She left a message and then emailed him the results. "That's that," she said as she closed down her laptop. "Now we wait for him to do his thing, I guess."

"He knows how dangerous this man is. He'll be motivated to follow up."

Ellery stood up and shoved her hands in her pockets. She nodded in the direction of his suitcase. "Looks like you're all packed."

Reed cast a begrudging look at his carry-on, which had taken him all of ten minutes to prepare. Easy in, easy out. In six hours he would be back inside his empty apartment. More important, from McGreevy's perspective, Reed would be back at his desk the next morning, with Ellery once again confined to his past. At least they had managed to go the past thirty-six hours without any sort of threat or vandalism. Reed walked to the window and looked down onto the street at the passersby, none of whom seemed to be skulking about. Still, he felt distinct unease. "I don't like the thought of leaving you here alone when we still don't know who's been threatening you," he said as he turned to her.

Ellery was all business this morning, with her hair pulled back and her shirt tucked in, almost as though she were still in uniform. "We've discussed this already. You can't stay here—I won't let you."

He knew this, of course he did. There was no way he could live out his days on her lumpy, furry couch. "Maybe you could stay with someone else for a while. A friend, or . . ."

"No, that's not—that's not necessary." Her face faltered,

just for a second, and Reed realized suddenly that he had hit a tender spot. Maybe she didn't have any friends—how could she, given her insistence on living her life in anonymity? Ellery drew herself up and squared her shoulders. "I have double locks. I have my gun. If anyone slips a note under my door again, I'll be sure to contact Detective Banyon."

"And me."

She tilted her head as if considering. "And you," she allowed at last. This would have to do for now. "Now let's get going before you miss your flight."

She drove him to Logan in the rented SUV, and this time, Reed barely registered the passing scenery. It felt like he was always leaving her. When she pulled over at the terminal to drop him off, she set the car in park and took a deep breath. "This is it. Thanks again for coming up here. I'll be sure to let you know what Manganelli has to say."

"Call anytime," he said, looking into her eyes to show he meant it. "If there is anything I can do, please let me know." He'd said approximately the same words to her years ago without really meaning them; now it felt as serious as a wedding vow.

She stared back at him for a long moment and then gave a tiny nod. "I will."

This was the part where he was supposed to get out of the car, but instead, something made him reach over and take her hand. He heard her quick intake of breath but she did not pull away from him. Gently, he searched out the scars with his thumb. She remained rigid as he traced the barely perceptible lines. "If I felt these," he murmured, watching her face as he touched her. "If I felt these scars, I would think . . . this woman has walked through hellfire and come out on the other side. She must be very strong and incredibly brave."

Ellery clenched her hand in a fist and turned to the window. "It's not so brave when you don't have a choice," she said thickly.

"Ellery." She wouldn't look at him. He took her wrist and put his lips to the scars. He could feel the tension in her, the rapid flutter of her pulse against his mouth. He let his lips linger a moment in a ghost of a kiss. "There's always a choice," he said as he released her.

She balled her hands together in her lap, nodding at him, although he wasn't convinced she actually believed him. "Go," she said hoarsely. "Get out of here."

He left the warmth of the car for the wind-whipped concrete sidewalk. Ellery pulled away so fast the tires screeched a little in her wake. Reed made his flight easily and took his usual seat by the window. The roar of the jet engines vibrated his body, preparing for takeoff, and he felt the plane gaining momentum down the runway. Faster and faster it hurtled, as though rocketing from the earth, until at last the ground fell away completely. Untethered now, Reed forced himself to watch as Boston grew smaller and smaller in the background, until it became gray and indistinct. No place he recognized at all.

# 9

Ellery was true to her word. After dropping Reed at the airport, she was extra cautious returning home, checking her rearview mirrors to make sure she was not being followed, taking care to park her rented car in a spot she could see from her apartment windows. If someone was watching and targeting her, it was possible that they were waiting for these first few moments when she was alone again. She kept her gun holstered to her hip and her coat unbuttoned as she walked to her building, but she did not see anyone lying in wait. At her door, she braced herself for the possibility of another nasty note, but she found only Speed Bump wagging on the other side. He snuffled her in greeting and then looked past her toward the hallway. Ellery closed the door and locked it. "Sorry," she told the dog. "He's gone home."

Bump nosed the crack at the bottom of the door, sniffing hard as though he could pick up Reed's scent. Ellery sighed at his fickle behavior and went to the living room to phone Manganelli again. She tried not to notice how empty it seemed now without Reed and his suitcase taking up space. Reed was one slightly larger than average man who had been in her home for two days. It's not like he'd had time to become a part of her landscape. Bump seemed to feel differently, though, as he ambled into the room and sat directly on her feet to get her attention. He looked up at her with baleful eyes, and Ellery frowned at him. "You realize your hero doesn't even like dogs, right? He thinks you smell."

Ellery tried Manganelli again on her cell phone, but she only got his voice mail, the same as before. She left another message asking him to call her back, and then she set the phone and her gun on the coffee table to wait. After a while, she put on music to try to distract herself—*Hallowed Ground* by the Violent Femmes—but she barely registered the different songs. Later, she took Bump for a walk, pausing to check her cell phone every time he stopped to sniff a snowbank. No one followed them as near as she could tell. But neither did anyone call.

It was not until Tuesday that she finally heard back from Manganelli. "Sorry," he told her. "I've been a little busy. You might have seen the stories about the two jewelry store holdups. The last one, on Saturday, the owner got shot. It's all hands on deck for this one."

Ellery didn't usually watch the news. It never had anything nice to say. "That's terrible. Did you catch the guy?"

"Guys, plural. There's two of 'em. And no, we're still running down leads. I'm actually calling you from the head because that's the only time I get a break right now. Look, I got the stuff you sent me. Thanks. I'll be sure to check it out as soon as I get a chance. Tell Markham I appreciate his help."

Ellery's heart sank. "But Reed found a pattern, and if it holds, there will be another attack soon. We don't have any time to wait."

"I'm sorry. I want to catch this SOB even more than you do, but I gotta follow the hot cases while they're still hot. This could still turn into a murder investigation if the owner doesn't pull through. Once we nail these assholes and things settle down again, I'll give the Mendoza case a fresh look."

"But—"

"I gave it a once-over," he cut her off. "The stuff you sent me. It's a few neighborhoods where the guy might live, plus the names of some sex offenders. You think we haven't already run those names ourselves?"

"Reed's list is more focused," Ellery said levelly. "You could maybe put someone else on the case while you're busy elsewhere."

"We're all busy right now. It's a shit-show around here, with the mayor calling every few hours to see if we have any new developments in the case. Turns out the owner of this jewelry store was a neighbor of his." She heard the sounds of running water and men's voices, suddenly loud, in the background. "Look, I gotta go. I'll check out the names, I promise—just give me some time."

He clicked off before Ellery could say anything further. She was surprised to find herself shaking, at how personal it all felt. Somewhere out there was another woman's life, about to be ruined, and no one was doing anything to stop it. Ellery went to the window and leaned her head against the cold glass. Night was falling, the sky turning purple, and faceless people streamed past on the sidewalks below. They were all hurrying home for the night, escaping out of the frigid winter and deep snow into the safety of their warm houses. Had the rapist already picked his next target? She imagined him on some anonymous street, standing in the deepening shadows, his eager breath steaming, his eyes following the woman in the upstairs apartment as she moved from room to room. Watching her. Waiting for the time when he could make himself invisible and climb inside.

At the start of the survivors' group meeting, Miles met Ellery's eyes the moment she walked through the door, almost like he had been waiting to greet her. He smiled broadly and raised his paper cup of coffee in cheerful salute. Ellery gave him a hesitant wave but opted to take an open seat next to Wendy. The woman had her hoodie pulled up over her bald head, her hands hidden inside her sleeves. She acknowledged Ellery's arrival with a quick glance. "Any news?" she asked, not sounding hopeful.

"Maybe," Ellery told her. "Agent Markham did an analysis of potentially related cases and he's given Detective Manganelli some names to follow up on. There's no guarantee, of course . . ."

"Names?" Wendy perked up, her dark eyes were shining. "Let me have them. I can check them out and maybe I'll recognize the guy."

Ellery drew back, surprised. "You said you didn't see his face. That he wore a mask."

"I might recognize his shape, his voice for sure, with all that disgusting stuff he said to me. Please?"

For a half second, Ellery considered it. She could take Wendy around to each of these guys and maybe something would stand out to her. Manganelli would have to act if they could narrow down the suspects to one guy. But then she took in the desperate pleading in Wendy's reddened eyes, how her fingernails were chewed down to the quick, and she saw a woman just barely hanging on. If they tried out all of Reed's eleven names and nothing came of it, Wendy might be worse off than before. Ellery shook her head, her own eyes wet with regret. "I'm sorry, no. It's not safe."

Wendy recoiled, looking angry. "I can handle it."

"I'm sure you can. But Wendy, you may or may not recognize the guy. We can be damn sure he would know you."

Wendy stiffened as this thought went through her, and then she sagged in her seat once more, brooding again, no longer looking in Ellery's direction. Ellery looked instead at Myra, who was being wheeled into the room by her husband. Patrick didn't so much as glower her way, but Myra held Ellery's gaze for a long moment, her mouth pursed as though she might have something to say. Before Ellery could find out one way or another, Dr. Sunny got the group session under way. "Today I'd like us to talk about gains and losses. The situations that brought you here are all admittedly painful and difficult. Each of you is healing from these wounds, but it's okay to acknowledge that some losses will be permanent. So I'd like us to go around the room and share that, if you can, to say the words out loud. What has been lost to you that cannot be repaired? And on the other side, what have you gained from your experiences? This isn't to say that what has happened to you is worthwhile or just, but that we can find unexpected gifts or knowledge even from the most trying of circumstances. So I put it to you all: what, if anything, do you have now that you did not have then?" She smiled gently. "Who would like to start? Alex?"

Alex was wearing a Patriots sweatshirt over his considerable belly. He looked like he hadn't shaved in a couple of days, and Ellery wondered if maybe the holidays were getting to him. It was hard enough to appear normal even on a regular day, let alone when the entire damn universe was covered with twinkling lights and "Joy to the World" blared on every other street corner. Alex coughed twice and looked at the floor before speaking. "Uh, well, the first one is easy. I lost Nate. My buddy. He's gone and nothing will ever bring him back. I dream about him sometimes, and it seems so real. Like, I can hear him laughing and joking around with me, giving me crap about my pathetic love life. In the dreams, I want to tell him: don't go into the store. Let's just keep walking, okay? I can hear the words in my head but they won't come out of my mouth. We just talk about other useless shit until I wake up, and of course he's still dead." He shook his head as if disgusted with himself. "As for something I gained? I dunno. I guess there's Nate's kids, his two boys. I knew 'em pretty good before this whole thing happened, but now, I make sure to go over and see them at least once a week. They're good kids. They didn't deserve this crap. I told the older one, Mikey, I'd coach his Little League team this spring, and he seems pretty happy about that."

"That's great, Alex, that you're reaching out to Nate's kids. I bet their mom is grateful, too."

Alex waved her off. "Elaine's okay with it."

The group lapsed into silence again and Dr. Sunny nudged them. "Would anyone else like to share?"

Tabitha scooted her chair forward, the metal feet dragging loudly across the floor. "I'll go," she said brusquely. "Here's what I lost: three years of my life. My asshole of a husband threatens to kill me, I managed to hold him off with a knife, and yet I'm the one who got sent to jail."

"Well, he died," Alex replied, not in a challenging way, but only stating the facts. "It's not like the cops could question him."

Ellery looked at Tabitha, reassessing. *Not just your average boring housewife after all,* she thought.

"Yeah, well, some people can just blow a guy away and call it self-defense and the governor acts like they're a big hero for it," Tabitha replied, her eyes on Ellery. "Not all of us are that lucky."

Ellery felt herself flush and she looked away. No part of her history could be called lucky.

"What about something you learned or gained from the experience?" Dr. Sunny interjected, trying to keep the discussion on track.

Tabitha studied her manicure for a long minute and did not answer. Then she huffed a short breath. "I said nothing," she began again. "I said nothing when Ryan started telling me when I should be home at night, and which friends I could see. He was right—some of my friends didn't like him. So why should we socialize with them? Why socialize at all? Isn't that why we got married, to be together all the time? 'I'll be your best friend, babe,' that's what he said. 'I'll do everything for you.' It sounded so sweet at first. So then . . ." She broke off, hesitating. "The first time he hit me, there wasn't anyone left to tell. My friends were all gone. Ryan promised it wouldn't happen again, and I made myself believe him. I didn't believe him the second time, but I didn't leave him, either. I just took it, for years. Well, I won't take anything anymore. I'm not some little mouse who sits by and lets people take advantage of her. If I have a problem, I speak up. I'll yell if I have to. But I'm through with making nice or putting up with other people's bullshit. It's my life now. No one else gets a say."

Ellery watched her, riveted. Tabitha's long face was pink with emotion, her body posture daring anyone in the room to challenge her. She locked eyes with Ellery, and this time, Ellery did not look away. She barely heard Miles when he started talking.

". . . my wife. I will miss her every day until I die. I feel sad not just for me, but for the kids who didn't get to have her as their teacher, and for the world that lost her beautiful music. I wish I'd thought to record more of it, you know, when she would mess around at our piano, playing those jazz tunes.

I guess I always figured there'd be more time." He took a deep breath and spread his hands. "I don't think I gained much by losing her, truth be told. But I do have you all." He flashed a self-conscious smile and looked around, lingering just a moment longer on Ellery. "And I've joined up with a group to fight for stricter sentencing on DUIs. Maybe . . . maybe we can stop the next drunk from getting behind the wheel."

"That sounds like a smart, healthy use of your time and experience," Dr. Sunny replied. "Thank you for sharing it with us. Myra, did you want to say something next?"

Ellery felt a stab of sympathy for the woman at being put on the spot like this. Who could find something positive in the death of your child? Myra twisted her hands in her lap, looking fretful. When she spoke, her voice was low and hoarse, almost inaudible. "I lost Bobby," she whispered. "It's been twenty-six years and I think about him every day. I think . . . if only I'd left him home that night. Patrick, sick as he was, still could have kept an eye on him. I think . . . why did the fire take him and not me? He was the innocent one in all of this." Her eyes watered and she pulled out a crumpled tissue from her sweater pocket, which she used to blow her nose. "There is nothing I wouldn't do to go back and fix it. Nothing. The family got money from the insurance, yes, but no amount was worth Bobby's life." Her voice wobbled again. "I guess, though, lately I've been thinking about Patrick. He could've left me half-burned in that hospital bed. Who wants an invalid for a wife? A cripple? He was still a young man. Now with money. He could've left me there and started over, but he didn't. He's taken care of me all these years. So maybe that's what I get: forgiveness."

Forgiveness. Ellery turned the word over in her mind, pondering the implications. Did Myra mean that Patrick forgave her for bringing Bobby with her to the store that night? She'd said Bobby "was the innocent one." Who then, was the guilty? Ellery was so busy wondering about the meaning of Myra's words that she failed to realize Dr. Sunny was talking to her. Only when she felt the eyes of the room on her face did she snap out of it. "Um, what?" she asked, embarrassed to have been caught not paying attention.

"I wondered if you'd like to share your thoughts on gains and losses," Dr. Sunny said.

"Me?" It hadn't occurred to her that she would be asked to contribute, too. In her head, she was still using the group as research, a way to learn more about Wendy's and Myra's cases. She was there as an observer, not a participant. Everyone was looking at her with an air of expectancy now, and she frantically searched herself for what to say. Something she lost. There was so much, it was hard to know where to even start the list. Her bike (it had never been recovered); her virginity; her smooth, unmarked body; her privacy. Her very name and place of birth. Maybe it was because her mother had asked her to come home for Christmas, but this was what she settled on. "I lost my home," she said, her voice clipped, overloud in the room with its low ceilings. "It doesn't matter that I had happy memories there because they all fall apart under the weight of that one night. I could see my bedroom window when he took me. I was that close. Almost home." She reached out and grasped at the air. Her hand fell empty and heavy in her lap. "My mother still lives there in the same apartment, right where it happened, because to her, it's the place where my brother was. To me, it's the place where Francis Coben could have killed me. It can't ever be home again."

She looked around and saw Miles was nodding at her with sympathy. Tabitha's gaze was more probing. She wasn't sorry for Ellery just yet. "And anything you've gained?" Dr. Sunny inquired.

Ellery groped around mentally for an answer. "I, uh . . ."

Her cell phone buzzed in her pocket. Even though everyone was watching, she pulled the phone out for a quick look. Maybe it was Manganelli saying he'd caught the rapist. The text glowed on the home screen, and it was from Reed: *All ok? Just checking in.*

Ellery smiled and sniffed and shoved the phone back in her pocket. "I think . . . I think maybe I got a friend."

Dr. Sunny smiled, too. "That's a lovely gain, even if it comes at great cost. Thank you for sharing with us." She turned to Wendy, who was now slouched low in her seat. "Wendy? Would you like a turn?"

Slowly, Wendy righted herself, as if pulling against the tide. "I used to feel kinda stupid coming here with you all," she said after a beat. "Most of you lost family or friends—people in the grave 'cause of what happened to you. Nobody died in my house that night." She drew a long shaky breath, and when she spoke again, her voice was teary. "But when I look back at my pictures from before it happened, it's like I don't even recognize myself. Who's that girl hanging with her girlfriends at the bar? Who's that guy kissing her cheek and looking at her like he loves her? I don't know her. I don't have her life anymore. She's gone, and he killed her. That's who died—me." She broke off to swipe angrily at the tears rolling down her cheeks. "So I'm gone but he's still out there walking around free as a bird, ready to do it to someone else. You'll have to excuse me if I don't see anything good about that."

When the meeting broke up a short while later, Ellery stopped Wendy before the other woman could pull her usual vanishing act. "You lived," she said, planting herself between Wendy and the door. "He set out to destroy you, but it didn't work. You're still here, working to stop him, waiting to put him away. He underestimated you, Wendy. He might think you're broken, that you're powerless, but you aren't. One day he'll know it, I promise you that."

Wendy's eyes became huge inside her gaunt face. "This don't feel like victory," she replied.

"Not yet. But it isn't over yet. Come on, let me buy you a sandwich. I need to eat something, and I could use the company."

"Mine?" Wendy asked wonderingly, but she didn't try to flee.

"Ms. Hathaway?"

Ellery turned to find Myra Gallagher pushing herself around the row of chairs. "Just one sec," she said to Wendy, and she hurried over to help Myra so the woman wouldn't have to struggle any further. "Call me Ellery," she said. "Please."

"This has to be quick," Myra replied in a hoarse whisper. "Patrick will be along any second, and I don't want him to see us talking. I wanted to ask you if you'd talked to Jacob. My son. Patrick said you'd been looking for him."

Ellery felt herself color under the sharpness of the woman's gaze. "Yes, I stopped by his house a week or so ago, but he wasn't there. I haven't tried to talk to him since."

"No one has seen him. He isn't at home and he didn't show up for work this week. We're worried sick that something's happened to him."

"Has he ever done this before?" Ellery asked. "Gone off without telling anyone?"

The truth was written on Myra's face. "Not for a long time." Her shoulders rose and fell with her sigh. "Jake's had some troubles, yes, but that was in the past. It . . . it wrecked him, too, what happened to Bobby."

Ellery knew that Jake's trouble with the law had preceded the Gallagher store fire, but she held her tongue. "I haven't even met Jake," she said. "But I can try to help you look for him if you like."

"Oh, no no," Myra assured her in a rush. She looked around Ellery to see if Patrick was approaching. "Patrick would never hear of it. I'm sure Jake will turn up soon enough."

Ellery bit her lip. She had not planned to raise the topic with Myra, but since the woman had brought it up, she couldn't resist asking. "Jake was there the night of the fire—did you know that?"

Myra looked up in horror, her blue eyes bright with emotion. "No, he wasn't.

"He was. I've seen a photograph that shows his face among the crowd."

"No, you must be mistaken. He—he wasn't there."

"Where was he?" Ellery knew from the reports that Jake's whereabouts were unaccounted for the night the store burned up.

Myra's chin quivered. "Jake's a good boy. Whatever struggles he had, they were my fault. Mine and his father's. Jake's paid enough for our mistakes." Her face went pale as she caught sight of Patrick coming up the walkway toward the hospital. "Get away," she said, waving Ellery aside. "He'll see you."

Ellery did as she asked, watching from around the corner as Patrick greeted his wife with a kiss on her cheek and began wheeling her away. *Forgiveness,* she thought again, remembering Myra's earlier words. Maybe Myra wasn't talking about herself at all. Maybe she'd had to forgive one son for killing the other.

Ellery took Wendy out to one of the ubiquitous burger and shake shops that seemed to have sprung up all over Boston. At Ellery's urging, Wendy ordered a cheeseburger, fries, and a chocolate shake, but Wendy just stirred a fry around in a pool of ketchup and didn't eat much. "I used to love cooking," Wendy said. "All kinds of it. Carnitas, frijoles, pasta primavera, butter chicken with all the fixings. I made a pineapple upside-down cake that was kind of famous in my family. My boyfriend Joe, he ate three slices at a time. *Tastes like love,* he used to tell me." She gave a wistful smile.

"Sounds delicious," Ellery said. "I'd love to try it one day."

Wendy's smile disappeared. "Yeah, well, I can barely heat a

can of soup now. You know what happened when I got out of the hospital?" She looked up at Ellery as if measuring her. "I threw out all the food in my fridge. I looked at all of it and I thought, how can I eat this now? This is happy food. I was happy when I bought it. It felt like a million years ago, like it had been someone else who did the shopping. I pulled it all out and put it straight in the garbage."

Ellery remembered that feeling of having to relearn how to eat again. Three days in the closet with only occasional sips of water, only when Coben felt like giving them to her, it had left her feeling so powerless over her own body that she'd found it confusing to hold a fork those first few days. "It gets better," she told Wendy gently. To prove it, she smiled and ate a fry.

Wendy pushed aside her food and folded her arms across her chest. "That FBI man. Is he still working on my case? Running down those names?"

"Reed had to go back to Virginia," Ellery said with regret. "Detective Manganelli is working on the list of names." She hoped she'd sold this white lie, which wouldn't be untrue for much longer. The rapist had nearly killed Wendy, and Manganelli had to know the next woman might not be as lucky.

"Reed," Wendy mused as she picked up another fry. This one actually made it to her mouth. "He's the one you were talking about today, isn't he? The friend you got."

"Yes."

Wendy nodded to herself. "And he knows everything that happened to you, right? What Francis Coben did with the farm tools?"

Ellery willed herself not to flush. "Yes, he knows."

"Must be nice. My friends, they sent flowers after it happened. They came to visit me once or twice. But most of them couldn't stand to look me in the eyes. Like they were imagining it, what he did to me. Eventually, they stopped coming at all. Now my sister's kicking me out, too." Her eyes welled up. "There's no one left."

Impulsively, Ellery reached across the table and grabbed Wendy's hand, hard. "Yes, there is."

That night, Ellery texted Reed back: *All's quiet here. Got your promotion yet?* She waited, watching her phone as she fed the dog his dinner, but Reed did not reply. Probably he was with his daughter. Or maybe on a real date, one that didn't end with fire. She checked her email and voice mail messages again for any sign of Manganelli, despite the fact that she knew very well he hadn't called or written. The jewelry store robberies were still unsolved, and the owner had died the day before. It might be a week yet, maybe longer, before he would even think to get back to Wendy Mendoza's case.

Ellery pulled up the list of names that Reed had given her and scrolled through them for the hundredth time. She had each one memorized by now. *Victor Cruz, 114 Elm Street. Max Johnstone, 440 Central Street, Apartment 2. Dwayne Redford, 21 Park Avenue.* It would be far too risky to take Wendy around to each one, but there was no reason Ellery herself couldn't go to check them out. "I won't talk to them," she assured Bump, who was sitting in the kitchen with her, looking hopeful next to his freshly empty dish. "I just want to see them, watch where they go. Maybe I can give Manganelli something more to go on."

She knew even as she said the words that he wouldn't welcome her involvement in his case, but since he couldn't be bothered to work it, she would fill in for him in the meantime. Wendy deserved as much. She grabbed a bottle of water from the fridge, holstered up her weapon, and snatched her phone from the counter. It buzzed in her hands, a response from Reed. *No promotion yet. Just cleaning my bathroom like a regular schmoe. What are you up to?*

She hesitated with the phone in her palm. He'd be furious with her. *Walking the dog,* she texted back quickly. *He says hi.*

Then she was gone.

241

# 10

Back in his nondescript town house, Reed felt no sense of homecoming. The place always looked exactly the same, as though preserved with a hermetic seal. Before, when he'd had to leave Sarit and Tula to travel for work, they'd lived entire lifetimes in his absence, and he would come home to a new, unexplained crack in the stairs, a refrigerator decorated with fresh, brightly colored scribblings, and a novel set of in-jokes that he couldn't follow. *Fill me in,* he'd say. *What did I miss?* And Sarit would oblige with a chatty, wide-ranging narrative that included piles of laundry and playdates and a new story she was researching on the most valuable home improvements people were making in D.C. and didn't he think they might consider adding solar panels? *Wait, slow down,* he'd say, but they never listened. They kept growing and changing until suddenly his family lived somewhere entirely different, a place he could no longer reach.

The noise and chaos was coming for a visit, though, as Sarit was to drop off Tula shortly for an overnight stay. Reed had prepared one of her favorite dishes—pan-fried chicken with biscuits and gravy, salad on the side—fully aware he was sucking up but not caring in the least. All's fair in love and divorce. He'd put on a Bach concerto to fill the void in the meantime—Bach, with his jaunty pointillist melodies, was perfect for chopping—and leaned over the counter as he scrolled through his phone, looking for any connection there. Ellery still hadn't answered his last message from hours ago, when he was hungry at work and he'd tried to be funny:

*Have reached vending machine levels of desperation. M&M decision time: plain or peanut?*

The message was retrieved two minutes after he'd sent it, but Ellery hadn't replied. *Maybe she's just busy,* he'd told himself as he'd made his selection (no peanuts). But then he'd had to wonder . . . busy doing what? She was out of work and at loose ends now. If she hadn't replied, it was because she didn't want to, not for lack of time. He couldn't be checking in on her safety all the time like some hovering grandpa type, and his painful efforts at a hip, breezy texting relationship had been rebuffed. *Go,* she'd said to him, *get out of here,* and it had sounded like it hurt her, like maybe she'd really meant the opposite, and he'd practically had to throw himself out of her car. He had to face the possibility that her words were genuine and that she truly didn't want him hanging around, even on the fringes of her life, that he would always be a living, breathing reminder of the worst thing that had ever happened to her.

The next series of texts on his phone did nothing to improve his spirits. They were all from his sisters regarding the big family history project Kimmy had going for their father's Christmas present.

> KIMMY: Reed! Time's running out! Do U have ur results back??!

Reed had been ignoring her if only for her use of "ur" for "your." But then his other sisters got in on the act:

> SUZANNE: Kimberly would like me to relay to you the fact that Christmas is rapidly approaching. I told her I was sure you had a calendar on your phone like the rest of us, but that I would oblige her and remind you. PS. What does Tula want this year? XXOO
>
> LYNETTE: It only seems fair that if we have to have our spit analyzed, then so should you. We're family, after all.

Reed switched over to his email program and called up the message from the DNA testing company that had the link to retrieve his results. His finger hovered over the screen. DNA was the holy grail of criminal investigation, the blood or sweat or hair you always hoped you'd find, an inexorable human stain that linked the perpetrator to the victim. DNA could reach out across the decades like fingers from the grave and solve a case that had at one time seemed impossible. It was black magic. It was impenetrable science. It was a laser in the dark, zeroing in on a single suspect. *That's him. That's the guy.*

Reed had grown up without any connection to his DNA. He'd had to look beyond his biology and decide for himself what kind of man he was, this mixed-race orphan boy plunked down in the middle of a modern-day southern fairy tale. *Our little prince,* his mother used to call him, and Reed had often lain in bed at night and imagined it were true; he was secretly royalty and his mother, the queen, had been forced to abandon him for his own safety. Finding out his mother had been a teenager living on the edge of poverty until the day she'd been murdered had left Reed with few answers and more questions, and he felt sure that the DNA results would do the same. His life was not a mystery to be solved.

He jerked his finger away from the phone just as the front door burst open and Tula bounded into the room, her backpack and coat already flying. "Daddy, Daddy!" Reed was never more sure of who he was than when he heard that word. He opened his arms and Tula flung herself into his embrace.

"I missed you," he said as he kissed her warm head several times. "Have you been growing again when I wasn't looking?"

"Daddy. It's only been a week. I have to check my room

'cause I think I left my Twilight Sparkle here last time." She wriggled away from him and dashed toward the stairs.

In the doorway, Sarit tilted her head at him as she folded her arms across her chest. "If it isn't the father of the year," she said, but in such a way that Reed knew he'd screwed up somehow. He waited for her to come out with it. "You're so thrilling, apparently, that even Disney World cannot compete. Tula is refusing to go on the trip because she wants to stay here with you."

Reed didn't even bother to hide his grin. "She does?"

Sarit glowered at him. "This isn't good news, Reed. Six-year-olds are supposed to want to go to Disney World. They aren't supposed to be worried that their fathers will be home lonely at Christmastime. I tried telling her that you will be with your parents and your sisters, but this held no sway with her. Maybe you could talk to her?"

"I think we should let her make up her own mind. Isn't that what you were always preaching to me about? Respecting her autonomy."

"That's for when she wants to wear her ballerina skirt over her dungarees," Sarit replied in a clipped voice. "Not for when she decides her own custody arrangement."

"We decided the initial arrangement," he reminded her. "You're the one who changed the plans. Tula is simply holding to the original schedule." Sarit opened her mouth to protest again, and Reed held up his hands. "I'll talk to her," he said, and Sarit relaxed. "But I won't talk her out of it."

Sarit considered a moment, tapping a finger against her lips. "Fair enough." She sniffed the air. "I must confess I do miss your cooking. Fried chicken?"

"Tula's a fan."

Sarit snorted. "Always her favorite things when she's at Daddy's house, right?" Before Reed had formed a response to this jab, she continued, "Any word on that promotion?"

"Nothing will be formalized until later this year, but it's looking good." McGreevy had given him an approving nod when he saw Reed back at his desk yesterday morning. However, Reed was surprised to see Sarit looking hopeful about his possible advance. "You want me to take this job?"

She rolled her eyes at him. "Yes, of course I want you to take it. It's all I've ever wanted, to have more of you in our lives. In Tula's life. I just didn't know I had to leave you to make it actually happen." They stared at each other for a moment, and Reed saw an openness, a vulnerability to her that he hadn't witnessed for several years, back when they were together in every sense of the word. The intimacy disappeared as Sarit pushed herself away from the doorjamb with a sigh. "You're her favorite because you're in short supply," she informed him tartly. "If you're around more, it evens the odds."

"Ah, the truth hurts."

"It always does," she agreed, and then she frowned at the suitcase still sitting by the stairs. "You're going away again?"

"No, I just haven't unpacked. You know how it is."

"You were in Boston last Thursday, Reed. Your clothes will be moldering in there."

"I didn't get back until Sunday," he said, somewhat defensive. His poor housekeeping had always been a sore spot.

"Sunday." She raised her eyebrows. "I thought this was meant to be a quick trip."

"It was," he said, and did not elaborate. But since it was Sarit, he didn't have to.

"You saw her, didn't you? Abigail."

"Ellery." Sarit had never met her. She knew her only as the girl from Reed's story, a character in the book they had written together. Sarit had been hungry for details after the events of the summer, but Reed had told her only what was in the newspaper. Sarit, who prided herself on always getting the inside scoop, had not been pleased. "I saw her."

Sarit's frown deepened. "You saw her—for four days? Reed. You're not *seeing* her, are you?"

Heat prickled the back of his neck. "No, of course not."

"Oh, good," she replied, relieved, and now it was his turn to frown.

"What's that supposed to mean?" She'd been seeing that

Randy guy for months now, the man who wanted to take Reed's daughter on her first trip to Disney World.

Sarit shouldered her purse as if to leave. "Well, think about it—it wouldn't be healthy at all. You're like a god in her world."

Reed laughed and shook his head. "You clearly don't know her at all."

The red spots that appeared on Sarit's brown cheeks told him he'd said the exact wrong thing. The girl who'd been Abby belonged to both of them in a way, but Ellery was all Reed's. Sarit raised her chin and shot Reed a warning look. "I'm just saying, Reed. It would never work. What on earth would you tell people when they asked how you two met?"

This barb landed on its mark, right in his chest, and Sarit turned on her heel to call her good-byes up to Tula. Reed stood there wordless for a few more minutes, and then he slowly climbed the stairs to go find his daughter. She was sitting on the floor of her room, reunited with Sparkle Pony or whatever the heck the purple creature's name was. "Tula." Reed's knees creaked as he crouched down next to her.

"Hmm?" She barely looked up from where she was combing the animal's unruly mane.

"Your mom told me you turned down the trip to Disney World because you're afraid I might get lonely."

Tula's hand stilled and she looked at the rug. "Mama has Randy and Amanda. You don't have anyone."

"That's not true. I'll be with Nanny and Papa and all your aunts. I would love for you to be there, too, but you don't have to stay home from the trip because of me. I'm a grown-up old dad, you see, and you do not have to feel responsible for me."

She looked up at him, her large dark eyes guileless. "I am, though. Love means being responsible. That's what Dr. Hargreaves said in church. Mama doesn't think I listen because I like to draw in the program when he's talking, but I can hear him just fine even if my hands are busy." She shrugged. "'Sides, you told me we could go this summer, right?"

It took Reed a moment to find his voice. "Ah, right. Yes."

She flashed an impish grin. "I'd rather go with you anyway—Amanda gets sick on the rides." She made a horrible barfing noise and pretended to vomit all over her bedroom in dramatic fashion.

"Thanks for that," Reed said, pretending to wipe it off his trousers while Tula dissolved into a gale of laughter. "Now . . . why don't we eat?"

Over the next few days, he picked up his phone approximately a dozen times to contact Ellery, but each time he put it down again. She'd said she would contact him if there was a problem, and to be truthful, she had reached out to him twice before for assistance, so he had to take her at her word. What he needed was a legitimate reason to call her so that it wouldn't seem like he was checking up on her. So this was why he was still working on the Gallagher fire in the background, just a tab or two open, easily hidden if McGreevy happened to pass by. Thus far, however, he had no new developments to report.

The first thing Reed did was to scan the press photos from the scene of the fire so that they could be enhanced using the FBI's powerful software. Reed had to make do with his own limited skills because he did not want to engage the actual experts and risk McGreevy finding out that he was still mucking around in the case. Despite his meager abilities with the technology, Reed was able to sharpen and clarify the picture well enough that he was now 100 percent certain that Jacob Gallagher was there the night the family store burned down. Reed also spotted Luis Carnevale in several shots, but this wasn't surprising, since no one disputed Luis was at the scene. Despite looking closely, Reed did not see any sign of a black middle-aged drifter with a distinguishing birthmark on his face who might have gone by the name of The Blaze.

He looked up the other Gallagher brother, David, but didn't find anything incriminating there. Dave's Pizza had expanded to two locations in Providence and the restaurants seemed to be doing well, with more than $250,000 in profits amassed last year between the two of them. Dave had been arrested for assault in 1995 but no charges were filed. Reed made a note to try to find out more. As far as the public record went, David Gallagher had been clean ever since.

"Markham!" At the sound of McGreevy's voice, Reed straightened up and clicked the window closed on his computer.

"Yeah, Puss?"

"I need to ask a favor. I've got the deputy chief meeting at four, and he's going to want to grill me about this." He handed Reed a file. "We have to get the Florida office something today, ideally before the evening news, because this is a hot one. Sanderson's got a profile worked up on their possible sniper, and he's concluded that the two shootings in Tampa are the work of the same offender. Read it over and tell me what you think of his conclusions, especially as to motive. Before we officially pull the pin on this one, I want to make sure we've double-checked every line so it doesn't blow up in all our faces."

"Sure, but I'm not familiar with all the facts of the case."

"You don't need to know all the facts. Just make sure Sanderson cites his sources right, okay? I want another set of eyes on this before we go to the chief with it and all hell breaks loose."

*A sniper,* Reed thought with a sigh as he opened the file. *And boom goes the dynamite.*

Sniper attacks were rare and terrifying, an irresistible media cocktail that guaranteed confirmation of an active shooter in a major American metropolis would be headlining the news not just in Florida but nationwide. No wonder McGreevy was gun-shy. The Bureau had worked the last notorious sniper attacks in D.C. in 2002, and their theory—that it was the work of an angry white man—had turned out to be entirely wrong when two black men were ultimately arrested.

Reed himself had never worked a sniper case, but his reading of Derek Sanderson's report suggested it was careful and thorough. The first Tampa shooting had occurred in the morning outside a coffee shop, where a fifty-three-year-old African-American man had been gunned down as he walked out with a pair of lattes. The man's wife had been waiting outside with their pet poodle, and she got to witness the whole thing. The second shooting took place the following afternoon, when a twenty-three-year-old college student named Brittney Albert was shot and killed walking from a Walmart to her parked car. The sniper's kill wasn't clean this time, though: he hit Brittney with his second shot, but the first one hit Brittney's friend, Karen Woods, who had been walking beside her. Karen was taken to the hospital in critical condition but was expected to live. Inexperience? A slip of the finger? Maybe the sniper had been gunning for both young women. The .223 caliber bullets recovered at each scene had been declared a forensic match, but that told them little about the gun, as they could have been fired from as many as seventeen different types of rifles.

Reed scanned through Sanderson's profile and found nothing that seemed especially controversial. The shooter was most likely a white male, thirty-five to forty-five years old, with military training. He enjoyed creating fear in others but was outwardly unemotional himself. He was far enough away at the time of the killings that he wouldn't have heard the screams or seen the blood. His targets were somewhat impersonal. The shooter would however relish all the media attention and the atmosphere of terror he had created. It was when Reed got to the end that he found the part that probably made McGreevy break into a cold sweat: Sanderson theorized that the sniper was partly motivated by racial hatred. He believed that Karen Woods, who was black, had been the real target—not her white friend Brittney Albert. The reason for Sanderson's conclusion was an inked "88" on the roof of the building believed to be the origin of the shots. The double eights were potentially a white power symbol signifying "Heil, Hitler" because *H* was the eighth letter of the alphabet.

Reed blew out a long breath and closed his eyes as he considered. Brittney was shot second. If Karen was the target, why keep going after she fell down? He picked up Sanderson's profile again and found the other agent's potential theories: either the killer flat-out missed and he was really aiming to finish off Karen, or possibly he was punishing Brittney for associating with Karen.

It felt a little thin to Reed and he spent some time combing over the facts of the case. He read an article or two about what was known regarding the psychology of snipers (not much) and some research into white terror symbols (frightening stuff). He noted that Sanderson was concerned enough about Karen's safety that he suggested she be linked up with FURS, also known as the Florida division of Urgent Relocation Services, a kind of temporary witness protection. Ultimately, Reed called up Sanderson in Florida and had him walk him through the case.

"The eighty-eight was fresh at the scene," he told Reed. "Tampa had a hard rain two nights before, so the ink would have been washed out if it had been left any earlier."

"Still," Reed countered. "It's a stretch."

"This guy is racially motivated," Sanderson insisted. "I'd stake my career on it."

Reed tapped the file lightly on his desk as he considered. "I think you already have. I'd distribute what you have to the task force but hold back motive from the press at this stage. You don't need the city any hotter than it's about to get."

There was a tense silence on the other end of the phone.

"You have something you want to add, Sanderson?" Reed asked finally.

"It's just that—don't you think we ought to tell 'em? Don't you think people with brown skin ought to know they might be walking around with a target on their back?"

Reed, as someone who, in the right light and with a summer tan, was one of those brown-skinned people himself, gripped his end of the phone a little tighter. "I think unfortunately, Sanderson, they probably already know that. Until you can back up your theory with something stronger than a piece of graffiti—whose meaning is still open to interpretation— discretion is the better part of valor. When we know more, they'll know more. You hear what I'm saying?"

"Yeah," Sanderson said after a beat. "I hear you."

When he hung up with Sanderson, Reed wrote up some notes for McGreevy, including his support for Sanderson's idea to loop in FURS for Karen Woods. They had temporary housing and people who could bring her groceries, so as to keep her out of sight while the law enforcement personnel figured out whether she was still in danger.

*FURS,* Reed thought as he wrote it out. *Sounds like a convention for those people who like to dress up in fuzzy costumes and rub on each other.* Other states, he knew, had related acronyms. In Texas, it was TURS. In California, CURS. Up Ellery's way, it was MURS.

MURS. Reed stopped typing and rubbed the side of his head. What was it that drifter had said before he disappeared after the fire? Reed dug out the hastily stuffed-away files from the bottom drawer of his desk and started sifting through them for the witness statement. That guy who talked to The Blaze right before he disappeared. It took him ten minutes of searching but Reed found what he was looking for: "He said he was going to Mars. Can you believe that?" Mars. MURS. Reed tried saying the two words under his breath, testing them out. Could work. *You cops disappeared him,* Bertie had said. *The Blaze didn't run. He had help.*

Reed pawed through the file and his notes until he found The Blaze's real name: Earl Stanfield. Then he looked up the number for the MURS field office, and ducked into an empty office to make the phone call. Within minutes, he was speaking with a nice woman by the name of Jennifer Teagarden. She was very sorry, but she couldn't be handing out information on previous clients over the phone, not even to the FBI, not even if it had been a quarter century since the client in question might have utilized their services. Reed would need a warrant.

"How about," Reed said, trying for his most charming voice, "how about if you could just tell me whether MURS was involved with the arson investigation in 1988 in any capacity? Could you do that for me?"

"I would love to help you," Ms. Teagarden replied. "I would. But I'm afraid I couldn't even look that up if I tried. We don't code our cases by associated criminal investigation."

"What about the referring officer? Is that part of your record?"

"Yes." Her tone was wary now.

Reed stood at the office door, the phone pressed tight against his ear. He could hear McGreevy's voice out in the hallway, talking to someone. *If you hang up now,* he told himself, *you're always going to wonder.* "Could you check if Russell McGreevy might have referred a client?" he asked tightly, his eyes screwed shut. His stomach felt like lead.

He heard her click-clack at some computer keys. "Russell McGreevy has referred several clients to us over the years," she replied. "I'm afraid that's all I can tell you."

"Was one in 1988?"

"Sir, I've told you all I—"

"Was one of them in April of 1988?" He was almost shouting now, his voice hoarse with desperation. *Please say no,* he thought. *Just say no.* It would almost be easier if she refused him.

Ms. Teagarden said nothing for a long moment. He could hear her breathing on the other end. He felt her tension and knew he could break it with just the slightest nudge.

"Please," he said, softer this time. "There is a man's life at stake here."

Still she hesitated. Reed felt his heart cage-dancing against his ribs.

"April 29, 1988," she said in a rush, and then she hung up the phone.

Reed kept his phone to his ear long past the point where the connection went dead. McGreevy's footsteps were coming closer now, his voice getting louder. "Markham?" The door handle rattled, making Reed jump. "Markham? Where are you? We need to talk."

# 11

Ellery had a list of eleven very bad men and no way to watch all of them at once. She'd started with Victor Cruz. He was big and strong looking and she could imagine him climbing through someone's window with a knife. Fifteen years ago, Cruz had been a high-school dropout living with his mother and his mother's shih tzu. One day, he'd locked the dog in the basement and suckered a fourteen-year-old neighbor girl to help him look for it. Then he'd trapped the girl and sodomized her in his childhood bedroom to the point that she'd needed corrective surgery afterward. Cruz had been sentenced to thirty years for the crime but was out in only eight. He'd been arrested only once since then, for public intoxication. Ellery tailed him for three days and nights. Cruz spent his mornings panhandling in Downtown Crossing and his afternoons drinking the profits away in his rented room on Elm Street. His home was a poor cousin to the one the rape victims tended to live in: a stand-alone duplex with cheap siding, mismatched front doors, and a black mailbox with a warped lid. There were no grand porches and balconies to be found here; only chipped concrete steps, a rickety fire escape, and a chain-link fence. Ellery had sat in her freezing rental car for six hours each night, rationing the sips of tea from her thermos, watching the blue flickering light of the TV that came from Cruz's bedroom. He'd never stepped outside.

The trouble was, Ellery knew, these creatures could play dead for a long time. In Chicago there'd been an old man who liked to sit on the stoop of his building, two blocks from where Ellery lived. His name was Simon and the kids called him "Simple Simon" behind his back. He'd had missing teeth and a cane and moved like molasses, but his eyes were always on the children. *Hey, there, girl,* he'd call when they passed. *Come over here! Do you want a piece of candy?* He'd take a Jolly Rancher from his pocket and hold it out in his twisted, clawlike hand. Ellery's mother had told her to stay away from Simon because he liked to "do stuff" to little kids, and Ellery had been happy to comply as she'd just thought Simon was completely gross, with his saggy skin and gap-toothed grin. Some of the older kids, especially the boys, had liked to toy with Simon. They'd play along and take his candy, then run away cackling. *Suck on this, old man!* No one was ever really scared, not until the time when Ellery was in high school and a seven-year-old girl with pretty beaded braids and a gap-toothed smile of her own had disappeared. She'd turned up dead in Simon's apartment only hours later. The police had known right where to look. Simon hadn't touched a child in decades, at least that anyone could prove, but the cops hadn't been fooled for an instant because they'd known the truth: he had never really changed.

So Ellery knew better than to think these eleven men had been rehabilitated. She followed them one by one, shadowing their lives and watching for any sign that might indicate they were active again. They blended back into their communities surprisingly well, disappearing into these rocky, difficult neighborhoods that had forged them. Victor Cruz barely left his one square block. She'd become bored with him after a few days of flat-out nothing, and she'd switched to Archie Freeman. Freeman commuted by the T each day to work as a fry cook at a greasy spoon in the heart of Mattapan—or, as it was known to the cops, Murderpan. The array of buildings told a familiar story: a liquor store next to a check cashing joint next to a bail bondsman; grim concrete facades and a coating of graffiti over all of it. The Christmas decorations here were faded from years gone by, tinsel thin and drooping. But Ellery saw beyond the surroundings to the hardworking people who lived here, like the middle-aged waitress in the diner where Archie worked, busting her ass during the lunch rush, or the school bus driver who waited at each stop to make sure each of his charges safely reached the sidewalk. Archie, meanwhile, was a rat among them. He was short and scrawny, older than the other men on her list, face wizened by age. He'd done twelve years for a rape he'd committed back in the 1990s, when an unsuspecting woman hailed his cab and he'd decided not to drive her home. Ellery concluded fairly quickly that he was not the man who'd attacked Wendy Mendoza; he did not fit the description of a large, powerful man. Still, she hated to leave him there unattended, smoking cigarettes in back of the restaurant, his cold, hard gaze tracking the schoolkids as they walked on by.

Reluctantly, she'd shifted her attention to Michael "Mick" Murphy, who looked like a reasonable suspect on paper. He'd done two stints for aggravated rape, and his weapon of choice was a switchblade, rather similar to the kind of knife that Wendy remembered from her attack. Problem was, Ellery had yet to lay eyes on the guy. She'd been parked in view of his listed address—a brick tenement building in the slice of Cambridge between MIT and Harvard—for the better part of two days and hadn't seen a trace of Murphy. The rich biotech companies had built up enormous glass facilities that cast shadows over some of the poorest neighborhoods in the city, so now billionaire CEOs were shopping at the same 7-Eleven as the hookers and the pimps. Ellery had availed herself of it twice yesterday to pick up a sandwich and some bottles of Coke, dashing back to her car as soon as possible to make sure Murphy hadn't slipped out of his hidey-hole in the meantime. It grew dark, then darker still, as the commuters emptied out of the surrounding area, leaving only the folks who had to live there.

Ellery's phone trilled in her pocket, making her jump. No one ever called her. She fished it out and saw the ID flash across the screen: Markham, Reed. She hesitated for a second, her finger poised above the screen. She'd been ducking most of his texts because she didn't want to lie to him about what she was doing. If they weren't talking, then technically she wasn't lying. Reed had apparently stepped up his game and now was daring her to ignore the phone call, too. She considered answering, but then a tall guy with broad shoulders came loping up the street toward Murphy's building. Could be him, but she was too far away to see his face in the dark. She dismissed Reed's call and jumped out of her SUV to hurry after the guy.

The cold wind stung her eyes and she buried her face in her scarf, partly for warmth and partly to protect her identity. The man reached the building and used a key to get inside. By the time Ellery reached the stoop, he had disappeared. She cupped her hands against the glass door and peered inside, but she saw only a dimly lit corridor with no one in it. She bit back a curse and looked around, but there was no one else nearby. She was forced to lurk around the corner in a shadowed parking lot, her back against a fence. It took the better part of an hour of standing there, shifting back and forth until she was so cold her toes were frozen, but finally a heavyset woman carrying a bag of groceries came huffing up the sidewalk toward the building. Ellery fell into step behind her like she belonged there, and the woman didn't seem to notice.

"Here, let me get that," Ellery said when the woman unlocked the door. The woman barely grunted a response, but she allowed Ellery to hold the door for her as she hauled her groceries inside. Ellery cased the mailboxes first, looking for Murphy's name, but the boxes had only numbers on them. She knew he was supposed to be in apartment 217, so she pushed into the stairwell and started to climb. A flickering fluorescent bulb revealed peeling gray paint and various initials and sayings carved into the wall. Ellery opened the door onto the second floor and looked up and down the empty hall. Her heart rate picked up as she set foot into the corridor. Thus far, she'd tailed the men only from afar, making sure she stayed on her own turf. She gave her gun a reassuring pat from the outside of her leather jacket as she started down the hall toward apartment 217.

There was no name on the door, either. She cocked her head to listen for a moment but couldn't make out any signs of life from inside. She knelt down and looked at the crack at the bottom of the door; all was dark.

"You lookin' for something?"

Ellery shot to her feet at the sound of a male voice behind her. A large African-American man had materialized from the apartment across the hall and one door down, and he did not look pleased to see her. "Uh, I heard this was Mick Murphy's place," she said, nodding at 217.

"Used to be."

He didn't elaborate and he was still standing between her and the exit. Ellery licked her lips and tried again. "You know where I can find him?"

The guy smirked. "I look like some kind of secretary? He was here, now he ain't. As long as he took his trashy Celtic punk-ass music with him, I don't give a damn where he went."

*Ah, so that's how it is,* Ellery thought. This guy liked information, or he wouldn't be a self-appointed hall monitor, and he didn't like Mick Murphy. "Thing is, Mick owes me some money," she said.

"Yeah?" He didn't seem all that interested yet.

"Knocked me up," she said, and this did get the man's attention. "Told me to get rid of the problem. Only he was supposed to pay half. Now I got the clinic leaning on me to pay the bills, and I don't have all the money, you know what I'm saying?"

"Fuck that shit," the man said with a glower. "His idea to get rid of it, then he's gotta pay. Cheaper now than if you had a kid."

"Yeah," she said with relief. "It's only fair."

"I heard he couldn't pay the rent. Went to live with his cousin a few blocks over, but I don't know where. Prolly you can find him drinking down at Sully's place." He shook his head with disgust. "They sell four-dollar beers on Wednesday nights and play his shitty music all the time."

"Thanks," Ellery said. "I owe you one."

He chuckled without humor as he moved out of her way. "Good luck gettin' your money. I don't think the landlord ever saw a penny."

Ellery took the steps two at a time back down to the front door and out again into the freezing night air. She already had her phone out so she could look up the location of Sully's pub, and she saw it was just two blocks to the west. After a moment of internal debate, she left her car parked where it was and headed toward the bar on foot, jogging lightly through the dark streets. Her phone rang again in her hand, showing Reed's name, and she hushed it this time by setting it to silent. She could call him when it was over, when she could share the good news: *we got him.*

When she reached Sully's, she had to wrestle with a heavy wooden door that had been warped by weather and time.

It pulled free at last and she staggered over the threshold, only to realize she'd made a terrible mistake: she was the lone woman in the joint. One by one, the men all turned to stare. Ellery could either turn tail and run or pretend like she meant to be here, so she avoided all eye contact and made her way to an open stool. Sully's was one narrow room dominated by a long wooden bar that had seen better days. The low ceiling trapped the scent of alcohol, wet boots, and fried food. The bartender, a bald man with an extensive waistline, bellied up to her on the other side of the bar. "What are you having?" he asked.

"Sam Adams, whatever's on tap," she said, acutely aware of all the eyes on her. She risked a glance around and spotted her quarry at the opposite end of the bar. Mick Murphy was big even sitting down, with broad shoulders that stretched the wool of his black peacoat. The shot glass all but disappeared in his large hand. He looked up to catch her staring, and she ducked her head so fast she got dizzy.

"Here you go, miss." The beer sloshed slightly as he put it in front of her. No dainty napkin for this place. His emphasis on the word "miss" bore a trace of malevolence, or maybe it was the way he didn't move away after serving her. "Ain't seen you in here before," he said, looming over her.

"Just passing through." She took a couple of sips of beer. "It's good, thank you," she added, hoping he would take the hint and leave her alone.

"You like that? I can buy you another." The man to her right slid over one stool so that they were almost rubbing elbows. He had lank hair and crooked front teeth. His bloodshot eyes suggested he'd been here early and often. "Better yet, try something harder. Hey, Ryan, get the lady some of that Three Ships. That's good shit, right there."

"No, thank you," Ellery said, leaning away from him as he pushed into her personal space. "I just came for one beer."

"One? Aw, honey. No one stops at just one."

"Sam's right," said another guy, who materialized behind her. He took the stool on her left. "Two's always better than one." This guy was older, mid-forties, with a double chin and a thick plaid shirt with a rip in the sleeve. She could see what looked like a homemade tattoo sticking out underneath it. He slung a heavy arm over Ellery's shoulders. "I bet we could all have some real fun together."

"I'm not looking for fun," she said, shrugging him off.

"Ooh, she's feisty! I like it when they fight a little, don't you, Sam?"

"You know it."

They were talking like she wasn't even there as they both pressed closer, surrounding her on either side. She glanced across the room and saw Murphy watching with naked interest. Predatory men. A vulnerable woman. He couldn't have ordered up a better show on Pay-Per-View. She'd bet he was stroking himself under the bar right now. Anger flared up in her, and she shoved the closest guy aside. "I said back off."

He held up his hands in mock innocence. "Aw, we were just havin' a little fun. What's the matter, honey? Don't you like fun?"

Ellery pulled out her wallet and tossed a ten on the bar. "Keep the change."

"What's your hurry? Come on, stay a while . . ."

The one called Sam grabbed her arm when she tried to leave. She went rigid and looked down at where he held her. "You don't want to do that," she said evenly.

"You don't know what I want." He licked his lips and smiled. "Not yet, anyway."

"Let me go."

"After you agree that I can buy you a drink."

Her heart was pounding. She'd been so focused on the power-hungry, stalker rapist that she'd forgotten the rest of them: the lazier ones who simply seized upon an opportunity. "I said no," she repeated, enunciating every word. She let her jacket fall open to reveal her gun. "Now let me go."

No one was watching the Celtics game on the TV anymore. They had all turned toward her and Sam. He was considering his options and he didn't like what he found. Temper flashed in his eyes, and he squeezed her arm painfully one time before releasing her with a flourish, like a magician conjuring a bouquet. "Like I care," he said. "You ain't so special."

The bartender gave her a level stare. "You'd best get out of here," he growled. "And don't come back."

Ellery escaped back into the night and ran down the block, stopping only when she was around the corner and out of sight of the bar. She bent over at the waist, gasping for air, struck anew by how stupid she had been. She was not on the job. She had no backup. She wanted to flee back to her safe, high-rise apartment, lock the doors, and never worry about Mick Murphy or any of the others again. Manganelli would investigate them all eventually on his own time. She could be like Reed and just go home.

*Home.* Just the thought of it was tempting. Her warm, soft bed was far across town but she could feel it, with its clean white sheets and weighty quilt that could erase her from the world if she pulled it high enough. She leaned her back against the cold brick wall and took deep, steadying breaths until the knot in her stomach released itself. Tomorrow was another group session, and she would either have to skip it or face Wendy, knowing she'd abandoned the poor woman to Manganelli's whims. Bed wasn't safe for Wendy. She had red-rimmed and haunted eyes, as though she might never see a peaceful sleep again. Ellery steeled her spine, squared her shoulders, and went back around the corner, past the front of the bar until she found a bus stop with its half-shell shelter.

From this vantage point, she could see anyone coming or going from the bar, but they could not see her. She shoved her frozen fingers in her pockets and sat down on the hard metal bench to wait.

It took another hour before Murphy appeared, just before closing time. He staggered out onto the icy sidewalk and swayed slightly. Ellery had been right in her assessment: he was big, close to six and a half feet—all of him in danger of toppling over. He turned abruptly and started walking right toward her, so she quickly slid behind the bus stop and held completely still, not even breathing as Murphy lurched on past. When she dared peek again, she saw him heading down the block alone. Carefully, she edged out from her hiding spot and started a stealthy pursuit. He was slow, possibly from the liquor, with an uneven gait and a periodic cough that halted him a few times. Once, he glanced back over his shoulder but Ellery caught his head turning and tucked herself into the nearest doorway. Her heart thrummed in her chest as she waited out the ticking seconds to see if she'd been made, but Murphy did not double back. She heard his cough again, fainter in the distance, and realized he'd continued on his way.

Tentatively, she emerged from the shadows once more, like an animal scenting the air, and crept along after him. The streets were slick and silent. She could hear her own heightened breathing as she tried to keep her footsteps light. Suddenly, Murphy made a sharp turn down a more residential street. Her stomach dropped when he disappeared from view, and she scrambled to catch up to him. The side street was darker, thanks to a burned-out streetlamp, and her eyes struggled to adjust. She heard more than saw him: a scuffling noise down the block. She proceeded cautiously, turning her head this way and that to try to locate the source of the sound she'd heard. That barking cough reverberated through the night, and she whipped around to find him. The street appeared empty.

Waving tree branches cast moving shadows on the ground. She inched forward some more and heard footsteps—not in front of her but to the side. He'd gone between the houses, she realized, down an alleyway that had access to the fire escapes. Maybe he was climbing up the side of a building right now. Ellery took out her gun and plunged into the darkness after him. She went slowly, her attention focused on the fire escapes on either side of the alley. Murphy was huge; he had nowhere to hide among a collection of iron bars. She passed an industrial-sized Dumpster and a chest-high pile of snow. No sign of Murphy.

She was just about to give up, lowering her gun, when out of nowhere came a lead pipe. It caught her squarely on the forearm, and she cried out as the gun fell out of her grasp. She heard it hit the ice and go sliding toward the street. There was no way to go after it because Murphy was swinging at her again. "You following me, you little bitch?" he hissed at her.

She ducked one blow but he just kept coming with the pipe.

"You want a piece of this? Yeah? Come and get me."

He caught her arm again, then her shoulder. She jerked to the side and his next blow caught the Dumpster instead, sending an unholy clang through the alley. "You don't fuck with me," he said as he took a fierce cut. Her arms throbbed but the pain didn't touch her. She was wild-eyed and determined to get to the gun.

"No woman wants to fuck you," she yelled back, breathing hard. "That's why you have to go out and rape them."

He howled something nonsensical and swung the pipe at her head, barely missing. He swung again, and again, and she dodged him twice before he caught her on the backswing and knocked her off her feet. When he careened forward, she raised her boots to his groin level and kicked with all her might. He screamed when she connected, then he reeled back against the bricks. Ellery used the momentary freedom to get back on her feet, but before she could go search for her gun, Murphy was coming at her again. She caught the end of the pipe with her hand, blocking his attack. She shoved hard and he actually stumbled backward. It was a ray of hope: for a huge man, he didn't seem especially strong. He redoubled his efforts and tried to shake her free from the pipe.

Her brain rattled inside her head but she held fast. He cursed at her again and twisted sharply so the end of the pipe caught her in the jaw. The flash of pain was enough to loosen her grip and he had the pipe to himself again. She saw the gleam of victory in his eyes as he raised it high. Desperate, she hurled herself backward out of his reach, only to catch the sharp edge of the Dumpster with the back of her head. Pain and dizziness overwhelmed her; she felt herself falling into the snow. She saw Murphy's enormous shadow. Darkness was coming up on her fast. *This is it,* she thought hazily, bracing for the final blow. Instead, she heard a gunshot. *Am I hit?* The thought flitted through her just before unconsciousness swallowed her up, and then she thought no more.

When she came to, blue lights from the police cars were spinning crazily at the end of the alley. It hurt just to look at them. "Police," called an authoritative male voice from the darkness. She heard the squawk of their radios. "We have a report of gunfire."

Ellery held the back of her head as she tried to sit up. Her arms ached and a surge of nausea overwhelmed her. She turned to the side and dry heaved into the snow.

Only when the officer's flashlight shone over her did she see she was retching into a pool of blood. Her hand was wet and cold, and she saw her fingers were stained with blood. "Ma'am, are you hurt?"

"I—I don't know." Her head felt cracked in two. "What happened?"

"Easy. Just stay down there," he said when she tried to get up. "I was hoping you could tell me what happened. Starting with: who is this?"

He trained his flashlight just a few feet away, and she saw Mick Murphy lying motionless in the street. He'd landed on top of his pipe. "Oh my God," she breathed, inching backward away from him. "Is he dead?"

"Lady, you were the one who was here. Are you okay? Did you see who shot him?"

Another officer came tramping down the alleyway. He was holding a flashlight in one hand and a gun in the other. "I think I found the weapon in the garbage can just outside," he said. "This is recently fired."

"That's—that's my gun," Ellery said.

There was another wail of sirens as the ambulances arrived on the scene. The first cop trained his flashlight on Ellery's face, making her wince. "I don't think you'd better talk no more," he advised her grimly. "Not 'til you get your head examined."

The cops accompanied her to the hospital, where they were all met by a Detective Natasha Rhodes from the Cambridge PD. The first thing Rhodes wanted to do was run a gunshot-residue test on Ellery's hands. It came back negative. "Everything else will have to wait," said the ER physician, a thin bald guy with wire-rimmed glasses. "Unless you'd like her to bleed to death while you're interrogating her."

Rhodes held up her hands. "Do your thing, doc. I can wait."

Ellery looked up from her place on the stretcher in alarm. "Bleed to death?"

His mouth twitched in a small smile. "Got her to leave the room, didn't it? Now please try to follow my finger using just your eyes—don't turn your head. That's good."

Rhodes had to cool her heels in the waiting room for a few long hours while the doctors gave Ellery the full workup. They X-rayed her arms, which proved to be badly bruised but not broken, stitched up the wound at the back of her head, and gave her a CT scan to make sure her brains hadn't turned to mush. When it turned out she wouldn't need surgery of any kind, they blessedly let her have a Coke and a pair of pain pills. She was sitting propped up in a hospital bed with several ice packs pressed against her body when they let Detective Rhodes back into the room.

Rhodes carried a Styrofoam cup with smudgy brown lipstick prints on it. Ellery had to give it up for a woman who had the wherewithal to put on makeup before arriving at a middle-of-the-night crime scene. Her well-styled Afro and form-fitting black suit told Ellery that Rhodes took her fashion seriously. Ellery knew her own appearance was a complete mess, from the big scrape on her chin to the bloodstains dotting her light gray T-shirt. Was it her blood or Murphy's? Ellery figured that was what Rhodes was keen to find out.

"Ms. Hathaway," Rhodes said as she tossed the empty cup and pulled out a small notebook. "How are you feeling? Are you up for some questions?"

"Sure," Ellery said, although her voice sounded thin with fatigue. The clock on the wall read 6:08, meaning she had been up for twenty-four hours straight. Only the part where she'd passed out next to a dead guy and awoken to find the cops standing there with her gun as the probable murder weapon gave her the adrenaline to keep up with Rhodes's conversation.

"I had some time out there." Rhodes jerked her thumb back toward the waiting room. "So I looked you up. You like to live your life in the danger zone, don't you?"

"Trouble seems to find me," Ellery muttered as she adjusted the ice pack on her arm.

"Once, sure. Maybe twice. A third time, and a person might start to think you go looking for it. Why don't you tell me what happened tonight in that alley?"

"What happened to the man who was with me?" If Mick wasn't around to tell his side, Ellery could make up any version she wanted. Of course, Rhodes saw through this ploy immediately, and she shook her head.

"Uh–uh. I ask the questions, you give the answers."

"Fine," Ellery said with a dramatic sigh, and she decided to hedge her bets with some half-truths. "I was walking by the alley and I heard a noise, like a scuffling sound. I thought I saw a man climbing up the fire escape on the side of the apartment building, so I went to investigate. I got partway into the alley when he attacked me with a pipe."

"You were passing by this alley at nearly two in the morning—alone."

Ellery held her gaze. "Yes."

"Where were you going?"

"For a walk."

"A walk." Rhodes glanced up from her notes with a skeptical expression. "It's fifteen degrees out there, and you live downtown. What are you doing walking through the underbelly of Cambridge in the middle of the night?"

"I can't sleep most nights. If you've looked me up, then you know why." Ellery had the Coben card in her back pocket, and she'd learned when to play it.

The strategy worked because Rhodes moved on. "So he hit you with a pipe—then what?"

Ellery recapped the fight until she got to the part where she slammed her head on the Dumpster. "I fell down, very woozy," she said. "Everything was swimming and I couldn't see well. I felt he was still there, and I thought he was going to hit me again. That's when I heard the shots. I don't remember anything after that."

"So you didn't see the shooter?" Rhodes looked surprised.

"No. Was it my gun that was used in the shooting?"

Rhodes hesitated a moment and then gave a short nod. "Looks that way. Ballistics will have to confirm."

"I didn't kill him."

"I realize that," Rhodes said, slightly irritated. "You don't see me with my handcuffs out, now, do you? The shot came from twenty yards away and patrol found you unconscious about three feet from the body. I'd say you're lucky you didn't wake up dead! But I've had a lot of experience with bullshitters, Ms. Hathaway, and you're piling it up so deep, I'm going to need hip boots."

"I've told you everything I can remember."

"Yeah, but that isn't the same as everything you know." There was a heavy pause, but Ellery didn't make any move to fill the silence. Finally, Rhodes sighed and made a show of putting her notebook away. "Maybe we'll get lucky," she said. "Turns out, one of the neighbors in the apartment building caught part of the incident on camera."

Ellery sat up with a jerk, and then regretted it as pain lanced through the back of her skull. "Uh, what?"

"He heard the fight. Ran to the window to try to film the thing." She shrugged. "Everyone wants to be a viral star these days. From what I can tell, this guy had no hope—the picture is dark and blurry—but it seems to back up your story." She put a little more emphasis than was necessary on "story." "There are some images of the shooter at the end. Our tech boys are trying to clean up the video to see if we can get a clear picture."

"Oh. Can I see it?"

"No, you may not. You're not on the job, Ms. Hathaway. You'd do well to remember that. Because stunts like tonight? That's not the way to get it back."

Ellery opened her mouth to reply but did not get a chance to say anything because the door flew open and Reed burst into the room. He looked pale and disheveled, with his glasses on crooked and his coat hanging open. "Thank God," he breathed when he saw her.

She blinked in surprise. "What are you doing here?"

"I've been calling you for a day and a half! Last night, the phone finally picks up only it's not you on the other end, it's some guy who identified himself as Officer Pisarro. He tells me you've been taken to the hospital in an ambulance. Then he hung up! What the hell else was I supposed to do?"

"I'm sorry, you are?" Rhodes was frowning at the man who had crashed her party.

"Reed Markham, FBI." He flashed his credentials at her but his eyes were still on Ellery, looking her over to assess her injuries.

"He's my official biographer," Ellery supplied as she leaned back in the bed with a tired grimace, but Reed did not look amused.

"What happened?" Reed asked, advancing toward her. "You look like you got hit by a truck."

"By a lead pipe," Rhodes said. "A man named Michael Murphy was swinging the pipe."

Reed looked at her sharply. "Mick Murphy?" he asked.

"Yeah? You know him?"

"I, uh . . ." Reed glanced back at Ellery, who tried to signal with her eyes that he should *just stop talking*. He was pissed, though, because he ignored the signs. "Yes," he said firmly, turning back to Rhodes. "He's a sex offender. An especially vicious one." That last part was pointedly aimed at Ellery. "I did some consulting work for the Somerville Police Department related to a string of rapes, and Murphy's name was on the short list of suspects."

"I see." Rhodes narrowed her eyes at Ellery. "Anyone else have a copy of that short list?"

Here, Reed pulled back a bit, because he answered: "I

couldn't really say who had the list. Why?"

"Because someone took out Mick Murphy tonight. He's now down at the morgue."

Reed shot Ellery a *what-the-hell-did-you-do* glare, and she raised her hands in self-defense. "It wasn't me! Ask her. She knows."

"Ms. Hathaway wasn't the shooter," Rhodes agreed. "But whoever it was used her gun."

"I didn't see who did it," Ellery explained to Reed.

Rhodes made a beleaguered gesture at Ellery. "That's because your girlfriend here was lying in the snow with a gaping head wound at the time."

"I'm not his girlfriend."

"Oh, really! That's the part of your statement you want to clarify?"

A fresh wave of exhaustion crashed over her, and Ellery shut her eyes. She didn't have the energy to fight with this woman anymore. Reed must have sensed this, too, because he stepped between Ellery and the detective. "Maybe we could continue this conversation another time," he said. "She looks like she could use some rest."

"Sure," Rhodes said with false cheer. "And maybe with some rest, her memory will come back to her and she can explain what she was doing in that alley with Mick Murphy."

Ellery kept her eyes shut as she heard Rhodes make her

departure, because this would mean she was now alone in the room with Reed, and frankly, between the pair of them, she'd rather keep Rhodes. She felt Reed standing there, staring at her. "What on God's green earth were you thinking?" he said finally.

She forced her eyes open. Reed was blurry. "Manganelli wasn't even investigating," she murmured. "He's too busy. I couldn't keep going to group every week and telling Wendy there was nothing new on the case, not when we both know this guy is out there, stalking a new victim."

Reed raised his hands in frustration, wordless with disbelief at her apparent stupidity. He scrubbed his face several times and took a deep breath. "It's my own damn fault," he said, sounding morose. "I handed you that list. I should have known what you'd do with it."

She felt guilty now. "I'm sorry."

He gave her an annoyed look. "No, you're not."

Honestly, at that moment, she really was. She hurt all over and her brain felt like it was sparking inside her head. "Here's the ironic part," she said to Reed. "It wasn't him. Murphy. He's not our rapist."

Despite everything, Reed looked intrigued. "How do you know?" he asked in a low voice.

"He has a limp. Initially, I thought he was just drunk from his time at the bar, but when we were fighting, I could tell he had crappy lower body strength—the blows didn't have the force you would expect from someone his size. If it weren't for that Dumpster, I probably could've taken him down, and he had almost a foot on me in height. There's no way he was scrambling up the sides of apartment buildings like some cat burglar."

"So who shot him?" Reed asked, eyeing the door like Rhodes was out there with a stethoscope, listening.

"I have no idea. Truly." She paused and looked at her lap. "But whoever it was, he or she may have saved my life."

He reached for her hand and gave it a quick squeeze. "When the cops find whoever it is, we can be sure to thank them at the pretrial hearing. In the meantime, let's get you home, hmm?"

That offer sounded so appealing that she didn't even mind when he held her arm to help her out of the bed. She eased onto her feet and was pleased when they seemed to sustain her weight. She shuffled like an old woman to collect her discharge papers while Reed fetched them a taxi. He took pity on her because they rode back to her place in blessed silence. At her front door, she fumbled her keys twice before he took them from her hands and opened the lock himself. "I can do that," she protested weakly.

"Yes, but you don't have to. It's already done."

She removed her boots at the door, and then he steered

her gently toward the couch, with the dog sniffing and wagging happily after them. She gave Bump's head a clumsy pat as she put her legs up on the coffee table. "Sorry, buddy. I missed your walk."

"I'll take him out. You just sit." Reed tucked a throw pillow behind her head and unfurled a nearby blanket over her lap.

"What are you doing?" she asked him as he fussed.

"I'm taking care of you," he replied, all business.

"Oh." Her heart faltered and she clutched the edges of the soft blanket. She couldn't look at him all of a sudden. "I'm not sure how to do that," she admitted at last.

He touched her knee gently and smiled. "It's easy. You just have to sit there. Let me take Sir Sheds-a-Lot out to the curb and then I'll be back in a jot, okay? Don't you move."

"I don't think I could even if I tried," she murmured, settling in. Morning sunlight streamed in through all her windows but she shut her eyes and found relief in the darkness. She heard Bump's eager nails scratching on the wood floor and the jangle of his collar as he disappeared out the door with Reed. It seemed like they were gone only a few seconds before they reappeared again, jolting her from the netherworld. Reed was in the kitchen. She heard the sound of kibble hitting the dog bowl, and then Bump slurping down some water. A few moments later, when she felt the other end of the sofa sag, she forced open her eyes. "You didn't have to come all this way," she said. "I would have called you back eventually."

He rubbed a hand over his stubble. "Right. From the morgue, maybe."

"Did I say I was sorry?" she asked vaguely.

"I don't want you to be sorry. I want you to stop taking chances with your life."

She was sleepy again, her eyes drifting shut. "You forget. I'm living on borrowed time." Her hand tremor returned suddenly, and she opened her eyes to look at it, like it was disconnected from the rest of her. "I'm shaking," she observed with clinical detachment.

Reed looked concerned. "Are you cold?"

"No," she said slowly, even as the shaking seemed to spread throughout her body. Soon she was in a full-body shudder and she couldn't make it stop. "What—what's happening to me?"

"I don't know." He shifted to sit closer to her, peering into her eyes, pressing a hand to her forehead. "You don't feel hot. Your eyes aren't crossed." He dropped her hands abruptly and started pawing frantically at the papers the hospital had given them upon her release. "Maybe it's shock. I'm calling the doctor."

She wanted to protest but her teeth were chattering too hard for her to speak. Being out of control of her own body was the worst thing to happen to her today. Dimly, she heard Reed on the phone, his voice tight as he described her symptoms. "No," he said. "No, none of that. Uh-huh. Are you quite sure?"

She was still trembling under the blanket when he returned to the couch. "Weh—well? What is it?"

"They say it's probably the adrenaline wearing off," he told her, smoothing a gentle hand down her arm. "We're to call back if it doesn't stop in a few minutes."

She shivered, blinking back tears. "Minutes?" Her teeth clacked together and she clenched her jaw to try to make it stop. Nothing she did held back the tremors. "Reed?" She reached out her hand and clutched blindly for him, but instead of taking her hand, he folded himself carefully around her.

"I'm here. You're okay. Try to breathe."

She screwed her eyes shut, the full horror of the day, of her whole life, rushing back at her. "Make it stop," she whispered desperately. "When does it stop?"

He held her tight and kissed her head. "I don't know, honey." He sounded as helpless as she felt. "I don't know."

# 12

The buzzing of his cell phone penetrated his consciousness slowly, layer by layer, like a sander over a board, until at last Reed twitched himself fully awake and fumbled in the direction of the noise. His mouth felt filled with cotton and he struggled to get any words out. "Markham," he said, half hanging over the side of Ellery's couch.

"Where the hell are you?" McGreevy was on the other end, somewhere near traffic because Reed could hear the rush of cars going past.

"I'm up in—"

"Don't say Boston."

"—Boston."

"Jesus Christ. This girl must really have your pecker in a pretzel if you're playing kamikaze with your career for her. Did you forget that we're supposed to be getting on a plane to Florida in half an hour?"

Reed lay back on the sofa cushions and closed his eyes. The correct move now would probably be to reply that he'd meet McGreevy in Florida, go hop on a plane, and forget everything he'd ever known about a drifter named The Blaze. He hadn't told Ellery yet what he'd found; it wasn't too late to play dumb. Unfortunately, Reed had an IQ of 154 and dumb just wasn't in his repertoire. "Earl Stanfield didn't just wander off in the middle of the Gallagher fire investigation," he said. "He was placed in the MURS program—and I think you know that because you put him there."

Wherever McGreevy was walking to, he stopped dead in his tracks. When he spoke again, his voice was low and dangerous. "You were barely out of short pants when that store went up in flames, Markham. So whatever it is you think you know now, more than a quarter of a century after the fact, you're dead wrong."

"I know the task force must have been deliriously happy to find Luis Carnevale gift-wrapped at the scene. I've read the files, Puss—this investigation reeked."

"Reeked like the gasoline Carnevale had on his clothes. He didn't just happen to be there that night. He was jerking off to his masterpiece while a little boy burned up inside that store. Think about that nugget whenever your heart starts bleeding too hard for the guy."

Reed sat up and put his socked feet on the floor. He bent

in half under the weight of what he had to do, his head in his hands. "Firebugs answer the alarm calls the same as the firemen. You know that as well as I do. Carnevale said he heard the sirens and followed them there."

"And you believe him." McGreevy's voice was hard, threatening.

"I've been to the prison. I've talked to him."

"Then you know what he is."

Reed had no reply for this, so he said nothing.

"That man terrorized an entire city for more than two years," McGreevy continued. "He set nearly a hundred fires and caused millions of dollars in property damage. Two men were badly injured putting out the fires he lit—and for what purpose? Just so he could get his rocks off, like he was doing the night Powell caught him."

"What did Earl see?" Reed kept his question soft, as though his own life weren't hanging on the answer.

"Nothing," McGreevy bit out harshly. "Not one damn thing of probative value. He got a nice little apartment safe and sound—he may as well've won the lottery—and Carnevale got a ten-foot cell, which is right where he belongs."

"He wasn't convicted of any of the other fires, only the Gallagher store."

"We didn't need any others. There was enough evidence from that one to put him away for a good long time."

"I gather you all made sure of that."

McGreevy snorted derisively. "Shit, Reed. You can't frame a guilty man." Then he paused as if considering his next move. "Listen here: I want you to tread very carefully because you're walking down a lonely road—one you don't get to come back from once you get too far gone. You want to go chasing some garbled story from a drunk back in 1988—whatever. If you want to make some big outcry of injustice for an arsonist who jacks off at a fire, well then I can't stop you. But I was the junior man on that task force and anything I did, I did because someone else was telling me to—someone who knew better than I did what the stakes were. So I'm going to return that favor and offer you some advice: if you go turning over old rocks, then I guarantee something'll slither right out and bite your ankles."

"Is that a threat?"

"Words of wisdom from someone who's been there."

"I'll take that under advisement," Reed replied tightly.

"Take it to the airport. I want you back on the job in Florida by the six P.M. news conference tonight. If you don't show up there, then don't bother showing up at all." He paused meaningfully. "And that is a threat, so I suggest you treat it as such."

Reed hung up with McGreevy and tossed his phone aside onto the coffee table. He had a crick in his neck from sleeping on the sofa and was dressed in yesterday's clothes. He couldn't remember the last time he'd eaten anything. Maybe it wasn't wise to throw one's career away on an empty stomach. He foraged in Ellery's pantry for something edible and finally found one granola bar, expiration date unknown. He took his chances and wolfed it down with a tall glass of tap water.

His watch said it was just past ten in the morning. Ellery had stopped shaking sometime after seven and disappeared into her bedroom, practically fleeing his presence. He'd heard the lock click shut and there had been no sound from her since. Normally, he'd be happy to let her sleep, but with her head injury, the doctor had given orders to check on her every so often to make sure she wasn't exhibiting any serious signs of brain damage. Reed went down the shadowed hall to stand in front of her white door. He listened but heard only silence on the other side. Gingerly, he stretched out a hand to stroke the smooth, cool wood. This was how they'd met, the two of them, with him on one side of the door and her on the other. Sometimes he felt like it would always be between them.

He rapped gently and heard a boisterous *woof* in response, followed by the jingle of Bump's collar and the sound of him snuffling the crack by Reed's feet. There was a long stretch with no other action, and Reed was just wondering if he should find a way to jimmy the lock when he heard it slide open. Ellery drew back the door and stood there squinting at him as though the light hurt her eyes.

"You're alive," he said with some relief—another déjà vu moment in their nontraditional relationship. Bump stopped just long enough to give Reed's feet a cursory sniff before bounding off in the direction of the kitchen.

Ellery hummed a nonreply and rubbed the side of her head with one hand. Her hair was tangled and the scrape on her chin had turned a dull brick red. She seemed hazy and unsteady on her feet and he wasn't sure if he ought to be hauling her back to the hospital, lickety-split.

"How do you feel?" he asked cautiously.

"Like I've been hit with a lead pipe."

She ghosted past him, careful not to touch, and with that he had his answer: she was fine. He trailed after her to the kitchen, where he found her sitting on a high stool, slumped over the granite-covered island. Now that he knew she would be okay, he felt a grim sort of comfort at her distress: maybe she would learn her lesson this time. "That was an incredibly dangerous stunt you pulled in the alley last night," he said as he poured her a glass of water. "What was your plan if you had caught Murphy climbing up the fire escape?"

"To stop him." She accepted the glass and drank it halfway down.

"Ellery." He took the seat next to her, but she did not

look at him. He sighed. "I know you want to get this guy, but you can't be following around violent sexual predators on your own. There's a reason cops bring backup."

"No one is looking for him. No one. Manganelli's busy with some jewelry store heist, and meanwhile this guy is out there somewhere, planning which window he's going to crawl through next."

"It's frustrating. I get that." He hesitated. "There's always some guy, though. Someone out there doing harm or planning to—you can't be responsible for all of them."

She rubbed the spot between her eyes. "Wendy asked me for help. I promised her."

"You don't owe her anything."

Ellery looked him in the eyes for the first time. "That's rich, coming from you."

"What does that mean?"

"You're standing here in my kitchen because I didn't answer my phone for a few hours. So yeah—go ahead and lecture me about my overreaching sense of personal responsibility." She took up the glass of water and drained the rest of it while he fought off the heat he felt coloring his face.

He opted for a change of subject. "I'm going to go find some food, since it's been ages since I've eaten a proper meal and I figure I can take the animal with me to get some exercise. Would you like anything?"

"Yeah. McDonald's. I'd like an egg McMuffin with two hash browns and an extra-large Coke with lots of ice."

Reed made a face. "My arteries hardened just from that description."

"The ice is medicinal." She shifted slowly off her seat, her back to him again. "I'm going to go shower for about three days."

Reed took Bump out into the frosty, sunshine-filled day. He had left Virginia with just the clothes on his back, so he had to step carefully around the larger slush piles or risk ruining his work shoes forever. *Not that I'll need them if I don't get down to Florida by nightfall,* he thought to himself as he tied Bump's leash to a pole outside of the nearest McDonald's. He ordered Ellery the food she'd requested and then stopped at a sandwich shop a few doors down to get tuna and sprouts on whole wheat for himself. When he returned to her apartment, he found Ellery showered and redressed in jeans and a green sweatshirt, with bare feet and wet hair that curled at the ends. He felt a little guilty about admiring the firm shape of her rear end as she stood on tiptoe to reach the plates in her kitchen cabinets. Everyone seemed to think he wanted only to get into Ellery's pants, and he wondered if perhaps he was protesting the truth of that too much.

Ellery didn't notice his lingering gaze. She appeared more alert and definitely voracious as she devoured the McMuffin in a series of quick bites. "Not to seem ungrateful," she said around a mouthful of food, "but aren't you supposed to be at the FBI right about now?"

"Something like that. According to McGreevy, I'm to be in Florida by dark or I'm fired," he replied, matter-of-factly.

"What?" She blanched as she set down her enormous paper cup of soda. "You should go, then. Right now."

She pushed off the stool and tried urging him away from his sandwich and toward the door. "Wait, it's okay." He gentled her with a hand on her arm. "Maybe he actually means to go through with the threat—but I have my doubts."

Her gray eyes searched his. "Why?"

He guided her back to her stool. Once he told her, there was no going back. He might be able to keep mum about what he'd found, but Ellery never would. "It seems that Luis Carnevale and his lawyer were right all those years ago. That would-be witness, Earl Stanfield, may have had a hand getting out of town. I think the task force hooked him up with the Massachusetts branch of the Urgent Relocation Service, which is meant to be temporary. But in this case, Earl stayed gone." He told her about his suspicions and his conversation with McGreevy.

"Wow," she murmured when he'd finished. "Earl must've had quite a story if they were willing to take a risk like that."

"McGreevy claims not. He says the guy didn't actually

witness anything. I think he believes he was just smoothing out a weird wrinkle in the prosecution's case."

"He used one hell of an iron to do it. If they took a homeless guy and made him not-homeless—enough to buy his silence for good—that can't have been cheap."

Reed said nothing. He'd seen government budgets up close and personal, and they weren't inclined to be handing out money where it wasn't strictly necessary. He also knew how much power lay in the words "Federal Bureau of Investigation." He flashed his ID and people did what he told them to more often than not. Maybe The Blaze had been happy to relocate. Maybe he'd had no other choice.

"Where is he now?" Ellery asked.

"I don't know. I'm not sure anyone does." Once Carnevale had been convicted, no one would have cared much about the whereabouts of Earl Stanfield.

"We have to tell Bertie Jenkins." Ellery was already reaching for her phone.

"No, wait."

She halted and looked at him, surprised. "What do you mean, wait? The guy's been in prison for twenty-five years. Don't you think that's long enough?"

"Yes, but . . ." Reed spread his hands. "We don't have proof of anything at all. MURS wouldn't admit to relocating Earl Stanfield, and McGreevy would surely deny everything if asked in an official capacity. Furthermore, McGreevy is right about one thing: we don't know that Earl actually saw anything that would help prove Carnevale's innocence. He could very well be just a drunk with a mixed-up story. Worse, we don't know where he is or if he's even living. Without anything to substantiate our story, all we would be doing is giving a loud-mouthed lawyer the chance to drag the FBI's name through the mud."

Ellery's posture became closed, almost hostile. "Maybe they deserve it," she said hotly.

"Maybe. The point is we don't know." McGreevy had trained Reed, had gone to bat for him last year when his life had been imploding. They were yoked in a way that went beyond the usual chain of command: if Reed blew the whistle and destroyed the reputation of one of the Bureau's most decorated agents, the director might force McGreevy's resignation, but he wouldn't be shaking Reed's hand for the trouble. Reed could kiss any chance of promotion good-bye forever. Or, possibly worse, no one might actually care that the FBI had potentially railroaded an innocent man twenty-five years ago, and Reed wasn't sure how he was supposed to live with that outcome, either.

"So we look for him," Ellery said, sticking out her chin. "We find Earl Stanfield and see what he knows."

"I've done the usual searches already," Reed told her. "If he's still living, he's off the grid."

There was a sharp knock at the front door, making Ellery jump. "Now what?" she muttered as Bump went skittering toward the door, barking his fool head off. Reed followed her to see who it was, and the opened door revealed Detective Rhodes on the other side. "Ms. Hathaway, you're looking decidedly less green today. I hope you're feeling better." She did not wait to be invited in but crossed the threshold with breezy confidence, forcing Ellery to the side.

"Yes, thanks," Ellery replied as she shut the door behind the detective.

Rhodes nodded in his direction. "Agent Markham," she said slyly. "Still on the job, I see."

Reed cleared his throat, suddenly self-conscious that he was standing around dressed in yesterday's clothes. Then he realized Rhodes hadn't changed, either. "Ms. Hathaway, I wondered if you'd had any further ideas about the shooter from last night."

Ellery shook her head slowly. "I told you—I never saw them."

"Well, maybe this will help. The tech boys took that video and got it cleaned up as good as possible. This is the best view we got of the shooter. Does he look familiar to you at all?"

Ellery took the printed image from her and studied it for a long moment. "I'm not sure. I don't recognize him at all, but there is something familiar . . ."

Reed stepped nearer so he could look, too. The black-and-white photo was grainy and dark, but the face was clear enough to him. "I know him," he said, and both women turned in surprise. "That's Jacob Gallagher."

A furrow appeared in Rhodes's otherwise smooth brown forehead. "Who?"

"Oh my God, I think you're right." Ellery regarded Reed with wide eyes. "What the hell was he doing in that alley?"

"Saving your life, apparently."

Rhodes put her hands on her hips. "Hello? You two want to fill me in here? Who is Jacob Gallagher?"

"Have you heard about that furniture store fire from the 1980s?" Ellery said. "The one where the boy died. His name was Bobby Gallagher, and Jacob is his brother."

"And you know him how?"

"I've never actually met him," Ellery said as she handed back the police photo. "I know his mother, sort of. We belong to a group together."

Rhodes had her notebook out now. "What kind of group?"

Ellery hesitated. "Survivors of violent crime. Myra Gallagher, she was badly burned in the fire, and of course her son Bobby was killed."

Rhodes touched the side of her head like it was starting to ache. "And this has what to do with the other son, Jacob?"

Reed glanced at Ellery, both of them measuring how

much to say. "Jacob was at the scene the night of the fire," Reed said eventually. "He would have been sixteen at the time." He crossed to the coffee table and withdrew his laptop from his briefcase. Within a minute or so, he had called up the enhanced news photos that clearly depicted young Jacob Gallagher among the crowd shots from the night of the furniture store fire. For added measure, he showed Rhodes Jacob's current driver's license picture so that she could see the resemblance to the image of the shooter.

"You're right, it looks like the same guy," she said as she looked back and forth between the two photos. Then she trained her gaze squarely on Ellery. "So assuming the shooter is Jacob Gallagher—the question is, why? Why was he in the alley and why did he shoot Michael Murphy?"

Ellery was used to hard questions, and she didn't wilt under Rhodes's stare. "As I've said, I was unconscious at the time. Maybe when you find Jacob Gallagher, you can ask him."

Rhodes thinned her lips and narrowed her eyes. "This little revelation you two uncovered—that Jacob Gallagher was there the night his family's store burned up—does he know about it?"

"We haven't said anything to him," Reed replied, and Ellery looked at the floor. He suspected that meant she'd passed on the information to Myra, which meant Jacob could very well know they had been investigating him.

Rhodes clearly sensed this, too, because she shook her head and took out the photo of their shooter again. "I'll put my people on Jacob Gallagher and see what turns up," she said. "And in the meantime, I'd advise you both to stay away from him. If you see him anywhere, you don't confront him, don't ask him any questions—you call me, you got that?"

"He saved my life," Ellery said, plainly not intimidated by the thought of encountering Jacob Gallagher.

"Oh, yeah? We'll see about pinning a medal on him. Meanwhile, I'll ask you: how often do you have to visit the range to stay accurate with your weapon? Four times per year? More? I was down at Moon Island last month checking out the new recruits, and most of 'em couldn't hit the broad side of a barn."

"And your point is?" Ellery asked.

Rhodes shrugged. "Gallagher—if in fact this is him in the picture—he shot Murphy with your gun. That probably means he didn't have a gun on him, which also probably means he doesn't own one, because I'm thinking he'd bring it if he was planning on hanging around some back alley in the middle of the night. So there he is, standing at the end of the alley while the two of you are fighting back and forth in the dark. He sees the gun, grabs it." She pantomimed picking up the gun and aiming it in Ellery's direction. "He hits Murphy with one shot but the other two were wide to the right by about three feet, including one that hit the Dumpster not too far from your head."

Ellery blinked. Reed's breath caught in his throat. Rhodes dropped her imaginary weapon. "So my point is," she said with emphasis, "maybe Murphy wasn't the person who Jacob Gallagher was aiming at."

# 13

Night began in the midafternoon. The shortest day was coming, and with it, a reminder that Boston properly belonged one time zone over, out in the Atlantic Ocean somewhere. Ellery and Reed were sitting in her rented car in the hospital parking lot, but to Ellery, it felt like the edge of a cliff. He had the wheel—her head injury meant she shouldn't drive—and they took turns watching the clock count down the minutes until she had to be inside for group and he had missed the Florida deadline. She sat on her hands so she wouldn't bite her nails and regarded his face in the shadows. She could feel it slipping away from him, the future he'd thought he was going to have, and this was his reward: to sit in a cold, dark parking lot with her.

She had wondered off and on what it might be like to be someone's priority, to be number one, even if it was only for a short time. Her father had left when she was ten and never looked back. Had he seen the news later on? Had he heard what had happened to her? She liked to imagine he didn't know, that maybe he'd found a place far away where Francis Coben did not exist. Her mother had had to choose between the child who was dying and the one who'd made it out alive, and so it had been no choice at all. Once the injuries had healed, Ellery was on her own again. The only person to pick her, to choose her best of all, had been the man who'd locked her in a closet and threatened to chop off her hands. After that, anonymity and detachment had felt welcoming, like a lessening of pressure, a way to disappear.

She felt that pressure bearing down on her as she fidgeted in her seat next to Reed. *Don't do this,* she wanted to tell him. *I'm not worth it.* She couldn't let herself get used to him being there, because eventually he would have to go home again. Sooner or later he would realize everything he'd lost.

"You could still go," she said softly, and he tore his gaze from the clock.

They stared at each other in the low light and she couldn't read his expression. "It's done," he said finally. "Now we wait."

"Wait for what?"

"To see what happens next."

Ellery was no good at waiting, so she ducked out into the frigid wind, fighting its force all the way across the parking lot until she could escape into the relative quiet of the hospital corridor. She found the usual room with its familiar roster of faces. Miles gave her a crinkle-eyed smile and a little wave. Tabitha was scrolling through her phone and didn't bother to look up. Alex was making himself a coffee, while Dr. Sunny leafed through her notes. Ellery took an empty seat next to Wendy, who was slouched in her chair, her eyes fixed somewhere beyond the confines of the room. "Hey," Ellery murmured to her. "How's it going?" She was interested in the answer, but she was also watching the door for Myra's arrival. She wasn't sure exactly how to start a conversation this time: *Hey, did your son happen to take some shots at me? Any idea where he might be now?*

Wendy gave a tight, one-shoulder shrug. "My sister wants me to move out. She says it's been months since it happened and I should be over it by now. That if he wanted to come back for me, he would've. She says I freak her kids out, hanging around the house all day, crying at weird times."

Ellery's heart squeezed in sympathy and she felt useless all over again. "I'm sorry."

Wendy turned to her abruptly, her dark eyes flashing. "You think they'll ever kill him? Coben? He's been on death row forever. What are they even waiting for anymore? Stick the needle in already!"

"I—I don't know." Ellery swallowed. "It's not up to me."

Wendy shrank back into her seat, huddling down. "It should be."

"Okay, everyone, it's time to get started," Dr. Sunny called pleasantly, and the others took their seats. Ellery glanced at the door but Myra wasn't rolling through it. Maybe the cops had been to see her. Maybe she was off somewhere, hiding Jacob. Ellery considered myriad possibilities and only partially paid attention to what was happening around her. She deferred when it was her turn to talk, and Dr. Sunny let it go with a small frown. Alex was talking about his plans for the Christmas holidays, but Ellery was subtly using her phone to look up Myra Gallagher's address. Her search came back empty.

When the group broke up, Ellery hung back until she could approach Dr. Sunny alone. Dr. Sunny greeted her with a calm smile. "Ellery. Can I help you with something?"

"Myra wasn't here today."

"Yes, I noticed that. It's not unusual for her to skip a session or two here and there."

The group was not due to meet again until after the New Year, and Ellery couldn't wait that long. "I need to get in touch with her," she said. "Do you happen to have her address?"

Dr. Sunny paused from gathering up her things. "I'm sorry, but I can't share that information with you. It's confidential."

Ellery blocked her path to the door. "Please," she said. "It's urgent."

Dr. Sunny's normally impassive face appeared skeptical. "Urgent?"

"Myra might be in danger." It wasn't entirely a lie. If Jacob was going around shooting people, it was impossible to predict what he might do next.

"Then you should contact the police," Dr. Sunny said.

"I am the police." Ellery's frustration crept up a notch.

"No, you're not. And at the rate you're going, that situation is going to become permanent."

Ellery reined in her temper. She had temporarily forgotten the part about where Dr. Sunny would be reporting her every word and thought back to the brass. "I've done everything you asked me to, showed up to every session."

"Yes," Dr. Sunny acknowledged with a tilt of her head. "You're here, physically. You answer questions when asked. But your participation is limited and your attention often seems elsewhere. You volunteer almost nothing about your experience."

"What can I add that hasn't already been said? It's all out there already in books and movies and magazines." She waved wildly in the direction of the windows. "When I think about the gallons of ink that've been spilled already on Francis Coben, it makes me want to never mention him again. He wants me to talk about him—don't you get that? He'd love it if he knew you guys had me sitting in some shrink's office, reliving every minute in Technicolor detail. That'd be like a friggin' wet dream for him!"

Dr. Sunny did not appear moved by her tirade. "I'm not saying you need to talk about Coben. I want you to talk about you."

Ellery opened her mouth and closed it again. The woman didn't get it: there was no way to separate the two. Ellery shook her head and looked away. "I told you at the beginning, I don't go in for talking. I've told the whole damn story multiple times now, and the ending never changes."

"And it won't," Dr. Sunny agreed. "Not until you say the part of the story you've been leaving out."

Ellery looked at her sharply. "What's that supposed to mean?"

"You'll have to tell me. Whatever you've been afraid to say—whatever causes you to shut down every time we talk about your future—that's what you need to examine."

Ellery bit back a sarcastic reply about how nice it must be to sit around and examine one's feelings all day, but her time was better served trying to keep dangerous criminals off the street. Sure, it might mean fewer terrorized clients for Dr. Sunny, but busting a sadistic rapist or a deadly arsonist had to be viewed as an overall net benefit for humanity—whether they felt all sunshiny about that fact or not. "Right now, what I need is to reach Myra Gallagher. Maybe you have a phone number, or an email . . ."

"I'm sorry. I can't help you."

Back in the parking lot, Ellery found Reed checking his email on his phone. "Not fired yet," he remarked with grim humor as she climbed inside the car.

"Myra wasn't at group today. The doctor says she does that sometimes—skips a meeting—but the timing worries me."

"It does seem odd. Of course, she may be tied up with Detective Rhodes for all we know."

Ellery felt a prick of guilt about Rhodes and all the parts of the story she'd left out from telling the detective. Rhodes was out there crusading on her behalf with only partial information. "Myra Gallagher's address isn't publicly listed," she began, and Reed gave her a long-suffering look, no doubt because he imagined her asking him to use his FBI connections to dig up the information, despite the fact that he had no legal standing to do so. "But I was thinking about Jake, about how he stayed even after his brother died, about how everyone seems to stay, generation after generation, right in the same neighborhood, even when it might be better to get out. The Gallaghers had their store burn down. Their child died. Maybe . . . maybe they stayed, too."

"The address would be in the initial reports," he said, following her logic as he started up the engine.

A quick stop at her apartment allowed Ellery to dump some kibble in Bump's bowl and then to look up the Gallaghers' old address from the files that Bertie Jenkins had passed along to them. They had lived in a small house on Everett Street in East Boston at the time, and a quick check of property records indicated it had not been sold since 1982. Assuming the Gallaghers had been the ones to buy the place, there was a reasonable chance they still lived there.

Reed drove across town while Ellery swallowed a pair of painkillers and leaned carefully back in her seat. Even the soft leather headrest made the lump on her skull start to throb. She closed her eyes and willed the pain to subside, waiting for the blessed moment when the pills would do their work. Reed let her rest for quite a while before he finally asked the obvious question: "What are you going to say to her?"

Ellery kept her eyes shut for a few moments longer. All these years, Myra had been pinning her anger on Luis Carnevale, thinking the monster was locked safely in a cage, when the real danger was possibly lurking right within her own family. To have birthed two children, only to have one kill the other ... Ellery couldn't imagine how to face a truth that ugly. Myra might very well slam the door in her face and never speak to her again. It was only the slim chance that Jake could be, if not redeemed, then rescued before an overzealous cop shot him in the streets, which gave Ellery any hope at all. "If she's hiding Jake, she should know the truth," she said, opening her eyes to look at Reed. "She should know everything she's risking."

When they reached the address that Ellery had dug out

from the files, she wiped her palm against the foggy glass of the car window to peer at the house. "This has to be the place," she said when she saw the front steps had a cement wheelchair ramp constructed alongside them. It was a boxy two-story place wedged in between larger, if not grander, homes. The multicolored lights of a Christmas tree glowed from the downstairs window and there was an evergreen wreath hung upon the door. "Maybe you should wait here," she said when she saw Reed had unbuckled his seat belt to accompany her. "They are going to be even less likely to talk to me if I bring the FBI with me."

"I might well have ceased to be the FBI some hours ago," Reed replied as he got out with her. "Either way, I am not letting you go inside alone to a place that might be harboring the man who shot at you last night."

"That's just one theory. We don't know he was after me."

"Oh, no?" Puffs of his breath misted in the air. "You think he was out in the middle of the night following Mick Murphy, do you? Hell of a coincidence that would be."

Ellery didn't reply to this as she knocked on the Gallaghers' door. A moment later, a pair of blue eyes appeared behind the wreath: Patrick Gallagher. He took a look at them and then dropped the curtain again. It took a long moment before he opened the door. "What do you want?" he asked, his shadow falling over them.

"I'm here to talk about Jacob," Ellery said. "May we please come in?"

Patrick glanced over his shoulder. "It's suppertime."

"Please, it will only take a few minutes."

Patrick's frown deepened the creases around his mouth, but before he could object further, Myra came rolling up behind him. "Pat? Who is it?" There was a fearful edge to her voice, but she relaxed when she saw Ellery and Reed standing on her doorstep. "Oh," she said, not seeming too surprised. She took a deep breath. "Well, don't leave them standing there in the cold. You're letting all the heat out."

Grudgingly, Patrick drew back the door and let Reed and Ellery over the threshold. He led the group down a short hall and back to the humble kitchen. It had a low ceiling and faded wallpaper decorated with fruits and vegetables. The cabinets had been painted several times over, the latest coat a white that showed faint hints of the green beneath it. The ancient stove had a rust spot on one edge, but the stew simmering inside the pot gave off a rich aroma that made Ellery's stomach rumble. Patrick put a lid on it before drawing out one of the kitchen chairs, a solid piece with beautifully carved lines that echoed back to the family's doomed furniture business. "State your business," he said, not offering them a seat at the table.

"I imagine the police have been to see you already," Ellery said.

"They were here earlier," Myra answered softly. "Searched the place up and down. If you're thinking Jacob's hiding here with us, you're wrong."

"Did they tell you why they want to talk to him?"

Patrick fixed her with a dead-eyed stare while Myra twisted her hands in her lap. Silence stretched between them. "They think he may have killed a man," Myra said finally. "Something about a shooting. I said that can't be true: Jake doesn't own a gun."

"It was my gun," Ellery told them, and Myra raised her head in shock.

"What? What are you talking about?"

Ellery gave them a quick recap of the events from the alley, at least as she could remember them. "If your son is the shooter, then he saved my life. It's in his best interests to turn himself into custody so everything can get sorted out."

Patrick wasn't giving up his suspicions so easily. "What's the FBI got to do with this?" he asked, nodding at Reed. "What's he want with our boy?"

"I'm not here in an official capacity. I'm just along to try to keep Ellery safe. I'm sure you can understand."

"Jake wouldn't hurt her," Myra protested. "He wouldn't hurt anyone."

"He set that fire years ago," Ellery replied. "At school. Someone could have gotten hurt."

Myra bristled at the suggestion, drawing her knit sweater tighter around her. "That was a prank, a mistake. It was years ago, when he was just a teenager. Everyone—everyone makes mistakes."

"He was at the scene the night of the store fire," Reed said.

Myra's deformed fingers worried the edge of her sweater in fretful fashion. Ellery had told her this news already, so she was more interested in Patrick's reaction. He didn't bat an eye. "So what if he was?" he said curtly. "Don't make any difference now."

"They think he set it," Myra said, a tad impatient. "That's what they think."

"We aren't here to make accusations," Ellery replied. "We just wanted you to know, in case you're in contact with him, that Jake should talk to the police. Trust me, it'll go better for him if he's the one to come forward than if they have to track him down themselves."

Myra was shaking her head and muttering. "It's all a mess. It's all a damn mess." She shot Ellery an accusing glare. "Why couldn't you have left well enough alone?"

Ellery stiffened as if struck. For several moments, she was mute. "He was following me," she said, "not the other way around."

Myra covered her face with both hands. "I lost one boy," she said mournfully. "Now you want to take the other."

"No, I'm trying to keep him out of trouble."

"It's a damn sight too late for that," Patrick said. He rose slowly to his feet. "I think it's time you two were leaving."

Ellery wasn't going to push any harder, not when Myra was sitting there in her wheelchair with her head bent low and her fingers trembling. "Have Jake ask for Detective Rhodes," she murmured as she moved to leave. "She'll be fair with him."

Patrick marched them toward the door. It opened with a great whoosh, the wind slamming it back against the wall. "I know you think you're helping," he said, his voice low and hard. "But maybe you can leave my family alone now."

"I'm sorry," Ellery began, but Patrick held up a hand.

"Whatever Jake did or didn't do, whatever happened back then—it's my fault."

Ellery held her breath. This sounded like a confession. From the way Reed went still at her elbow, she knew he sensed it, too. Patrick shook his head faintly.

"My wife and boy were at that store because I sent 'em there. The place was going under. I felt like I was drowning along with it. I was short with Myra and the kids, shoutin' all the time because I couldn't make anything in my life go the way I wanted. Jake was in trouble at school and I didn't know it. I didn't set that fire but I might as well've. My house was all out of order, burning in a different way, and I did nothing to stop it." He raised his bleak eyes to hers. "So if you need someone to blame, you can look no further."

Ellery felt trapped by the weight of his gaze, a quarter century of misery in one man's eyes. But Reed was apparently not as moved. "Your brother, David," he said. "He was a co-owner in the business. He would've had the same financial problems you did."

The end of Patrick's mouth curled up in a gremlin's smile. "David," he said, as though the word left a bitter taste on his tongue. "You're wasting your time there. He wouldn't have burned that store—he didn't care about it enough. He left me to make every single decision down to the stationery. 'Bout the only time he visited the premises was after hours, when he liked to take a girl there to show her all the beds."

"He must have been happy to take the insurance payout," Reed said.

Patrick snorted. "Happy. Sure. As long as someone else filed all the papers." He nodded at the open door. "Best be going, then. If we see Jake, we'll tell him about your visit."


On the way home, they picked up the ingredients for what Reed was calling "a poor man's jambalaya," which he set about making in the kitchen while Ellery lay down on the couch with her earbuds in and her eyes closed. "The Magnificent Seven" by The Clash filled her ears, its cheery upbeat tempo at odds with the biting, sarcastic lyrics. She could go for a drink right about now, a little zing in her veins, just enough to lighten the thoughts in her head, which rumbled around like stones. She'd tried so hard but she hadn't helped Wendy or Myra. Jake was in the wind, and somewhere there was still a violent rapist on the loose. Dr. Sunny didn't seem inclined to give Ellery back her job, and maybe she was right: Ellery had solved precisely nothing, and all she had for her trouble was a lump on the head and a man sizzling sausage in her kitchen—a man she might have managed to drag into the quagmire with her.

Her heart lodged in her throat and she rubbed it to ease the ache. "I'm taking the dog out," she announced abruptly as she pulled the earbuds from her ears. Bump perked up at her words, thumping his tail in anticipation.

Reed turned from the stove, the spoon in his hands. "Give me a second. I'll go with you."

"No," she replied, more forcefully than she'd intended. She wanted some space. "I'll be fine for five minutes. I won't go farther than down the block."

"You aren't even armed anymore," he pointed out.

It was true that the cops had taken her gun as evidence. She held out her cell phone and pushed 9-1, showing the digits to Reed. "I have this," she said. "If anything happens, I just hit that last one and run like hell. Okay?"

Reed looked wary, but he agreed. "Five minutes. Then I come looking for you."

She shrugged into her coat and hooked up Bump's leash. Outside in the night air, she felt like she could breathe again. Bump set a leisurely stroll through the snowbanks, his ears making tracks as they went. Ellery refused to look up at the windows to see if Reed was watching. They walked a bit farther, until they were just out of sight of her building. The streets were empty and quiet so she could hear the sound of her boots on the pavement. When a second set of boots fell into step behind her, she grabbed the phone in her pocket.

"Wait, stop," said a male voice.

She stopped. Cautiously, she turned around. Jake Gallagher stood five feet away, looking ashen and worn, his hands held up to indicate he meant no harm. He had his father's curly dark blond hair and his mother's haunted eyes. "I'm calling the police," Ellery said, her thumb right above the 1.

"Don't! I'm not going to hurt you." Bump meanwhile felt no tension in the air. He strained toward Jake, wagging and sniffing. Jake gave a half-smile. "Hey, boy. Nice doggie."

"What do you want?" Ellery demanded, and Jake's smile vanished.

"What do *you* want?" he shot back. "Why're you all up in my family's business? Making my mother cry. Bringing back all those horrible memories for her and my dad. She said you're working with that lawyer, the one who wants to get Carnevale out. What the hell do you even care?"

"I'm not working with anyone. I was just trying to find out the truth."

"That was the truth," he said. "He burned that store just like they said! You and that lawyer are the ones trying to twist everything, trying to make him seem innocent."

"You were there that night," Ellery said, and his anger sputtered. He shut his mouth and shook his head. "What did you see?" she pressed. When he still said nothing, she waved her phone. "Fine, tell it to the cops."

"No, don't," he blurted, holding out his hands again. "I was there, yes. I didn't see him do it, but I saw he was there. The fireman caught the right guy."

"How do you know that if you didn't see him do it?"

"I just know, okay? Who the hell else was it going to be? He was the only one jerking off to the fire." He said the last words in utter disgust. "My brother was in there."

"You knew they were there."

"Of course I knew." He gave her an appraising look, as if measuring how much to say. "I followed 'em there."

"Why?"

He shrugged. "Bored kid, I guess. Not every day your mom and baby brother sneak out at night. I was curious is all."

"You said 'sneak.' I thought they were going to pick up tax papers."

"I didn't find that out until later."

There was something else right under the surface, something he wasn't saying. She tried a different tack. "You like following people, huh? You've been following me."

He eyed her, pride glinting. "Good thing I did. You'd be in a body bag by now. That guy was beating the crap out of you."

She wasn't feeling especially grateful right at that moment. "Why were you following me?"

He shook his head as if she were too thick for words. "To see what you were doing—what you were digging up about the fire. That asshole murdered my baby brother and you were trying to get him out! My family was doing just fine until you came along, sticking your nose in where it didn't belong. I know your story, too, you got that? I've seen the papers. You're not even a real cop anymore. Who the hell are you to go playing around with people's lives?"

The anger in his words vibrated through her and she remembered the note: GET BACK IN THE CLOSET WHERE YOU BELONG. "It was you," she said softly. "The one who put the note under my door." Jake turned his face away from her but said nothing. Her voice rose. "Did you also torch my truck?"

"I don't know nothing about that," he said, but he sounded unconvincing.

"I think I'll call the cops now. Let them decide."

He jerked his attention back to her. "No, wait. Let me do it. I don't want you trying to tell my story."

She held the phone back from him. "Tell me the truth then: what were you doing the night of the store fire?"

He threw up his hands in exasperation. "I told you! I followed my mom there."

"Why were you following her?"

He kicked at the snow. "I followed her sometimes. It was just something I did."

"Uh-huh. Sixteen-year-old boys don't follow their moms around for fun."

His shoulders rose and fell as he took a deep breath. "My dad accused my mom of running around on him, okay? They fought about it a few times. So I followed her, just to see."

Ellery's pulse picked up. She could visualize Myra from the pictures back then, the ones that had shown her whole and handsome, with thick burnished hair, a curvy figure, and bright blue eyes. "And what did you see?"

He shrugged. "Nothing. She went to the store just like was reported on the news. Who the hell has an affair in the middle of a furniture store? I told my dad later: he was crazy, imagining things. My mother was a good woman, and she did not deserve this." He held out his hand. "Now can I make the call?"

"Yes," she said as she pocketed her phone. Reed would

be crashing their little party at any second, and there was no way she was handing over her only lifeline in the meantime. "You can call from inside. I'd lead you but I'm pretty sure you know the way."

Detective Rhodes was only too happy to come collect Jake Gallagher, although she had plenty of side-eye left for Ellery as she did so. "Twenty cops out looking for this guy, this man you claim you've never met before, and he just up and turns himself in to you," she said, deadpan. "You're a regular miracle worker, Ms. Hathaway."

After she left with Jake, Reed and Ellery finally got to eat the food he'd made, and she surprised herself with how hungry she was. Reed smiled as he watched her eat. "You like it?"

She picked out a spicy flavored shrimp with her fork and popped it in her mouth. "It's delicious. If your mom taught you, I can't even imagine what a cook she must be."

"Mama's amazing. Daddy was always trying to get her to hire someone to help her, especially with the bigger dinners, but she wouldn't hear of it. When Suzanne hired a caterer for her wedding fifteen years ago, I think Mama cried for two days."

"How many people were going to be at that wedding?"

Reed grinned. "Only five hundred or so."

Ellery coughed on the water she was drinking. "I can barely work a microwave."

"I'll be sure to put the leftovers in your fridge before I go," he replied after a beat, and there was a strange silence as they both sat there with the reminder that he would be leaving.

After dinner, she was cleaning the kitchen when he cleared his throat behind her. "Uh, would you mind terribly if I borrowed your washer? I'm afraid these clothes might be ready to walk around on their own."

"Oh! Of course not. Here, let me show you." She showed him her small utility room with the stacked washer/dryer combo, and then she went to find her gray terry cloth robe. It would be a bit short on him but he could survive for a couple of hours. He emerged from the bathroom and she tried not to notice his lean, hairy legs. She escaped to the couch while he put his clothes in the washer. A few minutes later, he rejoined her, taking a careful seat at the opposite end.

"Well? What shall we do now?" he asked, as though he weren't sitting there practically naked.

She could barely look at him. "I don't know. Watch TV? Play cards? I have a deck around here somewhere."

"Sure, cards it is." He looked at her solemnly and then down at his single article of clothing. "Just anything but strip poker."

They played gin rummy, and he beat her four games

in a row. She would have blamed the head injury but she suspected he'd skunk her even if her brains weren't recently addled. "I'm beginning to think the southern gentleman routine is all an act," she grumbled as she dealt a fresh hand. "You must be cheating somehow."

"I learned everything about gin rummy from my father," he replied as he picked up his hand. "He liked to play it with real gin."

She glanced at him from beneath lowered lashes. "I should get a bottle and start plying you with it. Maybe then I'd win a game."

He opened his mouth to retort, but the washer sounded a loud buzzer from the back of the apartment. "You've been saved by the bell," he remarked as he climbed off the couch. "Enjoy the reprieve."

She watched him go and when he'd disappeared from sight she remembered suddenly that the dryer door had a faulty hinge that required a slight lift to close it. She followed Reed to the tiny utility room to alert him of this news and promptly collided with his elbow as he was loading in his clothes. He poked her in the ribs right where she was already sore and bruised. "Ow," she said, sucking in a shallow, painful breath.

Reed's eyes widened in horror and he reached out his hands to steady her. "I'm sorry, I'm sorry. I didn't see you there. Are you okay?"

She straightened up as the pain receded. "Yeah, I think so."

"Are you sure?" He rubbed her shoulders gently.

"Yes, yes. I'm fine." They were practically on top of each other now. Her laundry room was barely wide enough to hold one person and a basket. Strangely, she felt no desire to get out of the way. It was an odd enough sensation, having someone in her personal space and not being distressed about it, so odd that she let the moment linger. Maybe too long.

"Ellery?"

"Hmm?" She was looking at the split in his robe, which had fallen open to reveal an expanse of golden skin and a sprinkling of dark chest hair.

"You're sure you're all right? You seem kind of . . . woozy."

"Your hair," she said, apropos of nothing. She had raised her eyes to his head. "It's flatter than usual."

"Yes, well. Pardon me if I didn't take the time to gel it up properly before hopping a plane to make sure you were alive."

"I'm alive." She gave a calm smile, and he returned it.

"And I'm so glad," he murmured. His hands, still on her shoulders, seemed to be urging her forward, and she decided to let it happen. He folded her in gently as though she might break, and she held her breath in this barest of hugs. Hesitantly, she let her fingers find the sides of him where he was lean and strong through the robe. Her nose poked into his collarbone and he smelled like warm, clean male. She couldn't help herself: she opened her mouth and gave him a brief, experimental lick.

"Jesus!" He jerked in her arms but he must have liked it because he didn't let her go. No, he pulled her closer, his naked legs starting to mingle with hers, and one large hand came up to cup the back of her neck, his fingers twisting in her hair. Her tongue darted out again, addicted to the salt of him now, and he buried his face against the side of her throat. Yes, she could do this, she thought, arching her neck as his hands started to move on her body. She could give him something he wanted. Then his sacrifices wouldn't have been all for nothing.

Her heart hammered at the decision. This was usually the part where she went outside herself, where she pretended it wasn't happening until it was over. If she could do it with other men, she could surely do it with Reed. She squeezed her eyes shut and tangled her fingers in the robe. It felt weird. Personal and intimate in a way that made her squirm. He was using his nose to nudge her shirt off her shoulder, exposing her skin to his mouth. She gasped at the scrape of his stubble contrasted with the softness of his lips, and was suddenly dizzy. That felt good. *Too good.* Strange sensations rushed at her and she couldn't make them stop. She wrenched away from him, breathing hard, her mouth hanging open in shock. Losing control was not an option.

Reed looked shellacked, his eyes dark, still aroused. "Ah, sorry," he said, clutching his head. "I didn't mean—that is, I shouldn't have . . ."

She had backed away from him into the hall. "Forget it." She barely got the words out when the banging started at her front door.

They froze again, a new kind of tension. It was after midnight now. There was a brief pause and then the pounding happened again. "I'll get it," Reed said, cinching up his robe.

"No, I will."

They went together to the door, pushing past each other, but it was she who reached the locks first. She peered through the peephole and drew back in surprise. "I think it's for you," she murmured, deferring to him with a wave of her hands. He looked puzzled as he opened the door.

Russell McGreevy stood in the dim hallway, shoes dripping, a streak of snow marring his otherwise perfect black coat. "Well," he said with a scowl as he took in Reed's bathrobe and bare feet. "Isn't this cozy?"

# 14

McGreevy did not wait to be invited inside. He pushed past Reed and stalked into Ellery's living room, his coat trailing like a cape. Ellery shot Reed a look that was half question, half accusation. *What the hell is going on here?* Reed gave a guilty shrug and cinched her bathrobe more tightly around his naked body, trying to look more self-assured than he felt as he marched in to face McGreevy. Regardless of the differences in their attire, it was his boss who was in the wrong here, and Reed had a feeling he knew it, too. Otherwise, why show up at Ellery's place in the middle of the night?

McGreevy had taken up sentry at the far end of the room, peering out at the city lights down below. He did not turn around when Reed and Ellery entered, as though they weren't worthy of his attention. Reed halted near the sofa, and Ellery kept her distance from both men, hugging herself and looking warily from one to the other. Bump sat at her feet, whining softly at the tension in the room. For a long moment, the only sounds were the dog's mild protests and the far-off tumbling clothes in the dryer.

"Thought you were in Florida," Reed said finally, and McGreevy whirled to frown at him.

"Don't play cute with me."

"Who's playing cute? I'd say this is more cloak-and-dagger, what with the surprise visit at this late hour."

"Let's hope it's not too late," McGreevy replied testily. He raked Reed up and down with his eyes. "I trust you have actual clothes lying around here someplace." His gaze slid toward the hall, toward Ellery's bedroom, but Reed refused to take the bait. He folded his arms.

"Why does it matter how I am dressed?" If McGreevy thought he could order Reed onto a plane to Florida, he was sadly mistaken about where his line of influence ended.

"Just get dressed, will you?" McGreevy gestured at him impatiently. "I don't have much time."

Reed didn't budge. "Where are we going?"

McGreevy regarded him with pale eyes. "I've found Earl Stanfield. The Blaze, whatever. Before you blow up my career—and your own—I thought you should hear the whole story, right from the horse's mouth. Then you can decide whether your crusade is really worth it."

"Found him," Reed repeated ironically. "Right about

where you left him twenty-five years ago, is that it?"

McGreevy put a hand to his hip, causing his coat to gape open and reveal his gun. A power gesture to remind them: McGreevy was still head of the pack. Adrenaline started pulsing through Reed's body, making it harder to breathe. McGreevy took several deliberate steps closer, his head tilted, his eyes squinting at Reed. "You make it sound like I trussed him up and left him for dead in the countryside. You act like it was my idea. I took orders from about six different men on that task force—I didn't make a single move without their say-so."

"So you were just following orders to disappear a witness," Reed said. "Got it."

McGreevy closed the distance completely, to the point where Reed could smell him now—the wet wool and dried sweat, coffee breath and barely controlled fury. He resisted the urge to look away. "Must be nice," McGreevy said, "that view from your high horse. Impressing your girlfriend with the firm moral stance, are you?" He pounded a fist into his palm for emphasis. "Maybe she doesn't remember the last time the three of us were together, you'd let a murderer walk around right in front of you and never seen him coming. Maybe you were busy watching her ass instead. Is that it?"

"We were the only ones even looking for a killer," Reed reminded him.

"She could've died, Markham," McGreevy continued as

though Reed hadn't spoken. His face loomed so close now that Reed couldn't even bring him into focus. "Your Ellery could've died just like little Adam Kennedy died. Right on your watch. Hell, you could've gone down with her, and then we wouldn't even be standing here, having this conversation. You'd be dead. Instead, fate went a different way, and you were the hero. Funny how thin that line can be sometimes, isn't it?"

"Yeah, funny." Reed's voice was hard.

After another beat of silence, McGreevy backed away with a slight shake of his head. "And let's not forget how that whole mess ended. How I signed off on your official bullshit story without so much as blinking, even though your girlfriend was left standing over a dead body with a gun in her hand."

He twisted around to look at Ellery, who seemed to quiver in his sights. Heat flared through Reed, quick and hot. "As you so dutifully pointed out, she could have easily been killed herself. As could I."

McGreevy kept his gaze trained on Ellery as he answered. "That's what I'm trying to remind you, Markham. Sometimes the right outcome is all that matters." He waited a beat longer and then drew himself up abruptly. "Get your clothes. Let's go."

"Now? It's the middle of the night."

"And come the morning, if we're lucky, it'll be like this whole thing never happened. You have five minutes. I'll be downstairs in the car waiting."

* * *

It took Reed only three minutes to shed Ellery's robe in place of his freshly laundered jeans and shirt. Ellery herself had disappeared into her bedroom to change as well, so at least they didn't have to make eye contact or discuss what McGreevy had nearly walked in on with his ill-timed visit. She emerged dressed in black from head to toe, looking like a night prowler, and Reed had a flash of how that had gone two nights before. "Maybe you should stay here," he said. She was still battling a head injury and serious bruises. No wonder he'd been allowed to feel her up in the laundry room. He winced a bit at the memory, and how he'd pressed an unfair advantage.

"Screw that," she told him as she grabbed her jacket. "You wouldn't even know about this case if it weren't for me."

Reed had to admit she was right about this point so he made no further argument. Downstairs, they found McGreevy idling in a dark town car, its humming engine the only noise on the otherwise silent street. Ellery climbed into the backseat and Reed hesitated a fraction of a second about where to sit before taking shotgun. He sided with Ellery, always, but he wasn't going to have McGreevy chauffeuring them around like they were a pair of recalcitrant children.

McGreevy didn't make any chitchat, his mouth set in a grim line as he drove them out of the city. Reed couldn't see Ellery from his vantage point so he had no idea what she might be thinking or if she had taken McGreevy's veiled threat to heart. Reed and Ellery had lied on their reports last summer about the shooting, and McGreevy knew it. There was a sizable gap between what he knew and what he could prove, though, and Reed was counting on that crevasse to keep them safe. In the end, the right person had wound up dead, and maybe that was McGreevy's whole point. Reed glanced sideways at his boss, who felt the shift and returned his stare briefly. He had to refocus on the road as he left the highway for a curvy, dark exit—a turn so tight it belonged at a carnival. Reed gripped the side of his door and held on.

With low cloud cover and the lights of the city far gone by now, there was almost no illumination to guide their path. Yet McGreevy drove with confidence, as though on native soil. He took them farther from the main roads, the scenery growing sparser with tall bare trees that flashed like white sticks in front of the car's headlights. The black night hid a deepening forest, someplace you could hide a body where it might never be found. The leather creaked beneath Reed as he twisted in his seat, trying to get his bearings. "Just how far off did you put this man?"

"We're almost there," McGreevy replied neutrally.

Sure enough, the trees parted and it was like coming out of a tunnel. Houses sat in the shadows, far off from the road, with lots of space between. They passed a café and a gas station, both shuttered for the night. McGreevy took another abrupt turn that led them back closer to civilization. Brick buildings. A small grocery and a bank. Finally, he found the side street he was seeking and stopped the car in front of a nondescript two-story house that had been divided into two apartments. "I'll do the talking," McGreevy said as they got out of the car.

The house showed no signs of life. Wind whipped down the street, waving the branches like scarecrows in a meadow. "What did you tell Earl Stanfield about this?" Ellery asked as they mounted the rickety wooden steps.

"I didn't tell him anything." He pushed the doorbell hard, twice in a row.

Ellery looked at McGreevy with some horror. "So we're just showing up here in the middle of the night to rattle him?"

"You're the one who started this," he replied without looking at her. He pushed the bell and held it.

After a few more seconds, the porch light came on and then Reed heard uneven footsteps coming down the stairs. When the door opened, it revealed a tall, heavyset man with a shock of salt-and-pepper hair and skin the color and texture of a worn-out baseball mitt. His right cheek bore the telltale white birthmark in the shape of a flame. They had found The Blaze.

"Mr. Stanfield?" McGreevy held up his ID, and the man leaned forward, cross-eyed, to stare at it.

"Do you people know what time it is?" he asked as he straightened up.

"Mr. Stanfield, I'm Russell McGreevy. We met about twenty-five years ago, after the fire at the Gallagher Furniture store."

Stanfield blinked slowly with no hint of recognition. "You're sayin' I know you?"

McGreevy barely repressed a sigh. "Yes. I helped set you up here. May we come in?"

"You want to come in?" The man was looking around like he half-expected to find some hidden cameras playing a trick on him. "What for? I'm not in trouble, am I?"

"No, no trouble. We'd just like to talk to you."

"I got a phone for that," he said as he pulled back the door to admit them. "You can even call it during the daytime hours."

"I'm sorry about the hour," McGreevy replied. "This just couldn't wait."

Threadbare carpet covered the stairs, and the narrow passageway was lit by a pair of naked bulbs yoked to the ceiling. At the landing, Stanfield pushed open a creaky wooden door and they all followed him inside. He turned on a floor lamp and flopped into a nearby recliner. A giant television set, one generation before flat-screen, took up about a third of the room. For seating, the others had to choose between a lumpy faux leather sofa and a rocking chair that was missing one spindle from its back. Reed and McGreevy took the sofa while Ellery opted to stand, leaning one shoulder against the doorjamb.

Stanfield rubbed his face with two large hands. "State your business," he said. "I got to be to work at seven."

"My associates here would like to know about the night of the fire," McGreevy said. "They want to know what you saw."

Again, Stanfield looked at them as if they were playing some trick, his brow furrowed and his eyes narrowed. "The fire? That was a long time ago. What're you rousting me out of my bed about it now for?"

"There have been some questions about the fire's origins," McGreevy said.

"That lady lawyer." Stanfield pointed at McGreevy, smiling a little now that he'd caught on. "Yeah, I seen her on the TV, going on about her uncle. She's a cute young thing. Fiery. I like that."

"You talk to her?" McGreevy asked sharply, as though this possibility had just occurred to him.

"Naw. I remember the deal. Don't talk to no one." He shrugged. "What's it matter now, anyway? That guy, her uncle, he's up for parole."

"It matters if he didn't do it," Reed cut in, and McGreevy

turned to glare at him. Reed ignored the censure. "If you have knowledge that could exculpate him, then you need to say so, even now—no matter what kind of deal you made back then."

"I don't know anything about no exculpatin'. I told what I seen and I told the truth. Whatever you people did with it, it's no mind to me."

"What did you see?" Ellery asked, pushing away from the wall.

Stanfield glanced at McGreevy as if asking for permission. McGreevy nodded. "Go ahead. Tell them."

Stanfield took a deep breath and looked at the ceiling. "Been a long time. Real long. I don't like to think too much about that time in my life—not much worth dwellin' on. But yeah. I remember that night. It was April but you know how that goes in Boston—it was still colder than a witch's titties after it got dark, so I liked to stay in this little space across the street from the furniture store. One of the walls was part of a pet shop, see, and so they had to keep the heat on all night for the animals. The vent put out warm air that kept me from freezing my ass off. So that's where I was when the fire started."

"Back up a second," Ellery said. "You were sitting there, across from the furniture store . . . just watching?"

"He was drinking," McGreevy supplied. "A fifth of vodka, I believe it was."

"I just got done telling you how cold it was," Stanfield retorted. "I had to get warm any way I could."

"So you had a view of the front door—not the back." Reed was trying to visualize the moment.

"Yes, sir. Front door. I seen that poor woman and her boy go inside. Seemed like no time at all before the fire started—almost like it was waiting for them." He shook his head in dismay. "I went across the street to see if I could help but the flames were coming out the door. There wasn't nothing I could do."

"Did you see who set the fire?" Reed asked.

"You mean did I see someone with a gas can or flamethrower or what have you? No. I did see that guy, though—that dude who got arrested. He was there."

"Before the fire?"

Stanfield looked confused. "Before? I don't know. There was a lot of people who came around that night once the place started to burn. He was there after, I know that much for sure. Before the fire . . . I don't remember. It was a cold night. Not too many people on the streets, 'cept the ones who had no choice."

Reed glanced at Ellery. She widened her eyes in question because this certainly wasn't the smoking gun story they had expected to hear. Reed had come prepared, however. "I want to show you some pictures," he said. "Tell me if you recognize anyone from that night."

"Sure, okay."

Reed took out his laptop and powered it up to reveal a school photo of Jake Gallagher, taken around the time of the fire. "What about this person? Did you see him?"

Stanfield frowned as he studied the image. "Don't think so. Can't say for sure."

"What about this man?" Reed switched the image to reveal a shot of Luis Carnevale.

"Ha-ha, yeah, man. That's the guy they arrested—Cardinale or something." He grinned and bobbed his head, pleased with himself like a game-show contestant who'd won a prize. "Yeah, he was there. Definitely."

"What about him?" Reed showed an older picture of Patrick Gallagher culled from news footage at the time of the fire.

Stanfield chewed his thumbnail as he looked thoughtfully at the picture. "I know him, sure. He was the owner, right? Saw him lots of times."

"What about the night of the fire?"

Stanfield paused to think about it a moment and then shook his head. "Don't think so. I saw his wife and kid. Not him."

Reed had saved the best for last. He called up a picture of David Gallagher, his current favorite suspect. He used the clearest one: an older driver's license picture that revealed David's close-cropped reddish hair, his green eyes, one set slightly lower than the other, and his dimpled chin. There was an arrogance in the set of his mouth, almost a smirk, that made Reed want to smack him. He handed the laptop over to Stanfield for a good look. "Take your time," he said as the other man hunched over the screen.

"This is the brother," Stanfield said after a moment. "The other guy from the store. I seen him sometimes, but not as much as the first guy and the wife. When this dude showed up, it was often after closing time and he wasn't alone—you know what I'm saying?"

Reed played dumb. "No, what are you saying?"

"He used it like party-town, man. Girls and booze and stuff. Sometimes, he'd leave half an empty in the garbage out back. Maybe half of a pizza. Yeah, I was always happy when he showed up."

"The night of the fire," Reed prompted.

Stanfield shook his head and handed the laptop back to Reed. "Naw, he weren't there. I told you. The place was dark. No party. It was dark right up until the boom. Then you could've lit the whole sky. Sounded like the end of the world."

Reed looked down at his screen, where he clicked over to the smiling image of little Bobby Gallagher, the picture used at his funeral. "For some people," he said, "I guess it was."

Across the room, Ellery scuffed her boot on the floor. He could feel her frustration, and Stanfield apparently sensed it, too. "Is this what you wanted?" he asked, anxious to please. "Did I help?"

McGreevy's smile was genuine for the first time as he stood up to shake Stanfield's hand. "You helped a lot. Our apologies again for the interruption. I assure you we won't be bothering you anymore."

Back in the town car, they drove in silence for several miles before Ellery leaned forward from the rear. "I don't understand," she said to McGreevy. "That man witnessed nothing of consequence."

"Precisely what I have been trying to tell you."

"So then why hustle him out of town?"

McGreevy seemed to choose his words carefully. "Stanfield was a rambling drunk at the time, a hustler, eager for any kind of handout he could get. His timelines might easily get confused, or be purposely confused by someone with an agenda."

"Someone like the defense lawyer, you mean," Ellery said.

"We made sure he got a hand up, not a handout," McGreevy replied. "The case went forward without incident. It was win-win for everyone involved."

Ellery disappeared into the backseat again, seemingly deflated, and Reed turned his face toward the window. He saw only a hint of his reflection in the blue light from the dash. McGreevy was so satisfied, so sure they had grabbed the right man in Luis Carnevale all those years ago, and nothing Reed or Ellery had turned up called that conclusion into certain doubt. Stanfield was living proof of the uselessness of eyewitness testimony. He'd been staring right at the store and seen nothing that clarified the case. Or maybe there was nothing to clarify, and McGreevy and the task force had been right all along: Luis Carnevale set the fire.

Reed still felt unsettled when he recalled the picture of Bobby Gallagher, as though there was something left to learn from the picture of a grinning two-year-old little boy, with his miniature denim suspenders and ruddy-cheeked face. Perhaps it was just the sense of a life cut way too short, a purpose unfulfilled, and the understanding that no matter whom they arrested for his murder, it could never bring relief. A child's death would always feel unsolved.

Back in front of Ellery's building, McGreevy didn't even bother to get out of the car. "I'm going to catch the next available plane to Tampa," he said, with a meaningful look at Reed. "If you're smart, you'll go with me."

Ellery got out of the car without a word. Reed watched her go, feeling pained. He couldn't just leave without talking to her. "You go," he said to McGreevy. "I'll catch up."

McGreevy put the car back into gear, his mouth curved

in a wry smile. "Maybe. Right now, all you're doing is falling farther behind. There's no future to be had here, Markham. The sooner you realize that, the sooner you can get on with the rest of your life."

Reed got out, and McGreevy sped away from the curb, sending up an arc of salt and slush that caught Reed across the knees. He looked down at the mess with a shiver. There was no way he could ask to borrow Ellery's washing machine again. He went to the front door of her building, where he found her waiting to let him inside. She did so in silence and they rode up in the elevator the same way, with no hint of conversation. Once inside the apartment, she hung up her jacket gingerly, as though raising her arms gave her pain, and he remembered anew that she was injured.

"Look," he said, and she stiffened, her back to him, as though she'd been dreading this very moment. "About what happened earlier . . ."

"Don't mention it," she said swiftly, moving away from him without even turning around.

He followed after her, gaining ground so that she couldn't put a door between them before he'd had his say. "I didn't mean for that to happen. That is, I didn't think you wanted . . ."

"I don't." She turned around in the hallway but didn't meet his eyes. "I mean, forget it. It doesn't matter what I want."

He searched her. "It does to me."

He waited but she did not say anything further, just hunched in on herself and looked at the floor. He wanted to gather her into his arms and hold her until she relaxed, but he knew such action would probably have the opposite effect.

"I'm sorry," he said, "for taking advantage."

Her head snapped up. "Don't apologize. That's worse. You're . . . you have nothing to worry about, okay? You don't have to be sorry. It won't happen again."

"It won't?" He reached a hand toward her but then drew it back.

Pain swam in her eyes but she held his gaze steady. "No," she said hoarsely. "It won't." Then she turned on her heel and disappeared into the bedroom, closing the door with a firm click.

Reed stood there rooted to the floor for a long time, until Bump ambled over and sat down next to him. He leaned on Reed's leg as if to commiserate how hard it was to be on the wrong side of the door. Reed leaned down and patted him with a sigh. "She has to come back out eventually," he told the hound, who followed him back out to the living room.

Reed stretched out on the sofa, which was becoming like a second home to him. He had already memorized the shape of the serpentine crack on her ceiling. He should try to get some sleep but the events of the day buzzed like fireflies in his head, lighting up and disappearing again before he could get a close look. He did what he usually did when he needed to feel better, to feel calm: he took out his phone and called up pictures of Tula. Her smiling face always made him smile in return. There she was last Halloween, dressed as a butterfly princess, complete with antennae and a crown. Here she was wearing one of his aprons as they made pecan pie together, flour on her nose. Her nose was his nose, and he touched it now, feeling its familiar shape in the dark. He remembered the day she'd been born and how primal it had felt to hold her, his own flesh and blood. His own mother had been murdered but his father had apparently walked away before that. Reed couldn't fathom it then, holding tiny Tula, watching her delicate fingers curve around his thumb. How could anyone leave behind their own child?

He swiped through a few more pictures. Tula really was a delightful mix of both her parents. She had Sarit's long lashes. His almond eyes. Reed's reverie over his darling daughter popped like a soap bubble. In its place, he saw Bobby Gallagher's picture again.

A hot prickle broke out over Reed's skin, and he sat up on the sofa. As if propelled from the great beyond, he pulled out his laptop and powered it up so he could see Bobby's photo again. It looked just as he'd remembered. Young Bobby, with his mother's heart-shaped face and the fresh good looks of a wee Irish lad. Reed frowned and leaned forward to see the screen up close. He called up pictures of Myra and Patrick, and compared them to Bobby. Then he called up one of David Gallagher. Yes, there it was: green eyes, dimpled chin. Patrick had neither of these.

He heard Jake Gallagher's words echo back to him: *My dad accused my mom of running around on him . . . So I followed her . . . Who the hell has an affair in the middle of a furniture store?*

Reed sat back, gobsmacked at the revelation. After blinking in the semi-darkness for a moment, he took the laptop and went to Ellery's bedroom door. He knocked twice before she deigned to answer. "I don't want to talk about it," she said shortly, parting the door just a crack.

He shoved the laptop screen up to the narrow space so she could see the terrible truth that he had just discerned. "Bobby Gallagher wasn't Patrick's son. He was David's. Myra had been having an affair."

# 15

Maybe it was her lingering head injury or the lack of sleep, but Ellery felt fuzzy on the logic of why they were parked in front of Dave's Pizza just ahead of the oncoming lunch rush. "You're absolutely sure that Bobby Gallagher was David's son?" she asked Reed again.

Reed sat behind the wheel of her rented SUV because she was still in no shape for navigating, and truthfully, he was now the one driving this latest twist in their sub rosa investigation. His hands skimmed the wheel in a nervous fashion that did not reassure her. "Well, nothing would be certain without a DNA test, but the odds are strong given the pattern of inheritance for a cleft chin. Add in that they have the same green eyes . . ."

"Wonder if the family noticed."

Reed squinted at the pizza parlor in thoughtful fashion. "People see what they want to see. I can't tell you how many times I used to look at my parents and try to see a biological connection. I once convinced myself that Suzanne and I had the exact same shaped hands." He held them out for his own inspection. "In my case, though, I knew the truth."

"Maybe David knew the truth, too—is that what you're thinking? That he set the fire to get rid of Myra and his son?"

"I don't know what to think at this stage. But so far, we've found only one member of the family who routinely hung about the furniture store after hours, and that's David. I'm curious as to what he has to say."

Ellery took a deep breath to prepare herself for the exit, urging her sore body into motion. "Let's do it."

Inside, they got hit with a rush of warm, fragrant air infused with the scent of rising dough, oregano, and spicy tomato sauce. The restaurant had a single line of red plastic booths along the wall and about a dozen small tables and chairs to fill out the rest of the space. Behind the counter, an industrial oven roared out heat like a dragon, and white-aproned employees moved in concert, dodging one another as they hurried to get the food ready for arriving customers. The queue was already halfway out the door, as a group of nearby construction workers arrived en masse, hungry for pizza. "What'll you have?" a harried woman in a red bandana yelled at them across the counter.

"We'd like to speak to David Gallagher," Reed replied, his voice also raised above the din of surrounding conversation.

It took the woman a second to parse that his words were not a food order. "Dave's busy making pies," she said.

Reed held up his FBI identification. "Tell him we'll take two slices of cheese. To go."

The woman's eyes went round like pizza pies, and she clearly wanted to hand them off as soon as possible because her voice became authoritative and urgent. "Dave! You've got customers come to see you!"

A voice from beyond hollered back. "Can it wait?"

The woman looked Reed up and down. "Don't think it can!"

A moment later, David Gallagher appeared behind the counter, dusting flour off his hands, his cheeks pink from the heat. He had shaved his thick auburn curls close to the scalp, but the green eyes and dimpled chin said they had found the right man. "Can I help you?" he asked, his gaze fixed not on Reed or Ellery but on the restless line of customers behind them.

Reed once again held up his ID. "We'd like a couple slices and a bit of your time," he said, and David's frustration hardened into glum resignation.

"Sure," he said. "On the house. Nina, can you bring over a couple of cheese slices and a pair of Cokes for our guests? Thanks." He took off the apron and came around the counter, indicating the nearest empty booth with a sweep of his hand. "Please, sit."

Reed slid in first, and Ellery joined him. David Gallagher took the opposite side, his head bowed. He seemed to be gathering his inner resources, as if reaching down inside for a different version of himself to present to the law. When he looked up, he gave them a determined smile. "It's not every day I have the pleasure of serving the FBI," he said. "What brings you to my humble establishment?"

Ellery saw it then, the way he could turn on the twinkle in his eye, how he deliberately shifted his body posture to be open and welcoming. Women could end up in bed with such a guy and not know his true self until it was over. She thought of his ex-wife and the dropped assault charges and wondered how long it had taken the woman to see the light.

"We're interested in the fire that occurred at your furniture store," Reed said, and Ellery watched closely for David's reaction. Surprise was really their only weapon here.

David seemed less shocked than she'd anticipated, given the fact that the crime was more than two decades old. He leaned back casually in the booth, his expression inscrutable. "Oh, yeah? Is that because the guy's getting out . . . Carnevale? You think he might pull something else?"

It was Ellery's turn to be surprised. "Carnevale's getting out?"

David's brow wrinkled, as though he was starting to doubt their authenticity. "Yeah, he made parole. It was on the news this morning. That's not why you're here?"

"I don't watch the news," Ellery replied. A woman appeared at their table to drop off the pizza slices and the cans of Coke. Ellery's stomach gave an eager rumble at the enticing scent of melted cheese, but she forced herself to push it aside for now. "Carnevale's lawyer believed he didn't set the fire," she said to David.

He snorted with amusement. "Lawyers will say anything you want if you pay them enough."

"Are you speaking from experience there?" Reed wanted to know.

David said nothing for a moment, looking from one to the other, assessing them. "If you're feds, then you know my record: it's clean."

"Your ex-wife, Heather, might disagree," Reed said.

David waved them off, his hand still coated with flour. "Water under the bridge. She got remarried. We're good now."

"The night of the fire, you said you were home in bed with Heather," Ellery said.

"I said it because that's where I was."

"I looked up your divorce records," Reed told him. "They suggest that you weren't always in your bed when you were supposed to be. Heather filed on the grounds of marital infidelity."

Anger flashed across David's face, but he reined it in quick. "Like I said: it's old news. Was I the greatest husband in the world? No. Did she walk away with close to a hundred grand of my money after just three years of marriage? Yeah, she did. So let's say I paid for my sins, okay?" He frowned at them. "I don't see how this is any business to the FBI in any case."

"At the FBI, we have the luxury of deciding for ourselves what is and isn't our business," Reed told him.

"Suit yourself. I just thought you'd have more important things to do than sit around here asking me whether I screwed around on my wife twenty years ago."

"We're more interested in whether you screwed around on her twenty-nine years ago," Reed replied.

"Twenty-nine years ago we weren't even married."

"Yes, but Myra was," Reed said. "To your brother, Patrick."

At this, David froze, just for a fraction of a second. He didn't have a canned, ready response, and the shock of these names, after all these years, showed on his face. "Patrick and me, we don't talk anymore. After the fire, he went his way and I went mine."

"You fought over the store," Ellery said. "You wanted out, even before the fire."

"We inherited the place from our father. It was always his

dream, not mine. Patrick loved working in the shop, carving out some new fancy table leg or whatever the hell inspired him on that particular day. To me, a chair's something you sit on, not a piece of art. He wanted me to work the business end so he could be hammering and sawing all day. No, thanks. That wasn't how I wanted to spend my days."

"The store was in financial trouble before the fire," Reed said. "You both could have lost everything."

David's gaze turned fierce again. "Patrick did lose everything. He lost his son! Don't think for a second we looked on that fire as any kind of blessing."

Ellery wanted to look at Reed, to check his reaction to David calling Bobby Patrick's son, but she dared not give away their suspicions just yet. "It wasn't a blessing for him," she allowed, "but you got what you wanted."

David shook his head vehemently. "Not like that. I never wanted a fire. Bobby died, for Christ's sake. He was barely two years old. What kind of monster would have ever wished for that?"

"Maybe the person who set the fire didn't realize Myra and Bobby were in there," Reed suggested carefully.

David shrugged and pulled a Coke can toward him, popping the tab. "You'll have to ask Carnevale. I hear he'll be getting out any day now."

"Myra's story has always been interesting to me," Ellery

said. "The part where she took a young boy out late at night to a dark furniture store, supposedly in search of tax documents, seems odd. Couldn't it have waited a few more hours? It doesn't make sense that she'd be so desperate to get her hands on those papers that she'd go out with a two-year-old in the middle of the night. So I'm wondering if maybe she had another reason for being there."

David pulled his T-shirt away from his throat and rolled his neck. "Such as?"

"Maybe she was meeting someone," Ellery said.

"Maybe she was meeting you," Reed supplied a moment later.

David flashed a nervous grin but shook his head. "That's nuts. I just told you: I was home with Heather. Call her and ask her if you don't believe me."

"Right now, we're asking you," Reed said pointedly. "You're the one who was known to conduct romantic liaisons out of the furniture store after hours."

"Listen, I'm telling you: I wasn't there that night. I wasn't carrying on with Myra. The two of them were barely talking to me by that point."

"Ah, but earlier," Reed said. "Say around three years before the fire? How were your relations with Myra then?"

"Our relations, as you put it, were just fine. It was only when the business started falling into the crapper that things got tense. Besides, what sort of scenario are you generating here: you think I was trying to bed Myra in the store, and to set the mood, she brought her little kid along? It doesn't make any damn sense."

"Maybe she brought him along to see his father," Reed said.

David's left eye appeared to spasm. His hand clenched around the soda can. "Patrick was home sick," he said shortly. "You know that."

"Patrick doesn't have a cleft chin," Reed replied, and pulled out his cell phone to prove it. He called up the picture of Patrick Gallagher and held it up for David to see. David merely glanced at it.

"What's that got to do with anything?"

"I think the boy was yours."

Finally, they'd struck a blow. David's mouth fell open but only a faint wheezing sound came out. The can warped and bent under the force of his grip, and he started shaking his head, back and forth. "No," he said. "No, that's not possible. No."

They let him sit there denying it to himself. He seemed almost in a trance, as if the idea had taken hold of his brain and zapped away all other thoughts. The more David said no, the more possible it seemed that Reed had guessed correctly. If David hadn't slept with Myra, he would never be so rattled by the very concept.

"Myra told us," Ellery said. "About the affair."

She felt Reed stiffen by her elbow and knew she was taking a chance with this lie. Indeed, it seemed to yank David back to the table with them, as he twitched and focused a shrewd gaze on her. "Myra told you? She said we had an affair?"

He seemed to be measuring her, and so Ellery nodded for emphasis. David appeared to consider Myra's transgression, but then he gave a snap shake of his head. "No, I don't believe you. Myra would never admit to anything like that. Let me tell you about Myra, okay? She grew up one of eight kids, the youngest, always dirt poor and always ashamed of it. Then one day when she's around fourteen, this man shows up at the house, claiming he's her father, asking to see her. The family threw him out, but the damage was already done. Turns out, Myra's mother was actually her older sister, Maureen. The people she knew as her parents were actually her grandparents, and the family had been lying to her all this time. She was born on the wrong side of the sheets. She doesn't like to talk about it now, but it's true. Her whole world with Patrick was built on respectability, on making sure they looked like an upstanding Christian family. It about killed her when Jacob got arrested for setting that fire at school. Never mind getting the kid some help—Myra wondered what the neighbors would think."

Ellery was not going to let him derail the narrative. "You're saying you didn't have an affair with Myra. That there was no chance Bobby was your son."

Reed helpfully called up the photo of Bobby, and this time David did look. He stared long and hard, and finally reached to take the phone in both hands, cradling it gently. "I haven't seen his picture in years," he said, his voice full of emotion. "Man, he was a sweet little guy. Didn't say much but always had the biggest grin on his face . . ."

"You loved him," Reed said softly.

David blinked wet eyes. "Sure. We all did." He shoved the phone back in Reed's direction. "No one in the family ever would have hurt a hair on that boy's head. Not Myra, not me, and not—not his father." He gulped in air in a pained gasp. "You—you should go now. I don't think I can help you anymore."

"There are still unanswered questions from that night," Ellery said.

"Maybe there always will be," David said, bracing his hand on the table. "Maybe that's what we have to live with. It's been twenty-six years. The state says it's over with now— they're letting Carnevale out, they're moving on. Maybe we should all do the same."

They said little on the trip home. Ellery eased forward in her seat to fiddle with the radio until she found the news, and it didn't take long before Luis Carnevale's story came up in the rotation. Bertie Jenkins gave a breathless, excited interview. "We are thrilled that the board has recognized Luis's exemplary record while incarcerated and decided to set him free. Of course, we remain angry that he was ever locked up to begin with—the state fixated on Luis as the arsonist and never even investigated other people with motive to set fire to the Gallagher Furniture store. The twenty-five years he's served are twenty-five too many."

"Are you going to sue the state?" the radio interviewer asked.

"Now is not the time to discuss that," Bertie replied. "Now is the time to rejoice in Luis's freedom."

The piece closed with a comment that Luis would be released within the next few days to a group home of some kind, where he would continue to be monitored on parole. The Gallagher family declined to comment on his release. Reed switched off the radio but kept his eyes on the road. "Maybe Luis was the answer all along," he said. "Like Powell said, they locked him up and the fires stopped."

"Maybe." Ellery had turned her gaze to the window, watching the dark, bare-boned trees lined up along the stretch of highway. "Do you think Bertie will sue on Carnevale's behalf?"

"She wouldn't get very far if she did. You'd have to prove both that Luis Carnevale definitively did not set the

Gallagher store fire and that the state knew this fact at the time it arrested him and convicted him of the crime. I don't see that happening."

Ellery turned back to look at him. "If we told her about The Blaze . . ."

Reed tightened his hands on the wheel. Ellery understood that selling out The Blaze meant possibly taking down McGreevy with him. "I've thought about that," Reed said after a beat. "But what would he say—that he saw nothing that night? He's not the crucial witness Luis Carnevale made him out to be. He saw Myra and her son and no one else, no one except Luis after the fact."

"So that's it, then. Everyone just walks away."

"At this point, I'm not sure there's another choice."

Ellery looked away again, back out at the gray sky and passing scenery. She put her hand flat against the cold window and regarded its shape, how it mimicked the branches of the trees. From this angle she couldn't see the scars, but she felt them always, or rather, she felt the absence of feeling, as her dead, wizened skin refused to transmit the sensory input from the cool, smooth glass. She and Bobby Gallagher would be about the same age, if he had lived. Maybe he would have inherited the family store and shared Patrick's love of wood carving. Maybe he would have followed David into the restaurant business. Wherever he might have gone, there was a path out there somewhere in the world that was missing him. Ellery stroked the glass and felt his absence, the place he might have been.

Back at her apartment, Ellery escaped to her bedroom while Reed booted up his laptop to look for a flight home. She lay down gingerly, her bruises smarting even at the gentle contact of the pillows. Speed Bump jumped onto the bed and she winced at his enthusiastic snuggling. "Easy," she told him. "I'm walking wounded."

She scratched him behind his long ears, enjoying the quiet, until it was broken by Reed's voice on the telephone a few moments later. She couldn't make out what he was saying but didn't have the energy to eavesdrop anymore. He would be leaving soon, going back where he belonged, and they might never see each other again. He could get promoted all the way up to Lord President of the FBI and go on normal dates with normal women. She told herself she didn't care.

She picked up her own laptop, and the screen that flickered to life showed what she had been working on when she'd last logged off: all the possible names of the serial rapist. The next one on her list was Richard Hopkins, a thirty-year-old with a rap sheet nearly thirty pages long. He'd been in and out of the system starting with possession with intent to sell at age fourteen, and by the time he'd hit adulthood, he'd graduated to more serious felonies like assault (with a knife), attempted murder (again with a knife), and two counts of forcible rape. Despite all this, his longest stint inside totaled just three years. His victims, though, they all got life. Ellery could only imagine what Wendy's reaction might be if they finally arrested the guy and he did just a couple of years for his crimes.

Reed came to hover in her doorway. She saw him in her peripheral vision but waited until he cleared his throat to actually look in his direction. "Booked a flight?" she asked, her voice high and tight.

"Er, not yet. I was on the phone with Heather Soto, David Gallagher's ex-wife. For what it's worth she says his 'no hard feelings' story is complete bullshit, but she does still back up his alibi for the night of the fire. She says he was home in bed with her. He may actually be telling the truth."

"Right," she said, returning her gaze to the screen. "I guess that settles it then."

"Right. Settled." He didn't move from her doorway, but neither did he say anything else. She scanned a few dozen more faces and did not look at him. After a while, she heard him take a breath. "Okay, then. I guess I'll go book that flight . . . unless there's anything else you need from me."

She regarded him with a neutral gaze. "What else could I possibly need?"

Her curt words had the desired effect. His face fell and then he nodded to himself. "I'll make that reservation and get out of your hair."

He disappeared and Bump rolled his head backward to look up at her with huge brown eyes. "Stop it," she told him automatically. "He doesn't actually live here, you know."

She returned to her search, trying to get a line on Richard Hopkins. His latest parole had come just a year ago, but she found no current address for him. Information was easier to access when she had the power of a badge behind her. She couldn't simply phone up the parole board and ask for Hopkins's supervising officer. Outside in her living room, she heard Reed shuffling some papers and she regarded the empty space where he'd recently been standing. Maybe there was one last thing he could do for her.

Reed's footsteps started heading for the door, and Ellery scrambled off the bed as fast as her sore body could carry her. "Wait," she called out as she rounded the corner from the hallway. Reed stood with his hand on the doorknob, but he looked toward her, expectant. She swallowed. "Um, do you feel like getting a cup of coffee?"

He narrowed his eyes at her, appropriately suspicious. "You don't like coffee."

"Yes, but you do. What do you say? I'm buying."

"Uh-huh," he said, clearly not buying it. But at least

he'd moved away from the door. "And what else will be happening while we drink this coffee? You're not planning on surveilling another rapist, are you?"

"Of course not," she replied, and Reed visibly relaxed.

"Good."

"I have to find him first."

Reed looked to the heavens in beseeching fashion. "Ellery . . ."

"If you could call the parole board and get the address, I'll do the rest."

He glared at her. "Rest, yes. That's what you're supposed to be doing. You're still walking around with a goose egg on your head from your last encounter—an incident that ended with a dead man and the confiscation of your gun, if I'm remembering correctly. Hell, Detective Rhodes is probably sitting out there in her car, waiting for your next illegal maneuver so she can finally take you downtown!"

"Good! I hope she is watching. She can see what it looks like to work an actual case." Ellery went to the kitchen to get a glass of water, but she felt Reed following her. He continued to press his case as she stood at the sink.

"This isn't your case," he argued. "It isn't mine, either."

"Fine," Ellery said without turning around. "Go home then. I'll find another way."

He didn't leave. He stood there watching her until she

set down her empty glass and slowly turned to face him. His dark eyes looked her over probingly, and she had to force herself not to squirm under the intensity of his gaze. "Ellery," he said finally, "you won't ever stop them all."

She stuck out her chin. "One name. That's all I'm asking for."

Reed let out a thin sigh and shook his head, but then he checked his watch. "How many names are left on your list?"

She exhaled in a rush. She'd been holding her breath, holding in hope. "Four."

He waved his fingers at her. "Hand them over, and I'll see what I can do."

Reed worked the phones and fifteen minutes later, he was on the line with Darrin McKinney, parole officer for Richard Hopkins. Reed put him on speaker as he introduced himself and explained that he was interested in speaking to Hopkins.

"He's got up to something and I don't know about it?" McKinney asked. Ellery heard the sound of swift keyboard typing on McKinney's end.

"I don't know that he's done anything at all," Reed replied. "I'd just like to talk to him."

"Talk about what? Hopkins has been keeping his nose clean eight months now, as far as we know. Did a check-in with him myself just two weeks ago."

Ellery looked at Reed, who hesitated for a long moment. "It's about a rape."

Silence stretched on the other end. Then they heard leather creaking, as if McKinney had leaned back in his chair. "Hopkins is at 1244 West Selden Street," he said grimly. "I'll meet you there."

Darrin McKinney beat them to the redbrick apartment building, where he stood outside smoking next to a dirty snow pile. To Ellery, he looked more like a fisherman from the docks, with his weather-worn face, thick flannel shirt, and rubber-soled boots. He dropped his cigarette butt into the slush as they approached. "I didn't call to say we're coming," he told them as he nodded at the squat, rectangular building. "But he's bound to be home. He always is, these days."

The front door wasn't locked, and so the three of them easily entered the nondescript lobby with its wall of metal mailboxes and gray linoleum floor. They added their own muddy footprints to the scrum as McKinney punched the elevator button with his thumb. "Hopkins is in 412," he said.

"You're authorized to search the premises, isn't that right?" Reed asked as they entered the elevator car. It gave a heavy groan and then lurched into motion.

"Sure, yeah. Anything in particular I'm looking for?"

"Women's underwear. Jewelry. Driver's licenses."

McKinney gave a curt nod and hit the fourth-floor button again, harder this time, but the elevator continued its glacial ascent. Finally, the doors slid open to reveal a long, bare hallway with white walls and industrial-grade red carpet. "This way." McKinney led them to the left, muttering as he walked. "He was supposed to be low risk."

Ellery couldn't hide her surprise. "He raped a woman in his car at knifepoint and abandoned her alone in the woods in the middle of winter, barefoot and half naked. He's lucky he didn't end up with a murder charge."

"Yeah, but that was before." McKinney rapped on the door marked 412. "Hopkins? McKinney here, open up."

Ellery heard someone moving around on the other side, and she tried to prepare herself for Richard Hopkins's appearance. She'd seen a bunch of these guys now, men who might pass as ordinary on the street but they appeared permanently defiled in her eyes. You couldn't read about a man raping a fourteen-year-old girl until she'd bled from her rectum and ever hope to see him as normal after that. All of these monsters could be the guy they were looking for, but only one of them actually was. The problem was, she couldn't trust her gut to know him when she saw him. Her gut reviled them all.

Finally, she heard a chain come loose from the inside of the door, and it pulled back slowly. At first, there seemed to be no one there, and Ellery blinked to clear her vision. A man in a wheelchair rolled into sight. He had scraggly brown hair and two missing teeth. "Officer McKinney, you're back so soon. And you brought friends with you."

"They're from the FBI, Ritchie, and they have some questions for you. You don't mind if we come in for a minute, do you?" McKinney had already pushed his way inside, but Reed and Ellery hung back in the hallway.

She looked at Reed and shook her head slightly. Hopkins wasn't climbing in anybody's window.

"What happened to put you in the chair?" Reed asked from his spot in the hall.

Both McKinney and Hopkins turned to look at him. "Black ice," Hopkins replied, his gaze almost defiant. "I'd been out eight days last January, and I take the usual exit off the Pike when bam—" He slammed one fist into his other palm. "All of a sudden I'm upside down at the side of the road, crushed like a tin can."

Reed looked to Hopkins. "I don't think we'll need to ask any more questions. Thank you very much for your time."

"What? That's it?" McKinney stepped out into the hall, his arms spread in aggravation. "I came all the way down here."

"Sorry. He's not our guy." Reed turned and Ellery fell into step beside him.

"We still have three names."

"I have a plane to catch."

Behind them, Hopkins's voice echoed down the hallway. "You wanna watch yourself out there. I never saw it coming."

\* \* \*

Ellery had a mug shot for their next target, Aaron Butler, a white guy who had served an eight-year sentence for forcibly raping both his teenage cousin and her friend. He'd been seventeen at the time but was tried as an adult, which put him at thirty-five years old now, or squarely in the rapist's demographics. His crime had an extra element of cruelty to it that made him a good match to Reed's profile. Butler had tied one girl to a tree in the nearby woods while assaulting the other right in front of her. His weapon of choice was a knife. Ellery had already performed the usual checks available to her and come up empty. Butler had been released on parole ten years ago and was no longer in the system. Reed used the FBI resources to find an address for him over near the Roxbury Crossing T stop. The Orange Line connected easily to the Red Line, the rapist's preferred hunting zone.

Ellery circled until she found a place to idle, next to a hydrant that had been dug out of the snowbanks. Across the street, Butler's building had bars on the first-floor windows and crumbling brick at the top. No pretty flags or Christmas lights here. The only decorations were the strings of power lines tacked along the outside of the building.

"We don't have cause to search his apartment," Reed reminded her as they sat there with the roaring of the heater.

"I know it." The dashboard clock read past three P.M., and

Reed's flight loomed large over the approaching evening.

"So then what's your plan?"

She didn't have a plan. She just wanted to lay eyes on the guy. As Richard Hopkins had proved, sometimes that was enough. "I think," she began, and then stopped when the apartment building door opened to reveal a large hulking white man wearing a dark coat and Patriots beanie hat. "I think that's him."

From the quick, athletic strides he took down the street, Aaron Butler didn't have any trouble moving his legs. "Park the car," Ellery said, opening the door. "I want to see where he goes."

She slammed the car door on Reed's protest and half-jogged down the road in pursuit of the disappearing Butler. The sidewalks hadn't been cleared in all spots, forcing her to zigzag in and out of the street, around the thigh-high snowbanks until they reached the cleaner, wider main road. Butler had his cell phone out, checking it every few feet. He had not even glanced backward in her direction. She followed him another block, until the sharp-angled concrete facade of the Roxbury Crossing T station came into view. She heard rapid footfalls behind her and turned to find Reed had ditched their car and caught up. "He's on the move," she said, pointing to where Butler was opening the door to the station.

Reed patted his trousers. "I don't have the fare on me."

She tugged his arm and dragged him into the street. "We can both use my pass. Come on, hurry."

Both using her pass meant sliding them through as one unit, Reed pressed so close that she felt his breath at her ear. "This is illegal," he informed her as they squeezed through the turnstile.

Ellery couldn't be bothered to answer as the train lumbered into the station. "There he is."

They entered the same car as Butler but used different doors, observing him from the opposite end. Ellery found herself missing the days when everyone left stray newspapers on the subway. They would have provided a convenient cover. Butler didn't seem to notice them, though. He stood holding on to the pole even though there were seats available. He'd stuffed his hat in one pocket and put in a pair of earbuds, and his attention remained glued to his phone.

The subway car stopped abruptly, sending all the passengers lurching forward. Butler grabbed the pole higher, steadying his balance, and the move revealed a black leather bracelet ringed with large shiny metal studs. "Did you see that?" she asked, not taking her eyes off Butler. "It's on his right hand."

Reed's answer was low and tight. "I saw it."

"This could be him."

"We don't know that yet," Reed said, but he sounded like he was trying to convince himself, not her.

When they reached Downtown Crossing, Butler bounced

out of the car and onto the crowded platform, forcing Ellery and Reed to fight the tide of people pushing onto the train. "This is where you change for the Red Line," Ellery said, craning her head to try to catch sight of Butler amid the crush of commuters. She spotted him heading for the street exit, not the Red Line. "There he goes."

They followed Butler into the shopping district and drew up short when he stopped at a small bakery with a cupcake sign out front. SPRINKLES, it read. "Maybe he's hungry," Ellery murmured as they slowed their approach.

"Smells delicious," Reed replied, sniffing the vanilla-scented air.

Ellery peeked around the edge to peer in the glass storefront. She saw Butler behind the counter, putting on an apron as he grinned and gestured at one of the other workers. "He's working here." Ellery turned in a whirl and bumped into Reed. "He works in a bakery. Do you know what this means?"

"Yes. He might very well taste sweet. Ellery, wait—!"

"I promised you a coffee." He reached for her but Ellery had already pushed open the heavy glass door to the shop. Ellery entered the store with purpose, but then halted at the threshold like she was entering a crime scene. She scanned the bakery from left to right, taking in the buttercream walls, the display counter that spotlighted a colorful array of cakes and treats of all sizes, and the crowd of chatting customers lined up at the counter and bumping knees at the handful of two-person tables. "You wait for seats," she said to Reed, who had materialized right behind her. "I'll order."

She got in line without bothering to ask him what he wanted. Instead, she bobbed and weaved behind the row of people so she could get a better look at the people working at the counter. There were at least two men back there, but they all wore black baseball caps emblazoned with the company logo and she couldn't see their faces. Ellery waited impatiently, shifting from foot to foot, until she got to the front of the line. "What can I get for you?" A perky blonde with big eyes and a ponytail coming out of the back of her baseball cap greeted Ellery with a wide, white smile.

Ellery looked beyond her to the people filling the orders. The guy she wanted to see was busy at the coffee machine, his back to her. "I, uh . . ." She put her hands on the counter and stood on her tiptoes for a better look.

The blonde took a step back at Ellery's aggressive behavior. "The lemon custard cake is on sale," she said hopefully, gesturing at the display. "It's totally yummy."

"Him," Ellery said, pointing at the large man. "What does he recommend?"

The girl gave her a puzzled look but dutifully turned

to her colleague and called out, "Aaron! This lady wants a recommendation from you!"

He emerged from out of the shadows and Ellery's stomach turned over as she got her first up-close look at Butler. *Big, like a linebacker,* Wendy had said, and this man definitely fit the type. Butler stood over six feet tall and his hands were the size of oven mitts. He had broad, muscular shoulders and biceps that strained his gray T-shirt. His eyes met Ellery's and she saw him freeze under the intensity of her gaze, his expression instantly hostile. She didn't back down; she held his stare openly. He looked her over, very slowly, and then dismissed her as no concern, his posture relaxing, his jaw going slack. "Yeah, can I help you?"

"I think—I think you already have." She ordered two cupcakes, one vanilla, one chocolate, and a pair of coffees—whatever would get her out of the line and back to Reed as quickly as possible. She had no appetite. Adrenaline had zapped every instinct but the need to get him.

She set the food and coffees on the petite table and took her seat, meanwhile keeping her watchful gaze on Butler's every move. She tracked him around the shop as he brought out coffee or pastries for people and bused the tables clear of dirty dishes. He showed lithe, economical movement as he worked in and out of the cramped spaces. Ellery was so caught up in following him that she had momentarily forgotten Reed was with her.

\* \* \*

Reed had also sized up Butler and clearly had come to the same conclusion: this could be the guy. His whole body went on alert, vibrating energy like a tuning fork. He kept his gaze averted from Butler, but Ellery refused to give Butler an inch. She didn't care if he noticed that she was staring. Back behind the counter, Butler reached into the case and withdrew a pair of fluffy, frosted cupcakes. He looked like he belonged at a tea party, and he didn't appear cognizant of their keen interest in him.

"This doesn't actually prove anything yet, you know," Reed cautioned her, but his voice was tight.

"I know. But I was thinking." She swallowed because she knew he would hate the plan, that he would try to change her mind.

"What?" Reed stole a glance at Butler, too. Maybe she had a shot at this after all.

"Wendy said she thinks that she would recognize his voice. We could bring her down here, let her hear Butler say a few words. If she IDs him, then we finally have something we can take to Manganelli. We'd have proof."

Reed absorbed her proposal with a slight frown, but he didn't immediately nix it. She could see his mind whirling as he considered all the possible problems. "It wouldn't be legal proof," he said after a minute. "This wouldn't stand up in court."

"It wouldn't have to. Manganelli could investigate and get the real proof, evidence that would put him away for good. This guy took trophies, Reed." She kept her voice down but her tone was urgent. "You know as well as I do they're probably sitting in his bedroom right now. All it would take is a warrant to bust him, and for that, we just need probable cause. A voice ID from the victim would provide that, easy."

"You're forgetting one detail," Reed said grimly. "If he's the guy, he would recognize her, too. What's he going to do when she walks through that door?"

Ellery thought back on the warm, smiling Wendy in the photograph from before the rape, and compared her mentally to the new pared-down, hardened woman with the shaved head and neck tattoo. "I don't know that he would recognize her," she said finally. "But it's easy enough to put her in a hat and some dark glasses. It's not like he's expecting her." Sure, there was a risk, but a small one, as far as Ellery could see. More important, the payoff could be huge.

Reed leaned back in his chair, pulling away from her and their shared plan. She felt him slipping and she shifted closer, the feet of her chair scraping loudly against the floor. "Listen," she said, practically crawling across the table to him. "Listen to me. This is our chance. This is how we can nail this bastard, right here, right now. I can go get Wendy and be back in an hour. By nighttime, he could be locked up and off the streets and women can go to sleep without worrying he might come through their window with a knife!"

"Shh." He held up his hands and looked around guiltily, as though someone else might have caught wind of what they were saying. She remained stretched across the table, right in his face, prepared to argue further. He relented with a sigh. "Okay," he said softly, and she eased back in her seat. "Okay." He pulled out his cell phone. "I'll just go ahead and cancel my flight—again. You go find Wendy. I'll make sure Butler doesn't take off in the meantime."

She resisted the urge to grab him and kiss his cheek. "Thank you," she said in a rush, already rising from the table. "This will work. I know it will."

In reality, it took Ellery ninety minutes to track down Wendy Mendoza and explain the plan. She'd found the woman living out of a suitcase at a Motel 6, her life growing closer to the edge of oblivion. "How do you know it's him?" Wendy asked when Ellery gave her the news. She hadn't moved from the bed, where she lay with an open bag of chips and a half-full bottle of cheap white wine.

"We don't know. That's why we need you." Ellery couldn't understand why the woman was dragging her feet now. "All you have to do is come to the bakery and tell us if anyone seems familiar. I'll be with you. Agent Markham will be there. You'll be totally safe, I promise you."

Wendy stared blankly at the television while she considered. "All right," she said finally. "Let's do it." She heaved herself off the bed, looking older than her years. "Just let me pull myself together."

Ellery tossed her a blue-and-white-striped beanie hat. "Use this, just to be safe. We don't want him recognizing you."

Ellery waited in the parking lot, chewing her thumbnail and watching for Wendy to come out of her room. Night fell on the city like a blanket, dark and complete, despite the early hour. Ellery had about given up hope when the young woman appeared out of the shadows and climbed into her car.

Wendy disguised herself with a bulky winter coat, the beanie hat, a scarf, and a pair of red-tinted glasses. Her fingers bit into the leather seat but her voice was determined when she said, "I'm ready. Let's go."

They didn't exchange many words on the way back to Sprinkles. Ellery had only told Wendy that they thought her attacker might be in the café; she didn't reveal anything further about which man they suspected or whether he could be a customer or an employee. Wendy's identification, if she could make one, needed to be as clean as possible if Manganelli was to use it to secure a warrant. For her part, Wendy seemed strangely calm, her eyes fixed on the road ahead, as though she were already imagining her way into a better future. Ellery felt her plan coming together as she pulled the car to a stop about half a block from Sprinkles.

"Okay, remember what our goal is here," she said, turning to Wendy. "We just want you to hear the voices inside to see if you recognize anyone. We'll go in and order a coffee. We'll sit with Reed to drink it, and you just keep your ears open for anyone who sounds familiar. If you hear him, point him out to me quietly, and then we can alert Detective Manganelli."

Wendy nodded. "I can't believe this is almost over," she murmured in wonder.

"Let's hope so."

The two women entered the shop, which had dropped off in business since the earlier part of the afternoon. Perhaps a dozen customers remained, chatting and eating their sugary confections. Reed sat among a smattering of empty tables, with a fresh cup of coffee in front of him and an open newspaper in his lap. He looked up immediately at their entrance, his jaw set and his gaze wary. Ellery raised her eyebrows at him in question, and he inclined his head slightly in the direction of the counter. Ellery exhaled when she saw Aaron Butler busily restocking the display case with fresh cupcakes.

Ellery didn't want to taint the identification by rushing Wendy straight up to the suspect. "I'll go order," she said quietly. "You join Reed, okay?"

Wendy seemed more frightened now, moving stiffly across the room to where Reed sat. Ellery ordered yet another coffee that she wouldn't drink, this time from a buxom brunette, and tried not to look at Butler. Would he get suspicious at seeing her again? Maybe she should have put on a hat as well. A lump of tension started expanding in Ellery's stomach, rising like dough. "Those are for here," she told the woman at the counter. With any luck, Butler would be the one to bring them out to the table. Ellery paid the bill and went to rejoin her party.

Reed looked up with some concern. "Wendy's feeling a little anxious," he said softly.

"I don't hear him," Wendy said, sounding panicked. "I don't hear him!"

"Just give it a moment," Ellery replied soothingly. She dragged over another chair and sat by Wendy for support. "We just got here."

"But you know he's here, right? You know it's him?" She looked around wildly, about as subtle as a rhinoceros at ballet class.

Ellery shushed her. "Breathe," she said. "Listen. Let us know what you hear."

Wendy fell silent again, her hands balled up in her lap. Ellery looked at Reed across the table, and his eyes said, *This is not a good idea.*

*Relax,* she told him silently. *We've got this.*

The next few moments unfolded almost as if in slow motion, as if she expanded her consciousness into several simultaneous planes. Peripherally, she saw Aaron Butler approaching with the coffee cups on white china saucers, saw how they looked like doll toys in his large hands. He was coming, getting bigger, taking over her whole perceptual field. Wendy's hand jerked under the table. "Ladies," he said, and that's all it took, that one word like a bullet to the brain. Ellery had just enough time to think *oh my God this is it* before Wendy was in motion on the other side of her, rising from her seat.

Ellery turned around to reassure her and found herself looking down the barrel of a revolver. *GUN.* She had to swallow back the word and all her instinctive training. "Wendy, don't."

"It's him, it's him, it's him . . ." The gun wavered in her hands but she had it pointed right at Butler.

"What the fuck is this?" Butler stood with the hot coffee in his hands, coffee that could be a weapon at this short distance. Behind him, the other customers started murmuring to each other in fear. "Lady, you got a serious problem!"

"He's the one! He raped me!" Wendy's accusation tore out of her in an anguished howl.

"Okay, good. That's good. We'll get him." Ellery eased her

chair back carefully, with no sudden movements. She caught Reed's eyes. His hand went slowly to his own weapon. *No,* she thought, feeling the situation spiraling further out of control. *No, no, no.* "Wendy, please! Put down the gun. Let us handle it now."

"He raped me!" Her dark eyes bore into her perpetrator.

"This bitch is crazy," Butler spat out.

"Shut up," Ellery ordered him sharply, her attention still with Wendy. "You did good," she told the woman. "You got him." She rose cautiously, trying to put herself between Butler and the gun. If she could remove him from Wendy's sight, then Wendy might be able to hear reason again. "Now we can call Detective Manganelli and he'll take him away. I promise."

Wendy stepped sideways to keep the gun on Butler. She shook her head resolutely. "I'm gonna kill him."

The crowd gasped collectively. Butler's teacups rattled in their saucers. Ellery felt more than saw Reed draw out his gun, and she flung out her arm at him. "No!"

Too late. He was on his feet, his gun pointed at Wendy. "Put down your weapon," he ordered her. "No one needs to get hurt."

Wendy shook her head. Tears streamed down her face. "*I got hurt,*" she said mournfully. "I got hurt already so bad, like a knife in my gut, and every day, I bleed and I bleed. Now it's his turn."

"Wendy, please." Ellery's whisper floated over the tense, horrible silence. "Don't do this. You can walk away right now and he can't touch you, not ever again. You will feel better, I promise, but not if you shoot him."

"You did." Wendy looked at her, really looked at her, for the first time since it all started.

Ellery opened and closed her mouth. She had no reply. Wendy's words came back to her—*Can you sleep at night, now that he's dead?*—and she knew then that Wendy meant to kill Butler no matter what they did. She'd meant it all along. "No!" she cried out as she saw Wendy raise the gun again.

Ellery flung herself at the woman just as the first bullet split the air. Wendy kept firing even through the tackle, both of them falling through the air in a hail of gunfire. Bullets shattered the ceiling, raining down dust and shattered glass. People screamed and stampeded for the exit.

They hit the ground with a painful jolt, Ellery landing squarely on top of Wendy. She held her down simply by gravity, her ears buzzing and her heart pounding. She tasted blood in her mouth and wondered if she'd been hit. Wendy started sobbing. In the distance, Ellery heard the sirens begin to wail.

"Ellery," Reed said gruffly, kneeling near them. "Ellery, are you okay?"

She saw he had Wendy's gun. "I—I don't know." She rolled off of the other woman, taking care to keep her securely on the ground. Her legs felt like lead but she didn't have any gaping bullet wounds anywhere. "I think so."

"Come on," Reed said, helping her to her feet. "She's not going anywhere."

On the floor, Wendy covered her face with her hands and curled into a fetal position, still shaking with the force of her anger and tears. Ellery suddenly remembered Butler and she whirled around with a jolt to find him seated in a chair, his hands cuffed behind his back. There wasn't a damn scratch on him.

"You went for her, I went for him," Reed explained.

Ellery hugged herself as a chill went through her. "She wanted to be me," she whispered. "She did this because of me."

"No." Reed's touch on her shoulder was gentle. "She did it because she thought it was the only choice she had."

The shop, half darkened by the exploded lightbulbs, lit up again under the glare of the arriving black-and-whites. "But they'll lock her up for this," Ellery said, desperate and sad. Wendy had just shot up a trendy Boston hotspot with a bunch of rich white clientele. "She'll go to prison."

"I think," Reed said mildly as they looked down at Wendy, "I think it doesn't matter. I think she was already there."

# 16

Christmas Eve day dawned bright and clear, but Ellery felt no warmth or cheer inside. She sat in Sunny Soon's office because the good doctor had been rather forceful in suggesting Ellery make an emergency appointment. Some people, it turned out, still watched the news, and Dr. Sunny had gotten an eyeful on channel five. "You've mostly talked so far about Wendy Mendoza," Dr. Sunny said from her wingback chair. "Why don't we talk about you now?"

"She is me, or at least she wanted to be." Ellery felt like Dr. Sunny hadn't heard a word she'd said. "Maybe Wendy was right. Maybe we're the same. I shot William Willett dead and I'm not sorry for it, either. If the brass made me come here so that I can see the error of my ways, so they can get some sort of mea culpa out of me, then screw them. I may as well leave now because that isn't happening."

"So you wanted Wendy to shoot that man—Butler."

Ellery looked at her sharply. "No, of course not. She's not a cop. She has no training. She could have killed half the people in that place and now they'll probably lock her up for it. I'm just saying I understand why she did it. And if she'd managed to hit him in the process, I wouldn't have cried a whole lot of tears."

"Crying," Dr. Sunny said mildly. "Is that something you do often?"

Ellery folded her arms and met Dr. Sunny's gaze directly. "Not anymore."

Dr. Sunny wore a red cashmere sweater with a white blouse underneath. At her breast sat a Christmas pin, a wreath of some kind, with little studded jewels that gleamed in the sunlight. To Ellery it looked like a snake eating its own tail. "Let me ask you this," Dr. Sunny said after a beat of silence. "Do you want your job back? Do you want to rejoin the police force?"

"I keep coming here, don't I? I'm doing what they asked."

"You come here, yes," Dr. Sunny agreed with an incline of her head. "You answer my questions with questions, or with one-word answers. You attend the group sessions and instead of participating as a real member, you embark on personal investigations into the backgrounds of the other patients."

"Hey, Wendy asked me for help!" Ellery sat forward in her chair, belligerent.

Dr. Sunny's impassive face didn't react. "Did it not occur

to you," she said slowly, "that you could have said no?"

The question took the fire out of her, the protest dying on her lips. She slumped back in the chair and shook her head vaguely, looking past Dr. Sunny rather than right at her. "No one was helping her," she murmured after a moment. She knew even as she said the words how ridiculous they sounded. Sure, Butler was behind bars now, possibly for good after the police had raided his apartment and found the driver's licenses and panties and jewelry taken from his various victims. She recalled Reed's face when he'd read the report. *There were more women than we knew about.* Those women, yes, maybe Ellery had helped them indirectly, and she had helped the faceless ones who would have been next, the victims who were not to be. But Wendy Mendoza? She was locked up in the state psychiatric ward, headed for trial as soon as she was deemed fit. Ellery could not honestly say she'd helped Wendy even one little bit.

She sank lower in the seat. Of course they weren't going to give her the job back. She'd been a fool for thinking it was possible.

"Ellery," Dr. Sunny said softly. "What do you want? What kind of life do you want for yourself?"

Ellery chuffed a humorless laugh. "Does it matter?"

"Of course it matters. Why would you think it doesn't?"

Ellery straightened herself up and held out a hand to

tick off the explanation for Dr. Sunny. "First, I wanted my father to stick around—you know, at least until I was done growing up. That didn't happen. Then, I wanted my brother Daniel not to die. I mean, I prayed to God and everything, but Daniel just got smaller and smaller in the bed until he was gone for good. I should've known better by that time, seeing as how I prayed for my own death in Coben's closet but it never came. No, I was the *lucky one* who got to live. Then later, finally after everything, all I wanted was a nice job in a quiet town where no one knew what had happened to me. We all know how that worked out, don't we?"

She trembled as she finished her speech, exhausted from the burst of emotion. Dr. Sunny's dark eyes searched hers. "You prayed to be dead?" she asked softly.

Ellery cursed herself mentally for letting this detail escape. *Stupid girl,* she told herself, just as she had back in the closet, berating the mistakes that had landed her there. Her mother would be so angry. *Stupid, stupid.* For Dr. Sunny, she shrugged one shoulder. "Doesn't matter now. I survived. I—I wouldn't change that."

Dr. Sunny looked thoughtful. "You've nearly been killed twice in the past few days. First in the alley and then when you jumped in front of Wendy's gun."

"Yeah, but I wasn't killed, was I?" Her chin rose, defiant. She remained The One Who Got Away.

For the first time, Dr. Sunny favored her with something of a frown. "You were lucky. Again. But I can't help but notice a pattern in your words and actions that seems hopelessly fatalistic."

"Everything dies eventually," Ellery replied darkly.

"Yes, but maybe you would like to try living first?" Dr. Sunny sat forward, as energized as Ellery had ever seen her. "I won't sit here and pretend that you've had an easy road. You've been dealt some really harsh blows, the kind most people never experience, me included, so I can't say that I or anyone else has simple answers for you. But you're young, smart, and capable. You do have choices. So I ask you again: Ellery, what do you want?"

The dangerous question made Ellery's heart pick up speed, and a sweat broke out across the back of her neck. But this time, she didn't deflect or deny. She thought of everything she'd already lost and could never have again. She thought of the wide, blue expanse of Lake Michigan, the click–clack sway of the "L" train, and the juicy Chicago hot dogs. She thought of her tranquil little house near the woods, the one she'd bought with her own money, and how she'd had to abandon it last summer as another victim in Coben's unending deathly legacy. She thought of Daniel. She thought of her mom. They spoke on the phone sporadically, but Ellery couldn't remember the last time they'd really talked.

She thought of the nightmares and the daymares and the horrible claustrophobia that came from having a serial killer live inside your head. She could shake and scream and kick the walls but she never got him loose. She woke up sometimes gasping for air because she couldn't breathe from the weight of him on top of her.

Ellery swallowed against the thickening of her throat. She thought of Reed with his kind eyes and his lean, rangy body and the way he treated her like she was normal, even though he knew very well what she was. When he touched her, she felt hungry and eager, heightened instead of diminished, and it scared the hell out of her. She understood now that there were big emotions left out there that she hadn't grappled with, feelings she didn't think were ever meant for her. Reed made them flash up, hot and fast, with a delicious sort of terror.

Now he was gone. Yet another thing she could never have, so it was pointless to ask.

Ellery felt tears burn in her eyes but she refused to let them fall. "I want—" she said, and halted at her tremulous, scratchy voice. She cleared her throat and tried again. "I want peace."

Ellery smelled the smoke before she saw it. She stepped off the T to walk toward home and caught the faint charcoal scent of it mixing with the seaside air. At first she thought perhaps she'd imagined it, but then she turned the corner and saw the gray cloud in the distance, expanding over the city like a slow-moving storm. She jogged to her apartment building and didn't bother to wait for the ancient elevator. She took the stairs two at a time and arrived huffing and puffing in her living room, turning on the TV and sinking onto the sofa to find the news. Bump wriggled up to her, wagging and seeking her attention, but she paid him no mind because of the scene now unfolding on her television set.

The local news had broken into whatever usual programming occupied the afternoon of Christmas Eve. There was a male reporter standing in front of a smoking apartment building in downtown Boston. It looked like a bomb had taken out the top two stories, charred and half-caved in as they were. It was a four-alarm blaze, according to the news crawl across the bottom of the screen. Two people had been taken to the hospital. Ellery turned up the volume. "Carnevale was released only yesterday to this halfway house," the reporter said. "By all accounts, he'd been a model prisoner during his twenty-five years at Walpole."

"No," Ellery murmured, shaking her head. "No."

She could scarcely believe it when the picture changed to show Luis Carnevale being led away by BPD officers. As with his arrest at the Gallagher fire, Carnevale had not fled but rather stood with the crowd to watch the burn. He looked directly into the camera, not smiling for it but not hiding, either. *You knew what I was,* his gaze seemed to say. *You knew, and you let me go.*

The segment cut to reporters assailing Bertie Jenkins as she tried to leave her office. Her face was a rictus of grief. "How do you feel about your uncle now?" Someone shouted at her. "How does it feel to know you freed a murderer?"

Bertie held up her hand, as if warding off the questions like they were physical blows. Ellery cradled the remote control to her chest, her heart aching for this woman she barely knew. She'd learned last summer how silently the devil could fall into step beside you. On the screen, Bertie tried desperately to find the safety of her car, but the crowd kept pushing in, in. "No comment," she said, twirling dizzily under the cameras. The words came out as a plea. "Please— let me through. Let me through!"

Ellery snapped off the television and stared up at the ceiling, Bertie's anguished words ringing in her ears. *Let me through* implied an out, another side, a respite and a freedom. *She'll have to learn soon enough,* Ellery thought. *There is no through.*

Her mother called around nightfall, and Ellery lingered at the window while she spoke to her. "We have some lake flurries happening outside now," her mother said. "Seems we may get a white Christmas after all." Only ashes fell over the city of Boston tonight. Ellery was glad for the dark because it meant she could no longer see the smoke in the sky.

"Did you get the package I sent?" she asked.

"Yes, dear. The sweater is lovely, thank you. I love the peach color. Did you get the presents from me?"

"Yes, I'm saving them for tomorrow." Ellery looked at the unopened cardboard box sitting on the floor near her couch. She knew without looking what it would contain, because each year her mother sent variations on the same three items: wool-lined house slippers, a leather-bound day planner for the upcoming year, and a box of candy. Sometimes she threw in a new toothbrush.

"Open it now," her mother urged. "I'll wait."

"Mom, it's late."

"It's not too late. Open it."

With a sigh, Ellery retrieved a pair of scissors and slit open the box. House slippers, daybook, and candy, as presumed. But this time there was also a cylinder with plastic-capped ends. Ellery picked it up and uncorked one side to peer into the hole. There seemed to be some sort of paper within it, so she reached in to fish it out. It unfurled to reveal a faded Bruce Springsteen poster, with young Bruce and his guitar rocking out in front of an American flag backdrop. It had been vintage already at the time she'd found it in the second-hand store and tacked it over her dresser at home. She had spent hours looking at that poster and listening to his music, thinking he must have understood. Bruce sang while young Ellie had planned her getaway.

Her eyes watered, looking at it again now.

"Did you get it?" her mother asked eagerly.

"I got it. Thanks." She sniffed back the emotion and tried again, clear this time. "Thank you."

"I liked to look at him hanging there in the bedroom, because I know you liked to look at him. I used to think maybe you'd take him with you when you came home again ..." Her mother didn't have to complete the thought because they both knew by now how the story ended. "Anyway, it's better he's with you. It's—it's where he belongs."

"I'll hang him up in a good spot," Ellery promised. She carefully rolled up the poster and hugged it gently to her chest. "It's funny, I didn't realize you even saw him hanging there. I didn't think you understood how much he meant to me."

"Of course I understood," her mother replied. "You were my daughter. I was your mother." She paused. "We were the only two there."

Ellery hung up with her mother, took the dog on a last chilly walk, and finally dozed off to some schmaltzy Christmas Hallmark movie playing on her television. She slept fitfully, her dreams full of fire, until she awoke in the black of night, alone in her dark living room. The TV had turned itself off by timer. The dog lay snoozing on the floor.

Ellery felt the dream receding away from her, like waves returning to the sea, and left behind was a new truth lying at her feet. Her mother's words echoed in her head: *we were the only two there.*

*Of course,* Ellery thought. *The only two.* She had been blind not to have seen it before. Strangely calm, she got up as though propelled by an outside force and went outside into the silent, starry Christmas Eve. The frosty air nipped at her fingers and toes, and refrozen snow crunched under her footsteps. The roar of her car's engine felt overloud on this, a sacred night, but Ellery did not even consider turning back. Bobby Gallagher had waited twenty-six years for someone to name his killer, and she wouldn't delay him an extra second.

In the dark, with no traffic, Boston felt like the small city it really was. All those old neighborhoods, rich and poor, crammed on top of one another inside forty-eight jagged square miles. She reached the Gallaghers' house in less than ten minutes. Her footsteps resounded on the hushed street. Bright twinkling lights in all colors blazed away in the row houses, Christmas trees visible through the windows as the sleeping occupants waited to see if Santa would come down the chimney. Ellery herself used the front door. She pressed the bell hard and repeatedly until Patrick Gallagher appeared, dressed in a flannel robe and slippers, his hair matted on one side and his scowl firmly in place. "What in the hell is going on? Do you know what time it is?"

"I need to speak to Myra."

"The hell you say! It's Christmas. Leave my family alone." He moved as if to shut the door on her, and Ellery blocked him with her body.

"I can talk to her now, or I can come back in a few hours with the police. Your call."

He opened his mouth, possibly to curse her out again, but a soft voice stopped him. "Pat, let her in."

"We don't have to," he said, turning around to his wife. "She's not a cop and we don't have to do anything she says."

"Let her in," Myra repeated, her tone scolding. "It's freezing out there." She rolled back her wheelchair so that he could widen the door to admit Ellery.

Ellery blew on her hands as she entered the cramped hall. It barely held the three of them and Myra's chair. Though the light was dim, Ellery could see the wheel tracks on the wooden floor, worn by two and a half decades of use. "What's so awful important it can't wait until morning?" Patrick asked as he drew the robe more tightly around his body.

"I'd like to speak to Myra about that."

Patrick frowned, the wrinkles deepening on his grizzled

chin. "Whatever you want to say to Myra, you can say to me. We have no secrets."

Myra's blue eyes met Ellery's, and she did not look afraid. "No, dear. You go back to bed and rest. I'll just go make some tea and we can have a chat." She said this as though it were totally normal to have an unexpected visitor drop in at three in the morning on Christmas.

Patrick took some convincing. "I don't like this," he said, glaring at Ellery. "I don't like the way she keeps coming around here, poking her nose in where it don't belong."

"I know you don't, dear." Myra patted his arm in loving fashion. "Don't worry, I'll be fine, and this will be the last time she comes here, I promise you."

Ellery and Patrick exchanged a curious look, both of them apparently surprised by this certain pronouncement from Myra. Eventually, he harrumphed his way back to the bedroom, closing its door with an emphatic slam. Myra wheeled herself into the kitchen, and Ellery followed. "Please, sit," Myra said as she pulled the kettle off the stove and began to fill it with water. Ellery couldn't take her eyes off the woman's discolored, waxy skin. How terrified she must have been when the flames started up around her, and the child was gone.

"Do you like herbal tea?" Myra asked pleasantly. "I find chamomile helps me sleep at night."

"Anything is fine." Ellery still hovered near the door, not

taking the offer of a chair. She'd come here on a mission and she was prepared to fulfill it, but it was harder than she'd imagined, here in this simple kitchen with Myra.

"There," Myra said as she turned the gas on under the kettle. "It'll just be a moment." She turned and regarded Ellery. "I've been expecting you, you know."

Ellery raised her eyebrows. She hadn't known until an hour ago that she was coming, so this news came as a surprise to her. "Oh?"

Myra nodded. "Ever since a couple of days ago, when I saw what happened with you and Wendy. How you tracked down the man who—who hurt her. I knew eventually you'd turn up here." She hesitated, and her voice grew soft. "For me."

At the admission, Ellery groped blindly for a chair, because now she needed it. She lowered herself in, her eyes still trained on Myra. "You set the fire that night."

Myra's left hand started a tremor, and she stilled it with her right. A painful silence passed between them, but eventually, Myra answered with a single, short nod.

Ellery let out a shaky breath. There it was after all these years: the truth. It gave her no pleasure. "The Blaze—he saw you and Bobby at the store," she continued. "He didn't see anyone else before the fire. The prosecution thought he was a useless witness because they were looking for a third party, someone other than you who came into the store that night. But there wasn't anyone, was there? The Blaze got it right all along."

"Yes." The air seemed to leave her body with the word, exhausting her, leaving her limp in the chair.

"But why?"

Myra forced herself upright, her mouth a grim line. "For the money, of course. The store was going under, there was nothing that could be done to save it. We could only save ourselves. Jacob needed a lawyer. David wanted out so badly, and he was getting desperate. He and Patrick fought constantly, when they talked at all. He was angry, he was threatening—" She shut her mouth with a snap, as if to hold back the last, awful part, but Reed had already deduced it.

"He was threatening to reveal your affair," Ellery finished.

Myra clawed at her throat with one gnarled hand. "Yes," she said finally. "He was going to tell Patrick the truth unless I could convince Pat somehow to buy him out of the business. But there was no money for it! David just wouldn't hear reason on the subject."

Ellery bit her lip, wondering how far to push. Myra didn't seem to be holding anything back. Maybe she had just been waiting all these years for someone to come and ask her for the truth. "Did he know that Bobby was his son?"

Myra drew a sharp breath and held it in. She closed her eyes tight and shook her head. "No," she said after a long moment, releasing the breath in a rush. "I didn't want him to know. Patrick and I had patched things up, at least mostly, and he adored Bobby. David didn't ever want kids. What good would come from the truth?"

The teakettle's whistle pierced the room, and Myra rolled over to remove it from the stove. She dutifully doled out two cups of tea and carefully brought them to the table.

"The fire," she said, "was going to solve all our problems at once. The store would be gone, that terrible weight from around our necks. David would take his share and go away once and for all. We would have money to pay Jake's bills, to keep him out of the worst of the trouble and give him a second chance. And that's what happened, you know. That part worked just like I dreamed." She shot Ellery a pleading look.

Ellery shook her head. "Bobby died," she reminded her.

"Don't you think I know that?" Myra's cry exploded with anguish. "Don't you think I live with that every day, every waking hour? Of course I would take it back in an instant if I could. But . . . but . . ." Her chin started to tremble and she paused to gather herself. "An instant was all it took. I was naïve, stupid. I thought all you had to do was scatter some gasoline around the place and set a match. I didn't realize how far in I'd gotten. I didn't realize Bobby was no longer between me and the door. The curtains went up immediately and I couldn't see or hear anything. 'Bobby, Bobby—where are you?' I yelled and the fire seemed to leap into my mouth. It was like he'd vanished literally in a cloud of smoke. I couldn't find him. Later, they told me he got caught up in a backdraft. He'd never had a chance." She shook her head sadly.

"Why the hell did you bring him in there in the first place?"

Myra's mouth twisted into an ironic grimace. "I told the truth about that part. Pat was sick, his head in the toilet. Bobby woke up at night, like he often did, and he would climb out of his bed. Jake was off God knows where. It didn't seem safe leaving the baby at home on his own." She covered her face with both hands. "I should have just left him at home."

Her sorrow seemed to sink down to her very bones, and Ellery felt the stirrings of pity for her. Then she remembered the aftermath. "Luis Carnevale went to prison," she said, her tone hardening again. "You never said a thing."

Myra nodded, accepting the weight of this on her slim shoulders. "I was in the hospital for several months," she said. "Multiple skin grafts. No one liked to talk to me about the fire, and I sure wasn't about to bring it up. I didn't watch television. I didn't do much of anything except lie in bed and think about Bobby. I prayed hard to God to take me then, to let me be with my baby. I didn't deserve to live."

Ellery looked away. She saw the picture of the Virgin Mary that presided over the kitchen table. Twenty-six years Myra had sat here eating her meals under that painting, all the while swallowing back the truth.

"Finally, I realized I had it backward," Myra continued. "I didn't deserve to die. This was my punishment: to outlive my baby. To spend the rest of my days knowing that it was me who caused his death. By the time I even heard Luis Carnevale's name, he was already on trial. We'd had so many fires that year. Everyone said it had to be him." She gave a tiny shrug. "I guess I let myself believe it, too. Turning myself in wouldn't have helped anything. It wouldn't bring Bobby back. Jake, he was so fragile back then, so torn up by his dad and me fighting, by the store having problems—and then the loss of his brother. He needed me. I'd already lost one boy, and that was my fault. I wasn't about to unburden myself only to heap more trouble on my other son. Or on Pat. They had suffered enough for my sins."

Ellery sat back in her chair, the one carved with such care by Patrick Gallagher. She pictured him gently helping his wife to and from the car. He'd had a small life, maybe not a bad one, but was it the one he would have chosen if he knew the truth? "Your version of the story is tragic," she told Myra, "but it's also incredibly self-serving. You say you kept your mouth shut to help your family, but it also kept you out of prison."

Myra's gaze turned dull and distant. "Prison," she said finally. "I'm ready, if that's what you want. Lock me up and throw away the key."

Ellery tried to imagine a DA who would take this case on,

twenty-six years after the fact, and with another man sitting in jail for the crime. The state wouldn't care to admit its guilt, either, and Luis Carnevale would forever be reasonable doubt. "No," she said at length, her voice hard. "I think you've gotten away with it."

Myra looked up sharply. "Gotten away with it? Not in this lifetime." She glanced at the painting of the Virgin Mary, the one Ellery had admired earlier. "There'll be no rest for me in this life," she repeated, her voice hollow. "Nor, I would expect, in any life to come."

Christmas morning at the Markham manse inevitably featured a breakfast big enough for the family and several generations of their ancestors. Reed and his sisters had helped their mother prepare a buffet that included baked shells, seven-cheese ham-and-eggs, crispy bacon, chicken and biscuits, winter fruit compote, roasted vegetables, cranberry-orange tea bread, and six kinds of cookies. Tula and her cousins inhaled their food and went back into the family room to take turns shaking the presents and chasing each other around the tree.

Reed eyed the tower of food on his plate and remarked to his sister Kimmy, "I think Mama may have to let out my pants after this."

She shoved him playfully. "Hush. You're as trim as you ever were. Try birthing three kids and then we'll talk about middle-age spread."

The talk about her kids reminded him of his broken promise. He glanced at their father holding court at one end of the long table. Angus waved his fork in the air to make some dramatic point, and the people around him all laughed. Reed leaned closer to his sister. "Kim, I'm sorry I didn't help you out with your present for Dad."

She reached for her Bloody Mary with one hand and patted him with the other. "Don't worry about it. Lynette made me feel like an ass for even asking you. I think I forget sometimes that you're not blood. I can't imagine our family without you in it, and I certainly didn't want to make you feel singled out or different. I was thoughtless and I'm sorry. I hope you'll forgive me for making you uncomfortable with this whole DNA nonsense."

Touched, Reed reached around and squeezed his sister's shoulders. "No offense taken, I swear. Maybe I should go poking around in my genetic background, huh? Might be good for Tula."

"Uh, about that." It was Kimmy's turn to look down the table at their father.

"What?" Reed asked when he followed her gaze. "Didn't he like your ancestry present?"

"I didn't give it to him. For one thing, Daddy would be incensed if you weren't part of it. He'd probably disinherit me on the spot if he thought I left you out. But also, Mama let slip the other day what his big announcement is." She paused for effect. "Daddy's running for governor."

"Really!"

As if on cue, Angus finished up his dramatic tale with a flourish. "Conscience doesn't prevent sin. It only prevents you from enjoying it! Am I right, or am I right?" His wife and assorted relatives laughed and clapped.

Kimmy smiled and raised her glass in her father's direction. "Somehow I don't think he'd like his DNA floating around on the internet right now. What if it turns out he has some predisposition to a terrible disease? A reporter could get wind of it or something."

"I thought these records were confidential."

"Well, sure. It always is until it's not. Daddy's going to have a bigger target on his back now, and you know how nosy the press can be."

Reed wondered if this was some backhanded slap at Sarit, but he held his tongue. The children's noisy laughter rose to the level of shrieking from the other room, and Kimmy grimaced as she set aside her drink. "I suppose I should go tend to that before they shatter the glass doors."

Angus clapped his hands when he saw her get up from

the table. "Quite right, Kimmy," he said, rising as well. "We should all get in there soon, eh? What kind of monsters keep the children waiting on Christmas?"

The rest of the day passed in a blur of torn paper, delighted yelps, and never-ending food. By evening, Reed was happy to find a quiet end of the burnished leather sofa in his father's den. Tula lay asleep with her head on his lap, and Reed took out his phone. He had one last present to send. For himself, he'd purchased a piano—nothing fancy, just a nice upright that fit within the smaller confines of his condo. It was an admission, once and for all, that he would never be going home again. He'd run through some old favorites until the rust fell away, and then he'd recorded a slow, bluesy version of "Have Yourself a Merry Little Christmas." He sent it now to Ellery, with a short, albeit practiced, note:

*To a friend, who is dear to me indeed. May we be together when the fates allow. Merry Christmas, and happy New Year. —Reed*

His heart skipped a beat when he sent it because he didn't know how she would interpret it, or even how he wanted her to interpret it. He knew only that he couldn't stop thinking about her and the way her skin had tasted under his mouth. The woman clearly wasn't encouraging any sort of relationship. In fact, she'd shut him down entirely. Somehow, though, Reed knew he would see her again. It felt like fate.

His phone still in his hand, he browsed idly through the day's news: Santa had completed his mission, and children rejoiced the world over. On his lap, Tula sighed and clutched her plush yellow pony against her body. Reed stroked her hair and smiled. Maybe it wasn't Disney World, but his daughter seemed to have had a wonderful Christmas. Moments like this, when they were quiet, just the two of them, he considered saying to heck with everything and taking her to live on some remote island where the biggest problem was which beach to lie on. Knowing Tula, though, she'd miss the TV.

He clicked back over to his email program, where the link to his DNA results sat, still untouched. Now that he knew Kimmy wasn't going to go announcing all the results in some big family video presentation, he decided to look. He was a bit curious, and he figured he owed it to Tula. Steeling himself, Reed opened the link and verified his password. He held his breath as the information came up.

The page loaded slowly, and when it finished, the results showed the composition of his background as determined by his DNA sample. Reed was 63% European, with Scandinavia and Great Britain most strongly represented; 19% Central Asian and 11% Native American; 2% African and 5% unknown/undetermined. "So I'm your basic mutt," he murmured to himself, intrigued.

The phone rang in his hands, and he fumbled it, wincing as it nearly hit Tula in the head. "Hello?" he whispered.

"Reed? It's Ellery." She paused. "I got your song. Thank you."

He smiled, warming at the sound of her voice. "You're quite welcome. I hope you've had a nice Christmas."

There was an uncomfortable silence on the other end, and he kicked himself for not remembering this time of year was one of tension for her. "It's been okay, I guess," she said finally. "Bump and I went for a long walk. I called my mom and we didn't end up yelling at each other. I did a lot of thinking."

"Oh? Any thoughts in particular?" He tried not to sound too hopeful.

"About prison, actually," she said, and his hope evaporated. "The kind with cement walls, and the kind we make for ourselves. You can get paroled from the first kind. I'm not sure how you ever get out of the second."

His heart squeezed inside his chest. "I don't know, either," he said softly. "But we could talk about it, if you like."

She seemed like she was considering it, but then replied, "No. I mean, not today. It's Christmas, right? Did you have a nice day with your family?"

"I did, thank you." He gave her some quick highlights. "I finally just clicked through on those DNA results I told you about, the test Kimmy had us all take. My ancestors apparently come from all over the globe."

"Cool. Did they find you any famous relatives?"

"I didn't get that far. Let me check." He switched to the browser again and poked around until he found the "genetic connections" tab. *Maybe I'm secretly royalty,* he thought as he opened it. Only this link didn't call up long-dead ancestors. Instead, it listed people within the database who had similar genetic profiles: Kimberly, Lynette, and Suzanne. Confused, Reed clicked "more information." Maybe they had tagged him as a relative, he thought. That's why the system had linked all of them together.

The screen showed a silhouette of a person next to Kimberly's name. Predicted relationship, it said, half-sibling. Possible range: aunt. Confidence: 98%.

The results came up the same for Lynette and Suzanne. Three tests couldn't be wrong, could they? He had to be related to them, genetically related. The phone started to slip out of his hand, which was now coated in sweat. Dimly, he heard Ellery's voice come through, tinny and far away: "Reed? Are you there?"

He opened his mouth but no sound came out. He felt hot and dizzy, like he might throw up.

"Reed? Is that still you?"

Reed couldn't reply. He was no longer sure of the answer.

## Author's Note

Reed Markham's mother, Camilla, was Latina and native to Puerto Rico. Some readers may be curious why Reed's genetic analysis does not mention anything about "Latino" DNA or refer to any Latin American countries in the results. The reason is that "Latino" is a racial construct, like "white," or "black," and so one would not see "Latino" DNA listed as part of the analysis.

Reed's analysis identifies his ancestry as European, Asian, African, and Native American. Due to human migration patterns, essentially everyone currently living in the Americas is some variety of European, Asian, African, and/or Native American ancestry. Reed's mixture of all of these is what one might expect for someone who identifies as biracial with one parent of Latina heritage and one parent of Caucasian heritage.

## Acknowledgements

When you write about sexual violence, sometimes those words resonate with survivors, and they come forward to say "Me, too." Thank you to all the women who have bravely shared their stories with me. I see you and you are beautiful.

There is one name on the cover of this book but a small army of people standing behind it. Many thanks to my astute and essential editor, Daniela Rapp, for invaluable feedback and advice. I'm grateful as well to my agent, Jill Marsal, for wise counsel and support.

I would be nowhere without #TeamBump, the badass beta squad who helps me get the words on the page. You guys make the work fun and push me to be better. Thank you, Katie Bradley, Stacie Brooks, Ethan Cusick, Rayshell Reddick Daniels, Jason Grenier, Suzanne Holliday, Shannon Howl, Robbie McGraw, Michelle Kiefer, Rebecca Gullotti

LeBlanc, Melanie Rose, Jill Svihovec, Dawn Volkart, Amanda Wilde, and Paula Woolman.

I write around the edges of a crazy busy life, and every precious hour counts. I am fortunate to have not one but two sets of nearby grandparents who help me find the time: Brian and Stephanie Schaffhausen, and Larry and Cherry Rooney. Love you all.

The source of all my writing starts at home, with the two people who complete me: my husband and fellow book enthusiast, Garrett, who has a storyteller's soul and an engineer's mind, and our beloved daughter, Eleanor, who has somehow managed to survive having a published author for a mother without getting mobbed for autographs in the elementary school hallways.

## About the Author

Joanna Schaffhausen is a scientific editor who previously worked as an editorial producer for ABC News, where she advised and wrote for programs such as *World News Tonight, Good Morning America* and *20/20*. She lives in the Boston area with her husband and daughter. *The Vanishing Season* is her first novel.

# THE VANISHING SEASON

*Joanna Schaffhausen*

Fourteen years ago, teenager Ellery Hathaway was victim
number seventeen in the grisly murder spree of serial killer
Francis Michael Coben. She was the only one who lived.

Now Coben is safely behind bars, and Ellery has a new
identity in a sleepy town where bike theft makes the
newspapers. But each July for the last three years, locals
have been disappearing. Then Ellery receives strange messages
hinting that the culprit knows exactly what happened to her
all those years ago. When she tries to raise the alarm, no one
will listen, and terrified she may be next, Ellery must turn
to the one person who might believe her story…

"A chilling, breathless dive into fear"
Carol Goodman

"A twisted story with an unforgettable protagonist"
Shannon Kirk

"A gripping debut"
Hallie Ephron

**TITANBOOKS.COM**

For more fantastic fiction, author events, exclusive
excerpts, competitions, limited editions and more

VISIT OUR WEBSITE
**titanbooks.com**

LIKE US ON FACEBOOK
**facebook.com/titanbooks**

FOLLOW US ON TWITTER
**@TitanBooks**

EMAIL US
**readerfeedback@titanemail.com**